DA

Biography Today

Profiles of People of Interest to Young Readers

Sports

Volume 9

Cherie D. Abbey
Managing Editor

615 Griswold Street • Detroit, Michigan 48226

Cherie D. Abbey, *Managing Editor*
Kevin Hillstrom and Laurie Hillstrom, *Staff Writers*
Barry Puckett, *Research Associate*
Allison A. Beckett and Linda Strand, *Research Assistants*

Omnigraphics, Inc.

* * *

Matthew P. Barbour, *Senior Vice President*
Kay Gill, *Vice President — Directories*
Kevin Hayes, *Operations Manager*
Leif Gruenberg, *Development Manager*
David P. Bianco, *Marketing Consultant*

* * *

Peter E. Ruffner, *Publisher*
Frederick G. Ruffner, Jr., *Chairman*

Copyright © 2003 Omnigraphics, Inc.
ISBN 0-7808-0654-9

The information in this publication was compiled from the sources cited and from other sources considered reliable. While every possible effort has been made to ensure reliability, the publisher will not assume liability for damages caused by inaccuracies in the data, and makes no warranty, express or implied, on the accuracy of the information contained herein.

This book is printed on acid-free paper meeting the ANSI Z39.48 Standard. The infinity symbol that appears above indicates that the paper in this book meets that standard.

Printed in the United States

Contents

Preface 5

Tori Allen 1988- 9
American Rock Climber, Winner of a Gold Medal in Speed
Climbing at Age 14 at the 2002 X Games

Layne Beachley 1972- 25
Australian Professional Surfer, Five-Time World Champion of
Women's Surfing

Sue Bird 1980- 42
American Professional Basketball Player with the WNBA
Seattle Storm, Winner of Two NCAA Championships with the
University of Connecticut Huskies

Fabiola da Silva 1979- 56
Brazilian Professional Aggressive In-Line Skater, Winner of Six
Gold Medals in the X Games

Randy Johnson 1963- 68
American Professional Baseball Player with the Arizona
Diamondbacks, Five-Time Winner of the Cy Young Award,
and Co-MVP of the 2001 World Series

Jason Kidd 1973- 86
American Professional Basketball Player with the New Jersey
Nets and Five-Time NBA All-Star

Tony Stewart 1971- 104
American Professional Race Car Driver and 2002 NASCAR
Winston Cup Champion

Michael Vick 1980- 124
American Professional Football Player with the Atlanta
Falcons, First Overall Pick in the 2001 NFL Draft

Ted Williams (Retrospective) 1918-2002 138
   American Professional Baseball Player with the Boston Red
   Sox, Six-Time Major League Batting Champion

Jay Yelas 1965- 161
   American Professional Fisherman, 2002 Bassmasters Classic
   World Champion and FLW Angler of the Year

Photo and Illustration Credits 178

How to Use the Cumulative Index 179

Cumulative Index 181
   (Includes Names, Occupations, Nationalities, and
   Ethnic and Minority Origins)

Places of Birth Index 217

Birthday Index 229
   (By Month and Day)

The Biography Today Library 239

Preface

Welcome to the ninth volume of the **Biography Today Sports**. We are publishing this series in response to suggestions from our readers, who want more coverage of more people in *Biography Today*. Several volumes, covering **Artists, Authors, Performing Artists, Scientists and Inventors, Sports Figures, and World Leaders,** have appeared thus far in the Subject Series. Each of these hardcover volumes is 200 pages in length and covers approximately 10 individuals of interest to readers ages 9 and above. The length and format of the entries are like those found in the regular issues of *Biography Today*, but there is **no duplication** between the regular series and the special subject volumes.

The Plan of the Work

As with the regular issues of *Biography Today*, this special subject volume on **Sports** was especially created to appeal to young readers in a format they can enjoy reading and readily understand. Each volume contains alphabetically arranged sketches. Each entry provides at least one picture of the individual profiled, and bold-faced rubrics lead the reader to information on birth, youth, early memories, education, first jobs, marriage and family, career highlights, memorable experiences, hobbies, and honors and awards. Each of the entries ends with a list of easily accessible sources designed to lead the student to further reading on the individual and a current address. Obituary entries are also included, written to provide a perspective on the individual's entire career. Obituaries are clearly marked in both the table of contents and at the beginning of the entry.

Biographies are prepared by Omnigraphics editors after extensive research, utilizing the most current materials available. Those sources that are generally available to students appear in the list of further reading at the end of the sketch.

Indexes

A new index now appears in all *Biography Today* publications. In an effort to make the index easier to use, we have combined the **Name** and **General Index** into one, called the **Cumulative Index**. This new index contains the names of all individuals who have appeared in *Biography Today* since the series began. The names appear in bold faced type, followed by the issue in which they appeared. The Cumulative Index also contains the occupations, nationalities, and ethnic and minority origins of individuals profiled. The Cumulative Index is cumulative, including references to all individuals who have appeared in the *Biography Today* General Series and the *Biography Today* Special Subject volumes since the series began in 1992.

The Birthday Index and Places of Birth Index will continue to appear in all Special Subject volumes.

Our Advisors

This series was reviewed by an Advisory Board comprised of librarians, children's literature specialists, and reading instructors to ensure that the concept of this publication—to provide a readable and accessible biographical magazine for young readers—was on target. They evaluated the title as it developed, and their suggestions have proved invaluable. Any errors, however, are ours alone. We'd like to list the Advisory Board members, and to thank them for their efforts.

Our Advisory Board stressed to us that we should not shy away from controversial or unconventional people in our profiles, and we have tried to follow their advice. The Advisory Board also mentioned that the sketches might be useful in reluctant reader and adult literacy programs, and we would value any comments librarians might have about the suitability of our magazine for those purposes.

Your Comments Are Welcome

Our goal is to be accurate and up-to-date, to give young readers information they can learn from and enjoy. Now we want to know what you think. Take a look at this issue of *Biography Today*, on approval. Write or call me with your comments. We want to provide an excellent source of biographical information for young people. Let us know how you think we're doing.

Cherie Abbey
Managing Editor, *Biography Today*
Omnigraphics, Inc.
615 Griswold Street
Detroit, MI 48226

editor@biographytoday.com
www.biographytoday.com

Tori Allen 1988-

American Rock Climber
Winner of a Gold Medal in Speed Climbing at Age 14
at the 2002 X Games

BIRTH

Victoria Ann Allen—known to her family and friends as Tori
—was born on July 30, 1988, in Auburn, Alabama. Her father,
Steve Allen, and her mother, Shawn Allen, worked as Christian missionaries in Africa during her childhood. When Tori and
her younger brother, Clark, became interested in rock climbing,
their parents bought a climbing gym in Indianapolis, Indiana.

YOUTH

As Christian missionaries, the Allens agreed to spend several years in Africa spreading their religion and helping the local people. When Tori was four years old, the family left the United States and moved to Albertville, France, to receive missionary training. They spent a year there learning French, and they also attended the 1992 Winter Olympic Games. After Tori's parents completed their training, the family moved to Benin, a small country located on the Gulf of Guinea in West Africa, near Nigeria. They spent the next four years living in the village of Savalou among French-speaking Africans.

> *"I had a very original childhood," Allen recalled. "I grew up in a West African village. I spent my days in the village cooking with the women, selling in the market place with my favorite vendors, tying babies on my back, playing games in the courtyards. . . . I loved it there."*

"I had a very original childhood," Tori recalled. "I grew up in a West African village. I spent my days in the village cooking with the women, selling in the market place with my favorite vendors, tying babies on my back, playing games in the courtyards. . . . I loved it there." Growing up in Africa helped Tori get used to being the center of attention. "She was the only white kid in a village of 5,000, and people stared," her father noted.

One of Tori's favorite things about Africa was playing with her pet Mona monkey, Georgie. "She was just days old when we got her so she thought I was her mom," she remembered. "She just hung on my dresses and went everywhere with me—to school, to market, on walks, to church." Tori particularly enjoyed climbing trees with Georgie. In 1996, as the Allens concluded their scheduled mission and prepared to return to the United States, Georgie was bitten by a poisonous snake and died. But Tori never forgot her first pet and favorite playmate. Once the family settled in Indianapolis, Indiana, she began collecting the toy monkeys that would eventually fill her bedroom.

Tori was a very athletic girl who enjoyed all sorts of sports. She became an accomplished ballerina and figure skater shortly after moving to Indianapolis. But she discovered her best sport by accident in December 1998, when she accompanied her father on a shopping trip to Galyan's—an outdoor-equipment store that contained an indoor climbing wall. "We'd never done rock climbing until right before Christmas, when Dad and I went shopping at Galyan's," she recalled. "They had a climbing wall, and it looked like a blast. We put on some climbing shoes and just did it." The tiny girl impressed bystanders by making it all the way to the top of the wall on her first try. She soon returned to Galyan's with her younger brother, who also became hooked on climbing. A month later, Tori entered and won her first junior climbing competition.

EDUCATION

Allen was home-schooled by her mother until she was 13 years old. She entered Lawrence Central High School in Indianapolis as a freshman in the fall of 2001, and she expects to graduate in 2005. She is a good student and also competes on her high school track team in the pole vault event.

CAREER HIGHLIGHTS

Claiming Numerous Junior Climbing Titles

Climbing competitions usually take place indoors, on artificial walls covered with oddly shaped hand- and foot-holds, in order to ensure that all competitors face the same conditions. Competitions can be conducted under a number of different formats. In bouldering, for example, competitors must climb a predetermined route up a 20-foot wall. In speed climbing, competitors race to see who can climb to the top of a 60-foot wall and tag a buzzer first. In difficulty events, competitors can win either by finishing the most climbs in a series or by reaching the highest point on a route. In dyno events, competitors start off by using a certain set of holds and must jump upwards to grab another set of holds.

Thanks to the controlled conditions indoors, this sort of climbing is not dangerous when it is done properly. The competitors wear sling-shaped harnesses connected to ropes that are held by spotters on the ground. The ropes remain slack when the competitors are climbing, but they become taut and catch the competitors if they slip off the wall. "The kids have never had so much as a bruise [from competitive climbing]," Shawn Allen said.

Within a few months of her first climbing experience, Allen was winning climbing competitions across the Midwest. After winning her age group at the Ohio River Valley Regional Tournament, she qualified for the 1999 U.S. Competition Climbing Association (USCCA) Junior National Championship. Allen defeated 30 top young climbers from all over the United States

Tori Allen (left) competes in speed climbing against Evi Neliwati of Indonesia (right) at the X Games.

to claim the junior title and be named to the U.S. Junior National Team. Her brother, Clark, finished third in his age group and also made the national team. In September 1999, they went on to compete against 90 kids from six countries at the Touchstone International Tournament in San Francisco, California. Both of the Allen siblings finished first in their age divisions and earned the right to represent the United States at the 2000 Junior Olympic Games in Moscow, Russia.

Tori Allen went on to claim more than two dozen junior climbing titles over the next three years, including four consecutive Junior National Championships. In 2000 she won the junior division at the Gorge Games, a prestigious competition held each year in the Columbia River Gorge near Portland, Oregon. The Gorge Games feature climbing, kayaking, mountain biking, and other outdoor adventure sports. In 2001 Allen entered the adult competition at the Gorge Games. She was the youngest participant in any event, and most of her competitors in the climbing competition were 20 to 30 years old. But Allen easily won the bouldering event, climbing every route without a fall. She also finished third

One of Tori's favorite things about Africa was playing with her pet Mona monkey, Georgie. "She was just days old when we got her so she thought I was her mom. She just hung on my dresses and went everywhere with me— to school, to market, on walks, to church."

in the dyno event. "Getting first in the actual climbing competition was the main thing," her father said afterward. "The dyno thing is more like trick climbing." In the fall of 2001, Allen defeated adult competitors once again to win the women's bouldering event at the Outdoor Rock Climbing World Championships in Orlando, Florida.

Setting World Records with Outdoor Climbs

In addition to participating in organized climbing competitions, Allen enjoyed challenging herself by climbing natural cliffs outdoors. In 2000, for example, she successfully climbed a route called Harvest in Kentucky's Red River Gorge. In rock climbing, different routes are ranked between 5.0 and 5.15 (from easiest to hardest), based on their degree of difficulty. Climbs that are rated above 5.10 are further divided into a, b, c, and d levels (from hardest to easiest). Harvest was rated as 5.13a, making it a very difficult climb. In fact, an average person would require many years of training and practice before they could master the route. By completing Harvest, Allen set a world record as the youngest person ever to climb a route with a 5.13a degree of difficulty on the first attempt.

In September 2001 Allen established another world record as the youngest woman ever to climb to the summit of a famous mountain called El Capitan in Yosemite National Park in California. She spent three days climbing 3,000 feet up a route called The Nose. She was accompanied by the famous speed-climber Hans Florine and a film crew that captured the feat on video. Allen kept an online diary of her experiences on El Capitan. "Right now I am camping out on a ledge called Dolt Tower," she wrote. "I am about 1,500 feet in the air and I am getting ready to go to sleep in my hammock hanging from the rock. Everything you do on a rock face is an experience; from sleeping to going to the bathroom. The second one is especially hard for girls."

> "
>
> *"Right now I am camping out on a ledge called Dolt Tower," Allen wrote in her online diary about her experiences climbing El Capitan in Yosemite.*
>
> *"I am about 1,500 feet in the air and I am getting ready to go to sleep in my hammock hanging from the rock. Everything you do on a rock face is an experience; from sleeping to going to the bathroom. The second one is especially hard for girls."*
>
> "

Upon reaching the summit, Allen only got to enjoy her accomplishment for a few minutes before she had to return to the real world. "Hans and I got to put a rock on the summit tower and sign the summiteers' paper in the box," she recalled. "After we had summitted 'The Nose,' we got the joy of hiking eight-and-a-half miles down the back side of it. To make it worse, I had 30 pounds of gear on my back. I have never been so happy and so tired in my life." Swarms of reporters met Allen at the bottom of the mountain. After completing a series of interviews, she returned to her motel room to catch up on her homework.

Taking Up Competitive Pole Vaulting

At the time Allen climbed El Capitan in 2001, she had just started classes as a freshman at Lawrence Central High School. She had also joined the school's track team as a pole vaulter. In the track and field event known as the pole vault, athletes run at full speed while carrying a long, flexible pole.

At the end of the runway, they plant the end of the pole in a small box set into the ground. Holding the other end, they use the pole to launch themselves high into the air. The goal is to propel their bodies over the top of a crossbar that rests gently between two uprights or stanchions. The winner of the pole vault event is the athlete who goes the highest without knocking down the crossbar. Pole vaulting requires a wide range of athletic abilities, including speed, coordination, timing, strength, body control, and courage.

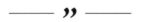

> *Girls' pole vault was not a sanctioned event in Indiana high school athletics, so Allen was forced to practice with the boys' team at Lawrence Central. She felt that it was unfair for her to have to compete against boys who were much larger and stronger than she was. "A 15-year-old girl can't bench press as much as a 15-year-old boy, so it's ridiculous to put us against each other," she stated. "It's just not right."*

Allen was inspired to begin pole vaulting competitively after watching American Stacy Dragila win the first gold medal ever awarded in women's pole vault at the 2000 Olympic Games in Sydney, Australia. (For more information on Dragila, see *Biography Today Sports*, Vol. 6.) Allen immediately showed great natural ability in the pole vault. In fact, she was invited to attend an elite pole vault camp at the University of Nebraska in the summer of 2001.

Girls' pole vault was not a sanctioned event in Indiana high school athletics, however, so Allen was forced to practice with the boys' team at Lawrence Central. She felt that it was unfair for her to have to compete against boys who were much larger and stronger than she was. "A 15-year-old girl can't bench press as much as a 15-year-old boy, so it's ridiculous to put us against each other," she stated. "It's just not right." To demonstrate her point, Allen noted that the Indiana state record for boys' high school pole vault (16 feet, 9 inches) was nearly a foot higher than the world record for women's pole vault held by Dragila.

Upon doing some research, Allen found out that girls' pole vault was a sanctioned high school athletic event in 42 other states. Girls in these states had the opportunity to earn college scholarships in pole vaulting and possibly qualify for the U.S. Olympic Team. Allen and her parents eventually decided to file a lawsuit against the Indiana High School Ath-

letic Association (IHSAA) to force them to sanction the event. The lawsuit argued that Indiana violated Title IX—a 1972 law that prohibited people from being excluded on the basis of sex from any education program or activity that received federal funding—by not giving Allen the opportunity to compete in girls' pole vault.

Unfortunately, as of the end of 2002 it did not appear that the situation would be resolved soon. The commissioner of the IHSAA claimed that the state was not discriminating against Allen because she was free to compete on the boys' pole vault team if she wanted to. He also took a poll of state track coaches and found that only 30 percent favored adding girls' pole vault to the list of sanctioned events.

Meanwhile, Allen managed to win the pole vault event at her county's freshman track meet despite competing against boys. After competing for only two years, she improved her best jump to 10 feet, 7¾ inches and set a national record for girls her age. She also won the youth girls division at the USA Track and Field Junior Olympics in the summer of 2002. Allen remained hopeful that Indiana would sanction her event before she graduated from high school. "I hope this comes not just for me," Allen said. "I know there are other girls who also would like to pole vault."

Allen celebrates after winning the speed climbing event at the Summer X Games in Philadelphia, August 2002.

Winning a Gold Medal at the X Games

In addition to pole vaulting, Allen continued with her climbing training. By the beginning of the 2002 indoor climbing season, Allen was one of the top-ranked climbers in the United States. She regularly competed against—and defeated —the best adult women climbers in the nation. In April, for example, she won the U.S. National Championships in indoor climbing in San Francisco, California. In July she overcame a fall on the first route to win another gold medal at the Gorge Games. Although some of her older competitors did not like losing to a teenager, most of them respected her talent and appreciated her energy and hard work. "There are some women who basically want a rule to be made that you have to be a certain age to compete [in the adult events]," her mother acknowledged. "Other women see a lot of the future of the sport in Tori. . . . The women are coming around. They see how hard she trains, how much work she puts into it. It's pretty hard not to like her."

In August 2002 Allen made her first appearance at the X Games in Philadelphia, Pennsylvania. The X Games are sometimes called the Olympics of alternative or extreme sports. The annual event features sports like skateboarding, wakeboarding, street luge, speed climbing, and motocross. Athletes from around the world compete in a variety of events for medals and more than $1 million in prize money. It attracts thousands of spectators as well as a national television audience. Over 200,000 spectators attended the 2002 X Games, and hundreds of thousands more watched events broadcast on prime-time television. Allen competed in the speed-climbing event. Since her competitors included many experienced European speed-climbing specialists, the 14-year-old Allen was not expected to win the event.

But Allen thrilled the pro-American crowd by scaling the 60-foot wall in 13.417 seconds — breaking the record set the previous year by nearly four seconds — to win the competition and claim $20,000 in prize money. She thus became the first American woman to win an X Games medal in speed climbing. "My competition was tough, many gold medal winners," she noted. "But I just tried as hard as I could to get to the top of the wall without slipping."

Allen was pleased with the outpouring of support she received from the crowd in Philadelphia. She hoped that her success would help attract more Americans to the sport of climbing. "I hope this really gets Americans into the sport, to show that we can compete with anyone in the world," she stated. "I think me being in this and winning helped draw a big crowd. It was pretty cool to hear the crowd going like that." In September 2002, Allen claimed another high-profile victory against international competition by winning gold medals in both the speed climbing and difficulty events at the Youth World Championships in France.

Promoting the Sport of Climbing

At five feet tall and under 100 pounds, Allen might seem to be an unlikely champion in a sport that requires

"I am not obsessed with what I eat but I try to always make good decisions about eating, sleeping, and other activities," Allen said about her training program.
"I would never do anything to intentionally hurt my body and that is why I am totally against drugs, drinking, and smoking. I am proud of my hard work and my reputation. I don't plan on ruining things by giving in to the people around me who are making poor decisions."

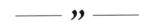

strength and a long reach. Climbing experts attribute her success to her flexibility, her strength in comparison to her weight, and her "positive ape index" — a climbing term that describes someone with exceptionally long arms and fingers.

Allen also works hard to stay on top of her sport. She climbs four days per week for about four hours each time. She concentrates on endurance for two of these days, and on power for the other two days. She also runs, lifts weights, participates in kickboxing, and trains for the pole vault. "I am not obsessed with what I eat but I try to always make good decisions about eating, sleeping, and other activities," she explained. "I would never do anything to intentionally hurt my body and that is why I am totally against drugs, drinking, and smoking. I am proud of my hard work and my reputation. I don't plan on ruining things by giving in to the people around me who are making poor decisions."

Allen has received a great deal of media attention for her climbing feats. She has been featured in every major climbing publication, for example, as well as in various newspapers and in *Sports Illustrated*. "She's accessible and energetic, and she has already become a great ambassador for this sport," said junior climbing official Jeanne Niemer.

Although Allen knows that many people would find climbing scary, she finds it exhilarating. "I love heights," she said. "To think you're so high up there and that you're in charge, you know?" Allen tries not to think about specific routes or holds, and instead tries to let her body take over. She believes that trying her best can take her a long way. "My dad bought me one of those inspirational pictures called 'Perseverance.' It says, 'You can't let go and still win.' So I don't let go," she explained. "I hate falling. It just frustrates me. But if it's a really hard move, I'll just jump and go for it. I never look down. I always look up. If you never reach for your goals, you're never going to get them!"

—— *"* ——

"In Kentucky I grabbed a nice hold to rest on and all of a sudden a flying squirrel popped out, jumped onto my shoulder, and leapt off.
I was so shocked, I couldn't scream. Another time I was climbing and I just got past a hard part, clipped a clip and reached around a ledge where a spider nest had just hatched. There were lots of little ones and they climbed all over me. . . ."

—— *"* ——

Allen admits that she prefers climbing on indoor artificial walls instead of outdoor natural rocks. Part of the reason for her preference is that she has had a number of strange and unexpected experiences while climbing outdoors. "In Kentucky I grabbed a nice hold to rest on and all of a sudden a flying squirrel popped out, jumped onto my shoulder, and leapt off. I was so shocked, I couldn't scream," she remembered. "Another time I was climbing and I just got past a hard part, clipped a clip and reached around a ledge where a spider nest had just hatched. There were lots of little ones and they climbed all over me. I was freaking out. When I got down it looked like I had chickenpox from all of the bites. And then my favorite one: I was climbing this route, not super-hard, and a bee landed on my lip. I bit at my lip and I heard this crunch. My lip was so swollen I couldn't talk. That was nasty."

As both a climber and a pole vaulter, Allen has experienced many positive things through sports. She hopes to share her experiences with young girls in order to encourage them to take advantage of opportunities to participate in sports. "I am responsible for making sure that all the little girls out there right now will continue to have unlimited opportunities in athletics. As a matter of fact, I am responsible to see that they have MORE opportunities than exist for them right now,"

"I was freaking out. When I got down it looked like I had chickenpox from all of the bites. And then my favorite one: I was climbing this route, not super-hard, and a bee landed on my lip. I bit at my lip and I heard this crunch. My lip was so swollen I couldn't talk. That was nasty."

she stated. "Not only am I going to continue to be a good role model, I am going to be an encourager to young girls and a spokesperson for what sports have done in my life. . . . I am going to start with rock climbing and move out from there. Look for me—I'll be the one leading the parade of smiling girls who have discovered the fun, fulfillment, and friendship in athletic participation in any sport they want!"

FUTURE PLANS

Allen hopes that her future will hold a trip to the Olympic Games as an athlete, either in rock climbing or in pole vault. "I want to go to the Olympics," she stated. "That's my life dream." So far it seems as though pole vault might provide her best opportunity to compete. Women's pole vault was included as a medal sport for the first time in the 2000 Olympics in Sydney, Australia. While rock climbing has not yet been sanctioned as a medal sport, it has been included in the Games as an exhibition sport.

Allen also plans to attend college in the future. She hopes to earn an athletic scholarship as a pole vaulter. She is considering attending Pepperdine University in California because of its proximity to natural cliffs for rock climbing. "Have you seen the rock out there?" she said. "How could you not want to get out there every day?"

As far as a future career, Allen wants to be either a kindergarten teacher or a spy. She has even set aside some of her earnings from climbing to start an all-girls' kindergarten someday.

HOME AND FAMILY

Allen lives in the Rocky Ripple neighborhood of Indianapolis with her family. Her parents are very supportive of her athletic goals. In fact, a year after she started climbing competitively they bought Climb Time, the Indianapolis climbing gym where she practiced. "We wanted to be with our kids," her father noted. "We didn't know the first thing about climbing." Nevertheless, the Allens turned Climb Time into a successful business. They gave the facility a thorough cleaning, replaced all the floor padding, repaired the existing holds, and added thousands of new holds to create diverse routes for climbers of all abilities. Thanks to their hard work, membership in the gym increased from 20 to 200 and monthly revenue doubled from about $11,000 to $23,000.

HOBBIES AND OTHER INTERESTS

Allen has a collection of over 500 toy monkeys. She often climbs with a tiny Curious George doll clipped to her belt in memory of her first climbing partner, Georgie the monkey. In fact, monkeys have become sort of a trademark for Allen — she often throws tiny monkey dolls to the crowd at climbing competitions.

Thanks to her success in climbing competitions and her bubbly personality, Allen has signed endorsement deals with 10 different companies. Her agent predicts that she could earn as much as $100,000 in sponsorship and prize money in 2003. Allen says that she will use part of earnings to help a family in Benin buy a house. She would also like to buy a pet monkey, but her parents are not so sure about the idea.

Allen wants to share her love of climbing with others and tries to help spread the popularity of her sport. For example, she does some coaching and has started a youth climbing club at her parents' gym. She also designs her own climbing clothes and hopes to start own line of clothing someday. "I think my success will help others," she noted. "I just want climbing to be big. Really big."

In her spare time, Allen enjoys going to the movies. She also plays electric bass guitar in the youth group band at her church and volunteers at the Indianapolis Children's Museum.

HONORS AND AWARDS

U.S. Climbing Competitions Association (USCCA) Junior National
    Champion: 1999, 2000, 2001, 2002
U.S. Junior National Team: 1999, 2000, 2001, 2002
World Record: 2000, as youngest person to on-site a 5.13a difficulty climb,
    Red River Gorge, KY
World Record: 2001, as youngest woman to summit El Capitan, Yosemite
    National Park, CA
Gorge Games, Women's Bouldering: 2001, first place; 2002, first place
X Games, Women's Speed Climbing: 2002, first place
USCCA Adult National Champion: 2002
Youth World Champion, Speed Climbing: 2002
Youth World Champion, Difficulty Event: 2002

FURTHER READING

Periodicals

ESPN: The Magazine, Aug. 19, 2002, p.94
Indianapolis Business Journal, Jan. 21, 2002, p.57
Indianapolis Monthly, Mar. 2002, p.224
Indianapolis Star, July 28, 1999, p.D1; Aug. 12, 1999, p.B1; Oct. 19, 1999, p.D6; May 22, 2001, p.D4; July 18, 2001, p.E1; July 24, 2001, p.E1; Mar. 8, 2002, p.B1; Sep. 10, 2002, p.D1
Jack and Jill, Mar. 2000, p.16
Lexington (Ky.) Herald-Ledger, Oct. 14, 2001, p.C12
News Journal (Wilmington, DE), Aug. 18, 2002, p.J2
Philadelphia Inquirer, Aug. 17, 2002, p.E7
Sports Illustrated, Aug. 20, 2001, p.22
Sports Illustrated Women, Mar. 1, 2002, p.33; May 1, 2002, p.56
Washington Post, Aug. 15, 2002, p.C12

Online Articles

http://www.delawareonline.com/newsjournal/sports/specials/2002xgames/news/18teenmakes ("Teen Makes Quick Climb to Top," *Delaware News Journal,* Aug. 18, 2002)

ADDRESS

Tori Allen
P.O. Box 502568
Indianapolis, IN 46236

WORLD WIDE WEB SITES

http://www.toriallen.com
http://www.womensportsfoundation.org

Layne Beachley 1972-

Australian Professional Surfer
Five-Time World Champion of Women's Surfing

BIRTH

Layne Beachley was born on May 24, 1972, in Sydney, Australia. She was the adopted daughter of Neil Beachley, who worked as a marketing manager, and his wife Valerie. Her adoptive family also included an older brother, Jason. Layne's biological mother, Margaret Nickerson, made contact with her in 1998, and they have remained in touch since then.

YOUTH

Beachley grew up as a tomboy who enjoyed playing outdoors with a group of neighborhood boys. She was very well-coordinated and learned to ride a skateboard at the age of two. "I remember stealing my brother's skateboard during one of his birthday parties and charging down the street, only to return home with half of my big toe missing," she noted. By the time she was three, Beachley could ride her skateboard while her father ran along and towed her behind him on a rope.

Beachley's childhood home in Sydney was located a short bus ride from Manly Beach, where her father taught her to surf at the age of four. "I just pushed her out on the board and told her to stand up, and she did," her father recalled. Beachley started out by riding the waves created by a passing ferry along the shoreline, surfing on a styrofoam board. "She always had amazing balance," her brother recalled. "She used to jump fully clothed on a surfboard, plane to the other end, and get out without getting wet." At the age of five, she began paddling out to the edge of the roped-off swim area and then surfing back in, often running into swimmers along the way.

Sadly, Beachley's adoptive mother died from complications of surgery in 1978, when Layne was six years old. "I remember Dad coming home and telling me and I put my face in my pillow and cried for a while and that was it," she noted. "I don't think I really understood the implications of it all." Being so young, Beachley retained only limited memories of her mother. "I don't have a clear recollection of her," she stated. "I do remember sitting on her lap early in the morning drinking the dregs out of her coffee cup. That must be why I have never liked coffee. I also remember the tantrums I would throw when she called me in

> "Joan is a wonderful, nurturing woman who was the only mothering influence I would ever accept," Beachley recalled about the family friend who cared for her after her mother's death. "I was a wretched child. I just wanted to play, to be outdoors, to be a tomboy. She let me do my thing, skateboard down the street at 100 miles per hour or ride my bike around the block and disappear or play tennis in the middle of the road, hit golf balls up the hill, climb trees. I was very hyperactive. If it was light, I was outside."

from playing outside for my afternoon nap. I still have the homemade blanket she used to cover me with."

Following his wife's death, Neil Beachley depended on a family friend, Joan Tate, to help him care for the children. Tate played the role of a nanny — picking the children up after school, fixing them meals, allowing them to stay at her house when their father went out of town for business — but she also became a mother figure for young Layne. "Joan is a wonderful, nurturing woman who was the only mothering influence I would ever accept," she recalled. "I was a wretched child. I just wanted to play, to be outdoors, to be a tomboy. She let me do my thing, skateboard down the street at 100 miles per hour or ride my bike around the block and disappear or play tennis in the middle of the road, hit golf balls up the hill, climb trees. I was very hyperactive. If it was light, I was outside."

Throughout her childhood, Beachley continued to spend a great deal of time at the beach. She learned early on that she faced an uphill battle as a girl involved in surfing — a sport dominated by boys. The boys around Sydney tended to be very protective of their favorite surfing spots, claiming that girls were not allowed on certain parts of the beach. Beachley ignored their warnings and often tried to surf in the boys' territory. "They'd pick me up by my wrists and ankles and heave me over the beach wall," she remembered. "I'd get right up, run back over the wall, and give as good as I got — and get thrown over again. This would sometimes happen two or three times a day. I think that had a lot to do with who I am now."

Beachley entered her first surfing contest at the age of 13, around the same time that she got her first fiberglass surfboard. At first, she did not really view surfing as a potential career. Instead, she planned to be either a professional tennis player or a stockbroker. She actually took a job in the stock exchange at one point, but it did not take long for her to migrate back to surfing. "After a couple weeks I realized, nope, that's not it," she recalled. "I was an athlete."

EDUCATION

Beachley attended McKellar Girls High School in Sydney, where she competed on the girls' surfing team. She won scholastic titles at the regional and state levels, then went on to compete in the National Scholastic Titles at Bells Beach in 1988. She earned her HSC — the equivalent of an American high school diploma — the following year.

Beachley rides a wave to her second consecutive ASP world surfing title, 1999.

CAREER HIGHLIGHTS

Joining the Pro Tour

Once Beachley decided to become a professional surfer, she worked hard to achieve her goal. She began competing on the Association of Surfing Professionals (ASP) World Championship Tour (WCT). In professional surfing events, competitors earn championship points and prize money by progressing through early group stages into later knock-out rounds. The last surfer remaining after a series of head-to-head matchups is the winner.

Beachley began competing on the WCT part-time in 1990. But without sponsors to provide equipment and help with travel expenses, she had to pay her own way by working at a series of odd jobs in restaurants, surf shops, and clothing stores. In 1991 she joined the pro tour full-time. She traveled to 15 competitions around the world between March and December, lugging six surfboards with her everywhere she went. "At first it was a real struggle," she acknowledged. "Long plane rides, not knowing where I was going, where to stay, how to get there, foreign languages, foreign food, being away from friends and family and the comforts of home for long periods of time. There is a lot more to doing the world tour than just surfing, but I was open to the experience."

Beachley trained very hard during her early years on the WCT. In fact, she seemed to spend more time working out than practicing on her surfboard. "I was kind of psychotic about it," she admitted. "I'd run up sand dunes with logs on my back. I'd ride a bike for 20 miles, run four miles, do 100 sit-ups, then run back and do another 100 sit-ups. Just stupid things. I'd wake up feeling like death. Sick with the flu, I'd go out and cycle at 5:30 a.m. in the pouring rain to make myself feel better. Otherwise, I'd feel guilty. . . . It made me mentally tough but physically ill. I over-trained. . . . But without that training, I wouldn't have come this far. [There are] times in competition when you just cannot go any further, and you have to push yourself. That's what the training prepared me for."

Beachley claimed her first professional surfing victory in 1993 at the Diet Coke Women's Classic at Narrabeen, Australia. "That's when my career changed for the better," she said of her first professional win. "I started believing in myself, which is what makes a huge difference, especially in competition. From then on I won at least one event every year."

"At first it was a real struggle," Beachley acknowledged about joining the pro tour. "Long plane rides, not knowing where I was going, where to stay, how to get there, foreign languages, foreign food, being away from friends and family and the comforts of home for long periods of time. There is a lot more to doing the world tour than just surfing, but I was open to the experience."

Beachley won another event in 1994 and finished the year ranked fourth in championship points. American Lisa Anderson won the world title that year. Beachley claimed her third professional victory in 1995 and moved up to second in the world rankings behind Anderson. Beachley broke through to win five out of 11 WCT events in 1996, but inconsistent performances in the remaining events left her third in points at the end of the year, as Anderson claimed her third consecutive world championship.

By the end of the 1996 season, Beachley developed chronic fatigue syndrome. Her doctors blamed the condition on overtraining, too much traveling, and a poor diet that did not recognize her allergies to yeast and wheat.

———— **"** ————

"I was kind of psychotic about training. I'd run up sand dunes with logs on my back. I'd ride a bike for 20 miles, run four miles, do 100 sit-ups, then run back and do another 100 sit-ups. Just stupid things. I'd wake up feeling like death. Sick with the flu, I'd go out and cycle at 5:30 a.m. in the pouring rain to make myself feel better. Otherwise, I'd feel guilty. . . ."

———— **"** ————

"I wasn't allowed to surf for over a month," she recalled. "I couldn't stay awake past eight o'clock at night, I couldn't get up before ten in the morning. I was dog-tired. It would be a beautiful sunny day outside and all I could do was sit on the couch and watch videos, then by four in the afternoon I was in tears, suicidal, because I couldn't go surfing, couldn't go training, couldn't do anything I wanted to do."

Beachley recovered during the off-season by making changes in her diet and cutting back on her training. She had another good year in 1997, winning two events and making the finals of many others. But she finished second in the world rankings once again, as Anderson claimed her fourth consecutive championship. At this point, some critics claimed that Beachley did not have what it took to be a champion. The media started referring to her as a "bridesmaid," meaning that she stood in the shadows while her rival Anderson took the spotlight.

Winning Her First World Championship

During the off-season, Beachley became romantically involved with fellow surfer Ken Bradshaw. Bradshaw, an American who was 20 years older than Beachley, was a legend in the world of surfing known for his mastery of big waves. He originated the sport of "tow-in surfing," in which surfers use motorized watercraft to tow them into the path of huge waves that break up to a mile offshore. Bradshaw used this method to ride waves up to 80 feet high, or the equivalent of a 10-storey building, at Outer Log Cabins off Hawaii. Bradshaw became Beachley's boyfriend, mentor, coach, and traveling companion, and he played a large role in her later success. "Before I met Ken I doubted myself so often," she admitted. "I was afraid to win and step above everyone. He made me believe in myself."

In addition to gaining Bradshaw's help, Beachley made some other changes before the 1998 season. She remained in Hawaii for several months in order to improve her technique in the small surf that she often encountered in women's contests. "I had to change my strategy and learn how to surf small waves," she explained. "I get more of an adrenaline rush out of surfing big waves than just surfing in general. When there's power behind me, I don't have to put so much power into the wave; it's already under my feet. I can just generate my technique without having to concentrate on placing myself in a position on a wave where I can get the most power out of a turn."

Beachley had a phenomenal year in 1998. She won three of the first four events on the pro tour on her way to claiming five victories for the year. In the meantime, her rival Anderson struggled with a back injury for much of the season. Beachley's early success helped her clinch the world championship with three events remaining. She captured her first world title by 2,420 points—the largest point margin in the history of the sport—and took home $75,300—the most prize money ever earned in a single season by a female surfer. She also stopped Anderson's string of consecutive championships at four.

Beachley was thrilled finally to become the world's top female surfer. But Bradshaw made sure that winning did not reduce her competitive drive. "I spent eight years getting to number one and I was almost relaxed and happy with that," Beachley recalled, "until Ken came up and said, 'You are the best women's surfer there is. Why can't you dominate for five years? Lisa [Anderson] won four consecutive. I'm setting you this goal: you win five world titles.' So basically Ken sets my goals and I go out and achieve them."

Meeting Her Birth Mother

In addition to achieving one of her professional goals in 1998, Beachley also accomplished one of her personal goals—meeting her birth mother. Beachley had done some searching for her birth mother several years earlier, but she was only able to find limited information. In 1998, however, her birth mother, Margaret Nickerson, managed to find her. Nickerson explained that she had given her daughter up for adoption because she was 17 years old, unmarried, and due to leave Australia and return to Glas-

— " —

It made me mentally tough but physically ill. I over-trained. . . . But without that training, I wouldn't have come this far. [There are] times in competition when you just cannot go any further, and you have to push yourself. That's what the training prepared me for."

— " —

gow, Scotland. "She said she desperately wanted to keep me but she really didn't have the resources to do it," Beachley noted. "She had to go back to Scotland, and a single mother wasn't socially accepted, so she had to give me up."

After speaking several times on the telephone, Beachley agreed to meet her birth mother in California, where Nickerson lived. The two women have met several times since then, and they are working together to define their relationship. "I tried to push her away a couple of times because I'm so focused on my career," Beachley admitted. "We are creating a friendship, but I think she wanted a bit too much, too soon." Beachley claims that she has no hard feelings toward Nickerson for giving her up for adoption. "There's not an inch of resentment," she stated. "I have no problem with it because I love the way I was brought up. I loved my childhood. It created who I am, and I wouldn't change who I am for the world. Every experience I had was part of me."

"I would like to be regarded as the best surfer ever. When you achieve your goals, you set higher ones, and after winning the title, I know the talents I have. I guess this season, I've got higher expectations more than anything."

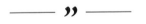

Defending the World Title

As the 1999 WCT got underway, Beachley was determined to prove that her first world championship had not been a fluke. "I would like to be regarded as the best surfer ever," she stated. "When you achieve your goals, you set higher ones, and after winning the title, I know the talents I have. I guess this season, I've got higher expectations more than anything." At the same time, Beachley realized that her competitors would be equally determined to knock her off the throne. "I'm the one the other girls are going to target," she acknowledged. "I've got a bullseye this year and everyone's going to be aiming at it."

Beachley turned in another fine performance in 1999. She won five events —despite suffering a torn knee ligament in the middle of the season— and successfully defended her world championship. Some people discounted her achievement, though, because her main rival, Anderson, had taken the year off to recover from injuries. "It's a lot of work being world champion," Beachley noted. "It's so much easier being number two. No one comes up to you and says, 'You suck, you don't deserve to be world

Beachley surfing at Bells Beach in Victoria, Australia, April 2001.

champion.' Or, 'You shouldn't have won today, you weren't on.' When you're number two, everyone gives you encouragement. They say, 'You can do it, you're the greatest, you deserve to be there.' I've learned not to take these things personally. I remember when I was number two, wanting to take Lisa out. That's what makes a true champion, being able to stay in there, handle the criticism, the ridicule, and the attention."

Beachley silenced many of the critics in 2000, when she won four WCT events to capture her third consecutive world title. Her most satisfying victory came in the season-opening Billabong Pro in Australia in March, when she defeated Anderson head-to-head in the final. "I placed so much importance and emotion on the first contest victory that I felt like I had achieved it all," she remembered. "I came against Lisa Anderson in the final, and for the last two years the critics have been saying I wouldn't have won the two world championship titles if it hadn't been for her absence because of her back injury. Finally I got to beat her outright, fair and square—it was a major accomplishment and I finally got to silence all the critics."

Beachley started out strong in the 2001 season, but then the European leg of the pro tour was canceled following the September 11 terrorist attacks on the United States. As a result, the world championship came down to the final event in Hawaii. Beachley came into the event leading by only 30 points, which meant that 10 of her competitors remained in the running to win the title. "I have never gone to Hawaii with less than a 600 point lead so it's a lot of pressure on me," she admitted. To make matters worse, Beachley's practice time was limited by a painful neck injury.

When Beachley lost in the quarterfinals to South African Heather Clark, she figured that her hopes of winning a fourth consecutive world championship were over. She was so upset about her poor performance that she stayed out in the water afterward, sitting on her board and crying. "I just wanted to cry like I'd never cried before," she explained. "I had to let go, I had to go through that emotional grieving." To her amazement, however, all of the other title contenders were knocked out of the competition one by one. She ended up winning the championship and equaling the record of four straight titles held by Lisa Anderson. "I was hoping it would be a lot more convincing than that," she said later. "I wanted to win. I didn't want to wait for other people to lose. But you can't have it your way all the time."

> "I remember chasing the thing down and everyone just backing off because it was one of the biggest that came through," Beachley recalled about riding a 30-foot wave. "As soon as I let go of the [tow] rope and I was going down the face I knew it was the biggest thing I'd ever ridden. I looked back at this 30-foot barrel behind my head and I was just telling myself, 'Stay standing, stay standing—all you have to do is stay on your feet and you'll be fine.' Meanwhile, I was going faster and faster. It was insane."

Beachley knew that her close call in 2001 would only give her competitors greater confidence going into 2002. "They've had a taste of what it's like to get close and next year will be tougher," she stated. "I'm going to have to work on some new moves and surf with more power and speed. I'm sure the judges get sick of seeing the same old stuff."

Conquering the Big Waves

While she was winning her fourth consecutive world championship in 2001, Beachley was also earning a reputation as the world's best female big-wave surfer. She had always enjoyed riding large waves, and her association with Bradshaw had introduced her to tow-in surfing. On January

Beachley surfing at the Billabong Pro event, the second ASP tour event of the 2001 season, in Tahiti.

12, 2001, she rode the biggest wave ever surfed by a woman—a 30-footer at Outer Log Cabins. "I remember chasing the thing down and everyone just backing off because it was one of the biggest that came through," she recalled. "As soon as I let go of the rope and I was going down the face I knew it was the biggest thing I'd ever ridden. I looked back at this 30-foot barrel behind my head and I was just telling myself, 'Stay standing, stay standing—all you have to do is stay on your feet and you'll be fine.' Meanwhile, I was going faster and faster. It was insane."

In 2002 Beachley became the only woman to join a group of elite men surfers in the Billabong Odyssey—a $1 million, three-year quest to ride the world's biggest waves. She joined the group after Bradshaw's usual jet-ski partner suffered an injury. "I'm one of the boys and I don't consider myself just a girl in this situation," she stated. "When you're against Mother Nature, it's survival of the fittest, survival of the strongest—it's not gender biased. The reason I rode that 30-foot wave so successfully was because I was mentally and physically prepared for the worst wipeout of my life. You've got to prepare yourself for the worst possible scenario and then hope for the best." As part of the Billabong Odyssey, Beachley surfed a 33-foot wave at Todos Santos Island off the Mexican coast. "I wasn't really that challenged by it at all," she said afterward. "I didn't get my hair wet."

Beachley actually preferred riding big offshore waves to surfing at some of the WCT locations, where the waves break in shallow water over dangerous reefs. Her least favorite spot to surf is Teahupoo in Tahiti, which features razor-sharp coral that is nearly exposed as large waves approach it. She suffered broken ribs and herniated discs in her neck there once, but she came back to win a competition at the same place in 2001. "I'm so comfortable in big waves when there's deep water," she explained. "I'm not going to hit anything, just go down deep, and I'm very comfortable underwater, getting tossed around, like in a washing machine. I can relax very easily. I have good lung capacity, I'm prepared for it. But reefs scare me. When I'm getting scraped across reefs, I'm getting skin torn off me, I'm not good with that."

> "I'm so comfortable in big waves when there's deep water. I'm not going to hit anything, just go down deep, and I'm very comfortable underwater, getting tossed around, like in a washing machine. I can relax very easily. I have good lung capacity, I'm prepared for it. But reefs scare me. When I'm getting scraped across reefs, I'm getting skin torn off me, I'm not good with that."

Claiming a Record-Breaking Fifth Consecutive Championship

As the 2002 WCT season got underway, Beachley was distracted by a change in her personal life—she and Bradshaw decided to end their relationship after nearly five years together. The main reason for the breakup was that Beachley wanted to live in her native Australia, while Bradshaw wanted to remain in Hawaii. "I miss my home, and Ken's place is Hawaii," she stated. "Traveling with me also stopped him from pursuing his dream, which is traveling around the world looking for the biggest waves to surf." The former couple parted on good terms and remain friends. "He and I are still prepared to work with each other in regards to my career and his big wave surfing," Beachley said. "But the romantic side of the relationship is over."

Beachley put a great deal of pressure on herself as the 2002 season began. She badly wanted to win a fifth consecutive world championship in order to beat Anderson's record of four straight titles, as well as to claim her place in history as Australia's most successful surfer. But this desire made her overly anxious in the first few events of the WCT season. "I'm trying too hard," she explained. "I came out all guns blazing this year and just put way to much expectation and pressure on myself." Though her performances were consistent, Beachley did not record her first victory until October at the Roxy Pro in France. None of her competitors had won more than one event either, though, so the victory moved her into first place in the point standings with only one event remaining.

Beachley entered the season-ending Billabong Pro in Hawaii with a 340-point lead over her closest rival. But she fell on the first wave of her quarterfinal match and was knocked out of the competition. Her mistake opened the door for her competitors, three of whom were poised to take away her title by winning the event. Once again, Beachley found herself watching and waiting to see whether luck would bring her another championship. The finals were delayed a week due to poor weather conditions, which gave Beachley even more time to ponder her situation. When the day of the competition finally arrived, she tried to calm her nerves by free-surfing out of earshot of the announcers. "I can't stand to sit on the cliff and watch it all unfold without my participation in it," she explained.

Just as had happened the previous year, Beachley's top rivals were eliminated from the competition one after the other. The contest organizers eventually sent someone over to where she was surfing to inform her that she had won her fifth world championship. "It was deja vu. It's a really frustrating way to win," she stated. "I'm in a state of disbelief. The guys on the jet ski came out and said, 'You've won, you've got to come in.' I said, 'I don't believe you.'"

By claiming a fifth consecutive world title, Beachley became the most successful surfer in Australian history. No other Aussie has ever won more than four world titles. In fact, only American Kelly Slater has won six career world championships, and his titles did not come in consecutive years. Beachley's 24 wins between 1993 and 2002 on the ASP World Championship Tour also tied fellow Australian Wendy Botha for most career professional surfing victories by a woman. Yet Beachley was not ready to stop there. "Now that I've won the five, I'm sure some of them are thinking, 'Well, she's got what she wanted and that's it, Layne Beachley's done,'" she acknowledged. "But the goal is now six. I'm determined to continue achieving."

Promoting the Sport of Surfing

Beachley—whose nickname is "Beast"—believes that part of her job as world champion is to promote the sport of surfing, especially among young women. "I want to continue to be a role model for all female ath-

Beachley takes part in a ceremony in Fiji in which she is welcomed to the island, prior to the Roxy Pro event in 2002.

letes and lead the way into a new era of women's surfing," she stated. Toward this end, Beachley agreed to appear as herself in the 2002 feature film *Blue Crush*. The movie follows the adventures of a group of independent-minded teenaged girls who live in Hawaii and love to surf. It features exciting scenes of surfing action, many of which were provided by Beachley's competitors on the pro tour.

Beachley is gratified that surfing has been gaining popularity among women. In fact, 100 women competed on the pro tour in 2002 — twice as many as five years earlier. "It's fantastic to see so many women getting involved and inspiring each other," she noted. Makers of surfing equipment and apparel responded to the trend by expanding their offerings for women. At the same time, though, Beachley points out that professional women surfers still earn far less money than their male counterparts, and that women's competitions are often held in less-desirable locations.

Although she admits that the life of a professional surfer has some negative elements, Beachley loves her career. "It gets a little tedious at times," she said. "You learn to be comfortable living out of a suitcase and moving house every week or two. But I won't have this job for my whole life, so all in all it's not too bad getting paid to see the world." She always tries to behave in a manner that makes her a good representative for her sport. "It's my responsibility as a world champion to be a role model and inspiration," she noted. "I've never done drugs, I've never tried pot, never had a puff of a cigarette. I'm completely drug-free."

Beachley recognizes that surfing involves an element of danger, but she claims that this only makes the sport more fun. "I've never suffered a wipeout to the point where I want to give it away," she stated. "It just makes me more motivated to get back out there. You just get tossed around like you're on spin cycle, then you're on rinse, then you're on washing, and then you're on spin again . . . and then you're spat out. I pretend I'm a rag doll and start joking with myself. It's all mental. You've just got to accept that you're going to take the biggest poundings of your life and be able to relax under extreme duress. That's the secret. So there . . . you can all go out there yourselves and do it now."

The ups and downs that Beachley experienced early in her career taught her a great deal about herself and helped her to become a five-time world champion. When she is asked to give advice to beginning surfers,

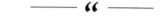

"It's my responsibility as a world champion to be a role model and inspiration. I've never done drugs, I've never tried pot, never had a puff of a cigarette. I'm completely drug-free."

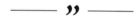

she tells them to set goals, work hard to achieve them, and learn from their mistakes. "If you fight for something I think you appreciate it a lot more. I wouldn't change any of the adversity I've endured over my career because it's character-building. It's who I am. I was not born a world champion or a big-wave surfer. It stems from desire and commitment and sacrifice. You've got to know what you want from life, then go out and get it," she said. "What doesn't kill you makes you stronger! Every mistake is a learning experience no matter how many times you may make the same error. Believe in yourself and surround yourself with people that believe in you too!"

HOME AND FAMILY

When she is not traveling to surfing competitions around the world, Beachley lives in Dee Why, Australia. She says that spending time away from Australia always makes her anxious to return home. "I miss my family and friends," she explained. "I miss the Australian culture, the sense of humor, the sarcasm. I miss being understood."

Beachley is not married, though she has been linked romantically with several well-known men. After breaking up with legendary big-wave surfer Ken Bradshaw in 2002, she began dating Kirk Pengilly, a member of the rock band INXS.

HOBBIES AND OTHER INTERESTS

In her spare time, Beachley enjoys reading, watching movies, playing tennis, and practicing yoga. She also does promotional activities on behalf of her sponsors, which include Billabong, Oakley, Baby G, Gallaz, Island Style, and Boost. During the off-season, she sometimes appears as a sports analyst on an Australian television station. Beachley has invested some of her prize money in real estate, and she owns three homes near Sydney in addition to the one she lives in.

HONORS AND AWARDS

Women's World Champion (Association of Surfing Professionals — ASP): 1998, 1999, 2000, 2001, 2002

FURTHER READING

Books

Gabbard, Andrea. *Girl in the Curl: A Century of Women in Surfing,* 2000

Periodicals

Age (Melbourne), Aug. 28, 1998, Sport sec., p.7; Mar. 18, 2000, Saturday Extra sec., p.1; Dec. 22, 2002, Sport sec., p.12
Australian (Sydney), Dec. 5, 2001, p.20; Jan. 14, 2002, p.22; Mar. 18, 2002, p.30; May 13, 2002, p.21; June 3, 2002, p.27; July 12, 2002, p.33; Dec. 10, 2002, p.16; Dec. 24, 2002, p.14
Herald Sun (Melbourne), Dec. 8, 2001, p.74; Dec. 16, 2001, p.12; Dec. 18, 2002, p.76
Honolulu Advertiser, Nov. 11, 2002, p.D1
Los Angeles Times, July 19, 1999, Around Town sec., p.2; July 23, 2000, p.D9
Orange County (Calif.) Register, Aug. 2, 1998, p.C13; Apr. 13, 2000, p.D14
Sunday Telegraph, Mar. 14, 1999, Sport sec., p.125; Nov. 12, 2000, Local sec., p.30; Jan. 20, 2002, p.55; Jan. 26, 2003, p.I24

Surfer, Apr. 2002, p.46
Times (London), Sep. 13, 1999, p.54

Online Articles

http://www.ausport.gov.au/fulltext/1998/sportsf/sf980410.htm
   ("The Sports Factor Transcript," *ABC Radio National,* Apr. 10, 1998)
http://sixtyminutes.ninemsn.com.au/sixtyminutes/stories/2000_04_09/story_
   144.asp ("Live Q & A with Layne Beachley," *60 Minutes,* Apr. 9, 2000)

ADDRESS

Layne Beachley
Association of Surfing Professionals
P.O. Box 1095
Coolangatta, QLD
4225 Australia

WORLD WIDE WEB SITES

http://www.surflifeforwomen.com/2001/surfers/bios/professional/bios_
   layne1.php
http://www.aspworldtour.com

Sue Bird 1980-

American Professional Basketball Player with the
WNBA Seattle Storm
Winner of Two NCAA Championships with the
University of Connecticut Huskies

BIRTH

Suzanne Brigit Bird—known as Sue for short—was born on
October 18, 1980, in Syosset, a quiet suburb on Long Island in
New York. Her father, Herschel, was a medical doctor special-
izing in cardiac rehabilitation. Her mother, Nancy, worked as a
nurse at Syosset High School. Sue has an older sister, Jennifer.

YOUTH

Bird showed a strong competitive streak even as a child, when she hated to lose at board games like Candyland and Risk. She was an athletic girl who enjoyed playing all kinds of sports, including soccer, tennis, track, and basketball. She honed her basketball talents by playing pickup games against neighborhood boys. One childhood friend recalled an incident when he beat her in a game, then took off his shirt and started to make a victory lap around the court. He was shocked when the basketball came flying across the court and hit him in the stomach. "I was just throwing the ball," Bird said innocently. "I didn't mean to hit you there."

Bird began playing organized basketball at the age of seven in a league organized by the Amateur Athletic Union (AAU). "My sister, who is five years older, played intramurals at a young age and I became interested by attending her games," she recalled. She ended up playing for a top-notch girls' team called the Liberty Belles, which won a regional championship and traveled to Salt Lake City, Utah, to compete for the AAU national championship. Bird played in a number of competitive leagues over the next few years. During this time, she developed into a complete player. "I

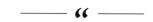

"I have the ability to shoot the ball. I can go by you. I can pull up. I don't have one superior strength in my game. I just do a lot of things pretty good, and it makes me a pretty good player."

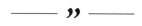

have the ability to shoot the ball. I can go by you. I can pull up," she explained. "I don't have one superior strength in my game. I just do a lot of things pretty good, and it makes me a pretty good player."

Bird's parents separated when she was 15 years old, and they eventually divorced. Though this situation was difficult for Bird, she remained close to both parents and learned a great deal from each of them. Her father tended to be blunt and often pointed out her mistakes, while her mother was always supportive and emphasized the positive. "I had one telling me the truth and one being ultrasupportive," Bird remembered. "It probably shaped my personality. They're so different, and I have both of them in me."

EDUCATION

Bird attended Syosset High School for two years. She was an honor roll student and earned varsity letters in soccer and track. But it was on the basketball court that she truly excelled, starting at point guard and averaging 20 points per game during her freshman year. In her sophomore season she averaged 17.7 points, 6.0 rebounds, 5.6 assists, and 5.4 steals per game.

Before the beginning of her junior year of high school, Bird decided to transfer to Christ the King, a private Catholic school in Queens, New York, that was known for its outstanding girls' basketball program. Christ the King had won seven consecutive state championships and produced a number of great women's basketball players, including WNBA star Chamique Holdsclaw. (For more information on Holdsclaw, see *Biography Today*, Sep. 2000.) Several of Bird's AAU teammates attended Christ the King, and Bird wanted to join the Lady Royals in order to face tougher competition on the court. "It's two different levels of competition," she explained. "I knew if I played against the best, it would make me a better player." Bird's parents rented an apartment in Middle Village, Queens, a few blocks away from her new school. They took turns living there with their daughter during the week, and spent weekends in Syosset.

Some people criticized Bird's decision to change schools. They accused Christ the King of recruiting players, which is not allowed in high school basketball. But Bird denied these charges.

"Not at any point did any of the coaches ever approach me in a way, like, come to Christ the King," she said. "I had played with these girls in AAU and AAU started in sixth grade. So it was friends [that helped convince me to change schools]." Bob Mackey, one of Christ the King's assistant basketball coaches, marveled at how Bird brushed off the criticism and remained focused on her goals. "She was going through a lot then, with the criticism for transferring and her parents getting divorced," he stated. "She was on top of everything, though. She was on top of her books, her basketball, and life. All around her there was adversity and she never let the problems get her away from life. I think it all prepared her for the college level."

During her junior year, Bird averaged 17.4 points, 6.5 assists, and 5.0 steals per game. She led the Lady Royals to a 23-3 record and the New York State High School Championship. In her senior season, Bird averaged 16.3 points, 3.9 rebounds, 7.3 assists, and 8.5 steals per game. Her strong performance at point guard helped Christ the King post a perfect 27-0 record and claim both the state and national championships. At the end of her high school career, Bird was honored as the player of the year for New York City and New York State for 1997-98. She was also named a high school All-American by *Parade* magazine.

Bird's basketball talents attracted the attention of many college scouts, and she received a number of scholarship offers from the nation's top women's basketball programs. Upon graduating from Christ the King in 1998, Bird decided to attend the University of Connecticut (UConn) in Storrs. "I have goals and I feel Connecticut is the place that will help me achieve them," she noted. "They have the greatest fans. The support is unbelievable." Bird went on to make the dean's list as a student at UConn. She graduated with a bachelor's degree in communications in 2002.

CAREER HIGHLIGHTS

College — The University of Connecticut Huskies

Bird entered UConn as part of one of the best recruiting classes in the history of women's basketball. She joined the Lady Huskies along with three other highly recruited players — center Tamika Williams and forwards Swin Cash and Asjha Jones. Many experts predicted that this group might be capable of winning four National Collegiate Athletic Association (NCAA) national championships.

Bird won the starting point guard job for the Lady Huskies as a freshman. She only started eight games in 1999, however, before suffering a season-ending knee injury. Bird was disappointed to miss most of her freshman season, and she found it very frus-

Bob Mackey, one of Christ the King's assistant basketball coaches, marveled at how Bird handled criticism and remained focused on her goals. "She was going through a lot then, with the criticism for transferring and her parents getting divorced," he stated. "She was on top of everything, though. She was on top of her books, her basketball, and life. All around her there was adversity and she never let the problems get her away from life. I think it all prepared her for the college level."

trating to watch from the bench. But the injury helped her realize that she had taken the game and her talent for granted. She vowed to come back and play with greater intensity from that time on. "I was dying to be out there. It's really hard to sit there and know there's nothing you can do. It's a helpless feeling," she noted. "Because of that experience, I value each game much more. You have to play every game like it's your last because it could be."

Bird playing for Connecticut against Seton Hall, February 2002.

Bird also used her time on the sidelines to watch her teammates. She memorized their tendencies and noticed their strengths and weaknesses. When she was ready to return to the lineup, she used this information to improve her game. "I got to see what our team likes to do, what individuals like to do," she recalled. "Even though I didn't actually get playing experience, I got watching experience. I was there every step of the way. . . . I kind of took notes. And I think that's kind of helped me."

Without their star point guard on the floor, UConn struggled in the 1999 NCAA tournament. The highly touted Lady Huskies ended up being upset by Iowa State in the regional semifinals. But Bird came back during her sophomore year to average 10.9 points and 4.3 assists per game. Her contributions helped lift her team to the NCAA championship against their arch-rivals, the University of Tennessee Lady Volunteers. When the season concluded, Bird was honored as the Nancy Lieberman-Cline National Point Guard of the Year for 2000.

By her junior year, Bird had gained a reputation as a go-to player who was capable of making key plays in pressure situations. One of the biggest moments of her college career came in the 2001 Big East Conference championship game. She hit a clutch shot at the buzzer to beat the top-ranked Notre Dame Fighting Irish by a score of 78-76 and give UConn its eighth consecutive conference title. The Lady Huskies reached the Final Four of the NCAA tournament that year, but they lost in the semifinal round. Bird once again averaged 10.9 points per game but increased her assist average to 5.0. She earned her second Nancy Lieberman-Cline National Point Guard of the Year award, and she was also named to the All-Big East Conference team.

A Perfect Season

As Bird's senior season got underway, UConn was the number one women's basketball team in the nation and the favorite to win the NCAA championship. The Lady Huskies' starting five—Bird, Cash, Jones, Williams, and sophomore guard Diana Taurasi—were widely regarded as the best in the game. Although each player possessed outstanding individual talents, it was the way they played together as a team that was most impressive. Many people credited Bird with the success of her team. As the point guard, she was the leader on the court. She brought the ball down the floor, called plays, distributed passes, and helped her teammates reach their potential. "If we get everyone involved and the offense and defense is flowing, we're really impossible to stop," Bird acknowledged.

In addition to being a good ballhandler and playmaker, however, Bird was also a strong shooter. Throughout her college career, she engaged in a constant battle with Connecticut Head Coach Geno Auriemma, who always tried to convince her to shoot more. "For Sue it was always like, 'Who can I pass to now?' rather than taking the shot herself," Auriemma noted. "And I wanted her to shoot more because she's a natural scorer who is very difficult to defend because defenders know that while she's a very good shooter, she loves to pass." Bird tried to follow her coach's instructions, but

> **“**
>
> *Connecticut Head Coach Geno Auriemma always tried to convince Bird to shoot more. "For Sue it was always like, 'Who can I pass to now?' rather than taking the shot herself," Auriemma noted. "And I wanted her to shoot more because she's a natural scorer who is very difficult to defend because defenders know that while she's a very good shooter, she loves to pass."*
>
> **”**

shooting never came as naturally to her as passing and creating scoring opportunities for her teammates. "It's not really a battle," she said of her ongoing struggle with Auriemma. "I think he just wants certain things out of me so it'll help the team. It's not that I'm against that. It goes against some of my personality traits. I'm definitely willing to chip in and do whatever I need to do and fill a role. He's still going to get mad at me if I pass up a shot but I think I've been doing a much better job."

Part of the secret of the Lady Huskies' success was the close relationship that developed among the team's senior starters. Bird shared an off-campus apartment with the three other members of her recruiting class — Swin Cash, Asjha Jones, and Tamika Williams. Bird learned a great deal from her African-American roommates. "Coming to college and rooming with someone of another race gave me a different view of what people have to go through," Bird noted. Her teammates also talked about that learning experience. As Swin Cash explained, "The biggest thing she's learned from me is just that there's another side to the world," Cash said. "Where I come from — growing up in public housing and seeing drugs and alcohol and things she may not have experienced — I think it helps her to understand how society looks at people like me. I think it has helped her understand what it's like being African-American in the here and now."

> "When you're in high school thinking about college, you have all these ideas about how your career is going to play out and all these fantasies. I did have high expectations. What's happened this year, what's happened in my career, has outdone what I thought."

Thanks in part to the bond among the four senior starters, UConn exceeded all expectations in 2002. The Lady Huskies finished the season with a perfect 39-0 record to match the best season ever in NCAA women's basketball (set by Tennessee in 1998). They led the nation in scoring average with 87.7 points per game, and set a new NCAA record by holding opponents to an average of 50 points per game. In fact, only one opponent ever came within 10 points of defeating the Lady Huskies all year.

UConn defeated the Tennessee Lady Volunteers by a score of 79-56 in the semifinals of the NCAA tournament. Bird scored 18 points in that game, which was attended by the largest crowd ever to watch a women's basketball game. Then the Lady Huskies went on to face second-ranked Oklahoma in the NCAA finals. Though Bird struggled a bit early in the game, she nailed six straight free throws down the stretch to help ice the victory, 82-70. UConn thus became only the fourth team in NCAA history to go undefeated and claim the championship. Bird averaged a team-high 18.5 points during the season-ending tournament.

Tamika Williams (left), Diana Taurasi (center), and Sue Bird celebrate their win against Oklahoma in the NCAA Final Four championship, March 2002.

Bird completed her college career with a total of 1,378 points, 585 assists, and 243 steals. Her career averages were 11.7 points and 5.0 assists per game. She left UConn as the school's all-time career leader in three-point shooting percentage (45.9) and free throw percentage (89.2), and also set a school record for most assists in a season (231 during her senior year). The Lady Huskies posted an amazing record of 114-4 with Bird in the lineup.

Looking back on her days with UConn, Bird admitted that her college basketball career had unfolded in an even more spectacular fashion than she had hoped. "When you're in high school thinking about college, you have all these ideas about how your career is going to play out and all these fantasies," she noted. "I did have high expectations. What's happened this year, what's happened in my career, has outdone what I thought."

At the end of her senior year, Bird received many postseason awards in recognition of her individual performance and her contributions to her team's remarkable season. She earned her third consecutive Nancy Lieberman-Cline National Point Guard of the Year award, for example, and was named Big East Conference Player of the Year. She also was named a Kodak All-American and the Naismith Player of the Year. To top off her outstanding college career, she received the Honda Award and the Wade Trophy. Bird accepted all of these honors with humility, always sharing credit with her coaches, teammates, and family. "When you have teammates who are just as talented as you are, it's kind of weird to get all the attention," she said.

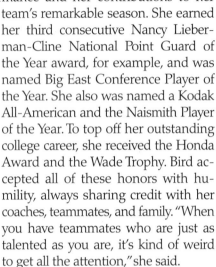

> **"**
>
> *Bird felt reluctant to leave her college teammates. "Sometimes I find myself sitting in the locker room like a dork just thinking about how teams in the WNBA are probably not as close as we are," she explained. "How they don't eat pregame meals together and things like that. I'm going to miss how we just hang out here. I'm going to miss that the most."*
>
> **"**

WNBA — The Seattle Storm

Upon graduating from UConn in 2002, Bird planned to begin a career as a professional basketball player in the Women's National Basketball Association (WNBA), which plays in the summer. Although she looked forward to joining the WNBA, she also felt reluctant to leave her college teammates. "Sometimes I find myself sitting in the locker room like a dork just thinking about how teams in the WNBA are probably not as close as we are," she explained. "How they don't eat pregame meals together and things like that. I'm going to miss how we just hang out here. I'm going to miss that the most."

Bird was selected as the first overall pick in the 2002 WNBA draft by the Seattle Storm. She thus became the only guard ever taken with the top pick in the draft. "Point guards like her don't come along very often," said Storm Coach Lin Dunn. "She has great court vision and surprisingly good

The University of Connecticut placed four players in the first six picks of the 2002 WNBA draft. From left to right: Tamika Williams, Sue Bird, Swin Cash, and Asjha Jones.

speed and quickness. She can score, pass, and handle the ball, and she can lead. Her presence on the floor makes everybody better." Bird's starting salary with the Storm was $57,500, but she was expected to make ten times that amount through endorsement contracts.

Bird was excited that her fellow seniors from the Lady Huskies were also selected high in the draft. In fact, UConn dominated the 2002 WNBA draft the way they had dominated the NCAA, with four players among the first six picks. Cash was selected second overall by the Detroit Shock, Jones was taken fourth overall by the Washington Mystics, and Williams went sixth overall to the Minnesota Lynx.

Perhaps the biggest adjustment Bird had to make upon entering the WNBA was playing for a losing team. The Storm had posted a 10-22 record in 2001, and it had notched a dismal overall record of 16-48 during its first two years of existence. Bird was not accustomed to losing. She had lost only three games during her high school career with Christ the King, and only four games during her career at UConn—a total of seven losses in six years. Some observers pointed out that she could lose that many games in a month as a member of the Storm. "I personally really, really, really don't like to lose, so that's probably going to be a problem," Bird admitted.

In the first game of her professional career, Bird scored 18 points and dished out six assists. But she also committed five turnovers as she struggled to adjust to the greater size and quickness of WNBA players. "I thought at times Sue looked like a rookie and at times she looked like an all-pro player," Dunn said afterward. "She did some good things for us offensively and was able to get us some big buckets, but she can't have five turnovers." Though she initially struggled on the court, Bird made an immediate impact on the Storm with her star power. Her charm and positive attitude made her an instant favorite among fans, and her team saw a surge in ticket and merchandise sales as soon as she took the floor.

> "She's the best," said Christ the King Coach Bob Mackey. "Adults love her because basically they want to see their kids grow up like her. Kids love her. Players look to her. Sue always has it together. She's the complete package."

Bird improved steadily over the course of her rookie season. In August she scored a franchise-record 33 points against the Portland Fire to help her team make the playoffs. The Storm finished the 2002 season with a 17-15 record, which earned them fourth place in the Western Conference and the first playoff appearance in team history. Bird averaged 14.4 points and 6.0 assists during her rookie season. She was named to the All-WNBA Team and was runner-up in voting for the WNBA Rookie of the Year award.

Although the Storm lost to the Los Angeles Sparks in the first round of the playoffs, Bird had led the team to a remarkable turnaround. "As disappointing as it is, I see the future and there is a lot of promise in it," she stated. "This was still a successful season because we got into the playoffs."

NWBL—The Springfield Spirit

When the WNBA season concluded, Bird signed a contract to play winter basketball with the Springfield Spirit of the National Women's Basketball League (NWBL). This relatively new six-team league offered top WNBA players a chance to play professionally in the United States rather than in Europe during the off-season. The Springfield Spirit featured several former UConn players, including Rebecca Lobo, Kara Wolters, and Rita Williams. Bird's college roommate, Swin Cash, also joined the team in 2002. The Spirit hoped that the addition of Bird and Cash would help the team improve on its last-place finish of 2001.

*Bird drives past Teresa Witherspoon in this game between the
Seattle Storm and the New York Liberty, July 2002.*

Bird also became a member of the USA Basketball women's team, which
represented the United States in international competitions, including the
Olympics. She was the youngest member of the American team that went
9-0 and won a gold medal at the World Championships in China in 2002.
Barring injury, Bird is expected to become the starting point guard for
Team USA at the 2004 Olympic Games.

In recognition of Bird's outstanding year — which saw her lead teams to an
NCAA championship, a world championship, and the WNBA playoffs —
she was honored as the 2002 Sportswoman of the Year in the team category by the Women's Sports Foundation. People who knew her lined up to
offer praise for her accomplishments on the court, as well as her leadership
qualities off the court. "She's the best," said Christ the King Coach Bob

Mackey. "Adults love her because basically they want to see their kids grow up like her. Kids love her. Players look to her. Sue always has it together. She's the complete package."

HOME AND FAMILY

Bird, who is single, remains close to her family. Her mother attended all of her home basketball games when she played for Connecticut, and her sister made it to many games as well. Her father moved to Las Vegas, Nevada, after the divorce, but he traveled to see her play in the NCAA tournament and also watched several WNBA contests.

People often ask whether Sue Bird is related to former NBA star Larry Bird. The two basketball players are not related, though Sue sometimes teases fans by making up an elaborate story about a family connection between herself and the Boston Celtics legend. "I tell them he's my half-uncle," she admitted. "I'll make up a total story about how my grandfather, on my dad's side, was married to Larry Bird's mother and they had Larry. Then, my grandfather and Larry Bird's mother got divorced and my grandfather remarried and had my dad. It really gets them going, but he's not my uncle. I wish, though, but he's not."

HOBBIES AND OTHER INTERESTS

In her free time, Bird enjoys hanging out with friends, listening to music, and watching movies. She has a remarkable memory for movie dialogue and can come up with a quote to fit almost any occasion. She also claims that she can recall the score and virtually every moment of every basketball game in which she has ever played.

HONORS AND AWARDS

AAU All-American: 1997
New York State High School Player of the Year: 1997-98
New York State High School Tournament MVP: 1997-98
High School All-American (*Parade*): 1998
Nancy Lieberman-Cline National Point Guard of the Year: 2000, 2001, 2002
ESPN National Point Guard of the Year: 2001, 2002
All-Big East Conference: 2001, 2002
Big East Conference Player of the Year: 2002
Kodak All-American: 2002
Honda Award: 2002
Naismith Player of the Year: 2002
Wade Trophy (National Association of Girls and Women in Sport): 2002

National Women's Player of the Year: 2002
ESPY Award: 2002, Top Female College Athlete of the Year
WNBA All-Star Team: 2002
All-WNBA First Team: 2002
Sportswoman of the Year, Team Category (Women's Sports Foundation): 2002
Women's Basketball World Championship: 2002, gold medal (as member of Team USA)

FURTHER READING

Periodicals

Bergen County (N.J.) Record, Mar. 11, 2002, p.S3; July 2, 2002, p.S1
New York Times, Jan. 9, 2000, Sec. 8, p.7; Mar. 16, 2000, p.D4; Dec. 25, 2000, p.D1; Mar. 25, 2002, p.D1; Mar. 31, 2002, Sec. 8, p.2
Newsday, Dec. 10, 1995, p.28; Jan. 31, 1997, p.A55; Nov. 5, 1997, p.A74; Nov. 14, 2001, p.A96; Apr. 20, 2002, p.A31; Apr. 23, 2002, p.A58
Seattle Post-Intelligencer, Jan. 16, 2003, p.C2
Seattle Times, Aug. 10, 2002, p.D1; Aug. 18, 2002, p.C1
Sports Illustrated, Apr. 8, 2002, p.44; Apr. 11, 2002, p.20; July 1, 2002, p.48
USA Today, Aug. 2, 2002, p.C10
Washington Post, Apr. 2, 2000, p.D11

Online Databases

Biography Resource Center Online, 2003

ADDRESS

Sue Bird
National Women's Basketball League
P.O. Box 1361
La Jolla, CA 92038

WORLD WIDE WEB SITES

http://www.wnba.com/storm
http://www.nwbl.com/spirit
http://www.usabasketball.com/bioswomen/sue_bird_bio.html
http://seattletimes.nwsource.com/sports/storm/spotlight/suebird/
http://espn.go.com/page2/s/questions/suebird.html

Fabiola da Silva 1979-
Brazilian Professional Aggressive In-Line Skater
Winner of Six Gold Medals in the X Games

BIRTH

Fabiola (pronounced fab-ee-OH-lah) Oliveria Samoes da Silva was born on June 18, 1979, in Sao Paulo, Brazil. Brazil is the largest country on the continent of South America, and her hometown is a major city located near its Atlantic Coast. Her father, Ernesto, made a living by selling lottery tickets, while her mother, Claudette, worked as a housekeeper. Da Silva has a younger sister, Fabiana, who is also an outstanding athlete. In 1997, Fabiana won a gold medal in the 1,500-meter event at the Pan-American Games junior track and field championships. Da Silva grew up speaking Portuguese, and she later learned to speak English.

YOUTH

Although da Silva's family did not have much money, she had an enjoyable childhood. "Growing up in Brazil was fun," she recalled. "My parents worked hard and tried to give us the best they could. My sister and I learned pretty much how to do everything. We were very independent." Da Silva spent as much time as possible playing outdoors. She was a tomboy who liked swimming, volleyball, basketball, and skateboarding. "When I was little I always liked to play with the boys," she noted. "They had more fun toys than the girls."

Da Silva took up kickboxing at the age of 12. She was good enough to become the junior regional champion in her weight class within a year. But when an opponent broke her nose during a practice match, she decided to look for another sport. It was around this time that da Silva received her first pair of in-line skates.

Da Silva spent as much time as possible playing outdoors. She was a tomboy who liked swimming, volleyball, basketball, and skateboarding. "When I was little I always liked to play with the boys. They had more fun toys than the girls."

She had enjoyed skating with traditional roller-skates for several years. When her mother saw how much Fabiola liked skating, she saved up money from her housekeeping job to buy her some in-line skates. These skates cost the equivalent of $500 in American money.

After making the transition to in-line skates, da Silva found that they were much easier to maneuver than her old roller-skates. "When I first tried it out I felt weird and uncoordinated," she remembered. "It took me a while to feel comfortable, but after that I picked it up real quick." Da Silva started hanging around at a skate park called Rollerbrothers in Sao Paulo, where local teenaged boys went to practice doing tricks on their skateboards and in-line skates. Although da Silva was one of the only girls at the park, she quickly learned to perform tricks and stunts like the boys. "It looked cool, so I started doing it," she said. Before long, da Silva joined the other kids in forming teams and putting on amateur shows and competitions.

As she grew more interested in skating, da Silva began watching videotapes of the world's best skaters. She would replay their tricks over and over until she figured out how to do them. In 1995 two American superstars of professional skating, Chris Edwards and Arlo Eisenberg, visited Sao Paulo to put on a demonstration for the local skaters. "After they did their stuff, I got to skate a bit with them," da Silva recalled. "They really liked to see a girl skating out there! Afterwards, they asked me for my address, but I thought they were just being nice and that I wouldn't hear from them again."

> *"I would love to go to school but I travel so much that I don't have time for it. I would like to be a vet but I know I would have to choose study or skating. Skating is my life and it's what makes me happy. So I'll keep skating until my body can't take it no more and then in the future I'll go to school. I know school will always be there and skating is not forever."*

A few months later, however, da Silva received an invitation from the American skaters' sponsors to come to the United States to participate in a competition sponsored by the Aggressive Skaters Association (ASA). She was thrilled to make her first journey to America. "I was so excited," she remembered. "Everything was so cool. I kept saying, 'Wow, everyone speaks English. Wow, I'm in the USA. Wow, all these people can skate.'" The unknown 17-year-old girl from Brazil amazed onlookers by capturing first place in the "vert" competition at the 1996 ASA World Tour event in Miami, Florida.

In the vert (short for vertical ramp) competition, skaters glide back and forth through an 11-foot-tall, U-shaped tube called a halfpipe. They gain speed on the downward ramps and perform tricks at the top of the upward ramps. Skaters are judged on the difficulty, performance, flow, and style of their tricks. Competitors usually perform between 15 and 19 tricks within the 50-second time limit.

Da Silva thrilled the crowd at her first organized competition by sailing five to six feet in the air above the halfpipe and performing tricks that only the best male skaters would dare to try. She completed two 360-degree spins, an invert (a handstand performed on the coping at the upper edge of the halfpipe), and a backflip. When she finished, all the professional skaters who had been watching rushed over to congratulate her. "It was my favorite moment of skating," she remembered. "Everyone was coming up to me and telling me they liked me. They said, 'Oh, you're good. You are so good.' It made me feel good inside."

EDUCATION

After winning the first competition she entered in the United States, da Silva knew she had the talent to be a professional aggressive in-line skater. But her mother insisted that she complete her education first. For the first two years of her career, da Silva lived with her family in Brazil, went to school, and traveled five times per year to skating competitions around the world. She graduated from Goaquin Leme Prado in Sao Paulo — the equivalent of an American high school — in 1998.

Da Silva plans to attend college when her skating career is over. "I would love to go to school but I travel so much that I don't have time for it," she explained. "I would like to be a vet but I know I would have to choose study or skating. Skating is my life and it's what makes me happy. So I'll keep skating until my body can't take it no more and then in the future I'll go to school. I know school will always be there and skating is not forever."

CAREER HIGHLIGHTS

Winning Gold Medals at the X Games

Da Silva's surprise victory in Miami in 1996 earned her a sponsorship deal with Rollerblade, one of the leading manufacturers of in-line skates. Rollerblade paid for her travel expenses and gave her free equipment, and she competed professionally as a member of the Rollerblade Riders team. "I had no idea they would pay you money to skate," she said after receiving her sponsorship. Da Silva won a second ASA event in Queens, New York, and then appeared at the 1996 X Games in Newport, Rhode Island.

The X Games are sometimes called the Olympics of alternative or extreme sports. The annual event features sports like skateboarding, wakeboarding, street luge, speed climbing, and motocross. Athletes from around the world compete in a variety of events for medals and prize money. It attracts thousands of spectators as well as a national television audience. Da Silva continued her successful rookie season by claiming a gold medal at the X Games in the women's vert competition. She accomplished this feat even though she and her coach were not informed that the time of her event had been changed. Without having a chance to warm up beforehand, da Silva performed a flawless, high-flying routine.

Da Silva competing in the final round of the women's aggressive vertical in-line skating at the 1997 X Games. Da Silva went on to win the event.

Da Silva earned a second consecutive X Games gold medal in the women's vert competition in 1997, and she claimed a third straight gold medal in 1998. After graduating from high school in Brazil that year, she moved to Santa Rosa, California. She felt that living in the United States would benefit her career by bringing her closer to professional in-line skating events, sponsors, and fans. "One of the reasons I moved to the United States was to learn English better, so I could speak to all my fans, especially the kids, about the lifestyle of skating," explained da Silva, who grew up speaking Portuguese.

As a three-time champion, da Silva was the favorite in the women's vert competition at the 1999 X Games. Many people were surprised when she lost in the finals to Ayumi Kawasaki of Japan. But da Silva took the loss in stride and vowed to use the experience to her advantage. "There's been so much pressure on my back for three years," she admitted. "It's good if you don't win all the time and take a little break. Then you can get yourself right and come back stronger. That's my thinking. That's what I'm going to do."

True to her word, da Silva came back with a spectacular routine to reclaim the women's vert gold medal at the 2000 X Games. She performed a 720 (two full rotations in the air) and a flatspin (a handstand spin with the body parallel to the ground) to defeat Kawasaki by half a point in the finals. "I think the way I put tricks together worked," she said afterward. Then da Silva went on to capture gold in the women's park competition at the X Games. In the aggressive in-line skating events known as park or street competitions, skaters have 65 seconds to make their way through an obstacle course filled with benches, rails, and ramps. They make use of the obstacles to perform between 10 and 17 tricks, which are judged on their difficulty and flow. Da Silva capped off her outstanding 2000 season by winning the ASA World Championship in the women's vert event.

"I am not discriminating against girls. But sometimes girls say, 'Oh, I can't do that. I'm a girl.' I hate it when they say that. I want to die *when they say that."*

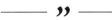

Competing against the Men

During the 2001 season, da Silva was the top-ranked female skater in the ASA for both street and vert events. She won the women's vert competition at the X Games once again in 2001 to claim her sixth gold medal. Unfortunately, she and her rival Kawasaki were the only women to qualify for the competition.

Though highly popular among men, the vert event did not attract many women skaters. Some women felt that it was too difficult to master or too dangerous, and they generally preferred the street or park competition. "I am not discriminating against girls," da Silva noted. "But sometimes girls say, 'Oh, I can't do that. I'm a girl.' I hate it when they say that. I want to *die* when they say that." Other women simply recognized that da Silva was so dominant in the vert that the best they could hope for was second place. The X Games ended up dropping the women's vert event from its schedule for 2002, and the ASA eliminated the women's vert competition that year as well. At this point, da Silva had claimed the ASA World Championship in women's vert three years in a row.

Da Silva was disappointed that her best event was being eliminated from the ASA Pro Tour and the X Games. But the cancellation of women's vert did not end da Silva's days of competition. Two years earlier the ASA had made a special rule, often called the "Fabiola Rule," that allowed her to compete in the men's vert. "You don't get motivated if you don't have somebody to push you," she acknowledged at that time. "With guys, you can't just put something easy together." Once the Fabiola Rule was put in place in 2000, da Silva competed in the men's vert at scattered regional competitions and often finished in the top 10. In 2001, she and Kawasaki competed in the men's division as well as the women's division at the X Games, although both women failed to make the finals of the men's vert competition.

> "I believe that girls can [compete against men] and I am going to keep skating and trying my hardest. In the beginning it will be hard, but in the future it's going to be good. I'm used to skating with guys most of the time. It's always been that way. To be honest, I don't care what people think, and I don't care if I skate with girls or boys. I just want to skate and have fun."

In 2002 da Silva had no choice but to compete against men full-time in the vert. "I believe that girls can do it and I am going to keep skating and trying my hardest. In the beginning it will be hard, but in the future it's going to be good," she said. "I'm used to skating with guys most of the time. It's always been that way. To be honest, I don't care what people think, and I don't care if I skate with girls or boys. I just want to skate and have fun."

Da Silva proved that she could be competitive in the men's division by finishing third at a 2002 ASA Pro Tour event in Dallas, Texas. She followed this accomplishment by taking second place in men's vert at the 2002 Latin American X Games in Brazil. "I hate when guys say girls can't do things," she stated. "In fact, I'd say that is what pushes me to be better. I just want to show that girls can do anything they want to." By the end of the 2002 season, da Silva was ranked 15th in the world in vert. She was the only woman included on the list of top competitors.

Da Silva recognized that some men did not appreciate losing to a woman. "Some people get upset, you know, 'cause it's that macho thing," she noted. "But who cares. All the girls are going to feel great." Another advantage to joining the men's division was that it gave da Silva the opportunity to compete for twice as much prize money as was offered in the women's division.

Da Silva skates at the 2002 Mobile Skatepark Series in Cincinnati, Ohio.

Reaching the Top of Her Sport

Da Silva is now widely regarded as the best women's vert skater in the world. She is also one of the most visible and respected athletes—among men or women—in her sport. In her home country of Brazil, she is known by her first name alone, like many of the country's top professional soccer players. Her fans around the world call her "Fab."

Despite her widespread popularity, however, da Silva remains humble and often tries to downplay her impact on in-line skating. "I don't want people to think of me as a big head," she explained. "It is so ugly on people, having a big head. You should be simple. I'm not like Michael Jordan. I'm just like everybody else."

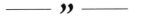

"I care about the way I carry myself. Kids look up to me. I try to stay in shape and keep my body good for anything that I do. No drinks or anything like that. I try to stay as healthy as I can. I work out and skate every day."

Da Silva feels that being a well-known athlete gives her a responsibility to be a role model for young fans. "I care about the way I carry myself. Kids look up to me," she noted. "I try to stay in shape and keep my body good for anything that I do. No drinks or anything like that. I try to stay as healthy as I can. I work out and skate every day." Da Silva has earned a reputation as a fair competitor who is always willing to share her tricks. "I like helping everyone," she said. "I don't like to hide my tricks. We should all try and help each other, because then we can have a great competition."

Da Silva plans to continue competing for another 10 years. She hopes that her influence will help attract more girls to the sport. "I just want to enjoy skating, try to push my sport, and get more girls involved," she stated. "And boys, too." Da Silva had the following advice for girls who are interested in aggressive in-line skating: "Make sure you wear all of your pads. Don't look at it as a 'guy sport.' If you feel comfortable, go out there and have fun. Do what makes you happy. It doesn't matter what it is."

HOME AND FAMILY

Da Silva, who is not married, lives in a townhouse in a quiet neighborhood in Santa Rosa, California. She shares her home with her dog, a Yorkshire

Da Silva on the half-pipe, 2002.

terrier named Chaci. Da Silva indulges her feminine side by sleeping in a large, princess-canopy bed.

Da Silva remains close to her family, although she does not see them as often as she would like. Early in her career, her mother used to accompany her as she traveled to competitions around the world. She eventually used some of her winnings as a professional in-line skater to buy her parents a beach house in Brazil. "My parents are real supportive in anything that I do," she said. "They love Rollerblading and they motivate me to do it more and more."

HOBBIES AND OTHER INTERESTS

In her spare time, Da Silva enjoys shopping, sleeping, and going to the beach. "I go to the beach a lot," she noted. "Maresias, in Brazil, is just beautiful—clean water, lots of trees, nice sand. Not many people go there, only the ones who live in the little town. It's almost deserted."

Da Silva has signed endorsement deals with a number of companies, including Rollerblade, Mountain Dew, The Gap, Cornnuts, 50/50 Frames, Levis, and Harbinger pads. She has also allowed her likeness to be used in several video games. Overall, Da Silva earns about $70,000 per year in sponsorship and prize money, which gives her a higher annual salary than her parents combined. "I could have never dreamed of being where I am today," she stated. "One day I was in Brazil skating and today I have this good, lucky life. It's like I won the lottery."

> *Da Silva had the following advice for girls who are interested in aggressive in-line skating: "Make sure you wear all of your pads. Don't look at it as a 'guy sport.' If you feel comfortable, go out there and have fun. Do what makes you happy. It doesn't matter what it is."*

HONORS AND AWARDS

ASA World Championships, Vert: 1996, first place; 1999, first place; 2000, first place; 2001, first place

ASA World Championships, Street: 1997, first place; 1999, third place; 2000, second place; 2001, second place

X Games, Vert: 1996, gold medal; 1997, gold medal; 1998, gold medal; 1999, silver medal; 2000, gold medal; 2001, gold medal

X Games, Park: 2000, gold medal

Gravity Games, Street: 1999, first place; 2000, second place; 2001, second place

Gravity Games, Vert: 1999, first place; 2000, first place; 2001, second place

FURTHER READING

Books

Savage, Jeff. *Top 10 In-Line Skaters,* 1999

Periodicals

Atlanta Journal and Constitution, May 19, 2002, p.D18
Cleveland Plain Dealer, Aug. 1, 2002, p.D10
Dallas Morning News, Apr. 28, 2002, p.B24
Honolulu Advertiser, June 28, 2002, p.T14
Orange County (Calif.) Register, Aug. 16, 2000, p.D1; Aug. 20, 2000, p.D11
Orlando Sentinel, May 4, 1998, p.C3
Philadelphia Inquirer, Aug. 18, 2001, p.C7; Aug. 16, 2002, p.D6
Providence Journal-Bulletin, Sep. 8, 2001, p.C1
San Francisco Chronicle, July 3, 1999, p.E8
San Francisco Examiner, July 3, 1999, p.D3
San Jose Mercury News, June 3, 1999, p.D1
Sports Illustrated for Kids, May 1, 1999, p.58
Sports Illustrated Women, Sep. 1, 2002, p.128

Online Articles

http://enquirer.com/editions/2002/06/01/spt_da_silva_still_just.html
("Da Silva Still Just One of the Guys," *Cincinnati Enquirer Online,* June 1, 2002)

ADDRESS

Fabiola da Silva
Aggressive Skaters Association
13468 Beach Avenue
Marina del Ray, CA 90298

WORLD WIDE WEB SITES

http://expn.go.com/athletes/bios/DASILVA_FABIOLA.html
http://www.rollerblade.com/skate/aggressive/bios/fabiola_int.html
http://www.sheshreds.com/in_her_view/dasilva_fab_02_03_09.html
http://www.asaskate.com

Randy Johnson 1963-

American Professional Baseball Player with the
Arizona Diamondbacks
Five-Time Winner of the Cy Young Award
Co-MVP of the 2001 World Series

BIRTH

Randall David Johnson, known to his friends as Randy and to
baseball fans as "The Big Unit," was born on September 10,
1963, in Walnut Creek, California. He was the youngest of six
children born to Rollen "Bud" Johnson, a police officer, and
Carol Johnson, a homemaker.

YOUTH

Johnson grew up in Livermore, California, southeast of San Francisco. He was an active boy who enjoyed playing basketball, baseball, and tennis, as well as skateboarding and riding motocross bikes. Always tall for his age, Johnson grew seven inches between the ages of seven and 12 and had reached six feet in height by the time he entered sixth grade. Being so much taller than other kids made him feel self-conscious, especially when he became the subject of teasing. "I used to be a real outgoing person when I was younger," he recalled. "But then I started getting noticed a lot for my height. I felt like I was in a three-ring circus and didn't know how to handle it."

One of Johnson's favorite activities as a boy was playing Little League baseball. As a left-handed pitcher, he tried to copy the style of Vida Blue, a famous left-handed pitcher for the Oakland A's. Johnson practiced pitching for hours at a time by throwing a tennis ball against the door of his family's garage. "I'd get in the street and do my windup, and after I threw the tennis ball at the garage door 70 to 80 times, the nails would start coming loose," he remembered. "My dad would have to hammer them back in." He also played catch with his father, who was an avid softball player.

"I'd get in the street and do my windup, and after I threw the tennis ball at the garage door 70 to 80 times, the nails would start coming loose. My dad would have to hammer them back in."

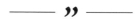

Johnson could always throw the ball very hard when he pitched in Little League, but he sometimes had trouble with his aim. This combination led some parents to complain that they did not want him to pitch because they were afraid their children might get hurt. Over time, as Johnson continued to improve, he began to think about making a career for himself in professional baseball. "I wanted to be a police officer because they help and protect people," he noted. "But the more I played baseball, the more I enjoyed it. That's when I started working really hard at baseball."

EDUCATION

Determined to be known for something other than his height, Johnson fooled around a lot in school and tried to be the class clown. His behavior sometimes affected his studies. "I was in the principal's office a lot because

I was kind of loud in the classroom," he admitted. "The teacher would say, 'You have to go to the principal's office because you're disrupting class.' Maybe I didn't learn as much as I would have liked in school, but that was my fault."

Johnson played baseball, basketball, and tennis at Livermore High School. As a senior, he led the league in scoring as a basketball player and pitched a perfect game (meaning that no opposing players reached base through either hits or walks) as a baseball player. By the time he graduated from high school in 1982, he had reached a height of six feet, nine inches. He was selected in the third round of the Major League Baseball (MLB) draft by the Atlanta Braves that year, but he decided to attend college instead of signing a pro contract.

———— **"** ————

"When I was younger and inexperienced, I was a very animated pitcher. I pitched with a lot of adrenaline. I was my own worst enemy when things weren't going well."

———— **"** ————

Johnson went to the University of Southern California (USC) on a dual scholarship for basketball and baseball, but he quit basketball after his sophomore year in order to concentrate on baseball. One of his teammates on the USC baseball squad was future MLB home run champion Mark McGwire. Johnson posted a record of 16-12 (16 wins and 12 losses) over three seasons as a college pitcher as he continued to struggle with his control. "I was like six-foot-ten and 180 pounds," he remembered. "I threw hard, but I'd usually hit the backstop about every other pitch." In June 1985, at the end of his junior year, he was selected in the second round of the MLB draft by the Montreal Expos. This time, Johnson decided that he was ready to play pro baseball.

CAREER HIGHLIGHTS

The Majors — Montreal Expos

Like most young players, Johnson spent his first few years in the minor leagues. In baseball, some players start their professional careers in the major leagues. But many more start playing for a team in the minor leagues, also called the farm system. The teams in the minor leagues are affiliated with those in the major leagues. There are a variety of minor leagues, which are ranked according to the level of competition. The top or

best league is Class AAA (called Triple A), next is Class AA, then Class A, then below that are the rookie leagues. Players hope to move up through the system to a Class AAA team and then to the major leagues.

Johnson started out with the Expos' Class A team in Jamestown, New York, then moved to the AA team in Jacksonville, Florida, before moving up to the AAA team in Indianapolis, Indiana. Throughout these years, Johnson gained a reputation as a moody and emotional player who struggled to control both his fastball and his temper. Still self-conscious about his height, he became annoyed when public-address announcers would introduce him as the tallest player in baseball, or when photographers would ask him to pose for pictures with the shortest player on the opposing team. He was easily flustered on the mound, too, and had a tendency to turn small mistakes into bigger ones. "When I was younger and inexperienced, I was a very animated pitcher," he explained. "I pitched with a lot of adrenaline. I was my own worst enemy when things weren't going well."

In 1988, a group of Montreal scouts came to watch Johnson pitch in Indianapolis. They were looking for young players to promote to the big leagues. Unfortunately, Johnson was hit in the wrist of his pitching hand with a line drive and had to leave the game early. Frustrated at missing his chance to impress the scouts, he smashed his right hand into the bat rack in the dugout. His left wrist turned out to be fine, but his right hand was broken. "Something had to give, and the bat rack was plywood three inches thick," he noted. This incident convinced the Expos to establish the Randy Johnson Rule, which allowed the team to fine players who hurt themselves in anger.

Despite the injury, Johnson posted a record of 8-7 with a 3.26 earned-run average (ERA—the average number of earned runs given up by a pitcher per nine innings) in 1988, which was good enough to earn him a promotion to the big leagues in the fall of that year. He thus became the tallest player in MLB history at six feet, ten inches. More importantly to Johnson, he went 3-2 with a 2.42 ERA with the Expos and earned a spot in the team's starting rotation for the following season. Unfortunately, Johnson did not last long as a starter for Montreal. He lost the first seven games he pitched and posted a dismal 6.67 ERA. He suffered from a lack of control that caused him to walk too many batters. As a result, he was sent back to the minor leagues for the remainder of the year.

Traded to the Seattle Mariners

In 1989, Johnson was traded to the Seattle Mariners. He played his first game for the Mariners in May of that year and defeated the New York Yankees by a score of 3-2. He went on to finish the season with a 7-9 record and a 4.40 ERA. Although his statistics were not particularly impressive, many people started to take notice of the velocity of the young lefty's pitches. During the 1990 season, Johnson improved to 14-11 and made the MLB All-Star team for the first time in his career. But the best moment of the season came in June, when Johnson pitched the first no-hitter ever by a Mariners hurler during a game against the Detroit Tigers. Johnson could not wait to call his parents afterward and tell them about his accomplishment. "I talked to my mom, she was crying," he remembered. "My dad, my biggest critic, wanted to know why I walked six."

Johnson became a solid performer for the Mariners, winning 13 games in 1991 and 12 games in 1992. He threw as hard as anyone in the majors and led the league in strikeouts during the 1992 season with 241. But he continued to have trouble controlling his pitches and also led the league in walks for the third consecutive year with 144.

Johnson also struggled to control his emotions, often showing fits of temper or sulking over bad calls. When he was not pitching, he acted as if he did not take the game seriously. He often clowned around on the bench and played practical jokes on teammates. He once wore a Conehead costume in the dugout, for example, and he once waved to the crowd with a fake arm that then fell out of his sleeve. Finally, Johnson continued to be sensitive about his height and the attention it brought him. "I'm known more for my height than my pitching," he stated. "It's like I'm a freak, a sideshow act. I suppose it's not rude to ask me how tall I am; people just want to know. But if you were 300 pounds and people kept asking how much you weighed, would you like it?"

Improving Consistency with the Help of a Legend

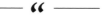

By the 1992 season, Johnson had become so frustrated with his lack of control that he considered quitting baseball. "I had a million dollar arm, but I wasn't thinking enough about how to be a pitcher," he remembered. In August of that year, however, he met with Hall of Fame pitcher Nolan Ryan and Ryan's former pitching coach Tom House. (For more information on Ryan, see *Biography Today,* Oct. 1992, and Update in the 1993 Annual Cumulation.) Ryan gave Johnson valuable advice about dealing with the pressures of being a big-league pitcher. "Nolan said he saw a lot of himself in me—an unproven pitcher who had shined sporadically," he recalled. "Nolan walked a lot of guys in his career, and he told me how he dealt with it. It was really beneficial."

"I'm known more for my height than my pitching. It's like I'm a freak, a sideshow act. I suppose it's not rude to ask me how tall I am; people just want to know. But if you were 300 pounds and people kept asking how much you weighed, would you like it?"

In the meantime, House helped Johnson correct a tiny flaw in his pitching mechanics that was affecting his consistency. "Tom noticed I was landing on the heel of my foot and spinning off toward third base," Johnson explained. "As a result, my arm dropped, I was wide open, I became a sidearm pitcher and was inconsistent with my release point and location." Making small changes in his pitching style and his attitude on the mound made a huge difference in Johnson's performance. "I owe everything to Nolan and Tom," he stated. "Because of them, I now consistently throw the ball in the strike zone, I walk fewer guys, and I strike out more guys."

In December 1992, Johnson's father died of heart disease. "After he passed away, I seriously thought about giving up baseball," Johnson recalled. "Baseball meant so little. I enjoyed the thrill of telling my dad how good I

Johnson warms up before pitching for the Seattle Mariners, April 1996.

was on a given night. When he passed away, I realized I had no one to call. Part of me had died too." Instead of quitting, however, Johnson decided to honor his father by becoming the best ballplayer he could possibly be. The loss of his father gave Johnson new perspective on what was important in life. He became a born-again Christian and started donating ten percent of his salary to charity. He also inscribed a cross and the word "Dad" on the palm of his baseball glove for inspiration. From that time on, Johnson approached his job with new confidence and maturity. "My heart got bigger," he stated. "Determination can take you a long way. After my dad died I was convinced I could get through anything."

Emerging as One of the Best Pitchers in Baseball

When the 1993 season began, Mariners fans saw a new and improved Johnson. Up to that point in his career, his win-loss record was a mediocre 49-48 and he had led the American League in walks for three straight seasons. But over the next nine years he would post an amazing 151-53 record. In 1993, Johnson led the major leagues in strikeouts for a second time with 308 in 255 innings, while walking only 99. He posted a 19-8 record that year with a 3.24 ERA. He made his second All-Star team and pitched two scoreless innings. "My teammates now come up and ask when I'm pitching, instead of asking when I'm throwing," he noted. "I think there's a big difference between someone who tries to go in there and strike everybody out instead of being a pitcher and thinking about the entire game."

"After [my dad] passed away, I seriously thought about giving up baseball. Baseball meant so little. I enjoyed the thrill of telling my dad how good I was on a given night. When he passed away, I realized I had no one to call. Part of me had died too."

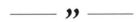

In 1994—with the season shortened due to a players' strike—Johnson became the Mariners' all-time leader in victories. He compiled a 13-5 record with a 3.19 ERA, led the league in strikeouts for the third straight year with 204 in 172 innings, and made his third appearance in the All-Star Game. Johnson was even more impressive in 1995. He went 18-2 for the year to set a new American League record for winning percentage, and he posted a 2.48 ERA. He also earned his fourth consecutive major-league strikeout title with 294 in 214 innings. His rate of 12.35 strikeouts per nine innings pitched broke the major-league record set by Nolan Ryan. Johnson was the starting pitcher for the All-Star Game, and he won the American League Cy Young Award—the award given annually to the top pitcher in each league.

"I can look you in the eye and tell you I have never enjoyed playing base-ball more than I do now," Johnson said during his phenomenal 1995 sea-son. "Not in Little League, not in high school, not in college. The word po-tential used to hang over me like a cloud. People would say, 'What kind of game are we going to get today?' Now I'm content. Right now I'm enjoy-ing every aspect of my life."

More important than his individual accomplishments, Johnson led the Mariners to the playoffs for the first time in the team's history. Seattle had trailed the California Angels in the standings by 11 games in August, but they came roaring back to tie on the last day of the season. The two teams played a one-game playoff to determine which one would win the divi-sion. Johnson took the mound for this game and pitched a 3-hitter. The Mariners' 9-1 victory gave the team its first-ever division title.

Next, the Mariners faced the New York Yankees in a five-game wild-card playoff series. They lost the first two games, but then won game three with Johnson on the mound. After Seattle won game four to tie the series, Johnson came back on one day's rest to pitch three shutout innings in the deciding game, which the Mariners won 6-5 in extra innings. Seattle then moved on to the American League Championship Series, where they faced the powerful Cleveland Indians. Johnson won game three for the squad, then came back to pitch again in game six with the Mariners facing elimination. Although the left-handed ace performed well, he was clearly exhausted from the extra work of the playoffs. The Mariners lost 4-0 and were knocked out of the playoffs.

Struggling through Injuries and Trade Rumors

After a 5-0 start, Johnson went on the disabled list with a back injury dur-ing the 1996 season. He underwent surgery in August to correct a herniat-ed disk in his back. "There was no guarantee I would be back," he recalled. "I was on an operating table, so weak I couldn't pick up a cup of coffee." Although Johnson missed the remainder of the season, he worked hard to return to his former level of play. He came back strong during the 1997 season, posting a 20-4 record to become the Mariners' first 20-game win-ner. He also led the American League in strikeouts per nine innings and was runner-up for the Cy Young Award behind Roger Clemens.

The 1998 season proved to be a difficult one for Johnson. He was sched-uled to become a free agent in 1999, and Mariners' management decided that the team could not afford to sign their ace to a new contract. Negotiations between Johnson and the team broke down, and he became the center of a whirlwind of trade rumors. The uncertainty of the situation affected Johnson's play, and he posted a disappointing 9-10 record with a 4.33 ERA through July. Then the Mariners traded the big left-hander to the Houston Astros, a National League team that was picking up veteran players before the trade deadline in hopes of making it to the World Series. The trade seemed to rejuvenate Johnson, who won his first six starts and ended up 10-1 with a 1.28 ERA. Unfortunately, Johnson could not continue his magic in the playoffs. He was the losing pitcher in game one and game four as Houston was eliminated from the divisional championship.

At the end of the 1998 season, some people suggested that Johnson had intentionally played poorly in Seattle because he was angry with team management. Johnson admitted that the conflict with management had affected his play, but he denied that it was intentional. "People are going to want to know how I could be 9-10 with Seattle and 10-1 with Houston last year," he said. "I'll tell you exactly how I did it. Because I was happy. It's a five-letter word. I was much happier in Houston. I was happy with the environment I was in. I was trying in Seattle. If anyone's ever seen me on the mound, I pitch with a lot of emotion. When you've got an employer screwing with your head, it's kind of tough."

> *"People are going to want to know how I could be 9-10 with Seattle and 10-1 with Houston last year. I'll tell you exactly how I did it. Because I was happy. It's a five-letter word. I was much happier in Houston. I was happy with the environment I was in. I was trying in Seattle. If anyone's ever seen me on the mound, I pitch with a lot of emotion. When you've got an employer screwing with your head, it's kind of tough."*

Joining the Arizona Diamondbacks

Johnson became a free agent before the start of the 1999 season. Many teams were interested in acquiring him, so he had a choice of where to play out the remainder of his career. To the surprise of many baseball fans, he chose to join the Arizona Diamondbacks. The Diamondbacks were an expansion team that had lost 97 games in 1998, which was the team's first year in existence. But during the off-season Arizona acquired several proven veteran free agents, including a whole new starting pitching rotation. Johnson, who owned a home in Glendale, Arizona, signed a four-year contract worth $53 million to play for the Diamondbacks. "This com-

Johnson pitches for the Arizona Diamondbacks, May 2001.

ing year I'm going to be extremely happy," he stated. "It's pretty special to be part of a community you actually live in as well. I'm excited about that. This is where my home is, it's where I want my family to be, and where I feel I can make the biggest impact of the teams that wanted me to pitch for them."

Johnson continued to dominate with his new team. He posted a 17-9 record during the 1999 season and led the National League with a 2.48 ERA and 364 strikeouts. He came close to reaching Nolan Ryan's record of 383 strikeouts set in 1973. In addition, his ratio of 5.2 strikeouts for every walk was the second-best ever. Johnson's strong performance earned him the National League Cy Young Award, making him only the third pitcher ever to win the coveted award in both leagues. He also led the Diamondbacks to the playoffs, but they were knocked out in the division championship series. Johnson pitched in game one and lost, which meant that he tied the record for most consecutive post-season losses by a pitcher with six.

During the 2000 season, Johnson went 19-7 with a 2.64 ERA. He led the majors in strikeouts yet again with 347, and he became the 12th player in history to reach 3,000 career strikeouts. He tied a record by striking out 20 batters in one game against the Cincinnati Reds in June, and he recorded his 200th career victory in October. To top off his excellent year, Johnson won the Cy Young Award for the second season in a row.

A Spectacular Season

The 2001 season turned out to be the most satisfying of Johnson's career. With the addition of right-handed pitching ace Curt Schilling, the Diamondbacks put together the toughest pitching combination in baseball and went all the way to the World Series. Johnson posted a 21-6 record for the year with a 2.49 ERA. He led the majors in strikeouts for the eighth time with 372. The main difference this time was that Johnson did not have to carry the pitching load alone. His teammate Schilling went 22-6 during the 2001 season with a 2.98 ERA and 293 strikeouts. Johnson and Schilling carried their team, which had a 43-56 record in games when the two stars did not pitch.

In addition to their impressive performances on the mound, Johnson and Schilling became close friends off the field. They played golf together every time the Mariners took a road trip. The loser had to buy a golf shirt at the pro shop, and the winner got to wear it into the clubhouse so their teammates would know who won. Johnson and Schilling pushed each other to perform at a new level all year, but also reduced the pressure of being the lone ace on the pitching staff. "What helped most with Curt was that he's one of the few pitchers who knows the expectations put upon the ace in a rotation of five pitchers. So I can share with him experiences and feelings I couldn't share with anybody," Johnson explained. "I didn't have the burden I'd been carrying for years. I didn't have to come to the ballpark knowing I'd have to win this

"What helped most with Curt [Schilling] was that he's one of the few pitchers who knows the expectations put upon the ace in a rotation of five pitchers. So I can share with him experiences and feelings I couldn't share with anybody. I didn't have the burden I'd been carrying for years. I didn't have to come to the ballpark knowing I'd have to win this game. I felt like if we were pitching back-to-back games, if I didn't win, he would. And if he didn't, I would."

game. I felt like if we were pitching back-to-back games, if I didn't win, he would. And if he didn't, I would."

The Diamondbacks rode their two star pitchers into the playoffs, where they defeated the St. Louis Cardinals to win their division. Unfortunately, Johnson lost the game he started, which gave him a seven-game losing streak in the postseason dating back to 1995. But he broke the streak during the National League Championship Series, winning two games to help Arizona eliminate the Atlanta Braves.

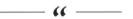

The 2001 World Series

"This is what every player in that clubhouse has waited for," Johnson said about making it to the World Series. "This is everybody's dream, to be here and to be playing the Yankees. It's the biggest stage in sports."

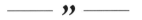

Arizona made it to the World Series faster than any other expansion team. There they faced the three-time defending champions, the mighty New York Yankees. The Yankees were big favorites going into the series, although some experts gave Arizona a chance thanks to Schilling and Johnson. "This is what every player in that clubhouse has waited for," Johnson stated. "This is everybody's dream, to be here and to be playing the Yankees. It's the biggest stage in sports." The Diamondbacks won the first two games on the strength of their aces, with Johnson throwing a three-hit shutout with 11 strikeouts in game two. But the Yankees came back to win the next three games by one run each. With his team down 3-2 in the series and facing elimination, Johnson won game six by a score of 15-2.

Schilling started the decisive game seven and performed well for seven innings. Then, in an unusual move, Diamondbacks Manager Bob Brenly brought in Johnson as a relief pitcher. "He said all along he's not going to play winter ball, so there's nothing to save it for," Brenly said. Johnson entered the final game with two outs in the eighth inning and his team behind 2-1. He got the next four outs to keep it a one-run game going into the bottom of the ninth. Then the Diamondbacks came back to win 3-2 on a bases-loaded single by Luis Gonzalez. Johnson received credit for the win, giving him three victories in the World Series.

Johnson and Schilling shared the honor of World Series Most Valuable Player. The duo went 4-0 in the World Series with a combined 1.40 ERA.

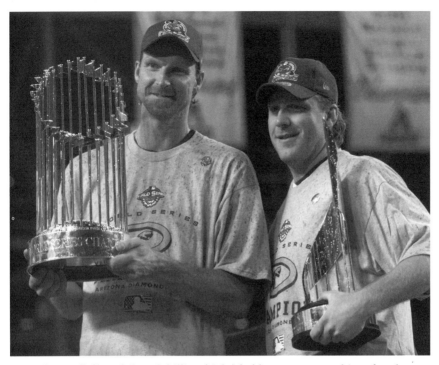

Johnson (left) and Curt Schilling (right) hold post-game trophies after the Diamondbacks won the World Series. Johnson is holding the World Series Championship team trophy, and Schilling is holding the Most Valuable Player award, which the two pitchers shared.

In fact, the two stars produced 224 of the 297 outs it takes a team to win a world championship through three rounds of playoffs. Afterward, Johnson won his third consecutive National League Cy Young Award. Schilling was the runner-up. "This has been a dream season. Not just because of the Cy Young Award but because another dream was fulfilled," Johnson said. "I know Curt's happy for me. I talked to him earlier today. He was calling me today to thank me for getting him to this next level where he's at. I thought that was the most flattering comment I've received to this point in my career."

Johnson noted that the World Championship meant more to him than a whole trophy case full of individual honors. "If you are not at the pinnacle of your profession, the Super Bowl, the NBA Championship, World Series, you kind of feel short on your career," he explained. "I felt that way last year when I received my Cy Young Award. I still felt like I was not a complete player because I had not been to the World Series. I had some indi-

Johnson's release.

vidual accomplishments, but this is a team game, and it takes 25 guys to get to the World Series."

In the 2002 season, Johnson continued his string of fine regular-season performances. He posted a 24-5 record with 334 strikeouts and a 2.32 ERA, topping the National League in all three categories. At the end of the season, he claimed his fourth consecutive National League Cy Young Award. Johnson thus became only the second pitcher in major-league history to win four straight Cy Young Awards, and he tied the record of five career awards set by Roger Clemens. The Diamondbacks finished the 2002 season with a 98-64 record to win their division, but they were swept in the first round of the playoffs by the St. Louis Cardinals. Johnson pitched in game one and allowed five runs in six innings.

In March 2003, Johnson renegotiated his contract with the Arizona Diamondbacks. He signed a new two-year extension to his contract worth $33 million. That brings the total value of the deal he originally signed to almost $65 million. Johnson's contract is the most lucrative annual deal for a baseball pitcher. But since he has earned a World Series trophy and five Cy Young Awards, including consecutive awards in the last four years, many agree he's worth it.

The Most Intimidating Pitcher of His Era

The Big Unit is widely considered to be one of the most intimidating pitchers of his era. His career statistics through the 2002 season — 224 wins, a 3.06 ERA, and five Cy Young Awards — speak for themselves. Johnson has also struck out 3,746 batters in his career, and his average of 11.21 strikeouts per nine innings is the best in major-league history. "I'm always trying to work on my control and get ahead of hitters," he stated. "That's pretty important for any pitcher, just being in control of the game more, dictating what's happening. I think I have a firm grasp on the majority of that, but there's always room for improvement."

Aside from his statistics, however, Johnson's sheer presence on the mound is enough to intimidate hitters. His size and his unusual windup make it seem as if he is releasing the ball closer to hitters than most other pitchers, plus his fastball has been clocked at up to 100 miles per hour. "I can be a little intimidating when I pitch because I'm so much taller than everybody and I throw hard," he admitted. "Hitters say it looks like I'm releasing the ball right on top of them." Johnson has proven to be nearly impossible for left-handed batters to hit. In fact, lefties have chalked up a dismal .197 batting average against him over the course of his career. Many top left-handed hitters schedule their days off when Johnson is pitching so they do not have to face him.

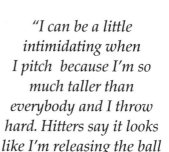

"I can be a little intimidating when I pitch because I'm so much taller than everybody and I throw hard. Hitters say it looks like I'm releasing the ball right on top of them."

Ever since he turned his game around during the 1992 season, Johnson has gained a new appreciation for his sport and a new acceptance of his height. "Now I know it's been a gift from God to be this tall and to be left-handed and to have a fastball," he stated. "I really have a great life. I'm playing a sport I love and get grossly overpaid doing it. I'm not ashamed to say that." Johnson has learned some important lessons along the way to becoming one of the best pitchers in baseball. "When things don't go your way, don't give up," he tells young fans. "Things haven't always gone my way. It took me a long time before I was able to throw the ball over the plate. There were times when I was really frustrated. You should always believe in yourself. If you do, your dreams can come true."

MARRIAGE AND FAMILY

Johnson met his wife, Lisa, at a charity golf tournament. They were married in 1993. The Johnsons have four children: daughters Samantha (born in 1994), Willow (1998), and Alexandria (1999), and son Tanner (1996). They live in Glendale, Arizona, in a home with eight-foot doorways and high counters in order to accommodate Johnson's height.

HOBBIES AND OTHER INTERESTS

Johnson has a number of hobbies. He is an accomplished amateur photographer whose work has been displayed in several art exhibitions. He also plays the drums and has had the opportunity to play with a few well-known bands, including Rush, Queensryche, and Soundgarden. Johnson also enjoys listening to music and maintains a collection of between 500 and 600 old records. "The reason I got into collecting vinyl is because there are a lot of bands I grew up listening to that only had one or two successful albums," he explained. "It's hard to find them in compact disc. So you have to get them on vinyl." Finally, Johnson is involved in charity work. He is active in the fight against homelessness and cystic fibrosis, and he also participates in the Make-a-Wish Foundation.

HONORS AND AWARDS

MLB All-Star Team: 1990, 1993, 1994, 1995, 1997, 1999, 2000, 2001
Cy Young Award (American League): 1995
Cy Young Award (National League): 1999, 2000, 2001, 2002
Warren Spahn Award as Most Outstanding Left-Handed Pitcher in
    Baseball: 1999, 2000, 2001, 2002
World Series Co-MVP: 2001 (with Curt Schilling)
Leroy "Satchel" Paige Award for Pitcher of the Year (Negro Leagues
    Baseball Museum): 2000, 2001
Co-Sportsman of the Year (*Sports Illustrated*): 2001 (with Curt Schilling)

FURTHER READING

Books

Bonner, Mike. *Randy Johnson,* 1999 (juvenile)
Christopher, Matt. *On the Mound with Randy Johnson,* 1998 (juvenile)
Sports Stars, Series 2, 1996
Stewart, Mark. *Randy Johnson: The Big Unit,* 1998 (juvenile)
Who's Who in America, 2002

Periodicals

Arizona Daily Star, Nov. 14, 2001, p.C1

Arizona Republic, Dec. 1, 1998, p.C1; Mar. 25, 2003, p.C1

Baseball Digest, Feb. 2001, p.42

Contra Costa (Calif.) Times, Mar. 25, 1996, p.B1; Aug. 15, 1999, p.B5; July 1, 2001, p.B1

Current Biography Yearbook, 2000

Los Angeles Times, Apr. 5, 1999, p.D1; Nov. 14, 2001, p.D1

Minneapolis Star-Tribune, Oct. 27, 2001, p.C1

New York Times, Mar. 31, 1996, sec. 8, p.8; Oct. 11, 2001, p.S1; Oct. 17, 2001, p.S1; Oct. 29, 2001, p.D9; Nov. 2, 2001, p.S6

People, Oct. 6, 1997, p.123

Seattle Post-Intelligencer, June 19, 1995, p.D1; Feb. 20, 1996, p.D1

Sport, June 1994, p.42; June 1999, p.54

Sporting News, July 11, 1994, p.13; Apr. 14, 1997, p.48; Dec. 8, 1997, p.86; Oct. 5, 1998, p.10; Dec. 14, 1998, p.80; May 22, 2000, p.33; Oct. 1, 2001, p.46

Sports Illustrated, Mar. 20, 1989, p.42; May 4, 1992, p.46; June 26, 1995, p.58; July 7, 1997, p.52; Aug. 10, 1998, p.32; May 8, 2000, p.52; Nov. 7, 2001, p.66; Nov. 12, 2001, p.36; Dec. 17, 2001, p.112

Sports Illustrated for Kids, Sep. 1995, p.54; Sep. 1996, p.60

Online Databases

Biography Resource Center Online, 2003, article from *Sports Stars,* 2000

ADDRESS

Randy Johnson
Arizona Diamondbacks
BankOne Ballpark
401 East Jefferson Street
Phoenix, AZ 85004-2438

WORLD WIDE WEB SITES

http://diamondbacks.mlb.com
http://www.bigleaguers.com
http://www.baseball-reference.com/j/jonsra05.shtml

Jason Kidd 1973-

American Professional Basketball Player with the
New Jersey Nets
Five-Time NBA All-Star
Perennial League Leader in Assists and Triple-Doubles

BIRTH

Jason Frederick Kidd was born on March 23, 1973, in San
Francisco, California. His father, Steve, worked as an airline
supervisor for TWA. His mother, Anne, worked as a book-
keeper for a bank. He has two younger sisters, Denise and
Kimberly.

Jason comes from a mixed racial background—his father is African-American, and his mother is white. "I was different from the day I was born," he stated. "I had two different cultures and two different backgrounds to learn from."

YOUTH

Kidd grew up as part of a wealthy, close-knit family on a ranch outside of Oakland, California. He was a competitive boy who loved playing sports. He started out playing soccer, which was his favorite sport until he began playing basketball in the fourth grade. He stood out immediately on the basketball court. During his first year, he led his Catholic league team to a major victory, scoring 21 of the team's 30 points.

Kidd perfected his game on the asphalt courts in Oakland's playgrounds. It was there that he was "schooled" by NBA All-Star Gary Payton. "I used to beat up on him to make him tough," Payton recalled. "He used to go home and tell his mother. But he'd come back every day and do something different to stop me from what I was doing to him."

"I was different from the day I was born," Kidd said about his mixed racial heritage. *"I had two different cultures and two different backgrounds to learn from."*

Kidd learned early on that the best way to be liked by the other players was to help them score baskets. Older boys often chose him to play on their teams because he passed the ball to them and made them look good. "Everybody wanted to score baskets," he noted. "I would get picked [for teams] a lot because they knew I wouldn't shoot." He practiced aiming his passes by throwing the ball at flies on a wall beside his house.

Neighborhood players also appreciated Kidd's fierce competitive spirit. In the sixth grade, for example, he charged right over a mailbox while playing in a neighborhood Thanksgiving football game. Such toughness is part of the reason he is often described as "a fullback with a basketball." Kidd's parents eventually convinced him to give up football. But he continued to play soccer and baseball, excelling at both.

Kidd's athletic ability always shined the brightest on the basketball court, however. He was so talented, in fact, that he began receiving college recruiting letters before he even started high school. "Everybody started saying how great Jason was," his father recalled. "We were flattered, but afraid to accept it. I guess by high school we started believing he might be something special."

EDUCATION

Kidd attended St. Joseph's of Notre Dame, a small Catholic high school in Alameda, California. He won the starting point guard position on the Pilots' varsity basketball team as a freshman. But when he posted poor grades in several of his classes, his parents threatened to pull him off the team. The threat convinced Kidd that he needed to pay more attention to his studies, and from that point on his grades improved.

At the beginning of his high school career, Kidd did not have a strong outside shot. He made up for this weakness with his masterful direction of the team's offense and his incredible passing abilities. But he also worked with his coach, Frank Laporte, to develop a reliable outside jump shot. During his freshman year, Kidd tallied 376 points, 263 assists, 278 rebounds, and 157 steals. His impressive statistics helped him earn a number of regional honors as well as the California State Frosh Player of the Year award. Kidd also garnered praise from college coaches like Jerry Tarkanian of the University of Nevada-Las Vegas (UNLV), who called him "the next Magic Johnson," referring to the legendary Los Angeles Lakers guard.

Kidd continued to excel on the court during his sophomore season, posting 645 points, 320 assists, 297 rebounds, and 168 steals. He was named player of the year for his league and region. By his junior season, Kidd was a renowned high school star. So many people came to watch him play that the Pilots often had to hold home basketball games at the Oakland Coliseum, where the NBA's Golden State Warriors played. Colleges across the country sent recruiters to watch the young star, and he received numerous scholarship offers. St. Joseph's took advantage of Kidd's popularity by marketing a line of sportswear under his name and auctioning signed basketballs. He also had his own trading card.

Prior to Kidd's junior season, Laporte chose to move the Pilots up a division in order to play against better competition, even though St. Joseph's had only one-third the enrollment of most Division I schools. Kidd rewarded his coach's confidence in him by leading the Pilots to the California Division I State Championships in both his junior and senior years. In his junior year, Kidd tallied 754 points, 237 assists, 309 rebounds, and 145 steals in leading his team to a 31-3 record. His performance helped him earn All-American honors from *Street and Smith* and *Parade* — two of the most respected rankings for high school basketball players.

Kidd continued to improve through his senior year, posting 886 points, 345 assists, 258 rebounds, and 249 steals to lead his team to a 32-3 record. He completed his high school career as the sixth all-time leading scorer in California prep history and the new state record holder for career assists with 1,155. His outstanding play earned him the 1992 Naismith Award as the nation's top high school basketball player, and he was also named national player of the year by *USA Today*. But while Kidd's amazing statistics and long list of awards received a great deal of media attention, it was his unselfish play and uncanny ability to feed passes to his teammates that gained the respect of his coaches and fellow players. Everyone agreed that Kidd's graduation from St. Joseph's of Notre Dame in 1992 marked the end of an era at the school.

CAREER HIGHLIGHTS

College — The University of California Golden Bears

Despite struggling with his college entrance exams, Kidd was recruited heavily by a number of top college basketball programs, including Arizona, Kentucky, Kansas, and Ohio State. Some experts even suggested that he was good enough to skip college and go straight to the NBA. His strong performance during a summer pro-am league in San Francisco — in which he was named most valuable player — proved that he could play at a professional level. "Jason Kidd is the only player I've seen in 32 years of coaching who could possibly skip college and go straight to the NBA," proclaimed University of California-Los Angeles (UCLA) Coach Jim Harrick.

> *Kidd learned early on that the best way to be liked by the other players was to help them score baskets. Older boys often chose him to play on their teams because he passed the ball and made them look good. "Everybody wanted to score baskets," Kidd noted. "I would get picked [for teams] a lot because they knew I wouldn't shoot."*

Although Kidd initially planned to attend an out-of-state college, he eventually decided to attend the University of California (commonly known as Cal) at the urging of his parents. Even though the university was not known as a basketball powerhouse, Kidd's parents had been impressed with Cal's head coach, Lou Campanelli, and his strong emphasis on academics. In addition, Cal was only a few miles away from Kidd's family

Cal point guard Jason Kidd dribbles the ball up court on a break during the Golden Bears Pac 10 game against the Washington State Cougars, 1993.

home, so he could continue to receive support from his family and friends as he began this new stage in his life. In addition, Kidd had played pick-up games at Cal while in high school and he knew several of the players. As the beginning of the 1992-93 season approached, Kidd expressed confidence that he would be a star at the college level. "I think the transition from high school to college is not that great for me as it might be for some players," he explained. "Playing with the pro players and college players in the summer, I have an idea of what it's going to take."

The year before Kidd joined the Golden Bears basketball squad, Cal posted a 10-18 record. Some experts predicted that Kidd could turn the team around within two seasons and lead them to the NCAA Final Four. Cal marketed their new star heavily. The team scheduled five home games at the Oakland Coliseum, which had more than twice as much seating capacity as the school's 6,578-seat Harmon Arena.

Despite these high expectations, the season got off to a rocky start. In the middle of Kidd's freshman year, Campanelli was fired amidst controversy. According to rumors, Campanelli had been pressuring his players in a negative and stressful way. But players and their parents denied these allegations. Todd Bozeman, the assistant coach who had recruited Kidd, took over the head coaching job.

"I think the transition from high school to college is not that great for me as it might be for some players," Kidd said. "Playing with the pro players and college players in the summer, I have an idea of what it's going to take."

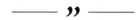

As the season progressed, the Bears continued to improve. The squad finished the season with a 21-9 record, earning the Bears an invitation to the NCAA tournament for only the second time in 33 years. Kidd excelled in the 1993 tournament. He hit several game-winning shots, including one against the Duke Blue Devils in the second round of the Midwest Regional. Kidd single-handedly eliminated the two-time defending national champions from the NCAA tournament, and in the process earned himself a spot on the cover of *Sports Illustrated*. Cal's surprising tournament run ended in the next round, however, when they lost to the University of Kansas Jayhawks.

Kidd ended his freshman season averaging 13 points, 7.7 assists, 4.9 rebounds per game. He also averaged 3.8 steals per game, which set an NCAA freshman record. Kidd became only the fifth freshman ever to be named to the All Pacific-10 Conference team. He was also named Freshman of the Year by *Sporting News* and *USA Today*. Impressive statistics were not Kidd's only contribution to his team's success, however. His court sense and hustle also helped motivate his teammates to play their best.

In his sophomore year of college (1993-94), Kidd led the nation in assists. He averaged 16.7 points and 9.1 assists per game, and also set a school record for career steals. Kidd was named a first-team All-American and the Pac-10 Conference Player of the Year—becoming the first sophomore and the first player from the University of California to earn that honor.

NBA—The Dallas Mavericks

Kidd did not return to Cal for his junior and senior years. Instead, he decided to make himself eligible for the 1994 NBA draft. He was selected as the second overall pick in the draft by the Dallas Mavericks—behind Glenn "Big Dog" Robinson of Purdue but ahead of Grant Hill of Duke. Kidd was thrilled to have the opportunity to play for the Mavericks. He had followed the team as a child and had even kept a Mavericks cap in his mother's car, dreaming that he would someday play in Dallas. He signed a contract worth $52.4 million over nine years.

Prior to starting his pro career with the Mavericks, though, Kidd had to deal with several legal problems. An airline clerk named Alexandria Brown claimed that Kidd was the father of her son, Jason Jr., born in 1993. Brown filed a paternity suit against Kidd, and he was ordered to pay child support. A young woman named Tameka Tate also sued Kidd for $250,000 for allegedly hitting and verbally abusing her. Due to conflicting stories from witnesses, however, the judge decided to drop the charges. Then, a month before he started playing for the Mavericks, Kidd left the scene of an auto accident that he was involved in and that he may have caused. He was arrested for speeding and misdemeanor hit-and-run, fined $1,000, and ordered to serve 100 hours of community service by coaching basketball at the Boys and Girls Clubs. Kidd later claimed that these experiences helped him mature. "When you do something bad, something good can come out of it," he stated. He received a great deal of negative press during this time, but he helped improve his reception in the Dallas community by making major contributions to charities.

Kidd joined a struggling team in Dallas, just as he had at Cal. In fact, the Mavericks had only managed to win 13 of their 82 games during the 1993-94 season. Kidd provided the team with a badly needed dose of hustle and playmaking ability. In his rookie year he averaged 7.7 assists and 1.9 steals per game, which ranked him in the top 10 in the NBA in both categories. He also posted four triple-double games (games in which he achieved double digits in three statistical categories—usually points, rebounds, and assists), the most in the NBA. Kidd suffered a season-ending ankle injury in February, and his team failed to make the playoffs. The Mavericks still

Dallas Mavericks guard Jason Kidd hangs over Golden State's Keith Jennings after he scored in Dallas, April 1995.

improved significantly over the previous season to finish with a 36-46 record in 1994-95.

Kidd shared Rookie of the Year honors with Grant Hill of the Detroit Pistons, and he was the only unanimous choice to the NBA All-Rookie team. He earned these honors despite the fact that he made only 38 percent of his shots from the field, a low percentage that showed how highly voters regarded his ability to pass off to teammates and to make plays happen. Kidd's outstanding play during his rookie season led many people to compare him to Magic Johnson. The great Los Angeles Lakers guard was Kidd's role model. "I will probably always pattern my game after Magic Johnson," he stated. "He was a total player. He always had fun on the court but at the same time he took care of business and he made everybody better around him. He brought his team to another level."

> *"I will probably always pattern my game after Magic Johnson," Kidd said about his role model. "He was a total player. He always had fun on the court but at the same time he took care of business and he made everybody better around him. He brought his team to another level."*

During his second NBA season, Kidd averaged 16.6 points per game and was named to the starting team for the annual All-Star game. But the Mavericks struggled that year and their record dropped to 26-56. Part of the reason for the team's decline could be traced to conflict between Kidd and another young star on the Mavericks, Jimmy Jackson. The two players had trouble getting along both on and off the court. As a competitive but quiet player, Kidd sometimes had problems communicating with his teammates. In fact, he once went six weeks without speaking to Jackson. Mavericks Coach Jim Cleamons tried to make peace between his two stars, but Kidd demanded to be traded.

The Phoenix Suns

In December 1996 the Mavericks traded Kidd to the Phoenix Suns for three other players. "This is for our future," said Suns Coach Danny Ainge. "Jason Kidd is a franchise player. He's a perennial All-Star. I knew he was unhappy in Dallas, and I think he'll be excited with starting over fresh in a new city. If he can rekindle that fire he had in his first and second years,

Phoenix Suns guard Jason Kidd hits a half-court shot just before the buzzer as Atlanta Hawks guard Jason Terry defends, January 2001.

he'll be a superstar." Although Kidd was sorry to leave Dallas and many good friends, he was excited to join one of the strongest offenses in the NBA. He chose the jersey number 32, which represented the triple-double statistics he hoped would someday become his season averages. Unfortunately, Kidd hurt his shoulder in his very first game in Phoenix and was out for most of the 1996-97 season.

Kidd came back in the 1997-98 season to repeat his feat of posting four triple-doubles, tying Grant Hill for most in the NBA. Making full use of his ballhandling and defensive skills, Kidd led the Suns to the NBA playoffs with a 56-25 record. Although they lost to the San Antonio Spurs in the first round, Kidd earned a spot as a reserve in the All-Star game that year.

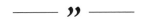

"I think that you cannot measure what's inside somebody's body, and what I mean by that [is] heart," Kidd said about his Nets teammates. *"These guys, my teammates, have been knocked down, been tortured in their short careers in New Jersey, and we surprised a lot of people."*

Kidd had an amazing season in 1998-99. He achieved seven triple-doubles (out of a total of 18 in the entire league) and averaged 16.9 points and an NBA-best 10.8 assists per game. He was also named the NBA Player of the Month in April. Unfortunately, the Suns again lost in the first round of the playoffs, this time to the Portland Trailblazers.

Kidd started out strong in the 1999-2000 season, but he fractured his left ankle in March. The injury forced him to sit out the last two months of the season and the first three games of the playoffs. He returned in time to help the Suns progress past the San Antonio Spurs to the second round of the playoffs, where they faced the Los Angeles Lakers. Although Kidd played well and achieved his first-ever triple-double in a playoff game, the Suns lost the series. His individual statistics remained impressive despite his injury. He led the NBA in triple-doubles with five and in assists with an average of 10.1 per game. He started in the All-Star game and was also honored for his defensive skills, making the All-Defensive Second Team.

In the fall of 2000, Kidd contributed his talents to the U.S. men's basketball team at the Olympic Games in Sydney, Australia. As the starting point guard and one of three captains, he helped Team USA bring home the gold medal.

The 2000-01 season marked the third consecutive year that Kidd led the NBA in assists (averaging 9.8 per game) and triple-doubles (with seven), and he was once again selected to play in the All-Star game. The Suns finished the season with a 51-31 record, but they were knocked out in the first round of the playoffs.

Kidd's off-court legal troubles also returned in 2001, when he was arrested for hitting his wife, Joumana, during an argument. He spent a night in jail, paid a fine, and underwent counseling with a sports psychologist. Kidd expressed remorse for his actions, sending a letter of apology to Suns season-ticket holders and making an apology to fans at mid-court after a home game. He blamed his behavior on career-related stress and the death of his father in 1999 from a heart attack. He also claimed that the arrest had a positive effect on him by helping him learn to communicate better and express his emotions in a more appropriate way. He said that the development of these skills not only improved his home life, but also helped make him a stronger team leader.

The New Jersey Nets

In July 2001, Kidd was traded to the New Jersey Nets. Many observers believed that the Suns decided to trade him because of the negative publicity his behavior had brought to the team. Despite such rumors, however, Kidd received a warm reception in New Jersey. In fact, he was named co-captain of the Nets—a team that had finished 26-56 the previous year and had not posted a winning season since 1997-98.

Kidd set a goal for his new team of winning 40 games in the 2001-02 season. He also promised to lead the Nets to the playoffs. New Jersey shocked many observers by winning seven of their first eight games under Kidd's dazzling on-court leadership, and the team continued to perform above expectations throughout the grueling NBA season. The Nets concluded the season with a 52-30 record, which marked the first time the team had won over 50 games in a season since its entry into the NBA in 1976. The Nets tallied the best record in the Eastern Conference, making them the top-seeded team heading into the 2002 playoffs.

New Jersey had only made it past the first round of the playoffs once before in its franchise history. But powered by Kidd's performance, the Nets progressed all the way to the NBA finals. He was the top scorer for his team in 11 of their 20 playoff games, and he even averaged a triple-double in the conference finals against the Boston Celtics—thus becoming the first player since Magic Johnson in 1983 to achieve triple-double stats in a conference championship. The Nets were swept in the finals by the defending champion Lakers, but they had come a long way in one season.

Kidd gave his teammates credit for the Nets' surprising run. "I think that you cannot measure what's inside somebody's body, and what I mean by that [is] heart," he stated. "These guys, my teammates, have been knocked down, been tortured in their short careers in New Jersey, and we surprised a lot of people." The 2001-02 campaign also marked Kidd's fifth appearance in the All-Star game of his eight-year career, and he finished second to Tim Duncan of the San Antonio Spurs in voting for the NBA's most valuable player.

It is Kidd's remarkable passing ability that most distinguishes his play. "I never talk to him about [his passing]," said Nets Coach Byron Scott. "It's just like Picasso when he's doing a painting — you don't bother an artist, you let him do his work."

One of the League's Best Point Guards

Today, Kidd is widely considered to be among the best point guards in the NBA. He is acknowledged as a strong all-around player who contributes by scoring, rebounding, and making assists, as well as by blocking shots and making steals. But it is Kidd's remarkable passing ability that most distinguishes his play. "I never talk to him about [his passing]," said Nets Coach Byron Scott. "It's just like Picasso when he's doing a painting — you don't bother an artist, you let him do his work." Rudy Tomjanovich, the head coach of the Houston Rockets who had coached Kidd in the 2000 Olympics, added: "That Kidd's a special player. He gets lost in the game. He's like Magic [Johnson] or [Larry] Bird or the special few who see things that other guys just don't see. He has a knack for making the big plays, and it there's a way to win, Jason Kidd will find it."

Kidd has played for three NBA teams, and all of them have improved their records with him at point guard. He ranks fourth all-time among NBA players in career assist average, at 9.4 per game, and ninth all-time in career steal average, at 2.11 per game. Kidd celebrated his 5,000th career assist in January 2002, and he hopes to beat John Stockton's record of more than 15,000 assists before his career is over.

Kidd plans to opt out of his current contract with the Nets and become a free agent in the summer of 2003. He hopes to stay with the Nets, but he

New Jersey Nets guard Jason Kidd starts the fast break as Chicago Bulls Tyson Chandler looks on, December 2002.

has asked for a seven-year contract worth approximately $120 million. This amount may not be feasible for the Nets — or any other NBA team — given salary cap restrictions. The Nets have said that they will do everything possible to keep Kidd in New Jersey. The team's best hope for keeping their star player may be to remain a contender for the NBA championship. Toward that end, the Nets acquired several promising players before the 2002-03 season, including seven-foot, two-inch center Dikembe Mutombo. "I'm not looking to go west," Kidd noted. "I'm looking to win a championship, and if New Jersey is the window of opportunity, then I have to take full advantage of that."

During the 2002-03 season Kidd began taking more shots per game, which raised his scoring average to 19.6 points per game but lowered his assists to 8.5 per game. By the beginning of March, the Nets had posted a 38-22 record and were leading their division. "The Nets will be a blueprint for any team out there," Kidd stated. "If you get a good group of guys who believe in each other and want one another to succeed and not be selfish, and nobody cares who scores the most or who has the winning basket, good things will happen. You'll see a lot of teams play our style."

> "The Nets will be a blueprint for any team out there," Kidd said about the 2003 team. "If you get a good group of guys who believe in each other and want one another to succeed and not be selfish, and nobody cares who scores the most or who has the winning basket, good things will happen. You'll see a lot of teams play our style."

MARRIAGE AND FAMILY

Kidd met his wife, Joumana Samaha, while he was playing in Phoenix and she was working as a local television reporter. They have a son, Trey (known as T.J.), who was born in 1999, and twin daughters, Miah and Jazelle, born in 2001. Kidd also has another son, Jason Jr., from an earlier relationship, during his college years.

Kidd and his family have lived in Saddle River, New Jersey, since he joined the Nets in 2001. Regarding the well-publicized incident in which he hit his wife, Kidd says that his abusive behavior is a thing of the past and that his marriage is stronger than ever. As his wife Joumana explained, "The important thing is that Jason made a mistake, acknowledged it, and did everything he could to make it better. We didn't sweep it under the carpet like a lot of people do. He's a role model and people saw him fall. And like one fan said to me, 'It's not how you fall, it's how you get up.'"

Kidd continues to attend counseling voluntarily to help him control his temper and avoid violent outbursts. He says that he no longer allows his career to interfere with his home life. "You can really get caught up in this job," he explained. "Family should always be number one, no matter what your job is. [The incident] helped me put things back in order and see them a lot clearer, not just at home but on the court, too. Any time [your] home is in order, you can do everything else well."

Kidd blows a kiss to his wife before every free throw. The tradition started when Joumana asked him to wave to her on camera when he was at an away game. He thought that would be embarrassing, but he blew her a kiss before shooting a free throw. The kiss has now become part of the ritual he uses to focus his concentration before he shoots.

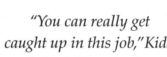

"You can really get caught up in this job," Kidd explained. "Family should always be number one, no matter what your job is. [The incident with my wife] helped me put things back in order and see them a lot clearer, not just at home but on the court, too. Any time [your] home is in order, you can do everything else well."

HOBBIES AND OTHER INTERESTS

In his spare time, Kidd enjoys playing golf and listening to rhythm and blues music. He has also collected baseball cards since he was a child. His most prized possession is his Ken Griffey Jr. card. He also collects basketball memorabilia.

Kidd has been involved in charity work throughout his NBA career. While he played with the Mavericks, for example, he bought 30 season tickets so that underprivileged children could attend games. After the terrorist attacks of September 11, 2001, Kidd donated 500 tickets for each of New Jersey's home playoff games to police, firefighters, and relatives of the World Trade Center victims. Kidd has also donated money to churches to build basketball courts. Some of his charity work is handled through the Jason Kidd Foundation, which hosts an annual charity golf event, and the Jason Kidd Basketball Scholarship Fund at the University of California.

Kidd is also active in product endorsements. He is the featured player in a new NBA Live video game, models Hugo Boss clothing, and appears in Pepsi and Nike commercials.

HONORS AND AWARDS

California High School Player of the Year: 1992
Naismith Award: 1992
National High School Player of the Year (*Parade*): 1992
National High School Player of the Year (*USA Today*): 1992
McDonald's High School All-American: 1992
NCAA Basketball National Freshman of the Year (*Sporting News*): 1992-93
NCAA Basketball National Freshman of the Year (*USA Today*):1992-93
All Pacific-10 Conference Selection: 1992-93
Pacific-10 Conference Player of the Year: 1993-94
First Team Collegiate All-American: 1993-94
Schick NBA Rookie of the Year: 1994-95 (with Grant Hill)
NBA All-Rookie First Team: 1994-95
NBA All-Star: 1996, 1998, 2000, 2001, 2002
First Team All-NBA: 1998, 1999, 2000, 2001, 2002
Olympic Men's Basketball: 2000, gold medal as member of Team USA

FURTHER READING

Books

James, Brant. *Jason Kidd*, 1997 (juvenile)
Gray, Valerie A. *Jason Kidd: Star Guard*, 2000 (juvenile)
Moore, David. *The Jason Kidd Story*, 1997 (juvenile)
Sports Stars, Series 1-4, 1994-98
Stewart, Mark, and Mike Kennedy. *Kidd Rocks: Rolling with Jason Kidd and the New Jersey Nets*, 2002 (juvenile)
Torres, John Albert. *Sports Great Jason Kidd,* 1998 (juvenile)
Who's Who among African Americans, 2001
Who's Who in America, 2002

Periodicals

Basketball Digest, Feb. 2001, p.32
Bergen County (N.J.) Record, Oct. 25, 2002, p.S1
Current Biography Yearbook, 2002
New York Times, Dec. 26, 2001, p.S1; Feb. 8, 2002, p.D1; Sep. 25, 2002, p.D1; Apr. 5, 2003, p.S4

San Francisco Chronicle, Mar. 21, 1992, p.D3; Nov. 5, 1992, p.C7; Aug. 15, 1994, p.A15; June 5, 2002, p.C1
Sport, Apr. 1994, p.54
Sporting News, Nov. 20, 1995, p.38; Jan. 6, 1997, p.29
Sports Illustrated, Nov. 22, 1992, p.68; Mar. 21, 1994, p.18; Oct. 3, 1994, p. 47; Nov. 11, 1996, p.94; Dec. 4, 2000, p.62; Jan. 28, 2002, p.58
Sports Illustrated for Kids, Feb. 1, 2000, p.30; Nov. 2002, p.27
Time, June 10, 2002, p.56
USA Today, Nov. 9, 1992, p.C9

Online Database

Biography Resource Center Online, 2003, article from *Sports Stars,* 1994-98

ADDRESS

Jason Kidd
New Jersey Nets
Nets Champion Center
390 Murray Hill Parkway
East Rutherford, NJ 07073

WORLD WIDE WEB SITES

http://www.nba.com/playerfile/jason_kidd
http://www.usabasketball.com/biosmen/jason_kidd_bio.html

Tony Stewart 1971-
American Professional Race Car Driver
2002 NASCAR Winston Cup Champion

BIRTH

Anthony Stewart—known as Tony—was born on May 20, 1971, in Rushville, Indiana. He was named after the legendary race-car driver A.J. (short for Anthony Joseph) Foyt, who won the Indianapolis 500 four times in his career. Tony's father, Nelson, was a traveling salesman, and his mother, Pam, was a receptionist in a doctor's office. Tony's parents divorced when he was a teenager, though they remained good friends. His mother later married Mike Boas. Tony also has a younger sister, Natalie.

YOUTH

Tony Stewart grew up in Columbus, Indiana, a quiet, middle-class suburb located less than 50 miles from Indianapolis Motor Speedway—site of the annual Indianapolis 500 auto race. His family home had a large garage in the backyard where his father was always tinkering with cars. Nelson Stewart competed in some amateur races as a hobby, and he often took the family to watch short-track races on nearby tracks. From the time he was a baby, Tony shared this interest in cars and racing. For example, he always wanted to look at his father's car magazines instead of picture books.

Throughout his childhood, Tony was attracted to anything with wheels on it. A favorite family photograph shows him sitting on his mother's vacuum cleaner while wearing a mixing bowl on his head as a helmet. As a boy he raced Big Wheels and bicycles against other kids in the neighborhood. Tony also enjoyed staging make-believe races with his toy cars on an oval-shaped, braided rug. "To him, the different braids made lanes; that was his racetrack," his mother recalled. "We'd haul that rug wherever we went, because that thing kept Tony busy for hours."

> *Stewart enjoyed staging make-believe races with his toy cars on an oval-shaped, braided rug. "To him, the different braids made lanes; that was his racetrack," his mother recalled. "We'd haul that rug wherever we went, because that thing kept Tony busy for hours."*

Starting to Race

When Tony was five years old, his father bought him a go-kart with an engine. He raced it around the backyard so often that he tore up all the grass. "Tony carved a definite oval into our backyard, and he would just go around and around on that go-kart," his mother remembered. "It wasn't long before we decided he needed to be out on a real track someplace." In 1978, when he was seven years old, Tony drove in his first organized go-kart race at a track in Westport, Indiana. He won his first championship in 1980 in the four-cycle engine rookie junior class at the Columbus Fairgrounds.

Before long, Tony and his father were traveling to races across the Midwest run by the International Karting Federation (IKF) and the World Karting Association (WKA). Although they could not afford the top-of-the-line karts and equipment used by some other teams, they were very successful—thanks to Tony's driving skill and Nelson's mechanical ability. Tony won the IKF Grand National Championship in 1983, and he claimed the WKA National Championship in 1987.

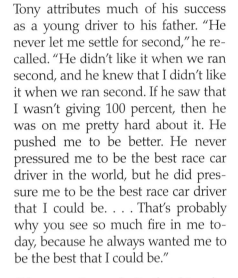

When Tony was five years old, his father bought him a go-kart with an engine. He raced it around the backyard so often that he tore up all the grass. "Tony carved a definite oval into our backyard, and he would just go around and around on that go-kart," *his mother remembered.* "It wasn't long before we decided he needed to be out on a real track someplace."

Tony attributes much of his success as a young driver to his father. "He never let me settle for second," he recalled. "He didn't like it when we ran second, and he knew that I didn't like it when we ran second. If he saw that I wasn't giving 100 percent, then he was on me pretty hard about it. He pushed me to be better. He never pressured me to be the best race car driver in the world, but he did pressure me to be the best race car driver that I could be. . . . That's probably why you see so much fire in me today, because he always wanted me to be the best that I could be."

Of course, Tony admits that his relationship with his father was not without conflicts. During his teen years, Tony went through a lazy, goof-around phase where all he wanted to do was hang around with his friends. One day, his parents went to visit relatives and asked him to mow the lawn while they were gone. When they returned, Nelson was furious to see that Tony had not mowed the lawn and instead spent the day playing baseball. That evening, a friend called to ask Nelson whether he knew of any good karts for sale. Nelson arranged to sell Tony's kart in order to teach his son a lesson about hard work and responsibility. Tony saw the buyer pick up his kart while he was belatedly mowing the lawn. "Seeing that kart disappear down the street absolutely destroyed me," he noted. "I finished mowing the yard, but I was literally crying my eyes out the whole time."

Luckily for Stewart's racing career, the situation turned out for the best. A few weeks later he was hired to race an enduro kart for a race team.

Enduro karts are also known as laydown karts because of the driver's position in the cockpit. They raced at large, well-known racetracks and went over 100 miles per hour. They provided an excellent training ground for young drivers who hoped to continue moving up through the ranks of auto racing.

Tony's parents divorced when he was in high school. Although he lived with his mother, he continued to go racing every weekend with his father. "Their divorce never stopped either of them from being a strong presence in my life," he noted. "Together or separately, they always provided the right amount of discipline for me." While his parents' divorce was difficult for him at the time, he later acknowledged that it was probably the best thing for everyone concerned.

EDUCATION

Stewart attended Columbus North High School. When he could make time in his racing schedule, he played trombone in the school's marching band. He graduated from Columbus North High School in 1989.

CAREER HIGHLIGHTS

After graduating from high school, Stewart moved up to race three-quarter (TQ) midget cars. These open-wheeled machines had more power than karts and usually raced on oval dirt tracks. In 1991 he was given an opportunity to drive sprint cars in a series organized by the United States Auto Club (USAC). He was so successful that he was honored as the USAC Sprint Car rookie of the year.

USAC sanctions races for three divisions of open-wheeled cars — midget, sprint, and Silver Crown. Over the next few years, Stewart was hired to drive cars in all three divisions. This experience helped him to become a more versatile all-around driver. "I [got] an education in racing that you couldn't have bought at any price," he stated. "All these rides took me to every sort of short track there is: dirt tracks, paved tracks, flat tracks, banked tracks, fast tracks, slow tracks. Because of that, I never fell into the common trap that snags so many young drivers: they develop a fixed style which helps them go fast at one type of track, but hurts them at another."

Although Stewart spent a lot of time racing in the early 1990s, he did not earn enough prize money to support himself. He worked at a series of odd jobs to help make ends meet. For example, he worked at McDonald's in Columbus, at a friend's brick plant, and as the go-kart track operator at a family fun center. "It wasn't an easy life in those short-track days," he re-

Stewart (foreground) battles with Robby Gordon (background) during the Indy Racing League Championship at Las Vegas Motor Speedway, September 1996.

called. "I slept in the backseat of my car more than once, too broke even to think about a motel room. I went to racetracks praying I'd win enough gas money to get back home."

In 1993 Stewart earned $3,500 in prize money at a single race. It was then that he decided to give up his part-time jobs and become a full-time race-car driver. The following year he won the USAC National Midget Championship. In 1995 he made history by winning the national championship in all three USAC divisions. Stewart thus became the first driver ever to hold the midget, sprint, and Silver Crown titles in the same year. In fact, only one other driver — open-wheel legend Pancho Carter — had won all three championships in his career. Winning USAC's Triple Crown required Stewart to compete in 58 national events over a ten-month season, always juggling the schedules of the three classes of races.

Joining the Indy Racing League

Stewart's success in the USAC ranks attracted the attention of John Menard, the owner of a team in the Indy Racing League (IRL). The IRL was founded by Tony George, owner of the Indianapolis Motor Speedway (home of the Indianapolis 500). George had become involved in a dispute with Championship Auto Racing Teams (CART), the organization that handled Indy Car racing in the United States. He felt that CART's rules had made Indy Car racing so expensive that it was impossible for young, talented American drivers to break into the sport. The popularity of Indy Car racing declined as more and more promising young drivers began racing stock cars in events organized by the National Association of Stock Car Auto Racing (NASCAR). Stock cars are like those sold in auto showrooms, but with souped-up engines, wide tires, and aerodynamic body work. Stock car racing provided a more affordable alternative to the sleek, high-performance, open-wheeled sports cars used in Indy Car racing. George blamed CART for the decline of Indy Car racing in the United States. He decided to form a new racing league for Indy Cars with the Indianapolis 500 as its centerpiece.

The IRL was created specifically to give young drivers like Stewart an opportunity to race Indy Cars. Stewart began competing for Team Menard during the 1996 IRL season and finished second in the first race he entered. For Stewart, the most exciting part of his rookie season was getting a chance to compete in the Indianapolis 500. "When you grow up an hour away from this place, it's just in your blood," he explained. "Growing up in Indiana, racing here is the biggest thing you can hope for." Stewart qualified second for the 1996 race with an average speed of 233.1 miles per hour. Another Menard driver, Scott Brayton, qualified on the pole (in the first position). Sadly, Brayton was killed in a crash during a practice session. Stewart started the race from the pole position and led 44 of the first 55 laps before falling back after a pit stop. Although he was forced to drop out of the race on lap 82 with engine trouble, he was still named Indianapolis 500 rookie of the year for 1996.

> **"**
>
> *"[I got] an education in racing that you couldn't have bought at any price,"* Stewart said about his experience driving race cars in all different divisions. *"All these rides took me to every sort of short track there is: dirt tracks, paved tracks, flat tracks, banked tracks, fast tracks, slow tracks. Because of that, I never fell into the common trap that snags so many young drivers: they develop a fixed style which helps them go fast at one type of track, but hurts them at another."*
>
> **"**

Stewart went on to claim IRL rookie-of-the-year honors that season. In 1997 he won the IRL championship for Team Menard.

As Stewart continued to demonstrate his driving skills in different types of race cars, he began to attract the attention of NASCAR teams. At this point, Stewart was not certain whether he wanted to race stock cars. For one thing, they were much larger than anything he had ever raced before (midget cars weigh less than 1,000 pounds, for example, while stock cars weigh over 3,000 pounds). In addition, he knew that the NASCAR circuit was highly competitive and that new drivers often had trouble being successful. He ultimately decided to ease into stock-car racing slowly.

Stewart signed a contract with Joe Gibbs Racing, a successful NASCAR team owned by the former coach of the Washington Redskins professional football team. At first he competed in both NASCAR and IRL events. He appeared in five races in the Busch Grand National Series — the second-highest NASCAR division, after the Winston Cup — during the 1997 season while also racing in the IRL. The following year he competed in all 11 IRL events as well as 22 Busch series races. Although Stewart enjoyed racing in both leagues, he knew that he would have to make a choice eventually. "I knew in the back of my mind that sooner or later, there would come a day when something would push me toward one form of racing or the other," he stated. "Maybe it would be a case of the two schedules having too many conflicts, or maybe I would simply discover that I wasn't happy enough in one series or the other. But at that point in my life I was doing my best to put that day off as long as I could."

Competing in the NASCAR Winston Cup Series

In 1999 Joe Gibbs decided that Stewart was ready to move up to the NASCAR Winston Cup series. Stewart left the IRL and committed himself to racing NASCAR, although he made sure that his contract still allowed him to race in the Indianapolis 500. The NASCAR Winston Cup racing season begins in February each year with stock car racing's most prestigious event, the Daytona 500 in Daytona Beach, Florida. The teams race at tracks around the country almost every weekend through November, for a total of over 30 events.

Throughout the season, the drivers earn points based on their finishing position in races. They also earn bonus points for leading the most laps in a race and a variety of other criteria. At the end of each year, the driver with the most points for the season is named the NASCAR Winston Cup Champion. The Winston Cup championship is recognized as one of the most difficult titles to attain in all of sports. The series features numerous

Stewart works on his car during the Winston 500, part of the NASCAR Winston Cup Series, at Talladega Super Speedway in Alabama, November 1999.

high-caliber teams and drivers, as well as lots of media attention and fan pressure. In addition, Winston Cup drivers must be able to handle a variety of tracks and conditions. For example, some races are held on small, half-mile oval tracks, like Martinsville in Virginia and Bristol in Tennessee.

Other events are held on twisting, asphalt road courses, like Watkins Glen in New York and Sears Point in California. Finally, some races take place on giant super-speedways, like Daytona in Florida and Talladega in Alabama.

Stewart immediately proved that he could compete in the Winston Cup series. The rookie surprised many observers by qualifying in the front row for his first race, the season-opening Daytona 500. He claimed his first victory in September 1999 at Richmond, Virginia, in just his 25th start. He ended up winning two more races that year—in Phoenix, Arizona, and Homestead, Florida—to become the first rookie to win three races in the modern history of NASCAR. Stewart finished the season ranked fourth in the Winston Cup point standings, which was the best finish for a rookie in over 30 years.

Perhaps the most impressive feat of Stewart's 1999 season came on Memorial Day, when he did "double duty" by racing in both the IRL's Indianapolis 500 and NASCAR's Coca-Cola 600 on the same day. After finishing ninth in the Indianapolis 500, he flew to North Carolina by helicopter, jumped into a completely different type of race car, and finished fourth in the Coca-Cola 600. He drove 1,080 miles (he withdrew from the Winston Cup race with 20 miles to go due to handling problems) to become the first driver ever to complete both races in the same day. Afterward, he was taken from his car in an ambulance and treated for dehydration and exhaustion.

During the 2000 Winston Cup season, Stewart proved that his rookie year had not been a fluke by winning a series-high six races. He claimed two victories at Dover in Delaware, and he also won at Michigan, New Hampshire, Martinsville, and Homestead. Unfortunately, his performances the rest of the year were inconsistent, so he could only manage a sixth-place finish in the season point standings.

Stewart had an up-and-down year in 2001. The season began on a tragic note when NASCAR legend Dale Earnhardt was killed during the Daytona 500. "It was hard to come to grips with the fact that the next time we went racing, Dale wouldn't be there," Stewart said later. "I had never seen a Winston Cup race, on television or from the driver's seat, that didn't have Dale in it." Stewart was involved in the multiple-car accident that took Earnhardt's life. In fact, Stewart's crash was the most spectacular part of the wreck. His car flew high into the air and then rolled end-over-end down the track, eventually coming down on the hood of his teammate Bobby Labonte's car. Luckily, Stewart came away with only a concussion and a bruised shoulder. He went on to win three races that year—at

Richmond, Sears Point, and Bristol—and finish second in the Winston Cup point standings. The victory at Richmond in May was the tenth of his career; he achieved that milestone in only 79 starts.

Stewart did "double duty" once again on Memorial Day, 2001. This time, he used a special diet and workout regimen to help him prepare for the grueling day. He ended up finishing sixth in the Indianapolis 500 and third in the Coca-Cola 600. He not only completed all 1,100 miles, but said he was ready to drive a short-track race later that evening. A writer for *Auto Racing Digest* called Stewart's performance "an almost unrivaled feat of skill, precision, and concentration."

Earning a Reputation as NASCAR's "Bad Boy"

Over the course of his first three Winston Cup seasons, Stewart was involved in several incidents—both on the track and off—that helped him earn a reputation as NASCAR's "bad boy." He often had trouble controlling his temper, which he attributed to his passion and intensity about driving race cars. "I can't help it; when it comes to my racing, I'm intense," he stated. "Everybody likes to win, and I'm no different. But I guess I'd have to add this: I'm not a good loser. In fact, I'm a bad loser, plain and simple, and I'm not ashamed of that."

> *Stewart often had trouble controlling his temper, which he attributed to his passion and intensity about driving race cars. "I can't help it; when it comes to my racing, I'm intense. Everybody likes to win, and I'm no different. But I guess I'd have to add this: I'm not a good loser. In fact, I'm a bad loser, plain and simple, and I'm not ashamed of that."*

One memorable incident took place during Stewart's rookie season in 1999. He and fellow driver Kenny Irwin collided several times in the first 150 laps of a 500-lap race at Martinsville. The last collision knocked Stewart's car into the wall and out of the race. As the remaining cars circled the track slowly under the yellow caution flag, Stewart got out of his car and waited for Irwin to come around. Then he removed the fireproof heel pads from the bottoms of his driving shoes and threw them at Irwin's windshield. Still angry, Stewart ran over to Irwin's car, leaned into the passenger-side window, and tried to grab his fellow driver. Stewart received a fine of $5,000 from NASCAR, and footage of this incident was replayed often on television to demonstrate Stewart's hot temper.

Stewart's Chevrolet Monte Carlo (#20) during a pit stop at the NASCAR Winston Cup Series MBNA 500 at Atlanta Motor Speedway.

Another incident took place at Daytona in 2001, during the Winston Cup series' first stop at the track following Earnhardt's death. Track officials put a new safety rule in place that prohibited cars from dropping below the yellow line on the inside of the track in order to pass. Stewart was charging toward the front of the field when he felt he was forced to drop below the line to avoid a collision. NASCAR officials waved a black flag at Stewart, signaling that he was required to pull into the pits as a penalty for breaking the rules. Stewart chose to ignore the flag and finish the race, believing that officials would later review the television footage and see that he had only broken the rules in order to avoid causing an accident. He ended up finishing sixth, but NASCAR penalized him by dropping him to 26th position. After the race, Stewart engaged in a heated argument with NASCAR officials and received a fine of $10,000. On his way back to his garage, he slapped the tape recorder out of the hand of a reporter who asked him about the incident.

Another high-profile incident occurred at Bristol in 2001. Stewart was running fourth when rival driver Jeff Gordon bumped into his car on the last lap of the race. Stewart spun out and ended up finishing 25th. After the race ended, Stewart followed Gordon onto the pit road and bumped into his car, causing Gordon to spin out in the pits. This incident earned Stewart another $10,000 fine and probation from NASCAR. Some members of the media started calling him "Tony the Temper" or "Tony Tantrum" because of his sometimes angry and aggressive behavior on the track.

Stewart added to his bad-boy reputation by making statements that some reporters or fans found insulting. For example, he once remarked that the fans at Talladega were the most obnoxious in all of NASCAR. He claimed that he never meant to offend people, but only tried to be honest in answering questions. "I'm not such a bad guy. Really. I don't enjoy being in the middle of controversy, and I don't like being 'NASCAR's bad boy,' which is a term I hear a lot," he noted. "I've been in hot water occasionally with the media, and with various officials. Sometimes it feels like I've gotten as much notoriety by misbehaving as I have by winning races and championships. I haven't ever looked for trouble, but it sure has seemed to find me."

——— " ———

"I'm not such a bad guy. Really. I don't enjoy being in the middle of controversy, and I don't like being 'NASCAR's bad boy,' which is a term I hear a lot. I've been in hot water occasionally with the media, and with various officials. Sometimes it feels like I've gotten as much notoriety by misbehaving as I have by winning races and championships. I haven't ever looked for trouble, but it sure has seemed to find me."

——— " ———

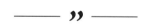

The 2002 NASCAR Season

The 2002 season started out badly for Stewart. After winning a practice race and finishing second in a qualifying race, he was an early pick to win the Daytona 500. But his engine failed just two laps into the race and he ended up finishing last. This turn of events meant that he started the season ranked 43rd in the Winston Cup point standings. Stewart came back to log two consecutive top-five finishes in the next two events, however, and then recorded a win at Atlanta in March. He went on to claim another victory at Richmond in May.

In August, though, Stewart's temper threatened to ruin what was beginning to seem like a promising season. He was thrilled to qualify on the pole for the Brickyard 400, a NASCAR race held at Indianapolis Motor Speedway. He hoped to win on his home track in front of his family and friends. But his car faded as the race went on and he ended up finishing a disappointing 12th. Frustrated and angry, Stewart tried to return to his garage without talking to any reporters. One free-lance photographer began chasing him, and Stewart turned around and punched the man. He received a $10,000 fine and was placed on probation by NASCAR. The incident embarrassed Stewart's sponsor, Home Depot, which fined him another $50,000. At this point Stewart decided to seek anger-management counseling. "I need to do something to make it to where I can control my anger better," he stated. "It's obvious over three-and-a-half years, I can't do it on my own, so I'm going to seek professional help and get somebody that can help me learn how to control my emotions."

The week after he punched the photographer, Stewart came back to claim his third victory of the season at Watkins Glen. He turned in consistently strong performances week after week to end up with a total of 15 top-five finishes over the course of the season. By the time the series moved to Talladega in October, Stewart had taken over the lead in the Winston Cup point standings with only six races remaining.

Traditionally, the Winston Cup champion acts as a sort of ambassador for NASCAR during the year of his reign. He is expected to attend press conferences and promotional events, and he is often asked to comment on rule changes and other racing issues. When it became apparent that Stewart might claim the 2002 championship, some people complained that he would not be a good representative for NASCAR. Stewart only added to this impression when he rejected the whole idea of being an ambassador, saying that he was trying to win a points title, not a political office.

But other people believed that Stewart—who has often been called a "racer's racer"because he cares more about winning races than about winning over fans or sponsors—would be a fine representative for the sport. "In the broad sense, a champion is called on to represent NASCAR, and I am convinced he can meet that challenge," said NASCAR official Jim Hunter. "He is definitely not vanilla. He is Neapolitan, and you get a little bit of everything with Tony Stewart. We know he can charm Godzilla when he wants to. We also know that when he puts on his game face and gets ready to race, leave him alone, get out of the way."

Winston Cup Champion

On November 17, 2002, Stewart clinched the 2002 Winston Cup championship by 38 points over Mark Martin at the season-ending event at Homestead, Florida. When the race at Homestead concluded, Stewart

2002 NASCAR champion Tony Stewart celebrates after finishing the Winston Cup Ford 400 at Homestead-Miami Speedway in Florida, November 2002.

found himself surrounded by a mob of fellow drivers, team owners, and crew members. "To have your peers come out there and congratulate you like that, I don't care what check Winston writes, I don't care how many trophies they give me, the feeling and satisfaction of seeing those guys out there is more than money can buy," he said.

> **When he clinched the 2002 Winston Cup championship, Stewart found himself surrounded by a mob of fellow drivers, team owners, and crew members.**
>
> **"To have your peers come out there and congratulate you like that, I don't care what check Winston writes, I don't care how many trophies they give me, the feeling and satisfaction of seeing those guys out there is more than money can buy."**

The prestigious Winston Cup Championship marked the ninth driving title of Stewart's amazing career. "If I had to retype my resume tomorrow, I'd put the Winston Cup championship at number one," he stated. "All of the championships I've been a part of were hard to acquire. None of them were easy. They had their unique set of circumstances, obstacles, and challenges to overcome. But my heart tells me that this championship—the Winston Cup championship—is my greatest accomplishment in racing."

The difficulties he had to overcome during the 2002 season made the championship even sweeter for Stewart. "To start the season off the way that we did—to be able to rebound from all that, along with all the other things we went through—and to have kept our focus to go out and get the most points week in and week out, I still have a tough time believing what we've accomplished," he noted.

Stewart won $9.16 million in prize money for the 2002 season, which ranked a close second behind Jeff Gordon's all-time earnings record. At the end of four seasons of NASCAR Winston Cup racing, Stewart had chalked up 15 victories, $21 million in earnings, and $85,000 in fines.

As it turned out, Stewart performed very well in his new role as Winston Cup champion. Officials, media, and fans alike found him to be warm, funny, and humble in interviews and public appearances. At the season-ending awards banquet, he drew laughs by presenting NASCAR officials with the certificate from his anger-management course. Stewart also amused reporters by pulling out a camera and snapping pictures of photographers at a press conference.

Stewart drives his #20 Chevrolet during the Winston Cup Food City 500 at the Bristol Motorspeedway in Tennessee, March 2003.

As the 2003 season approached, Stewart said that his plan was to relax, have fun, and keep things in perspective for the good of his race team. "I feel a little more relaxed going into this season, because I don't feel I have anything to prove. My goal this year is to have fun, strictly to have fun," he stated. "I'm just trying to be smart and look out for the team. Those guys went through a lot last year. We all went through a lot last year. I'm just trying to make things a little more efficient, a little easier to where those guys aren't worrying about, 'Well, what happens if he has a bad day?' It just makes life easier for all of us. I'm just trying to look outside my circle and say, there are more people involved here, and what can I do to help the race team?" At the same time, Stewart hoped to bring Joe Gibbs Racing another Winston Cup championship. "Winning one makes you want to win another, and we've done a lot of things to make ourselves better for this year," he explained.

Struggling with Fame

Stewart is widely recognized as one of the best and most versatile race-car drivers in the world. According to his namesake, the great A.J. Foyt: "In my lifetime, there's probably been only two or three guys I've known who could drive just about anything they sat down in. And Tony Stewart is one of 'em." Many NASCAR fans appreciate Stewart's work ethic, driving skills, and passion for racing. "Nobody in this sport ever gave me anything," he explained. "I was not a rich kid. I didn't have a single door open up for me because I was a famous driver's son, or a famous driver's brother. Any opportunity that came my way, I earned. Every ride I was ever offered was based on my performance, my reputation, or both."

―――― **"** ――――

"I'm well aware that you can lose your life doing what I do. But I believe this: I've got a better chance of dying of cancer than of getting killed in a race car. I've got a better chance of killing myself on some interstate highway than on some speedway. Sure, I have a risky job, but lots of folks do: firemen run into burning buildings, truck drivers crash, factory workers face all kinds of industrial hazards. There's danger in a hundred occupations. . . ."

―――― **"** ――――

Some fans also enjoy Stewart's honesty and willingness to speak his mind. "There are so many people who give the cookie-cutter answers down here," Stewart once said. "The people that support me are tired of that. I'm not here for a popularity contest." Most of his fellow drivers like and respect him, and say that he sometimes expresses frustrations that they all feel. At the same time, Stewart has alienated some race fans with his angry outbursts and aggressive behavior. In fact, he is one of the drivers most likely to be booed on the Winston Cup circuit.

Stewart admits that he has struggled to deal with some aspects of his fame. Although he tries to be accessible to the people who support NASCAR, Stewart wants fans to understand that drivers need to be able to live a normal life. "People ask what it's like to be a Winston Cup driver," he said. "Well, it's great, as long as that's all you want to be. But if you want to be a living, functioning human being at the same time, it has its drawbacks. I'll be the first to admit that I haven't always handled all this in the most graceful way. But, in my defense, when you grow up the way I did, you don't spend a lot of time preparing for how you'll react to being famous."

One of the aspects of the job that bothers Stewart most is the autograph-seekers that crowd into the team garages and pit areas where the cars are being prepared. "Sometimes they catch you at the wrong time, and you're intense," he explained. "You may be in a bad mood or maybe focused on something and not paying attention to them and they'll think that you're a bad person because they didn't get the autograph they wanted right then. Not that you didn't want to sign it right then. When I get focused on racing, that's all I'm worked about. I don't let outside distractions distract me." While Stewart willingly signs autographs at promotional events, he reserves the right to refuse to sign while he is working. "I'm sorry, but I don't feel like I owe anybody an autograph," he stated. "I don't feel like I owe anybody anything more than my best effort in the race they bought tickets to. On that score, I've never cheated anybody out of a penny."

Though several of Stewart's close friends have lost their lives in auto races, he says that his love for racing makes it worth the risk. "I'm well aware that you can lose your life doing what I do," he said. "But I believe this: I've got a better chance of dying of cancer than of getting killed in a race car. I've got a better chance of killing myself on some interstate highway than on some speedway. Sure, I have a risky job, but lots of folks do: firemen run into burning buildings, truck drivers crash, factory workers face all kinds of industrial hazards. There's danger in a hundred occupations. The difference is, I'll bet I love my job more than most people in those occupations love theirs. . . . There are millions of people who spend literally their entire adult lives doing work they can't stand. I am doing the only thing I've ever really wanted to do, the only thing that completely fulfills me. I'm a very lucky person. So if I don't make it out of the next race I run, don't cry for me. That's an order."

"The difference is, I'll bet I love my job more than most people in those occupations love theirs. . . . There are millions of people who spend literally their entire adult lives doing work they can't stand. I am doing the only thing I've ever really wanted to do, the only thing that completely fulfills me. I'm a very lucky person. So if I don't make it out of the next race I run, don't cry for me. That's an order."

HOME AND FAMILY

During the NASCAR season, Stewart—who is single—lives in Davidson, North Carolina, in a condominium on Lake Norman. He also used some of his Winston Cup earnings to purchase his boyhood home in Columbus, Indiana, and spends as much time there as possible. "The neighbors who were there when I was growing up are still here," he noted. "When I think about growing up, that's my house. I always know that if I get homesick I can go home for a day."

Stewart remains close to his family. His father attends many of his races, and his mother and sister are both involved in running his fan club and souvenir business.

HOBBIES AND OTHER INTERESTS

Stewart describes himself as a laid-back person off the racetrack. In his spare time he enjoys fishing, playing pool, and riding motorcycles and all-terrain vehicles (ATVs). He also likes to challenge his friends to races with remote-control cars or in simulated racing games.

Stewart is involved in charity work, though he tries to keep his good deeds private. He has used his own plane to fly sick children to races, for example, and he saved the life of an abused greyhound he heard about while racing in Florida. "I hate to say this because it will ruin my bad-boy image," he noted, "but deep down inside I am a caring person."

WRITINGS

True Speed: My Racing Life, 2002 (with Bones Bourcier)

HONORS AND AWARDS

International Karting Foundation Grand National Champion: 1983
World Karting Association National Champion: 1987
USAC Sprint Rookie of the Year: 1991
USAC Midget National Champion: 1994, 1995
USAC Sprint National Champion: 1995
USAC Silver Crown National Champion: 1995
Indianapolis 500 Rookie of the Year: 1996
Indy Racing League Rookie of the Year: 1996
Indy Racing League Champion: 1997
NASCAR Winston Cup Rookie of the Year: 1999
NASCAR Winston Cup Points Champion: 2002

FURTHER READING

Books

Mello, Tara Baukus. *Tony Stewart,* 2000 (juvenile)
Mitchell, Jason. *Driver Series: Tony Stewart,* 2002 (juvenile)

Stewart, Tony, with Bones Bourcier. *True Speed: My Racing Life,* 2002
Teitelbaum, Michael. *Tony Stewart: Instant Superstar,* 2002 (juvenile)
Utter, Jim. *Tony Stewart: Hottest Thing on Wheels,* 2000 (juvenile)
Who's Who in America, 2002

Periodicals

Auto Racing Digest, Apr.-May 2003, p.16
AutoWeek, July 6, 1998, p.44
Circle Track, Feb. 2000, p.28
Houston Chronicle, May 26, 1996, p.18
Indianapolis Star, Nov. 9, 2000, p.B2; Dec. 7, 2002, p.D1
Kansas City (Mo.) Star, Feb. 15, 1996, p.D1
New York Times, May 29, 2001, p.D4; Dec. 5, 2002, p.D4
Palm Beach Post, Nov. 15, 2002, p.H3
Sporting News, July 30, 2001, p.50; Dec. 24, 2001, p.53
St. Petersburg Times, May 24, 1998, p.C15
Sports Illustrated, Dec. 22, 1999, p.118; Nov. 18, 2002, p.107; Dec. 1, 2002, p.18
Sports Illustrated for Kids, July 1, 2002, p.37
USA Today, May 28, 1999, p.F8
Winston-Salem (N.C.) Journal, Jan. 9, 2003, p.C1

Online Articles

http://espn.go.com/magazine/flemfile_20020703.html
    ("Stranger at the Track,"*ESPN The Magazine,* July 3, 2002)
http://espnmagazine.com/2002/1516/althomy.html
    ("Trouble Seems to Stalk Stewart,"*ESPN Magazine,* Nov. 27-Dec. 3, 2002)

ADDRESS

Tony Stewart
Joe Gibbs Racing
13415 Reese Boulevard West
Huntersville, NC 28078-7933

WORLD WIDE WEB SITES

http://www.tonystewart.com
http://www.nascar.com/drivers/dps/tstewart00/wc/index.html

Michael Vick 1980-

American Professional Football Player with the
Atlanta Falcons
First Overall Pick in the 2001 NFL Draft

BIRTH

Michael Dwayne Vick was born on June 26, 1980, in Newport
News, Virginia. His mother, Brenda Vick, was 16 years old and
unmarried at the time of his birth. His father, Michael Boddie,
decided that he was too young to handle the responsibility of
raising children and left the family to join the military in 1984.

Boddie returned after a few years, however, and married Brenda Vick when Michael was nine. After rejoining the family, he took a job as a painter and sand-blaster in the Newport News shipyards. Michael has an older sister, Christina (born in 1979), a younger brother, Marcus (born in 1984), and a younger sister, Courtney (born in 1991).

YOUTH

Vick was raised in a three-room apartment in a public housing project in Ridley Circle, Virginia. Despite her young age, Brenda Vick taught her son valuable lessons about hard work and determination while he was growing up. While her mother watched the children, Brenda finished high school and worked at Kmart to provide food and clothing for her family. She eventually got a job driving a school bus. Throughout Vick's childhood, she often warned him and his siblings against repeating her mistakes, telling them, "Don't have children when you're young."

Vick first learned to throw a football at the age of three. He often played catch with his father, who was a very athletic man, in the courtyard of their apartment complex. As Vick grew older, he played in pick-up football games with his older cousin Aaron Brooks, who went on to play in the NFL with the New Orleans Saints.

Vick was a happy youngster whose curiosity often got him into trouble. When he was six years old, for example, he glued his eyelids together with Super-glue and had to wait a week before his eyelashes grew long enough for the glue to be cut out. After his father left the family, Vick started getting into trouble at school for being disruptive in class. His mother worried that he might get involved with a bad crowd if she didn't find something for him to do after school. She pushed him to join the neighborhood Boys and Girls Club, where he played a variety of sports with other children — including future NBA star Allen Iverson — and received coaching and guidance from volunteers. When he was not at the Boys and Girls Club, Vick could be found fishing and crabbing in the James River.

EDUCATION

Vick entered Ferguson High School in Newport News as a freshman in 1994. He started the year as the quarterback of the junior varsity football team, but he was promoted to the varsity team after throwing for 20 touchdowns in the first six games of the season. Ferguson High School closed during his sophomore year, so Vick transferred to Warwick High, also in Newport. He immediately earned the starting quarterback position on Warwick's varsity football team. In only his second game at Warwick, Vick set a district record by passing for 433 yards on only 13 completions.

Vick's coach at both of his high schools was Tommy Reamon, who had played professional football for the Kansas City Chiefs in 1976. Reamon paid special attention to Vick, enrolling him in summer camps and conducting private practice sessions to help him improve his passing and running skills. Reamon also put Vick through a tough conditioning program, which included lifting weights and throwing 100 passes a day. Finally, the coach helped Vick develop into a leader by emphasizing the importance of off-field behavior and communication skills. Vick formed a close relationship with Reamon and credits his high school coach for his later success.

> **"I lived in his shadow,"** Vick recalled about rival quarterback Ronald Curry, a four-time all-state selection from nearby Hampton High School. "At the end of my senior year I ended up second-team everything. The papers would have a huge picture of Ronald Curry, with poor little Mike Vick down in the corner about the size of a stamp. I never held it against Curry — just the opposite, I was happy for him. But being second was something I had to deal with, and deal with a lot."

During his senior year, Vick passed for 1,668 yards and 10 touchdowns, and added another 10 rushing touchdowns. Over the course of his high school career, Vick racked up 4,846 yards passing for 43 touchdowns, and 1,048 yards rushing for 18 touchdowns. Unfortunately, his terrific individual performances were not enough to turn the team into a championship-caliber squad. The team posted a 20-13 record over four seasons and never reached the playoffs with Vick as quarterback.

Despite the mediocre performance of his team, Vick received a great deal of national attention as a senior. He was rated the fifth-best quarterback prospect in the nation by *SuperPrep,* a college recruiting publication. He was also named to *Parade* magazine's high-school all-American team. Closer to home, though, Vick never even received first-team district honors. That award went to rival quarterback Ronald Curry — a four-time all-state selection from nearby Hampton High School. "I lived in his shadow," Vick recalled. "At the end of my senior year I ended up second-team everything. The papers would have a huge picture of Ronald Curry, with poor little Mike Vick down in the corner about the size of a stamp. I never held it against Curry—just the opposite, I was happy for him. But being second was something I had to deal with, and deal with a lot."

Upon graduating from Warwick High in 1998, Vick was heavily recruited by a number of strong college football programs, including Syracuse, Clemson, and Georgia Tech. On a recruiting visit to Syracuse, Vick went out for the evening with Donovan McNabb, the school's star quarterback. (For more information on McNabb, see *Biography Today*, April 2003.) McNabb was a senior at that time and wanted Vick to take his place after he graduated. Though the two African-American quarterbacks stayed in touch and eventually competed against each other in the NFL, Vick chose a different college. "I didn't want to walk in the same footsteps as [McNabb]," he explained. "I wanted to go to a place where I could start my own legacy." Vick ultimately decided to attend Virginia Tech because it would allow him to stay closer to his family. His younger brother, Marcus, followed in his footsteps and is expected to be the starting quarterback at Virginia Tech in 2003.

CAREER HIGHLIGHTS

College — The Virginia Tech Hokies

During his freshman year at Virginia Tech in 1998, Vick was red-shirted, meaning that he practiced with the team but did not appear in any games. According to college athletic rules, athletes are eligible to play a sport for up to four years. Major college football programs often red-shirt promising athletes during their freshman year to give them time to adjust to the college game while retaining their full four years of eligibility. Red-shirting allowed Vick to gain experience while keeping his four full years of college eligibility. His high school coach, Tommy Reamon, was the one who suggested that the Virginia Tech coaching staff give Vick a year to mature and prepare for college-level football. The Hokies posted a 9-3 record that year, including a victory over Alabama in the Music City Bowl.

The time Vick spent watching from the sidelines paid off during his second (or red-shirt freshman) year with the Hokies. As Virginia Tech's starting quarterback, Vick led the nation in passing efficiency with a rating of 180.4—the second-highest total ever and the highest for a college freshman in NCAA history. He also set a new school record by moving the ball for an average of 9.3 yards per play. Vick led his team to a perfect 11-0 season and a number two national ranking. The Hokies earned a spot in the

Michael Vick (#7) of the Virginia Tech Hokies.

2000 Sugar Bowl against the powerful Florida State Seminoles in a contest to decide the NCAA championship.

The Hokies got off to a poor start and found themselves down by a score of 28-7 early in the game. At this point, Vick gathered the team around him and said, "Yo, it ain't going down like this. Somebody's gotta step up. I guess it's going to be me." Led by Vick, the Hokies mounted a tremendous 22-point comeback effort to take the lead late in the third quarter. Florida State recovered, though, and ended up winning the game and the national championship by a score of 46-29. But Virginia Tech earned the respect of its opponents and football fans across the country with its gutsy performance.

Coaches and sportswriters reserved special praise for Vick's spectacular play against Florida State. Displaying both his rifle arm and dazzling footwork, he had ripped the Seminoles defense for 225 yards passing and 97 yards rushing by the final whistle. "I'm proud of my performance," Vick said after the game. "If I could change anything about this season, I wouldn't change anything. Even tonight. I wouldn't change a thing. We went out there and played as hard as we could. We showed everyone we are champions. There is no way we don't have the respect of this nation right now. I think everyone knows we are one of the top teams in the nation."

Vick received a number of prestigious awards at the conclusion of his stellar 1999 season. He was named Rookie of the Year and Offensive Player of the Year for the Big East Conference —making him the first Division I football player ever to win both awards in a single year. He also tied a record for highest finish by a freshman by ending up third in the voting for the Heisman Trophy, which honors the top player in college football each year. Vick's honors also included the inaugural Archie Griffin Award as the season's Most Valuable Player, as well as an ESPY Award as the nation's top college player.

"I'm proud of my performance," Vick said after the 2000 Sugar Bowl against the powerful Florida State Seminoles. "If I could change anything about this season, I wouldn't change anything. Even tonight. I wouldn't change a thing. We went out there and played as hard as we could. We showed everyone we are champions. There is no way we don't have the respect of this nation right now. I think everyone knows we are one of the top teams in the nation."

Vick turned in another strong performance during 2000, his second year of eligibility. He passed for 1,234 yards and ran for another 607 while leading the Hokies to another great season. The team finished with a 10-1 record, with the only loss coming against Miami while Vick was sidelined with an ankle injury. Virginia Tech earned a spot in the Gator Bowl, where they faced the Clemson Tigers. Vick passed for 205 yards and one touchdown and rushed for 19 yards and another touchdown against Clemson, leading his team to an impressive 41-20 victory. He was named the Gator Bowl Most Valuable Player afterward.

During his two seasons as Virginia Tech's quarterback, Vick attracted a great deal of media attention with his strong arm and quick release, as well as his speed and elusiveness as a runner. He was widely regarded as one of the best all-around athletes and most exciting players in college football. At the same time, his positive attitude and solid work ethic made him a well-liked and respected leader on his team. "People ask me all the time what his greatest attribute is, and I always say it's his personality," said Hokies quarterback coach Rickey Bustle. "He's the most levelheaded young athlete I've ever been around. He doesn't get frustrated, he doesn't get too excited. He has fun out there. He has a fun personality, a mature personality." One of Vick's teammates, senior guard Matt Lehr, added that "Considering all the attention he gets, the guy could be a problem. But Mike doesn't seem affected by it at all. He's still just one of the guys in the locker room. He's still quiet, considerate of others, a gentleman. Truth is, Michael Vick is almost too good to be true."

> **"**
>
> *Vick's positive attitude and solid work ethic made him a well-liked and respected leader on his team. "People ask me all the time what his greatest attribute is, and I always say it's his personality," said Hokies quarterback coach Rickey Bustle. "He's the most levelheaded young athlete I've ever been around. He doesn't get frustrated, he doesn't get too excited. He has fun out there. He has a fun personality, a mature personality."*
>
> **"**

NFL — The Atlanta Falcons

A few weeks after the 2001 Gator Bowl, Vick announced that he had decided to leave college early and make himself eligible for the NFL draft. Some people criticized his decision, claiming that he was not ready to play in the NFL. They said that he did not have enough experience after only two college seasons, that he was too dependent on his running ability, and that he was too small (at six feet) to be an effective pro quarterback.

But the Atlanta Falcons disagreed with such assessments. They traded three draft choices and receiver Tim Dwight to the San Diego Chargers in exchange for the first overall pick in the 2001 draft, which they used to se-

Vick (#7) of the Atlanta Falcons runs for yardage against the Carolina Panthers, October 2002.

lect Vick. Vick thus became the first African-American quarterback and the youngest player ever taken at number one. The Falcons signed Vick to a six-year, $62 million contract. Vick used $1.5 million of his signing bonus to buy his family a new home. "I'm proud of what he has done as an athlete," his father stated. "But I'm also proud of the man he has become."

When Vick joined Atlanta, the Falcons were in the midst of a rebuilding phase. The team had only made the playoffs six times in its 35-year history. After battling their way to a Super Bowl appearance in 1998, the Falcons had posted a dismal 9-23 record over the next two seasons. Nevertheless, the Falcons decided to bring Vick along slowly during his rookie season. He appeared in eight games in 2001, usually when the outcome was no longer in doubt. He started two games when Atlanta's regular starting quarterback, Chris Chandler, went down with injuries.

Although Vick struggled at times and made some rookie mistakes, he impressed his coaches and teammates with his unflappable calm on the field.

In his first-ever NFL appearance — against San Francisco in the 49ers' home opener — Vick came into the game with the Falcons stuck deep in 49er territory. The San Francisco crowd was screaming, trying to rattle the highly publicized rookie. Amidst all of the noise, Vick walked into the Falcons' huddle, calmly pulled a ChapStick out of his helmet, moistened his lips, and popped it back into his helmet. "Are you kidding me?" Atlanta running back Jamal Anderson remembered thinking. "He just started laughing, and then everyone else did too. And I'm thinking, 'This is the coolest guy on the planet.'"

Vick's rookie statistics were not overly impressive. He admitted that he had a hard time familiarizing himself with the more complex professional game. Vick completed 50 passes out of 113 attempts for 758 yards and two touchdowns. His completion rate of 44.2 percent would have placed him squarely at the bottom of the National Football Conference (NFC) rankings if he had thrown enough passes to qualify. But his biggest problem was committing turnovers. In fact, he once gave up three fumbles in a single game. On the plus side, Vick rushed 29 times for 300 yards, which gave him a solid average of over 10 yards per carry. The Falcons finished the season below .500 and failed to make the playoffs.

> *Vick became the first African-American quarterback and the youngest player ever taken at number one in the NFL draft. The Falcons signed Vick to a six-year, $62 million contract. Vick used $1.5 million of his signing bonus to buy his family a new home. "I'm proud of what he has done as an athlete," his father stated. "But I'm also proud of the man he has become."*

Things began to look up for Vick and the Falcons in 2002, though. Vick became Atlanta's starting quarterback and greatly improved his all-around game over the course of the season. He gave a hint of things to come in the season opener, when he completed his first 10 pass attempts. In the eighth game of the season, against the division-leading New Orleans Saints, Vick posted nearly 300 yards in total offense and scored two rushing touchdowns. He was voted NFL Player of the Week in recognition of his performance. A few weeks later, Vick set a single-game record for a quarterback with 173 yards rushing against the

Quarterback Michael Vick (#7) drops back to throw a pass during the game against the Miami Dolphins.

Minnesota Vikings. His total included a 46-yard touchdown run that allowed the Falcons to win the game in overtime. Although Vick missed six games at the end of the season due to a broken ankle, he still finished the season with nearly 3,000 yards passing and 777 yards rushing (top among NFL quarterbacks) for a total of 24 touchdowns. He was named to the NFL Pro Bowl team in honor of his performance.

The Falcons overcame an up-and-down season to make the playoffs for the fourth time in team history. In the first round, they registered a shocking upset of the Green Bay Packers in the notoriously chilly conditions of Lambeau Field. Vick impressed many observers with his poise during the game. In the second round of the playoffs, Atlanta faced off against the Philadelphia Eagles — a team that boasted its own athletic young African-American quarterback, Vick's old friend Donovan McNabb. The two stars had similar styles of play and were often compared in the media. "It's great to be compared to Donovan," Vick noted. "The things that he accomplished over the last three years of his career are the things I want to accomplish as my career goes on. We both bring a lot to the table. We're both the new breed of quarterback. It's the first time we both are going head to head. The whole world will be watching. I'm pretty sure you can expect a lot of excitement."

> "
>
> *When asked to name the most important factor in an NFL quarterback's success, Vick responded, "Self-confidence. That's everything, man. If you don't believe in yourself, you won't succeed. Intelligence is important. A never-say-die attitude. Obviously, ability is, too. A quarterback has to be able to elude fast guys and make incredibly athletic plays. . . . I had the chance to meet with [former NFL quarterback] Steve Young last July. I really looked up to him when I was younger. He told me that when things break down, it's up to me to make things happen. That's when good quarterbacks are at their best."*
>
> "

Unfortunately for Vick, he and his teammates failed to generate much excitement after the opening kickoff. Philadelphia successfully employed a defensive strategy that focused on limiting Vick's running opportunities. The Falcons lost the game 27-7 and were eliminated from the playoffs.

Quarterback Michael Vick (#7) scrambles with the ball during this game against the Minnesota Vikings, December 2002.

A New Breed of NFL Quarterback

Vick's athletic abilities far exceed those of a traditional quarterback. He can run 40 yards in 4.25 seconds, for example, which makes him one of the fastest players in the NFL. He also possesses a 40-inch vertical jump and can throw a football 80 yards. Like traditional passing quarterbacks, Vick has a laser arm and the ability to think quickly and strategically. But he also has the running speed and open-field moves of a traditional option quarterback. In fact, ESPN analyst Joe Theismann called Vick "the best running person in football." Steve Sabol, president of NFL Films, added that "He's hard to compare to another quarterback. I'd compare him to maybe Gale Sayers [one of the NFL's great running backs]. He's capable of creating a moment of pure wonder. I remember that was the same feeling I'd get when I'd watch Gale Sayers. [Vick is] one of the guys that widens the boundaries and extends the parameters."

Some of the strongest compliments about Vick's talents come from his fellow NFL players. "It's unbelievable, man," said Falcons cornerback Ashley Ambrose. "He makes it looks so easy. It's ridiculous. I've never seen anybody like that in my life." Norman Hand, defensive tackle for the New

Orleans Saints, claimed that "He's the best I've ever played against. We've never seen the likes of him in the NFL." "He's the hardest guy in the league to tackle—harder than any running back I've faced," added Chicago Bears linebacker Brian Urlacher. "He's going to be really good for a long time."

As he begins his third year in the NFL, Vick plans to continue to get better. His goals include winning the Super Bowl and being elected into the Pro Football Hall of Fame. "I feel like I'm a special person and a special talent, and that in time and with the grace of God I can be one of the best in the game," he stated. "I don't think the NFL has seen the likes of me, a quarterback who moves the way I do and throws the way I do. I'm not saying that with arrogance or anything. That is just the way I feel."

> "I feel like I'm a special person and a special talent, and that in time and with the grace of God I can be one of the best in the game. I don't think the NFL has ever seen the likes of me, a quarterback who moves the way I do and throws the way I do. I'm not saying that with arrogance or anything. That is just the way I feel."

When asked to name the most important factor in an NFL quarterback's success, Vick responded, "Self-confidence. That's everything, man. If you don't believe in yourself, you won't succeed. Intelligence is important. A never-say-die attitude. Obviously, ability is, too. A quarterback has to be able to elude fast guys and make incredibly athletic plays. The pass-rushers in the league—Julius Peppers, Jevon Kearse—are all so quick. I had the chance to meet with [former NFL quarterback] Steve Young last July. I really looked up to him when I was younger. He told me that when things break down, it's up to me to make things happen. That's when good quarterbacks are at their best."

HOME AND FAMILY

Vick, who has never been married, lives in Atlanta. He has a son, Michael Jr., who was born in July 2002. "I love this little man so much," Vick stated. "He's the person I pick up all those first downs on third [down] and 25 [yards to go] for, the one I take all those hits for." Michael Jr. lives with his mother in Vick's hometown of Newport News, Virginia. Vick remains close to his own mother and speaks to her every day.

HOBBIES AND OTHER INTERESTS

In his spare time, Vick enjoys fishing, playing video games, and breeding pit bulls. He is also the national spokesperson for Boys and Girls Clubs of America.

HONORS AND AWARDS

High School All-American (*Parade*): 1998
Archie Griffin Award: 2000
ESPY Award: 2000
Big East Conference Offensive Player of the Year: 2000
Big East Conference Rookie of the Year: 2000
Collegiate All-American (*Sporting News*): 2000
Top NFL Draft Pick (Atlanta Falcons): 2001
NFL Player of the Week: 2002 (Week 8)
NFL Pro Bowl: 2002

FURTHER READING

Periodicals

Atlanta Journal and Constitution, Apr. 29, 2001, p.D1
New York Times, Apr. 20, 2001, p.C18; Jan. 9, 2003, p.D1; Jan. 11, 2003, p.D1
Richmond (Va.) Times Dispatch, May 10, 1998, p.D7
Sports Illustrated, Jan. 13, 2000, p.68; Aug. 4, 2000, p.92; Sep. 23, 2002, p.52
Sports Illustrated for Kids, Winter 2002, p.32
Sporting News, June 5, 2000, p.61; Oct. 30, 2000, p.48; Mar. 5, 2001, p.29; Apr. 9, 2001, p.38

ADDRESS

Michael Vick
Atlanta Falcons
4400 Falcon Parkway
Flowery Branch, GA 30542

WORLD WIDE WEB SITES

http://www.atlantafalcons.com
http://www.nflplayers.com
http://www.jockbio.com/Bios/Vick/Vick_bio.html

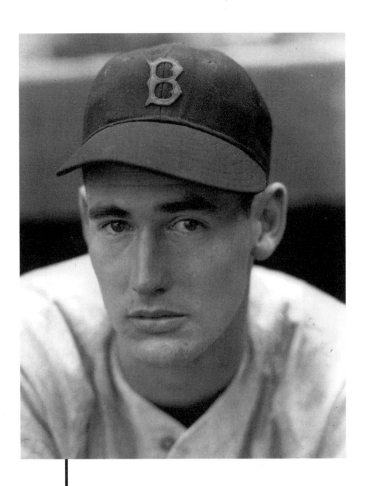

RETROSPECTIVE

Ted Williams 1918-2002

American Professional Baseball Player with the
Boston Red Sox
Six-Time Major League Batting Champion

BIRTH

Theodore Samuel Williams was born on August 30, 1918, in
San Diego, California. This is the date that Williams provided,
but there is some controversy surrounding the date because
his birth certificate originally read August 20. His mother, May
Venzer, was a lieutenant in the Salvation Army—a charitable

religious group—when she met his father, Sam Williams, who was then a soldier and later became a photographer. Williams had one brother, Danny, who was born two years after him.

YOUTH

May and Sam Williams raised their family in a modest home in San Diego that was purchased with the help of a friend. Although the Williamses were expected to repay the benefactor, May habitually poured her earnings back into the Salvation Army, and Sam earned little income as an occasional photographer. May worked long hours, and her commitment to the Salvation Army often required nighttime service. Sam's schedule was unpredictable also. In fact, May's and Sam's schedules were so erratic that the Williams boys were often locked out of the house awaiting a parent's return. Ted spent much of his time on those evenings swinging a bat in the backyard.

As a young boy, Williams developed a strong interest in hunting and fishing. This was fostered in part by an older neighbor who served as a sort of surrogate father to him during his father's frequent absences from the Williams household.

Williams's love affair with baseball began when he was 12 years old. "I can tell you exactly when it started," he recalled. "It wasn't when I was 10 or 11. It happened when I was 12. I had never followed major-league baseball. The only players I had ever heard of were [Babe] Ruth and [Lou] Gehrig. And then I read that Bill Terry had hit .400, and that really excited me. Four hundred! I don't think I even knew what you had to do to hit .400, but I could tell that it was something wonderful. I knew I wanted to

> *"I can tell you exactly when it started," Williams said about his love affair with baseball. "It wasn't when I was 10 or 11. It happened when I was 12. I had never followed major-league baseball. The only players I had ever heard of were [Babe] Ruth and [Lou] Gehrig. And then I read that Bill Terry had hit .400, and that really excited me. Four hundred! I don't think I even knew what you had to do to hit .400, but I could tell that it was something wonderful. I knew I wanted to do that, too. Hit .400. I was so excited that even though it was dark out . . . I got my little bat, ran out to our little backyard, and began to swing."*

do that, too. Hit .400. I was so excited that even though it was dark out . . . I got my little bat, ran out to our little backyard, and began to swing."

Williams's baseball swing was a constant preoccupation for him. Even during those early days in his backyard, he dreamed of playing on a major league field. With that goal in mind, the youngster studied how to be the best hitter he could be. By the time he was 14 years old, Williams was including himself in baseball games at a local park, forsaking Sunday school and other activities to play games with both adults and other kids. His mother was supportive of her oldest son's enthusiasm for the sport, even though she was discouraged by his lack of interest in the Salvation Army. She bought Williams a baseball glove and helped him make a baseball uniform. Still, when he had the opportunity to play baseball for money with a local team, she forbade it on the grounds that the team was sponsored by an establishment that sold liquor.

Williams's early skills on the baseball diamond helped him gain self-confidence. But like many other teenagers, he remained insecure about other things. He was particularly self-conscious about his physical appearance. He was taller than most of his peers—he eventually reached a height of six feet, four inches—and he had trouble gaining weight. He drank countless malted milk shakes in an attempt to add bulk to his frame, sometimes drinking four or five in a single day.

EDUCATION

After completing elementary school in the San Diego area, Williams moved on to Hoover High School. He quickly emerged as one of the top pitchers on the school's baseball team. But for all of his skills on the mound, he earned even more recognition for his hitting. Teammates and opponents alike marveled at his skill with the bat. His offensive prowess was so feared that teams occasionally walked him intentionally with the bases loaded.

Williams's exploits on various San Diego baseball diamonds soon attracted the attention of major league scouts. His father suddenly realized that his oldest son might be able to make a living playing baseball, and he subsequently became much more involved in the boy's baseball activities. Before long, Sam Williams was acting as his son's agent. He turned down modest contract offers from the New York Yankees and St. Louis Cardinals, convinced that a better deal would come along.

In the meantime, a new Pacific Coast League baseball franchise opened in San Diego. The Padres, as the team was called, immediately contacted

Williams to see if he wanted to play for them. Thrilled with the opportunity to stay at home and yet play professional baseball, Williams signed a contract to play for the team for only $150 per month, far less than he would have made with the Yankees or Cardinals. But the agreement also stipulated that Williams, who was only 17 years old at the time, could not be traded until he was at least 21. The contract also said that upon being dealt to a major-league team, his mother would receive ten percent of the money earned from the sale of her son's services.

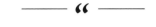

CAREER HIGHLIGHTS

The San Diego Padres of the Pacific Coast League

Williams made no attempt to hide the fact that he was awestruck to be a member of the Padres. "Everything was new," he remembered. "Seeing all the players and seeing them up close and getting that experience to be a professional ballplayer. . . . I thought I was in a fairyland. It was all like a dream for a year and a half."

Williams made no attempt to hide the fact that he was awestruck to be a member of the Padres. "Everything was new," he remembered. "Seeing all the players and seeing them up close and getting that experience to be a professional ballplayer. . . . I thought I was in a fairyland. It was all like a dream for a year and a half."

The Padres moved Williams off of the pitcher's mound and into the outfield, where he did not particularly distinguish himself. At the plate, however, he showed signs of being a big league hitter. He posted some notable hitting streaks during his one and a half seasons with the club, and during his second season he rang up 98 runs batted in (RBIs) and 23 home runs.

People affiliated with the Boston Braves and the New York Giants recognized that the young slugger had plenty of potential, and both clubs made offers to purchase Williams's services. Ultimately, though, the Boston Red Sox out-hustled the other teams to add Williams to its roster in 1938. The acquisition was controversial, though. In striking the deal with the Red Sox, the Padres had broken their promise to keep Ted Williams until the age of 21. To make matters worse, they refused to pay May Williams a percentage of the asking price even though her son's contract with San Diego explicitly called for it. Many believe that the Red Sox ended up paying May Williams the money she had been promised by the Padres in order to buy

Williams at bat in 1939 at Fenway Park in Boston.

her son's contract. After leaving San Diego, Williams continued to support his family financially, but he rarely visited home.

Life in the Minors

Soon after Williams arrived at the Red Sox training camp in 1938, Coach Joe Cronin recognized that the 20-year-old player needed more seasoning before he could play in a Red Sox uniform. His fielding was weak and he had some trouble with the higher-caliber pitching of the major leagues.

But he nonetheless attracted a fair amount of attention, in part because the town's sportswriters saw that the young slugger had a somewhat cocky attitude. Indeed, Williams's self-confidence was evident within days of his arrival in Boston, and stories about him soon began to circulate. One well-known story held that at one of the team's first batting practices, veteran star Jimmie Foxx stepped to the plate to take his swings. Another player turned to Williams and told him, "Wait until you see Foxx hit." Williams responded, "Wait until he sees me hit." Although Williams later claimed that the exchange never took place, he admitted that such a quote was not out of character for him.

At the end of spring training, Williams was transferred to Minneapolis, a minor league team for the Boston Red Sox. In baseball, some players start their professional careers in the major leagues. But many more start out playing for a team in the minor leagues, also called the farm system. The teams in the minor leagues are affiliated with those in the major leagues. There are a variety of minor leagues, which are ranked according to the level of competition. The top or best league is Class AAA (called Triple A); next is Class AA; then Class A; then below that are the rookie leagues. Players hope to move up through the system to a Class AAA team and then to the major leagues.

> *"I want to become such a great hitter that when I walk down the street people will say, 'There goes Ted Williams, the greatest hitter in baseball.' Then I'll be happy. That's all that interests me in this world — to be the greatest hitter in all baseball."*

After moving to the Minneapolis farm team, Williams received instruction from Hall of Famer Rogers Hornsby. Williams paid close attention to Hornsby's tips, because he was determined to make it to the major leagues. "I want to become such a great hitter that when I walk down the street people will say, 'There goes Ted Williams, the greatest hitter in baseball,'" he once said. "Then I'll be happy. That's all that interests me in this world — to be the greatest hitter in all baseball."

Williams quickly emerged as the most controversial player on the Minneapolis roster. He was the club's biggest home run threat and showed a flair for producing a hit when it was most needed. But even though he impressed people at the plate, he worried his coach in the field. He constantly argued with the fans, and on one occasion he simply sat down in the middle of the field during play. He also threw tantrums when his performance was not up to his standards or when teams intentionally walked him. On several occasions he threatened to quit the game altogether. He nearly destroyed his career when he punched a glass water cooler and shattered it, cutting his hand severely.

Playing for the Red Sox

Despite his immaturity, Williams moved up to join the Red Sox roster in 1939 and immediately made a name for himself. During his rookie year he led the league with 145 RBIs, beating out Yankee Joe DiMaggio—who would be compared to Williams throughout their careers—and teammate Jimmie Foxx for baseball's RBI title. His tremendous home runs made him a fan favorite, and within months it seemed that he had befriended countless police officers, fire fighters, restaurant employees, cab drivers, and children throughout the city. But Williams also attracted a fair amount of negative publicity. On one occasion he brought a gun to Fenway Park, where the Red Sox played, and shot several pigeons and a number of scoreboard lights. Many people expressed disgust about Williams's juvenile behavior, but the slugger ignored them.

After a while, the Boston sportswriters decided that Williams should have a nickname. Williams told them to call him "The Kid," a name that had been given to him by clubhouse assistant Johnny Orlando during his first day of training camp. Williams began to refer to himself in the third person as "The Kid," a nickname that everybody seemed to think was pretty appropriate. The name reflected not only his youthful exuberance, but also his sometimes childish mood swings and tantrums.

After posting such an amazing rookie year, Williams raised expectations for himself among the fans and the press. But during his second year in the league pitchers began to serve him more difficult breaking balls to hit, and he struggled at times. As his productivity at the plate dropped, his fielding began to suffer as well. Harold Kaese of the *Boston Transcript* subsequently wrote a critical column in which he claimed that Williams possessed "extreme selfishness, egoism, and lack of courage." Kaese went on to blame the young player's immaturity on "his upbringing. Can you imagine a kid, a nice kid with a nimble brain, not visiting his mother and father all of last winter?"

The personal attack stunned Williams. Writing in his autobiography, *My Turn at Bat*, he stated that prior to the clash with Kaese, "I was willing to believe a writer was my friend until he proved otherwise. Now my guard's up all the time, always watching for critical stuff. If I saw something, I'd read it 20 times, and I'd burn without knowing how to fight it. How could I fight it? . . . I was moody a lot. I'd go in spells. Jimmie Foxx was always in my corner, but he called me a 'spoiled boy' that year, and I guess I acted like one. If I got mad and didn't run out a ground ball, Cronin would chew me out, which was right, and I'd be sorry and full of remorse, so the next couple times I'd sprint like mad to first base even when I was a sure out. That was also the year I got booed for making an error and then for striking out, and the unfairness of it hit me. I vowed that day I'd never tip my hat again."

Williams at Yankee Stadium, selecting bats in the dugout before the game on July 1, 1941. At that point in the season he was batting .402.

1941 — A Year to Remember

Williams started the 1941 season with a bang. By May 15 he was hitting .339, with several impressive home runs under his belt. On that day Joe DiMaggio began a record-setting, 56-game hitting streak that played a part in his being named the Most Valuable Player for the year. But Williams began to make headlines of his own, as his batting average continued to spiral upward.

At one point in the season, Williams's batting average had climbed up to an incredible .427, and fans around the country debated whether the slugger would be able to keep a .400 average for the entire year. Williams was up to the challenge. For the remainder of the season, he not only kept his average above the .400 mark, but also contended for the "Triple Crown" — awarded to a player who leads the league in batting average, number of home runs, and number of RBIs (he ended up leading the league in average and home runs, but not in RBIs).

As Williams entered the last day of the season, he was batting .3995, which rounded to the .400 mark. Coach Cronin gave Williams the opportunity to sit out the final day and preserve the mark, but the Red Sox star decided to play in both games of the doubleheader that was scheduled. "If I couldn't hit .400 all the way I didn't deserve it," he later said. "When I got the first hit I felt a little more confident, then I hit a home run over the right field fence and from there on, *wrrooofff.*" By the time the doubleheader was complete, he had hit six for eight, earning a final average of .406. A year later Williams carved out another amazing season, winning baseball's Triple Crown with a .356 batting average, 36 home runs, and 137 RBIs. Once again, though, he was passed over as the league's Most Valuable Player, losing to New York Yankee Joe Gordon.

> *As Williams entered the last day of the 1941 season, he was batting .3995, which rounded to the .400 mark. Coach Cronin gave Williams the opportunity to sit out the final day and preserve the mark, but the Red Sox star decided to play in both games of the doubleheader that was scheduled. "If I couldn't hit .400 all the way I didn't deserve it. When I got the first hit I felt a little more confident, then I hit a home run over the right field fence and from there on, wrrooofff."*

Called into the Service in World War II

But Williams's focus soon changed. In December 1941, the Japanese bombed the naval base at Pearl Harbor in Hawaii. That marked the beginning of direct U.S. involvement in World War II. After the bombing, Williams's military draft status changed. Although he had been classified as III-A, signifying that his mother was dependent upon his income for her well-being, he was reclassified as I-A, making him immediately eligible for the draft. When he requested that the draft board review his reclassification, his patriotism was questioned in the press.

Williams subsequently enlisted in the U.S. Navy in 1942 as a second lieutenant in naval aviation. During his military training, he displayed amazing math skills for someone with only a high school education. His hunting background also made him one of the camp's top rifle marksmen. Instead of entering combat, though, he was made an instructor. He was transferred to a combat squadron shortly before the war ended, but as he prepared to leave San Francisco for battle, the war ended and Williams was discharged.

Williams enlisting in the U.S. Navy, 1942.

The Red Sox Win the Pennant

Williams returned to the Red Sox in 1946—the only year that he won the pennant (league championship) with the ball club. During Williams's career the powerful Yankees often beat out the Red Sox for the privilege of playing in the World Series, but in 1946 Boston would not be denied. Led by Williams, the Red Sox built an early lead in the division standings. By the halfway point in the season, he was leading the league in most offensive categories.

On July 14 of that year, in the first game of a doubleheader against Cleveland, Williams stroked three home runs. In the second game, Cleveland shortstop and manager Lou Boudreau tried a strategy that came to be known as the "Boudreau shift." He positioned all of the infielders on the right side of the field, where Williams usually pulled the ball. Instead of pushing the ball to the vast open area on the left side of the diamond, Williams tried to drive the ball through the crowded side of the field. As the strategy gained publicity, he felt continually challenged by other teams to defeat variations of the shift by hitting the ball through it instead of around it.

Williams's average dropped and—when it appeared that he would lose the Triple Crown because of opponents' shifts—he became frustrated. Still, the team rolled on and won the American League pennant. The owner of the Red Sox arranged a victory celebration, but Williams did not show up. Rumors of his lack of team spirit clouded the newspapers the next day.

Because the National League pennant race had not yet concluded, the Boston management set up an exhibition series to keep the team fresh. Williams got hit in the elbow by a pitch during the first game of the series, though, and he also struggled with a virus. He used neither of these factors as an excuse when he performed poorly in the World Series against the St. Louis Cardinals. Against a version of the Boudreau shift, he hit five singles and walked five times. He had no extra base hits and did not make a strong impact in the series, which the Cardinals won in seven games. Williams's critics seized on his mediocre performance. They claimed that he was not a clutch hitter and that he was more concerned with individual statistics than team victories.

The following season, Williams's stormy relationship with the press continued. In fact, the feud caused him to miss out on winning the Most Valuable Player award once again. He had rolled to a great year in 1947, hitting for a .343 average with 32 home runs and 114 RBIs. But he lost in the MVP balloting by one vote, as one of Boston's writers failed to place him among the league's top ten players. As a result, the award went to DiMaggio. Had that writer voted for Williams as even the ninth best player of the year, Williams would have won the honor outright.

Between 1948 and 1950, the Red Sox fell into a pattern under new Coach Joe McCarthy. They started out each season slowly, then began to close ground on the frontrunner, occasionally overtaking them, and then lost in the end. In 1949 Williams's team lost the pennant on the last day of the season, and Williams himself lost the batting championship during his last at-bat by walking instead of getting a hit. A hit would have made him the only player ever to win three Triple Crowns.

In the 1950 season Williams's image with fans declined when he spat and made obscene gestures toward them and members of the press during several games. One spitting incident even prompted the Boston management to issue an apology on behalf of Williams. Rumors began to circulate that Williams might be traded, but in the All-Star game that year he injured his elbow, limiting his trade value. An ensuing operation resulted in the removal of 15 bone chips. He lost some of his extension and power and had to tolerate stiffness in the elbow through the remainder of his career.

Williams in the cockpit of a Marine F9F-5 Panther jet fighter plane in 1952, training for service in the Korean War.

Called into the Service in Korea

In 1952 Williams was called into the Marines to fight in the Korean War. Although he had been relegated to the role of a pinch hitter for most of that season because of a leg injury, Williams was forced into the spotlight for what many thought would be his last day in the majors—April 30, 1952. He was presented with gifts, one of which was a book containing the signatures of more than 400,000 well wishers from across the country. In an uncharacteristic gesture of gratitude he tipped his hat to the crowd. On what many anticipated would be his last at-bat, he hit a home run against the Detroit Tigers.

During the Korean War, Williams entered into combat as a pilot. He flew in 39 missions, many of them as the wing man (partner aircraft) of one of

———— " ————

"The funny thing was I didn't feel anything," Williams recalled about the time in Korea when his plane was hit by anti-aircraft fire during an air attack. *"I knew I was hit when the stick started shaking like mad in my hands. Then everything went out, my radio, landing gear, everything. The red warning lights were on all over the place."*

———— " ————

America's most famous pilots — the war hero, astronaut, and U.S. Senator John Glenn. Williams came close to losing his life on at least one occasion in Korea. His closest call occurred when his plane was hit by anti-air-craft fire during an air attack. "The funny thing was I didn't feel any-thing," he recalled. "I knew I was hit when the stick started shaking like mad in my hands. Then everything went out, my radio, landing gear, everything. The red warning lights were on all over the place." Members of his squadron tried to communicate with him, but the radio was out and Williams did not hear their command to eject. He flew over the ocean with the intention of landing in the water. Much of the area was iced over, how-ever, and Williams pressed on for land. He finally located an airstrip and landed the plane, which by now was largely engulfed in flames. "He was coming in at 200 miles per hour," said one observer. "He skidded about two or three thousand feet in a burning plane on one of those old Marsden mattings that looked like a waffle. He didn't blow, and he got out of it. It was a miracle thing."

Williams was discharged from the service on July 10, 1953, due to a virus that often plagued him during the latter part of his baseball career. After returning home to the United States, Williams originally intended to relax and spend some time fishing, but his business manager convinced him to return to the Red Sox.

Williams did well throughout the remainder of the 1953 season, but broke his collarbone in spring training the following year. He finished the 1954 season with a .345 average, but missed out on the batting title because he had not taken the necessary minimum number of at bats. In 1955 Williams retired in order to avoid high alimony payments as part of a divorce settle-ment. He came out of retirement in mid-May and quickly showed that he was still among the league's best hitters. But once again, his limited num-ber of plate appearances disqualified him from consideration for the league batting title.

End of a Career

In 1957 Williams had a year that many consider to be as noteworthy as the magical 1941 season in which he hit .406. At the age of 39 he hit .388, a remarkable average for any player. He began to use a heavier bat — 35 ounces as opposed to 31 ounces — and began to concentrate less on pulling the ball. As he peppered the entire field with hits, teams realized that defensive shifts aimed at stopping him had lost much of their effectiveness. In September, however, Williams was victimized by the recurring virus that had been plagued him for the past several seasons. The slugger was kept out of the lineup for more than two weeks. When he returned, he set a record by getting on base in 16 consecutive plate appearances. He started the string with two home runs and hit two more over the course of setting the record. As the season entered its final days, it appeared that Williams had a chance to reach .400 again. Despite their sometimes ugly spats with the slugger, most fans and reporters rooted him on. But he fell just short in his bid for a second .400 season.

Bouts with food poisoning, a gimpy ankle, and pulled muscles kept Williams from getting off to a great start in 1958, and he was kept out of the starting line-up for the All-Star game for the first time since his rookie year. But Williams grew stronger as the season progressed and went on to claim his sixth batting championship with a .326 average.

The injury bug visited Williams once again in 1959. A pinched nerve in his neck forced him to change his batting stance, and his hitting suffered as a result. He hit .254 and was asked to retire at the end of the season. Instead, Williams demanded the opportunity to redeem himself in 1960. After the Red Sox agreed to sign him at the $125,000 salary he had made the previous year, Williams cut his own pay to $95,000.

In 1960 Williams hit for a .316 average and stroked 29 home runs, none more memorable than the last, which occurred on the final at-bat of his ca-

———— **"** ————

"He was coming in at 200 miles per hour," one observer said about the time Williams attempting to land his plane while engulfed in flames.
"He skidded about two or three thousand feet in a burning plane on one of those old Marsden mattings that looked like a waffle. He didn't blow, and he got out of it. It was a miracle thing."

———— **"** ————

reer. Recalling that homer, award-winning novelist John Updike wrote that the pitcher, Jack Fisher, "was low with the first pitch. He put the second one over, and Williams swung mightily and missed. The crowd grunted, seeing that swing, so long and smooth and quick, exposed. Fisher threw the third time, Williams swung again, and there it was. The ball climbed on a diagonal line into the vast volume of air over center field. . . . It was in the books while it was still in the sky. . . . Like a feather caught in a vortex, Williams ran around the square of bases at the center of our beseeching screaming. He ran as he always ran out home runs—hurriedly, unsmiling, head down, as if our praise were a storm or rain to get out of. He didn't tip his cap. Though we thumped, wept, chanted 'We want Ted' for minutes after he hid in the dugout, he did not come back."

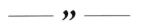

> *Williams's remarkable feat of maintaining a batting average of .406 over an entire season, which he achieved in 1941, has not been duplicated since.*
>
> *"I didn't realize how much .400 would mean to my life," he acknowledged. "I mean it had happened only 11 years before I did it, and I thought someone else would do it pretty soon. I felt there certainly would be other .400 hitters. I said that. I always said that. Now here it is, 50, 60 years later."*

The Kid's Legacy

Williams ended his career among the all-time leaders in nearly every offensive category. He finished with a lifetime .344 batting average, 521 home runs, and 2,019 walks. His .483 on-base percentage is still the highest in major-league history. His remarkable feat of maintaining a batting average of .406 over an entire season, which he achieved in 1941, has not been duplicated since. "I didn't realize how much .400 would mean to my life," Williams acknowledged. "I mean it had happened only 11 years before I did it, and I thought someone else would do it pretty soon. I felt there certainly would be other .400 hitters. I said that. I always said that. Now here it is, 50, 60 years later." Williams also led the league in walks eight times, in runs scored six times, in RBIs and home runs four times, and won two most valuable player awards. From the time that he retired, people have wondered about how much more spectacular his career could have been if he had not lost so many games to military service and injury.

Here is the powerful batting swing of Ted Williams, taken in 1957.

After retiring from baseball as a player, Williams was named to the Baseball Hall of Fame in 1966. He called his induction "the greatest thrill of my life. I received 280-some votes from the writers. I know I didn't have 280-odd close friends among the writers. I know they voted for me because they felt in their minds and some in their hearts that I rated it, and I want

153

to say to them: Thank you from the bottom of my heart." Williams impressed many people by using his Hall of Fame induction speech to recognize some of the great African-American baseball players who were denied an opportunity to play in the majors during segregation (a time in American history when people were separated by race, which had the effect of putting black people in an inferior position in society). "I hope that Satchel Paige and Josh Gibson somehow will be inducted here as symbols of the great Negro players who are not here because they were not given a chance,"Williams said in 1966. Thanks in part to his efforts, a special committee honoring players from the Negro Leagues elected Paige and Gibson to the Hall of Fame in the 1970s.

— **"** —

After retiring from baseball as a player, Williams was named to the Baseball Hall of Fame in 1966. He called his induction "the greatest thrill of my life. I received 280-some votes from the writers. I know I didn't have 280-odd close friends among the writers. I know they voted for me because they felt in their minds and some in their hearts that I rated it, and I want to say to them: Thank you from the bottom of my heart."

— **"** —

Williams remained involved in baseball following his retirement. He managed the Washington Senators for four years, from 1969 to 1973. He also served as a batting instructor from time to time with the Red Sox. Williams played in several nostalgic reunion games in the 1980s and was honored at Fenway Park on May 12, 1991, on the 50th anniversary of his accomplishment of batting .406. In a speech before the game, Williams alluded to his famous refusals to tip his hat to fans during his playing career, then said that "today, I tip my cap to a-a-a-l-l the people in New England, without question the greatest sports fans on earth." And he took a baseball hat out of his pocket and waved it in the air.

As the years passed, Williams became a beloved public figure in Boston and across the country. He seemed to mellow with age and became more open in interviews. Most people forgot about the controversies that had surrounded his career and focused instead on his legendary accomplishments. "I'm just a loveable old guy, now," he explained. Williams gradually gained a reputation as an avid fisherman, a spokesman for worthy charitable causes, and a promoter of the U.S. Marine Corps. In 1991, he received the Presidential Medal of Freedom—the highest honor awarded to civil-

Former Red Sox player Ted Williams (right) and former Yankee player Joe DiMaggio (left) wave to the crowd before the start of the 1991 All Star Game. Both Williams and DiMaggio played in the 1941 All Star Game, 50 years earlier.

ians in the United States. In a statement accompanying the award, President George Bush called him "an American legend, a remarkable figure in American sports, and a twice-tested war hero."

Williams always remained an enthusiastic fan and supporter of the game of baseball. "I think the ballplayers today, overall, are better than they've ever been," he once said. "I watch them on TV and they fly through the air. They make spectacular plays." Nevertheless, he added, "I wouldn't trade one day from the years I played. I just feel that I truly played in the greatest era."

The Passing of a Legend

In late 1991, Williams suffered the first of a series of strokes that left him partially blind and caused numbness on one side of his body. One positive outcome of his failing health was that it helped him to establish a closer relationship with his grown children. His son, John Henry Williams, moved to Florida to care for him and assumed responsibility for his business dealings. A few years earlier, Williams had fallen victim to a scam artist who convinced him to donate money and memorabilia to a joint business venture. The scam artist was eventually sent to prison for his actions, but Williams was unable to recover his money or legal expenses. John Henry was determined to see that no one would take advantage of his father again. He visited sports memorabilia shops across the country to uncover forgeries of his father's signature, then started his own, legitimate memorabilia business to provide his father with income.

In 1994 Williams participated in the opening of the Ted Williams Museum and Hitters Hall of Fame in Hernando, Florida. The following year, a tunnel under Boston Harbor was named after him. Williams made his final appearance in Boston in 1999, when he went to the All-Star Game at Fenway Park to take part in a celebration for the Team of the Century. When the former slugger came onto the field in a golf cart, he received a standing ovation from the crowd and was quickly surrounded by admiring current All-Stars as well as baseball heroes from years past.

In 2000 Williams had a pacemaker implanted in his chest to regulate his heartbeat, and the following year he underwent open-heart surgery. He died of cardiac arrest on July 5, 2002, in Inverness, Florida. As word spread of the legend's passing, tributes poured in from baseball fans, celebrities, and politicians across the country. "No one knows what kind of career numbers he would have had, and what records he would have broken, if he hadn't spent those five years as a pilot and member of the 'greatest generation,'" said John Kerry, the U.S. Senator from Massachusetts. "This guy was courageous, bigger than life, tough as nails, and he had that rare ability to sum up perfectly in his very character so many things — a generation, a game, a country. I'd say we won't see another like him."

> **"**
>
> *"No one knows what kind of career numbers he would have had, and what records he would have broken, if he hadn't spent those five years as a pilot and member of the 'greatest generation,'" said John Kerry, the U.S. Senator from Massachusetts. "This guy was courageous, bigger than life, tough as nails, and he had that rare ability to sum up perfectly in his very character so many things — a generation, a game, a country. I'd say we won't see another like him."*
>
> **"**

Williams is greeted at home plate by Joe DiMaggio (#5) and coach Marv Shea after hitting a dramatic ninth-inning home run in the All Star Game, July 1941.

The Red Sox honored Williams's memory the following day before a home game at Fenway Park. In a solemn ceremony, they mowed his number 9 into the leftfield grass where he once played, placed a single red rose in the bleacher seat where his longest home run had landed in 1946, and posted a message on the scoreboard that read, "At bat, number 9, batting .406." A U.S. Marine Corps honor guard raised the American flag to half mast and played taps. "There goes the greatest hitter that ever lived," the announcer said, as fans and players observed a moment of silence.

MARRIAGE AND FAMILY

Williams married and divorced three times. He had a daughter, Barbara Joyce (known as Bobby Jo), with his first wife, Doris Soule, to whom he was married from 1944 to 1955. He married Lee Howard in 1961, but their union was short-lived. In 1968 he married Delores Wettach, with whom he had a son, John Henry, and a daughter, Claudia. He lived in Crystal River, Florida, until his death in 2002.

Unfortunately, an ugly legal battle developed among Williams's children after his death. A few hours after he died, his two younger children — John Henry and Claudia — sent his body to a cryonics chamber in Arizona to be frozen. Cryonics is an unproven technology that is used to preserve bodies in hopes that they can be regenerated, or brought back to life, at some time in the future. But Williams's older daughter, Bobby Jo, and many of his friends were outraged by this action. They remembered that Williams had expressed a desire to be cremated, and his 1996 will supported their statements. Some people accused John Henry of trying to profit from his father's death by freezing his body and selling his DNA. But John Henry claimed that Williams had changed his mind about cremation, and he produced a note his father had signed in 2000 to prove it. "We believe in the potential for regenerative science to advance substantially in the next 100 years," John Henry Williams stated. "[My father's] attitude was, 'If there's a chance that we can be reunited in the future, let's take it.'" Bobby Jo filed a lawsuit against her half-siblings, demanding that Williams's body be returned to Florida to be cremated. But she eventually ran out of money to continue the lawsuit, so the legendary slugger's body remains frozen.

> ――― **"** ―――
>
> *Williams paid visits to children in hospitals throughout his playing career and for many years afterward, though he insisted that he receive no publicity for his efforts. "Look, it embarrasses me to be praised for anything like this. The embarrassing thing is that I don't feel I've done anything compared to the people at the hospital who are really doing the important work. It makes me happy to think I've done a little good. I suppose that's what I get out of it. Anyway, it's only a freak of fate, isn't it, that one of those kids isn't going to grow up to be an athlete and I wasn't the one who had the cancer?"*
>
> ――― **"** ―――

HOBBIES AND OTHER INTERESTS

Williams was an expert fisherman who enjoyed fishing in the coastal waters of Florida until a few years before his death. He even co-authored a book about fishing. In 2000 he was inducted into the Fishing Hall of Fame.

Williams was also an active solicitor, spokesperson, and patron of the Jimmy Fund, a charitable organization devoted to working with children and developing a cure for cancer. Indeed, Williams paid visits to children in hospitals throughout his playing career and for many years afterward, though he insisted that he receive no publicity for his efforts. "Look, it embarrasses me to be praised for anything like this," he explained. "The embarrassing thing is that I don't feel I've done anything compared to the people at the hospital who are really doing the important work. It makes me happy to think I've done a little good. I suppose that's what I get out of it. Anyway, it's only a freak of fate, isn't it, that one of those kids isn't going to grow up to be an athlete and I wasn't the one who had the cancer?"

WRITINGS

My Turn at Bat: The Story of My Life, 1969 (with John Underwood)
Fishing the Big Three: Tarpon, Bonefish, Atlantic Salmon, 1982 (with John Underwood)
The Science of Hitting, 1986 (with John Underwood)
Ted Williams's Hit List, 1996
Ted Williams: My Life in Pictures, 2001 (with David Pietrusza)

HONORS AND AWARDS

Player of the Year (*Sporting News*): 1941, 1942, 1947, 1949, 1957
American League Batting Champion: 1941, 1942, 1947, 1948, 1957, 1958
American League Triple Crown Winner: 1942, 1947
American League Most Valuable Player: 1946, 1949
1950s Player of the Decade (*Sporting News*): 1960
Baseball Hall of Fame: 1966
Manager of the Year: 1969
Presidential Medal of Freedom: 1991
Fishing Hall of Fame: 2000

FURTHER READING

Books

Baldassaro, Lawrence, ed. *The Ted Williams Reader,* 1991
Encyclopedia Britannica, 2002
Encyclopedia of World Biography Supplement, Vol. 19, 1999
Linn, Ed. *Hitter: The Life and Turmoils of Ted Williams,* 1993
St. James Encyclopedia of Popular Culture, 2000
Who's Who in America, 1997
Williams, Ted, and David Pietrusza. *Ted Williams: My Life in Pictures,* 2001

Williams, Ted, and John Underwood. *My Turn at Bat: The Story of My Life,* 1969

Wolff, Rick. *Ted Williams,* 1993 (juvenile)

Periodicals

Boston Globe, July 6, 2002, pp.A1, G13; July 8, 2002, p.C7
Current Biography Yearbook, 1947 and 2002
Esquire, Apr. 1999, p.116
Life, Feb. 1, 2000, p.35
New York Times, July 6, 2002, pp.A1, D1; July 9, 2002, p.A21; Dec. 21, 2002, p.D2; Dec. 29, 2002, p.F28
Palm Beach Post, July 11, 2000, p.C1
Sport, Nov. 1998, p.122
Sporting News, Nov. 14, 1994, p.42
Sports Illustrated, July 4, 1994, p.56; Dec. 25, 1995, p.15; Nov. 25, 1996, p.92; July 16, 2001, p.25; July 15, 2002, p.44; July 17, 2002, p.70
Time, July 15, 2002, p.72

Online Articles

http://sportsillustrated.cnn.com/baseball/mlb/features/1998/williams/1996.html (*Sports Illustrated,* "Rounding Third," Nov. 25, 1996)

Online Databases

Biography Resource Center Online, 2003, articles from *Encyclopedia of World Biography Supplement,* 1999, and *St. James Encyclopedia of Popular Culture,* 2000

WORLD WIDE WEB SITES

http://www.tedwilliams.com
http://www.boston.com/sports/redsox/williams/
http://www.baseball-almanac.com/quotes/quowilt.shtml
http://www.jimmyfund.org/abo/tedwilliams/

Jay Yelas 1965-

American Professional Fisherman
2002 Bassmasters Classic World Champion and
FLW Angler of the Year

BIRTH

Joel Andrew Yelas was born on September 2, 1965, in Honolulu, Hawaii. He has been known by the nickname Jay (taken
from his initials) since his childhood. His father, Joe Yelas, was
a high school teacher and administrator. His mother, Kim
(Griffiths) Yelas, was a kindergarten teacher. He has one younger sister, Lisa.

YOUTH

Yelas lived in a suburb of Honolulu until he was 12 years old. He loved being on the ocean and spent a great deal of time waterskiing and fishing for perch or crabs. Every summer Yelas and his family would visit relatives on the U.S. mainland. His maternal grandparents lived in Oregon, where the young boy learned to enjoy hiking, camping, and fishing for trout or salmon. "These times we spent together as a family gave me a love of sports and the outdoors," he stated. "This love is the foundation for all the decisions that brought me to the place I am today."

Yelas's paternal grandparents had a cabin on a lake in upstate New York. This lake was where he caught his first bass. "One morning when I was eight or nine years old, standing alone down on the dock of my grandfather's cabin, I threw out a black jitterbug and began reeling it in, working it slowly on the surface," he recalled. "When a 13-inch bass took the bait, I thought I would bust with excitement! That was the first bass I caught on my own."

> "One morning when I was eight or nine years old, standing alone down on the dock of my grandfather's cabin, I threw out a black jitterbug and began reeling it in, working it slowly on the surface. When a 13-inch bass took the bait, I thought I would bust with excitement! That was the first bass I caught on my own."

The Yelas family moved to the mainland permanently when Jay was in eighth grade. They lived in Phoenix, Arizona, for two years before moving to Santa Barbara, California. Yelas still enjoyed fishing and began to pursue the sport competitively during this time. "I transformed overnight from a happy-go-lucky kid out for a good time with Dad to a fierce competitor," he noted. "I began to live to out-fish everyone on the lake."

At first Yelas poured his energy into trout fishing. It was not until his junior year of high school that he discovered bass fishing. Yelas was trout fishing with a buddy at Lake Cachuma in California when "suddenly the hum of an outboard motor shattered our peaceful morning as a shiny, sleek bass boat slid into our sleepy little cove," he remembered. "Our new guests had my full attention. I watched in awe as the two anglers in their flashy bass rig jumped up, ran to the bow, and threw their trolling motor in the water. Without a sound, they picked up their crankbaits and stood side by side, as they quietly eased down the bank, casting and retrieving, casting and re-trieving." After watching the bass fishermen pull out a couple of nice-sized bass, the two teens decided that bass fishing looked like fun. When they tried it the following weekend, Yelas caught his second bass and became hooked on the sport. "It was on a crawdad Hellbender crankbait at Lake Cachuma," he remembered. "It was at this time, at 16 years of age, that I really got into bass fishing."

From this time on, Yelas went bass fishing every chance he got. He entered his first team bass fishing tournament in 1983, during his senior year in high school. Even though he snapped his rod during the competition, he decided to become a professional bass fisherman. "I remember the day I told my dad I was going to be a pro fish-erman," Yelas laughed. "His exact words were, 'Oh no you're not.' [But] he is my biggest fan these days."

"I remember the day I told my dad I was going to be a pro fisherman," Yelas laughed. "His exact words were, 'Oh no you're not.' [But] he is my biggest fan these days."

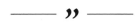

EARLY INFLUENCES

Yelas met Bill Sedar — a 68-year-old local bass-fishing expert — around the time that he decided to try to make a career for himself in fishing. Sedar became a close friend and mentor to the young man. "He was a barrel full of fishing knowledge, and I was quite the sponge," Yelas recalled. "He taught me more about bass fishing than anyone, and I credit him with laying the solid foundation for my career as a pro bass fisherman." Yelas continues to make a special trip to Lake Cachuma each year to fish with Sedar.

EDUCATION

Yelas attended Iolani, the private school where his parents taught in Honolulu, through the seventh grade. When the family moved to Phoenix, he completed eighth grade at All Saints Episcopal Day School, then trans-ferred to Sunnyslope High School in ninth grade. His family moved to California when he was in tenth grade, and he graduated from San Marcos High School in Santa Barbara in 1983. "I know moving to new schools and starting over is difficult for many kids," he noted, "but I learned to roll with the punches, making new friends and scouting out what new sports teams these schools had to offer."

Yelas caught his first seven pound bass on December 24, 1982, in California.

Yelas went on to attend Oregon State University, where he studied fisheries management. In order to prevent him from being distracted from his studies, his father made him sell his fishing boat before he started college. But Yelas buckled down and got such good grades during his freshman year that his father let him buy another boat. "Jay arranged his classes at Oregon State so he could fish Friday through Monday," his father noted.

Yelas started competing in team fishing tournaments during his sophomore year of college. Working with two different partners, he fished in every contest in Oregon over the next three years. In 1986 he and one of his partners, Jerry Harris, won the U.S. Bass Team Championship for the state of Oregon. In the meantime, Yelas stuck with his studies. He earned a bachelor's degree in Resource Recreation Management from Oregon State in 1987.

CAREER HIGHLIGHTS

Working His Way Up through the Pro Ranks

Once Yelas graduated from college, he was ready to begin his career as a full-time professional bass fisherman. His parents loaned him $30,000 to buy a new, 18-foot bass boat and to pay for fishing equipment and tournament entry fees. "Our deal was that if he got his degree, we'd support a try as a pro," his father explained. Yelas decided to focus his attention on several pro bass-fishing circuits in the West that were sponsored by various organizations. He moved to Phoenix, Arizona, in order to be at the center of these circuits.

Yelas started off his career with a bang by finishing sixth in the first professional bass-fishing tournament he entered—the 1987 U.S. Open at Lake Mead in Arizona—and collecting $8,000 in prize money. Thanks to his hard work and success, he was able to pay back his parents within a short time. Yelas spent the next three years fishing in every Western tournament he could find. He competed up to 40 weekends per year, and he spent the time between tournaments traveling and living out of his van. "I always looked at that period of time as being similar to a minor-league experience in baseball," Yelas explained. "I played every day, got lots of experience, had plenty of success, and after three years felt like I was ready for the big leagues. In bass fishing, that means the Bassmaster Tournament Trail."

When he was just getting started, Yelas competed up to 40 weekends per year and spent the time between tournaments traveling and living out of his van. "I always looked at that period of time as being similar to a minor-league experience in baseball. I played every day, got lots of experience, had plenty of success, and after three years felt like I was ready for the big leagues. In bass fishing, that means the Bassmaster Tournament Trail."

Bassmasters tournaments are sponsored by the Bass Angler Sportsman Society (BASS), an international fishing organization with 600,000 members. The Bassmasters Tournament Trail is a series of 10 high-profile tournaments that culminate in the season-ending Citgo Bassmasters Classic World Championship. Most bass-fishing tournaments take place over several days. The competitors have a limit, or maximum number, of fish that they can count toward their catch each day. At the end of the tournament, the angler whose total catch has the highest weight is declared the winner. Yelas entered his first Bassmasters tournament in April 1989 on Lake Mead. He placed 12th and caught the biggest fish of the entire event, a five pound, 12 ounce bass (5-12 in fishing shorthand). The following year he moved to Jasper in East Texas, near the Sam Rayburn Reservoir, to be closer to Bassmasters tournaments in the South and East.

> "
>
> *"I became a Christian on February 28, 1993, and I still thank God every day for revealing Himself to me. He filled a spiritual void in my life, making my life complete. I was amazed at how God changed my heart once I humbly prayed to receive Christ as my Savior. He doesn't demand that we conform to some list of good and bad things we must or must not do, but rather changes our hearts. He makes us want to do the right thing. He changes us from the inside out. This inner transformation is what many Christians refer to as being 'born again.'"*
>
> "

Becoming a Born-Again Christian

Throughout the early years of his pro career, Yelas's entire life centered around bass fishing. "I had turned into a selfish individual who traveled around the country doing something I loved without giving a rip about anyone or anything else," he admitted. "My world revolved around two things: me, and how many bass I caught." In his drive to be the best in his sport, Yelas was willing to try anything to get an edge over his fellow anglers. In the late 1980s, he began searching for a spiritual foundation that would help him reach his potential as a fisherman. He read many books about philosophy and religion during this time. He eventually became involved with the New Age movement, which encourages individuals to tap into the unlimited power within themselves. But Yelas continued to feel empty spiritually, and both his

The final day of the Bassmaster Classic Tournament, 2002.

fishing career and his family life suffered as a result. "When I look back now, I can see what a dangerous time this was for me," he recalled. "I set off on a spiritual journey without the Bible, the Truth, as my guide. It was like trying to boat across the ocean with the wrong map. I got lost."

Yelas had attended an Episcopal church regularly as a child, and he had learned many Bible stories and basic facts about the Christian faith. But it was not until 1993 that Christianity made a real difference in his life. While he was driving home from a fishing tournament in which he had performed particularly poorly, he prayed to God for guidance. It was at this time that he became a born-again Christian. "I became a Christian on February 28, 1993, and I still thank God every day for revealing Himself to me. He filled a spiritual void in my life, making my life complete," Yelas stated. "I was amazed at how God changed my heart once I humbly prayed to receive Christ as my Savior. He doesn't demand that we conform to some list of good and bad things we must or must not do, but rather changes our hearts. He makes us want to do the right thing. He changes us from the inside out. This inner transformation is what many Christians refer to as being 'born again.'"

A short time after he became a born-again Christian, Yelas experienced a string of successes in Bassmasters tournaments. In fact, he finished in the top 10 in half of his tournaments over the next two years. Yelas believes that God transformed his fishing career from this time on, helping him to become successful so that he would gain a platform to share God's message with others. "My conclusion is that it was a period of time in which God said, 'OK, now that you have given your life to Me, I am going to firmly establish you as a top pro so that I can use you in the future to share My gospel and tell other fishermen of My love for them,'" he noted.

During the three-day tournament, Yelas ended up catching 14 fish totaling 45 pounds, 13 ounces to become the 2002 Bassmasters Classic World Champion. "This is just the thrill of a lifetime for me. Winning the Classic makes your career as a professional fisherman," he said afterward. "What an unbelievably humbling experience it was.... The hand of God was on my fishing in a way that I have never experienced before in my entire career."

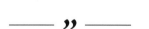

Establishing Himself on the Bassmasters Tour

Yelas won his first tournament on the Bassmasters tour—the Maryland Top 100 on the Potomac River—during the summer of 1993. He caught a total of 20 bass that weighed 54 pounds, 11 ounces and earned $46,000 in prize money, which he used to buy a house. In 1995 he won the second-biggest event of the year, the Bassmasters Superstars tournament on the Illinois River near Peoria. He claimed $50,000 in prize money and attracted the attention of several sponsors.

All the top professional fishermen are sponsored by companies that make fishing-related products. The sponsors pay the fishermen a salary in exchange for using their products, displaying their logos on boats and clothing, and making promotional appearances. Sponsorship money helps the top fishermen bridge the gaps in their earnings between tournament victories.

Yelas claimed the third Bassmasters tournament victory of his career in 1997 at the Missouri Invitational at Lake of the Ozarks. The following year he moved to Tyler, Texas. Over the next few years he posted a string of solid performances but failed to win any tournaments. He broke a four-year winless streak to capture his fourth career victory in 2001 at the Missouri Invitational on Table Rock.

By this time, Yelas had firmly established his reputation as a talented and consistent angler. He had qualified for the annual Bassmasters Classic—known as the Super Bowl of bass fishing—in 11 consecutive seasons by earning points for strong finishes in different BASS tournaments. Yet he had never done particularly well in the Classic. His best finish was third place in 1993, but he was never a threat to win that tournament. In fact, his total catch weighed eight pounds less than the winner's.

Winning the 2002 Bassmasters Classic Championship

Yelas struggled through the 2002 BASS events he entered. He won only $15,000 in prize money over the course of the season and barely earned enough points to qualify for the Bassmasters Classic. But he took great care with his preparations and pre-fishing practice sessions and entered the tournament with high hopes.

The 2002 Classic was held on Lake Lay near Birmingham, Alabama. Each of the 40 anglers that qualified for the tournament were issued two standard tackle boxes. They were allowed to fill these boxes, but they could not bring along any other fishing gear. Yelas spent 15 hours packing his boxes. His equipment included 60 crankbaits (diving lures with three hooks), 100 Berkley Power Worms, 100 6-inch Berkley Power Lizards, 40 Berkley Power Craws (plastic crayfish), 40 Berkley Power Grubs, 25 spinnerbaits in various weights, a variety of surface lures, 150 hooks, 60 sinkers, fishing line, scissors, a scale and measuring board, glue, a flashlight, sunglasses, and sunscreen. In a separate bundle he brought seven rods and seven reels.

Once the tournament began, Yelas concentrated his efforts on a spot he had discovered during pre-fishing practice. It was located at the north end of Lake Lay, about a quarter-mile from Logan Martin Dam. He noticed that when water was released from the dam, it flooded some shallow areas and created prime habitat for big bass. He fished this area using a prototype Berkley Jay Yelas Power Jig tipped with a Berkley Power Frog. Yelas's strategy worked so well that he led from the opening day of the tournament. In fact, he was ahead by nearly 10 pounds going into the final day. "It's been a dream week for me," he acknowledged. "Everything is going so much better than I anticipated. I predicted that 35 pounds would win the tournament, and I've got 35 pounds after just two days."

During the three-day tournament, Yelas ended up catching 14 fish totaling 45 pounds, 13 ounces to become the 2002 Bassmasters Classic World

Yelas landed the biggest bass at the 2002 Bassmaster Classic.

Champion. "This is just the thrill of a lifetime for me. Winning the Classic makes your career as a professional fisherman," he said afterward. "What an unbelievably humbling experience it was. . . . The hand of God was on my fishing in a way that I have never experienced before in my entire career." Yelas's catch for the tournament included the largest bass caught by any competitor each day, making him the first angler ever to sweep the daily "big fish" awards at a Bassmasters Classic. "I could do no wrong all week at the Classic," he acknowledged. "I caught the big bass every day of the tournament, an unprecedented feat in Bassmaster history."

Yelas's victory—the fifth of his career—was worth over $200,000 in prize money. But he maintained that the sweetest part was the support he received afterward. "The best part of winning the Classic for me has been all of the very sincere congratulations I have received from everyone," he noted. "Friends, acquaintances, fans, and peers alike have all been so very gracious in their congratulations. Everyone seems genuinely happy for me. Thank you. You don't know how good that makes me feel. It is the best part of winning."

Claiming the 2002 FLW Angler of the Year Title

Yelas capped off his 2002 season and cemented his place among elite sport fishermen by capturing the FLW Angler of the Year title. The FLW tour (short for Forrest L. Woods, the tour's founder) sponsors six major professional bass-fishing tournaments each year. It is the main national rival to the Bassmasters tour, though many top fishermen compete in both. Yelas had not participated in the FLW tour since 1997, when it made a rule requiring competitors to display only the logos of tour sponsors, rather than the logos of their individual sponsors. Out of respect for his personal sponsors, Yelas chose to fish only in tournaments that allowed freedom in endorsements. But in 2002 Yamaha outboard motors—one of Yelas's major sponsors—signed on as a sponsor of the FLW tour. Yamaha asked Yelas to participate in the tour, and he agreed.

On the FLW tour, fishermen earn points based on their finishing position over the six events. The winning angler in a tournament gets 200 points, second place earns 199 points, and on down the line. The competitor who accumulates the most points during the season wins the prestigious title of FLW Angler of the Year. Although Yelas performed consistently on the FLW tour in 2002, defending champion Kevin Van Dam performed better. In fact, Van Dam held a seemingly insurmountable lead of 28 points

"The best part of winning the Classic for me has been all of the very sincere congratulations I have received from everyone. Friends, acquaintances, fans, and peers alike have all been so very gracious in their congratulations. Everyone seems genuinely happy for me. Thank you. You don't know how good that makes me feel. It is the best part of winning."

entering the final tournament on Lake Champlain in New York. This meant that Yelas would have to finish more than 28 spots ahead of Van Dam in the standings in order to claim the Angler of the Year title.

Yelas recognized that he was not in a favorable position. "Kevin had such a big lead that I had virtually thrown in the towel and dismissed my chances of winning as nonexistent," he admitted. "Up until this tournament, Kevin had a perfect record as a closer. Every time in his career that he had led a tournament or an Angler of the Year race going into the last day or last tournament, he had always won."

But 2002 was a different story. Feeling very little pressure to perform, Yelas relaxed and finished ninth in the final tournament. In the meantime, Van Dam fell apart and finished 44th, handing Yelas the Angler of the Year title by seven points. "That's not much," Yelas noted. "That's just one fish in a season." The victory brought Yelas $25,000 and a new boat, as well as the opportunity to have his picture on collectors' boxes of Kellogg's Corn Flakes. It also demonstrated his consistency, just as his Bassmasters Classic victory had shown his ability to perform under pressure. "They're two entirely different titles," he explained. "The Bassmasters Classic says the most about somebody who can withstand the pressure and the spotlight. Angler of the Year shows consistency from tournament to tournament."

> "They're two entirely different titles," Yelas explained about winning the Angler of the Year title and the Bassmasters Classic tournament. "The Bassmasters Classic says the most about somebody who can withstand the pressure and the spotlight. Angler of the Year shows consistency from tournament to tournament."

Thanks to his dual titles, Yelas found himself in great demand over the next several months. He received hundreds of phone calls and e-mails from fans, the media, and sponsors. He did numerous interviews and made promotional appearances across the country on behalf of his sponsors. He also wrote a book. Titled *Jay Yelas: A Champion's Journey of Faith, Family, and Fishing: An Autobiography*, it was published in 2003. "It's not a how-to book about how to catch fish. It's just an autobiography about a fisherman," he stated. "My main motivation to write the book is to share the wisdom I learned over the years. If someone can take that book and read it and take something in it and apply it and give them a better quality of life, then my Classic victory wouldn't just benefit me, but help others, too."

Sharing His Love of Bass Fishing

Yelas has joined the ranks of the world's most successful professional bass fishermen. His victory in the 2002 Bassmasters Classic raised his career earnings to over $1 million, placing him sixth on the BASS all-time money list. He has posted five career victories on the Bassmasters tour, in addition to 15 finishes in the top three, and 47 finishes in the top 10. He has col-

*Yelas with the Bassmaster World Champion trophy, in the middle
of a fireworks display, 2002.*

lected paychecks in 66 percent of the events he has entered on the pro tour, and he has qualified for 12 consecutive Bassmasters Classics.

Despite his success, Yelas claims that making a career as a professional bass fisherman is not as easy as it might seem. "A professional fisherman today has to be part businessman, part public speaker and educator, and part salesman for his sponsors. You have to work at all facets of those things to be successful today," he explained. "A lot of people think, 'What an easy job that must be, fishing.' But it's fishing against the best fishermen in the world. It's not that easy."

Yelas's favorite lures are spinnerbaits, jigs, and crankbaits. "I consider the spinnerbait to be one of the most highly versatile lures known to man. And it is an excellent year-round bass bait."

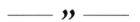

Yelas also dislikes some of the politics of his sport. For example, prior to the beginning of the 2003 season Anheuser Busch—the makers of Busch and Budweiser beers—signed on to sponsor the BASS Angler of the Year program. In order to participate in the program, competitors are required to put the Busch logo on their boats and clothing. Due in part to his religious beliefs, Yelas refuses to promote alcohol. He is angry that BASS entered into a sponsorship arrangement that would force anglers to promote a specific product against their will. Yelas ultimately agreed to participate in the Angler of the Year program, but he planned to refuse to accept any prize money from the program as a form of protest against the Busch sponsorship. "This will give me a great platform to share my faith with those who will listen," he explained. "A man who turns down $100,000 cash based on the principles of his faith will really have an audience. People will be curious. It will be an opportunity for me to glorify Jesus Christ, my priceless Lord and Savior!"

Although some aspects of his career can by difficult, Yelas still loves fishing. His favorite place to fish is Lake Powell in Arizona. "It's the most beautiful lake in the country with its deep, clear water and high red rock walls," he noted. "It's like fishing in the Grand Canyon. I can fish all day and never see another boat. Fishing is fair, but the lake surroundings with its history and natural beauty more than make up for it."

Yelas's favorite lures are spinnerbaits, jigs, and crankbaits. "I consider the spinnerbait to be one of the most highly versatile lures known to man," he

Yelas fishing with baby Hannah.

stated. "And it is an excellent year-round bass bait." The biggest bass Yelas ever caught was an 11 pound, 11 ounce monster from Lake Toho in Florida in 2001. His biggest one-day total catch in a tournament was five bass weighing 36 pounds, nine ounces, also from Lake Toho in 2001. It was the third-biggest stringer (total catch) in BASS tournament history.

Yelas enjoys sharing his love of bass fishing with others. "I've always loved to bass fish, and it's just a God-given talent," he said. "I still love it, and plan on doing it as long as the Good Lord lets me." Yelas feels that his sport has a lot to offer in terms of role models for young people and families. "I think people are disgusted with sports scandals and spoiled athletes and they're looking for positive things they can do with their kids," he stated. "One of the advantages pro fishing has over other sports is that fishermen are a good bunch of guys."

MARRIAGE AND FAMILY

Yelas met his wife, Jillian, in 1989 while he was living in Phoenix. Jill knew very little about bass fishing at that time. "When we met and Jay told me he was a professional bass fisherman, all I could think about was those Sunday shows on TV," she remembered. "I couldn't fathom it."

Yelas and his wife Jillian.

Yelas took the unsuspecting young woman on a fishing trip for their second date. "She never lets me forget that trip to the lake,"he said. "I put her in my boat, and proceeded to launch it by just backing down the ramp and stomping on the brakes. By the time I parked and made it back to the ramp, the wind had blown her 50 yards out into the middle of the lake. I yelled, 'Come and get me.' She yelled, 'How?' I said, 'Just put the trolling motor down.' She said, 'What's a trolling motor?' It turned into quite an event."

Yelas and his wife have two daughters, Hannah and Bethany. Both girls enjoy fishing and travel with their father to tournaments when their school schedules permit. "I'm on the road 240 days a year, and time away from family's the hardest thing,"Yelas noted. The family lives in Tyler, Texas, which Yelas describes as "a fantastic little city that has just about everything you would find in a big city."

HOBBIES AND OTHER INTERESTS

In his spare time, Yelas enjoys playing golf and gardening. He is an active leader in the Fellowship of Christian Anglers Society (FOCAS). He also makes promotional appearances for his sponsors, which include Skeeter boats, Yamaha outboard motors, Berkley power bait, Daiwa rods and reels, Motorguide trolling motors, Lowrance electronics, and Sadler Smokehouse.

WRITINGS

Jay Yelas: A Champion's Journey of Faith, Family, and Fishing: An Autobiography, 2003

HONORS AND AWARDS

Bassmasters Maryland Top 100, Potomac River: 1993
Bassmasters Superstars, New Orleans: 1995
Bassmasters Missouri Invitational, Lake of the Ozarks: 1997
Bassmasters Missouri Invitational, Table Rock: 2001

Citgo Bassmasters Classic World Champion: 2002
FLW Angler of the Year: 2002

FURTHER READING

Books

Yelas, Jay. *Jay Yelas: A Champion's Journey of Faith, Family, and Fishing: An Autobiography,* 2003

Periodicals

Arkansas Democrat-Gazette, June 11, 1995, p.C1
Baltimore Sun, July 27, 2002, p.C1; Dec. 22, 2002, p.D17
Boating World, Nov. 2002, insert sec., p.6
Dallas Morning News, Aug. 1, 2002, p.B13
South Florida Sun-Sentinel, July 27, 2002, p.C11; July 28, 2002, p.C14
Kansas City (Mo.) Star, Apr. 22, 2001, p.C13
New York Times, Aug. 18, 2002, sec. 8, p.12
San Diego Union-Tribune, Jan. 18, 2003, p.D2
USA Today, July 28, 1994, p.C1; Sep. 11, 2002, p.C7

ADDRESS

Jay Yelas
Alday Communications
144 S.E. Park
Suite 250
Franklin, TN 37064

WORLD WIDE WEB SITES

http://www.jayyelas.com
http://www.bassmaster.com
http://www.fishingworld.com/Pro-JayYelas/

Photo and Illustration Credits

Tori Allen/Photos: PatitucciPhoto.com; AP/Wide World Photos (pages 12 and 18).

Layne Beachley/Photos: Getty Images; AP/Wide World Photos; Pierre Tostee/Getty Images; Getty Images; Pierre Tostee/Getty Images

Sue Bird/Photos: AP/Wide World Photos.

Fabiola da Silva/Photos: copyright © Duomo/CORBIS; AP/Wide World Photos; Mike Simons/Getty Images.

Randy Johnson/Photos: Todd Warshaw/Getty Images; courtesy Arizona Diamondbacks; AP/World Photos; Ezra Shaw/Getty Images; J.T. Lovette/ Reuters; Mike Segar/Reuters.

Jason Kidd/Photos: AP/Wide World Photos; Otto Gruele/Getty Images; AP/Wide World Photos. Cover: AP/Wide World Photos.

Tony Stewart/Photos: Newscom.com; David Taylor/Getty Images; Jon Ferrey/Getty Images; Chris Stanford/Getty Images; Donald Miralle/Getty Images; AP/Wide World Photos

Michael Vick/Photos: Erik S. Lesser/Getty Images; Dave Knache/Virginia Tech; Erik S. Lesser/Getty Images; Elsa/Getty Images. Eliot Schechter/ Getty Images. Cover: Andy Lyons/Getty Images.

Ted Williams/Photos: AP/Wide World Photos.

Jay Yelas/Photos: BASS; courtesy Jay Yelas (page 164); BASS; courtesy Jay Yelas (pages 175 and 176).

How to Use the Cumulative Index

Our indexes have a new look. In an effort to make our indexes easier to use, we've combined the Name and General Index into a new, Cumulative Index. This single ready-reference resource covers all the volumes in *Biography Today,* both the general series and the special subject series. The new Cumulative Index contains complete listings of all individuals who have appeared in *Biography Today* since the series began. Their names appear in bold-faced type, followed by the issue in which they appear. The Cumulative Index also includes references for the occupations, nationalities, and ethnic and minority origins of individuals profiled in *Biography Today*.

We have also made some changes to our specialty indexes, the Places of Birth Index and the Birthday Index. To consolidate and to save space, the Places of Birth Index and the Birthday Index will no longer appear in the January and April issues of the softbound subscription series. But these indexes can still be found in the September issue of the softbound subscription series, in the hardbound Annual Cumulation at the end of each year, and in each volume of the special subject series.

General Series

The General Series of *Biography Today* is denoted in the index with the month and year of the issue in which the individual appeared. Each individual also appears in the Annual Cumulation for that year.

bin Laden, Osama . . . . Apr 02
Bush, George W. . . . . Sep 00; Update 00;
   Update 01; Update 02
Clarkson, Kelly . . . . Jan 03
Eminem . . . . Apr 03
Fuller, Millard . . . . Apr 03
Giuliani, Rudolph . . . . Sep 02
Holdsclaw, Chamique . . . . Sep 00
Lewis, John . . . . Jan 03
Roberts, Julia . . . . Sep 01
Rowling, J.K. . . . . Sep 99; Update 00;
   Update 01; Update 02
Spears, Britney . . . . Jan 01
Tucker, Chris . . . . Jan 01
Wood, Elijah . . . . Apr 02

Special Subject Series

The Special Subject Series of *Biography Today* are each denoted in the index with an abbreviated form of the series name, plus the number of the volume in which the individual appears. They are listed as follows.

Adams, Ansel .... Artist V.1	(Artists)
Clements, Andrew .... Author V.13	(Authors)
Chan, Jackie.................. PerfArt V.1	(Performing Artists)
Fauci, Anthony............... Science V.7	(Scientists & Inventors)
Kidd, Jason .... Sport V.9	(Sports)
Peterson, Roger Tory .... WorLdr V.1	(World Leaders: Environmental Leaders)
Sadat, Anwar .... WorLdr V.2	(World Leaders: Modern African Leaders)
Wolf, Hazel.................. WorLdr V.3	(World Leaders: Environmental Leaders 2)

Updates

Updated information on selected individuals appears in the Appendix at the end of the *Biography Today* Annual Cumulation. In the index, the original entry is listed first, followed by any updates.

Arafat, Yasir .... Sep 94; Update 94;
Update 95; Update 96; Update 97; Update 98;
Update 00; Update 01; Update 02
Gates, Bill .... Apr 93; Update 98;
Update 00; Science V.5; Update 01
Griffith Joyner, Florence......... Sport V.1;
Update 98
Sanders, Barry .... Sep 95; Update 99
Spock, Dr. Benjamin .... Sep 95; Update 98
Yeltsin, Boris .... Apr 92; Update 93;
Update 95; Update 96; Update 98; Update 00

Cumulative Index

This cumulative index includes names, occupations, nationalities, and ethnic and minority origins that pertain to all individuals profiled in *Biography Today* since the debut of the series in 1992.

Aaliyah . . . . Jan 02
Aaron, Hank . . . . Sport V.1
Abbey, Edward . . . . WorLdr V.1
Abdul, Paula . . . . Jan 92; Update 02
Abdul-Jabbar, Kareem . . . . Sport V.1
Aboriginal
  Freeman, Cathy . . . . Jan 01
Abzug, Bella . . . . Sep 98
activists
  Abzug, Bella . . . . Sep 98
  Arafat, Yasir . . . . Sep 94; Update 94;
    Update 95; Update 96; Update 97; Update
    98; Update 00; Update 01; Update 02
  Ashe, Arthur . . . . Sep 93
  Askins, Renee . . . . WorLdr V.1
  Aung San Suu Kyi . . . . . Apr 96; Update 98;
    Update 01; Update 02
  Banda, Hastings Kamuzu . . . . WorLdr V.2
  Bates, Daisy . . . . Apr 00
  Brower, David . . . . . WorLdr V.1; Update 01
  Burnside, Aubyn . . . . Sep 02
  Calderone, Mary S. . . . . Science V.3
  Chavez, Cesar . . . . Sep 93
  Chavis, Benjamin . . . . Jan 94; Update 94
  Cronin, John . . . . WorLdr V.3
  Dai Qing . . . . WorLdr V.3
  Dalai Lama . . . . Sep 98
  Douglas, Marjory Stoneman . . WorLdr V.1;
    Update 98
  Edelman, Marian Wright . . . . Apr 93
  Foreman, Dave . . . . WorLdr V.1
  Fuller, Millard . . . . Apr 03
  Gibbs, Lois . . . . WorLdr V.1
  Haddock, Doris (Granny D) . . . . Sep 00
  Jackson, Jesse . . . . Sep 95; Update 01
  Ka Hsaw Wa . . . . WorLdr V.3
  Kaunda, Kenneth . . . . WorLdr V.2
  Kenyatta, Jomo . . . . WorLdr V.2
  Kielburger, Craig . . . . Jan 00
  Kim Dae-jung . . . . Sep 01

LaDuke, Winona . . WorLdr V.3; Update 00
Lewis, John . . . . Jan 03
Love, Susan . . . . Science V.3
Maathai, Wangari . . . . WorLdr V.1
Mandela, Nelson . . . . Jan 92; Update 94;
  Update 01
Mandela, Winnie . . . . WorLdr V.2
Mankiller, Wilma . . . . Apr 94
Martin, Bernard . . . . WorLdr V.3
Masih, Iqbal . . . . Jan 96
Menchu, Rigoberta . . . . Jan 93
Mendes, Chico . . . . WorLdr V.1
Mugabe, Robert . . . . WorLdr V.2
Marshall, Thurgood . . . . . Jan 92; Update 93
Nakamura, Leanne . . . . Apr 02
Nkrumah, Kwame . . . . WorLdr V.2
Nyerere, Julius Kambarage . . . WorLdr V.2;
  Update 99
Oliver, Patsy Ruth . . . . WorLdr V.1
Parks, Rosa . . . . Apr 92; Update 94
Pauling, Linus . . . . Jan 95
Saro-Wiwa, Ken . . . . WorLdr V.1
Savimbi, Jonas . . . . WorLdr V.2
Spock, Benjamin . . . . Sep 95; Update 98
Steinem, Gloria . . . . Oct 92
Teresa, Mother . . . . Apr 98
Watson, Paul . . . . WorLdr V.1
Werbach, Adam . . . . WorLdr V.1
Wolf, Hazel . . . . WorLdr V.3
Zamora, Pedro . . . . Apr 95
actors/actresses
  Aaliyah . . . . Jan 02
  Affleck, Ben . . . . Sep 99
  Alba, Jessica . . . . Sep 01
  Allen, Tim . . . . Apr 94; Update 99
  Alley, Kirstie . . . . Jul 92
  Anderson, Gillian . . . . Jan 97
  Aniston, Jennifer . . . . Apr 99
  Arnold, Roseanne . . . . Oct 92
  Barrymore, Drew . . . . Jan 01
  Bergen, Candice . . . . Sep 93

Berry, Halle . . . . Jan 95; Update 02
Bialik, Mayim . . . . Jan 94
Blanchard, Rachel . . . . Apr 97
Bledel, Alexis . . . . Jan 03
Brandis, Jonathan . . . . Sep 95
Brandy . . . . Apr 96
Bryan, Zachery Ty . . . . Jan 97
Burke, Chris . . . . Sep 93
Cameron, Candace . . . . Apr 95
Campbell, Neve . . . . Apr 98
Candy, John . . . . Sep 94
Carrey, Jim . . . . Apr 96
Carvey, Dana . . . . Jan 93
Chan, Jackie . . . . PerfArt V.1
Culkin, Macaulay . . . . Sep 93
Danes, Claire . . . . Sep 97
DiCaprio, Leonardo . . . . Apr 98
Diesel, Vin . . . . Jan 03
Doherty, Shannen . . . . . Apr 92; Update 94
Duchovny, David . . . . Apr 96
Duff, Hilary . . . . Sep 02
Dunst, Kirsten . . . . PerfArt V.1
Eminem . . . . Apr 03
Ford, Harrison . . . . Sep 97
Garth, Jennie . . . . Apr 96
Gellar, Sarah Michelle . . . . Jan 99
Gilbert, Sara . . . . Apr 93
Goldberg, Whoopi . . . . Apr 94
Goodman, John . . . . Sep 95
Hanks, Tom . . . . Jan 96
Hart, Melissa Joan . . . . Jan 94
Hewitt, Jennifer Love . . . . Sep 00
Holmes, Katie . . . . Jan 00
Jones, James Earl . . . . Jan 95
Lee, Spike . . . . Apr 92
Locklear, Heather . . . . Jan 95
Lopez, Jennifer . . . . Jan 02
Mac, Bernie . . . . PerfArt V.1
Muniz, Frankie . . . . Jan 01
O'Donnell, Rosie . . . . . . Apr 97; Update 02
Oleynik, Larisa . . . . Sep 96
Olsen, Ashley . . . . Sep 95
Olsen, Mary Kate . . . . Sep 95
Perry, Luke . . . . Jan 92
Phoenix, River . . . . Apr 94
Pitt, Brad . . . . Sep 98
Portman, Natalie . . . . Sep 99
Priestley, Jason . . . . Apr 92
Prinze, Freddie, Jr. . . . . Apr 00
Radcliffe, Daniel . . . . Jan 02
Reeve, Christopher . . . . . Jan 97; Update 02

Roberts, Julia . . . . Sep 01
Ryder, Winona . . . . Jan 93
Shatner, William . . . . Apr 95
Sinatra, Frank . . . . Jan 99
Smith, Will . . . . Sep 94
Stewart, Patrick . . . . Jan 94
Thiessen, Tiffani-Amber . . . . Jan 96
Thomas, Jonathan Taylor . . . . Apr 95
Tucker, Chris . . . . Jan 01
Usher . . . . PerfArt V.1
Vidal, Christina . . . . PerfArt V.1
Washington, Denzel . . . . Jan 93; Update 02
Watson, Barry . . . . Sep 02
Watson, Emma . . . . Apr 03
Wayans, Keenen Ivory . . . . Jan 93
White, Jaleel . . . . Jan 96
Williams, Robin . . . . Apr 92
Wilson, Mara . . . . Jan 97
Winfrey, Oprah . . . . Apr 92; Update 00
Winslet, Kate . . . . Sep 98
Witherspoon, Reese . . . . Apr 03
Wood, Elijah . . . . Apr 02
Adams, Ansel . . . . Artist V.1
Adams, Yolanda . . . . Apr 03
Affleck, Ben . . . . Sep 99
African-Americans
  see blacks
Agassi, Andre . . . . Jul 92
Aguilera, Christina . . . . Apr 00
Aidid, Mohammed Farah . . . . . WorLdr V.2
Aikman, Troy . . . . Apr 95; Update 01
Alba, Jessica . . . . Sep 01
Albanian
  Teresa, Mother . . . . Apr 98
Albright, Madeleine . . . . Apr 97
Alcindor, Lew
  see Abdul-Jabbar, Kareem . . . . Sport V.1
Alexander, Lloyd . . . . Author V.6
Algerian
  Boulmerka, Hassiba . . . . Sport V.1
Ali, Muhammad . . . . Sport V.2
Allen, Marcus . . . . Sep 97
Allen, Tim . . . . Apr 94; Update 99
Allen, Tori . . . . Sport V.9
Alley, Kirstie . . . . Jul 92
Almond, David . . . . Author V.10
Alvarez, Luis W. . . . . Science V.3
Amanpour, Christiane . . . . Jan 01
Amin, Idi . . . . WorLdr V.2
Amman, Simon . . . . Sport V.8

An Na . . . . Author V.12
Anders, C.J.
  see Bennett, Cherie. . . . . Author V.9
Anderson, Gillian. . . . . Jan 97
Anderson, Laurie Halse . . . . . . Author V.11
Anderson, Marian . . . . Jan 94
Anderson, Terry. . . . . Apr 92
Andretti, Mario . . . . Sep 94
Andrews, Ned. . . . . Sep 94
Angelou, Maya. . . . . Apr 93
Angolan
  Savimbi, Jonas . . . . WorLdr V.2
animators
  see also cartoonists
  Jones, Chuck . . . . Author V.12
  Lasseter, John.. . . . . Sep 00
  Tartakovsky, Genndy . . . . Author V.11
Aniston, Jennifer. . . . . Apr 99
Annan, Kofi . . . . Jan 98; Update 01
Applegate, K. A. . . . . Jan 00
Arab-American
  Nye, Naomi Shihab . . . . Author V.8
Arafat, Yasir. . . . . Sep 94; Update 94;
  Update 95; Update 96; Update 97; Update
  98; Update 00; Update 01; Update 02
Arantes do Nascimento, Edson
  see Pelé. . . . . Sport V.1
architects
  Lin, Maya . . . . Sep 97
  Pei, I.M. . . . . Artist V.1
  Wright, Frank Lloyd. . . . . Artist V.1
Aristide, Jean-Bertrand . . Jan 95; Update 01
Armstrong, Lance.. . . . . . . Sep 00; Update 00;
  Update 01; Update 02
Armstrong, Robb . . . . Author V.9
Armstrong, William H.. . . . . Author V.7
Arnold, Roseanne . . . . Oct 92
artists
  Adams, Ansel. . . . . Artist V.1
  Bearden, Romare . . . . Artist V.1
  Calder, Alexander . . . . Artist V.1
  Chagall, Marc . . . . Artist V.1
  Christo . . . . Sep 96
  Frankenthaler, Helen. . . . . Artist V.1
  Gorey, Edward. . . . . Author V.13
  Johns, Jasper . . . . Artist V.1
  Lawrence, Jacob . . . . . Artist V.1; Update 01
  Lin, Maya . . . . Sep 97
  Moore, Henry. . . . . Artist V.1
  Moses, Grandma . . . . Artist V.1
  Nechita, Alexandra . . . . Jan 98
  Nevelson, Louise . . . . Artist V.1

O'Keeffe, Georgia . . . . Artist V.1
Parks, Gordon . . . . Artist V.1
Pinkney, Jerry . . . . Author V.2
Ringgold, Faith . . . . Author V.2
Rivera, Diego . . . . Artist V.1
Rockwell, Norman. . . . . Artist V.1
Warhol, Andy . . . . Artist V.1
Ashe, Arthur. . . . . Sep 93
Ashley, Maurice . . . . Sep 99
Asians
  An Na. . . . . Author V.12
  Aung San Suu Kyi . . . . . Apr 96; Update 98;
    Update 01; Update 02
  Chan, Jackie . . . . PerfArt V.1
  Chung, Connie. . . . . Jan 94; Update 96
  Dai Qing . . . . WorLdr V.3
  Fu Mingxia . . . . Sport V.5
  Guey, Wendy . . . . Sep 96
  Ho, David . . . . Science V.6
  Ka Hsaw Wa. . . . . WorLdr V.3
  Kim Dae-jung . . . . Sep 01
  Kwan, Michelle. . . . . . Sport V.3; Update 02
  Lee, Jeanette . . . . Apr 03
  Lin, Maya. . . . . Sep 97
  Ma, Yo-Yo . . . . Jul 92
  Ohno, Apolo. . . . . Sport V.8
  Pak, Se Ri . . . . Sport V.4
  Park, Linda Sue . . . . Author V.12
  Pei, I.M. Artist V.1
  Tan, Amy. . . . . Author V.9
  Wang, An . . . . Science V.2
  Woods, Tiger. . . . . Sport V.1; Update 00
  Yamaguchi, Kristi . . . . Apr 92
  Yep, Laurence . . . . Author V.5
Asimov, Isaac . . . . Jul 92
Askins, Renee . . . . WorLdr V.1
astronauts
  Collins, Eileen . . . . Science V.4
  Glenn, John . . . . Jan 99
  Harris, Bernard . . . . Science V.3
  Jemison, Mae. . . . . Oct 92
  Lovell, Jim. Jan 96
  Lucid, Shannon . . . . Science V.2
  Ochoa, Ellen . . . . Apr 01; Update 02
  Ride, Sally. Jan 92
athletes
  see sports
Attenborough, David . . . . Science V.4
Atwater-Rhodes, Amelia . . . . . . Author V.8
Aung San Suu Kyi . . . . . Apr 96; Update 98;
    Update 01; Update 02

183

Australians

Beachley, Layne . . . . Sport V.9
Freeman, Cathy . . . . Jan 01
Irwin, Steve . . . . Science V.7
Norman, Greg . . . . Jan 94
Travers, P.L. . . . . Author V.2
Webb, Karrie . . . . Sport V.5; Update 01;
 Update 02

authors

Abbey, Edward. . . . . WorLdr V.1
Alexander, Lloyd. . . . . Author V.6
Almond, David . . . . Author V.10
An Na . . . . Author V.12
Anderson Laurie Halse. . . . . . . Author V.11
Angelou, Maya . . . . Apr 93
Applegate, K. A.. . . . . Jan 00
Armstrong, Robb . . . . Author V.9
Armstrong, William H.. . . . . Author V.7
Asimov, Isaac . . . . Jul 92
Attenborough, David. . . . . Science V.4
Atwater-Rhodes, Amelia . . . . . . Author V.8
Avi . . . . Jan 93
Baldwin, James . . . . Author V.2
Bauer, Joan. . . . . Author V.10
Bennett, Cherie. . . . . Author V.9
Benson, Mildred. . . . . Jan 03
Berenstain, Jan. . . . . Author V.2
Berenstain, Stan. . . . . Author V.2
Blume, Judy . . . . Jan 92
Boyd, Candy Dawson. . . . . Author V.3
Bradbury, Ray . . . . Author V.3
Brody, Jane . . . . Science V.2
Brooks, Gwendolyn . . . . Author V.3
Brower, David. . . . . WorLdr V.1; Update 01
Brown, Claude. . . . . Author V.12
Byars, Betsy . . . . Author V.4
Cabot, Meg . . . . Author V.12
Caplan, Arthur . . . . Science V.6
Carle, Eric. . . . . Author V.1
Carson, Rachel . . . . WorLdr V.1
Childress, Alice . . . . Author V.1
Cleary, Beverly . . . . Apr 94
Clements, Andrew . . . . Author V.13
Colfer, Eoin . . . . Author V.13
Collier, Bryan. . . . . Author V.11
Cooney, Barbara . . . . Author V.8
Cooney, Caroline B. . . . . Author V.4
Cormier, Robert. . . . Author V.1; Update 01
Cosby, Bill. Jan 92
Coville, Bruce . . . . Author V.9
Creech, Sharon . . . . Author V.5

Crichton, Michael . . . . Author V.5
Cronin, John. . . . . WorLdr V.3
Curtis, Christopher Paul . . . . . . Author V.4;
 Update 00
Cushman, Karen . . . . Author V.5
Dahl, Roald . . . . Author V.1
Dai Qing . . . . WorLdr V.3
Danziger, Paula. . . . . Author V.6
Delany, Bessie. . . . . Sep 99
Delany, Sadie . . . . Sep 99
dePaola, Tomie . . . . Author V.5
DiCamillo, Kate. . . . . Author V.10
Douglas, Marjory Stoneman . . WorLdr V.1;
 Update 98
Dove, Rita. Jan 94
Draper, Sharon . . . . Apr 99
Dunbar, Paul Lawrence . . . . Author V.8
Duncan, Lois. . . . . Sep 93
Ellison, Ralph. . . . . Author V.3
Farmer, Nancy. . . . . Author V.6
Filipovic, Zlata. . . . . Sep 94
Fitzhugh, Louise . . . . Author V.3
Flake, Sharon. . . . . Author V.13
Frank, Anne. . . . . Author V.4
Gantos, Jack. . . . . Author V.10
Gates, Henry Louis, Jr.. . . . . Apr 00
George, Jean Craighead . . . . Author V.3
Giff, Patricia Reilly. . . . . Author V.7
Gorey, Edward. . . . . Author V.13
Gould, Stephen Jay . . . . Science V.2;
 Update 02
Grandin, Temple . . . . Science V.3
Grisham, John . . . . Author V.1
Guy, Rosa . . . . Author V.9
Gwaltney, John Langston . . . . . Science V.3
Haddix, Margaret Peterson . . . Author V.11
Haley, Alex . . . . Apr 92
Hamilton, Virginia . . . . Author V.1;
 Author V.12
Handford, Martin . . . . Jan 92
Hansberry, Lorraine . . . . Author V.5
Heinlein, Robert . . . . Author V.4
Henry, Marguerite. . . . . Author V.4
Herriot, James . . . . Author V.1
Hesse, Karen . . . . . . Author V.5; Update 02
Hinton, S.E. . . . . Author V.1
Hughes, Langston. . . . . Author V.7
Hurston, Zora Neale. . . . . Author V.6
Jackson, Shirley. . . . . Author V.6
Jacques, Brian. . . . . Author V.5
Jiménez, Francisco. . . . . Author V.13

Johnson, Angela . . . . Author V.6
Kamler, Kenneth . . . . Science V.6
Kerr, M.E. . . . . Author V.1
King, Stephen. . . . . . Author V.1; Update 00
Konigsburg, E. L. . . . . Author V.3
Krakauer, Jon. . . . . Author V.6
LaDuke, Winona . . WorLdr V.3; Update 00
Lee, Harper. . . . . Author V.9
Lee, Stan. . . . . Author V.7; Update 02
Le Guin, Ursula K. . . . . Author V.8
L'Engle, Madeleine . . . . Jan 92; Apr 01
Leopold, Aldo. . . . . WorLdr V.3
Lester, Julius . . . . Author V.7
Lewis, C. S. . . . . Author V.3
Lindgren, Astrid . . . . Author V.13
Lionni, Leo. . . . . Author V.6
Lipsyte, Robert . . . . Author V.12
Love, Susan. . . . . Science V.3
Lowry, Lois . . . . Author V.4
Lynch, Chris. . . . . Author V.13
Macaulay, David . . . . Author V.2
MacLachlan, Patricia. . . . . Author V.2
Martin, Ann M. . . . . Jan 92
McCully, Emily Arnold. . . Jul 92; Update 93
McKissack, Fredrick L. . . . . Author V.3
McKissack, Patricia C. . . . . Author V.3
Mead, Margaret . . . . Science V.2
Meltzer, Milton . . . . Author V.11
Morrison, Lillian . . . . Author V.12
Morrison, Toni. . . . . Jan 94
Moss, Cynthia . . . . WorLdr V.3
Mowat, Farley . . . . Author V.8
Muir, John. . . . . WorLdr V.3
Murie, Margaret. . . . . WorLdr V.1
Murie, Olaus J. . . . . WorLdr V.1
Myers, Walter Dean. . . . . Jan 93; Update 94
Naylor, Phyllis Reynolds . . . . Apr 93
Nelson, Marilyn. . . . . Author V.13
Nielsen, Jerri . . . . Science V.7
Nixon, Joan Lowery . . . . Author V.1
Nye, Naomi Shihab . . . . Author V.8
O'Dell, Scott . . . . Author V.2
Opdyke, Irene Gut. . . . . Author V.9
Park, Linda Sue . . . . Author V.12
Pascal, Francine. . . . . Author V.6
Paterson, Katherine . . . . Author V.3
Paulsen, Gary. . . . . Author V.1
Peck, Richard. . . . . Author V.10
Peet, Bill . . . . Author V.4
Peterson, Roger Tory. . . . . WorLdr V.1
Pierce, Tamora. . . . . Author V.13

Pike, Christopher . . . . Sep 96
Pinkney, Andrea Davis. . . . . . . Author V.10
Pinkwater, Daniel . . . . Author V.8
Pinsky, Robert . . . . Author V.7
Potter, Beatrix . . . . Author V.8
Prelutsky, Jack . . . . Author V.2
Pullman, Philip. . . . . Author V.9
Reid Banks, Lynne . . . . Author V.2
Rennison, Louise. . . . . Author V.10
Rice, Anne . . . . Author V.3
Rinaldi, Ann. . . . . Author V.8
Ringgold, Faith . . . . Author V.2
Rowan, Carl. . . . . Sep 01
Rowling, J. K. . . . . Sep 99; Update 00;
  Update 01; Update 02
Ryan, Pam Muñoz . . . . Author V.12
Rylant, Cynthia . . . . Author V.1
Sachar, Louis . . . . Author V.6
Sacks, Oliver . . . . Science V.3
Salinger, J.D. . . . . Author V.2
Saro-Wiwa, Ken. . . . . WorLdr V.1
Scarry, Richard . . . . Sep 94
Scieszka, Jon. . . . . Author V.9
Sendak, Maurice . . . . Author V.2
Senghor, Léopold Sédar . . . . . WorLdr V.2
Seuss, Dr. . . . . Jan 92
Silverstein, Shel . . . . Author V.3; Update 99
Sleator, William. . . . . Author V.11
Small, David. . . . . Author V.10
Snicket, Lemony . . . . Author V.12
Sones, Sonya . . . . Author V.11
Soto, Gary . . . . Author V.5
Speare, Elizabeth George . . . . Sep 95
Spinelli, Jerry. . . . . Apr 93
Spock, Benjamin . . . . Sep 95; Update 98
Stepanek, Mattie. . . . . Apr 02
Stine, R.L. Apr 94
Strasser, Todd . . . . Author V.7
Tan, Amy. . . . . Author V.9
Tarbox, Katie . . . . Author V.10
Taylor, Mildred D. . . . Author V.1; Update 02
Thomas, Lewis . . . . Apr 94
Tolkien, J.R.R. . . . . Jan 02
Travers, P.L. . . . . Author V.2
Van Allsburg, Chris . . . . Apr 92
Van Draanen, Wendelin. . . . . . Author V.11
Voigt, Cynthia. . . . . Oct 92
Vonnegut, Kurt, Jr. . . . . Author V.1
White, E.B. . . . . Author V.1
White, Ruth . . . . Author V.11
Wilder, Laura Ingalls. . . . . Author V.3

Williams, Garth . . . . Author V.2
Williamson, Kevin . . . . Author V.6
Wilson, August . . . . Author V.4
Wolff, Virginia Euwer . . . . Author V.13
Woodson, Jacqueline . . . . Author V.7;
   Update 01
Wrede, Patricia C. . . . . Author V.7
Wright, Richard . . . . Author V.5
Yep, Laurence . . . . Author V.5
Yolen, Jane . . . . Author V.7
Zindel, Paul . . . . Author V.1; Update 02
autobiographies
Handford, Martin . . . . Jan 92
Iacocca, Lee . . . . Jan 92
L'Engle, Madeleine . . . . Jan 92
Parkinson, Jennifer . . . . Apr 95
Avi . . . . Jan 93
Babbitt, Bruce . . . . Jan 94
Backstreet Boys . . . . Jan 00
Bahrke, Shannon . . . . Sport V.8
Bailey, Donovan . . . . Sport V.2
Baiul, Oksana . . . . Apr 95
Baker, James . . . . Oct 92
Baldwin, James . . . . Author V.2
Ballard, Robert . . . . Science V.4
ballet
   see dance
Banda, Hastings Kamuzu . . . . WorLdr V.2
Bardeen, John . . . . Science V.1
Barkley, Charles . . . . Apr 92; Update 02
Barr, Roseanne
   see Arnold, Roseanne . . . . Oct 92
Barrymore, Drew . . . . Jan 01
Barton, Hazel . . . . Science V.6
baseball
Aaron, Hank . . . . Sport V.1
Bonds, Barry . . . . Jan 03
Fielder, Cecil . . . . Sep 93
Griffey, Ken, Jr. . . . . Sport V.1
Hernandez, Livan . . . . Apr 98
Jackson, Bo . . . . Jan 92; Update 93
Jeter, Derek . . . . Sport V.4
Johnson, Randy . . . . Sport V.9
Jordan, Michael . . . . Jan 92; Update 93;
   Update 94; Update 95; Update 99; Update
   01
Maddux, Greg. . . . . Sport V.3
Mantle, Mickey . . . . Jan 96
Martinez, Pedro . . . . Sport V.5
McGwire, Mark . . . . Jan 99; Update 99
Ripken, Cal, Jr. . . . . . . Sport V.1; Update 01

Robinson, Jackie . . . . Sport V.3
Rodriguez, Alex . . . . Sport V.6
Rose, Pete . . . . Jan 92
Ryan, Nolan . . . . Oct 92; Update 93
Sanders, Deion . . . . Sport V.1
Sosa, Sammy . . . . Jan 99; Update 99
Williams, Ted . . . . Sport V.9
Winfield, Dave . . . . Jan 93
basketball
Abdul-Jabbar, Kareem . . . . Sport V.1
Barkley, Charles . . . . Apr 92; Update 02
Bird, Larry . . . . Jan 92; Update 98
Bird, Sue . . . . Sport V.9
Bryant, Kobe . . . . Apr 99
Carter, Vince . . . . Sport V.5; Update 01
Chamberlain, Wilt . . . . Sport V.4
Dumars, Joe . . . . Sport V.3; Update 99
Ewing, Patrick . . . . Jan 95; Update 02
Garnett, Kevin . . . . Sport V.6
Hardaway, Anfernee "Penny" . . . Sport V.2
Hill, Grant . . . . Sport V.1
Holdsclaw, Chamique . . . . Sep 00
Iverson, Allen . . . . Sport V.7
Johnson, Magic . . . . Apr 92; Update 02
Jordan, Michael . . . . Jan 92; Update 93;
   Update 94; Update 95; Update 99; Update
   01
Kidd, Jason . . . . Sport V.9
Lobo, Rebecca . . . . Sport V.3
Olajuwon, Hakeem . . . . Sep 95
O'Neal, Shaquille . . . . Sep 93
Pippen, Scottie . . . . Oct 92
Robinson, David . . . . Sep 96
Rodman, Dennis . . . . Apr 96; Update 99
Stiles, Jackie . . . . Sport V.6
Stockton, John . . . . Sport V.3
Summitt, Pat . . . . Sport V.3
Swoopes, Sheryl . . . . Sport V.2
Ward, Charlie . . . . Apr 94
Bass, Lance
   see *N Sync . . . . Jan 01
Bates, Daisy . . . . Apr 00
Battle, Kathleen . . . . Jan 93
Bauer, Joan . . . . Author V.10
Beachley, Layne . . . . Sport V.9
Bearden, Romare . . . . Artist V.1
beauty pageants
Lopez, Charlotte . . . . Apr 94
Whitestone, Heather . . . Apr 95; Update 02
Bennett, Cherie . . . . Author V.9
Benson, Mildred . . . . Jan 03

Berenstain, Jan .... Author V.2
Berenstain, Stan .... Author V.2
Bergen, Candice.................. Sep 93
Berners-Lee, Tim .... Science V.7
Berry, Halle .... Jan 95; Update 02
Bethe, Hans A. .... Science V.3
Bezos, Jeff .... Apr 01
Bhutto, Benazir .... Apr 95; Update 99;
    Update 02
Bialik, Mayim .... Jan 94
bicycle riding
    Armstrong, Lance...... Sep 00; Update 00;
        Update 01; Update 02
    Dunlap, Alison .... Sport V.7
    LeMond, Greg .... Sport V.1
    Mirra, Dave .... Sep 02
billiards
    Lee, Jeanette .... Apr 03
bin Laden, Osama .... Apr 02
Bird, Larry .... Jan 92; Update 98
Bird, Sue .... Sport V.9
Blackmun, Harry .... Jan 00
blacks
    Aaliyah .... Jan 02
    Aaron, Hank.................. Sport V.1
    Abdul-Jabbar, Kareem......... Sport V.1
    Adams, Yolanda .... Apr 03
    Aidid, Mohammed Farah ..... WorLdr V.2
    Ali, Muhammad............... Sport V.2
    Allen, Marcus .... Sep 97
    Amin, Idi .... WorLdr V.2
    Anderson, Marian .... Jan 94
    Angelou, Maya .... Apr 93
    Annan, Kofi .... Jan 98; Update 01
    Aristide, Jean-Bertrand .. Jan 95; Update 01
    Armstrong, Robb .... Author V.9
    Ashe, Arthur .... Sep 93
    Ashley, Maurice .... Sep 99
    Bailey, Donovan............... Sport V.2
    Baldwin, James .... Author V.2
    Banda, Hastings Kamuzu ..... WorLdr V.2
    Bates, Daisy .... Apr 00
    Battle, Kathleen .... Jan 93
    Bearden, Romare .... Artist V.1
    Berry, Halle.................... Jan 95
    Blige, Mary J. .... Apr 02
    Bonds, Barry.................... Jan 03
    Boyd, Candy Dawson......... Author V.3
    Boyz II Men .... Jan 96
    Bradley, Ed. .... Apr 94
    Brandy .... Apr 96

Brooks, Gwendolyn .... Author V.3
Brown, Claude.............. Author V.12
Brown, Ron .... Sep 96
Bryant, Kobe .... Apr 99
Canady, Alexa............... Science V.6
Carson, Ben................. Science V.4
Carter, Vince........ Sport V.5; Update 01
Chamberlain, Wilt .... Sport V.4
Champagne, Larry III............. Apr 96
Chavis, Benjamin....... Jan 94; Update 94
Childress, Alice .... Author V.1
Collier, Bryan.............. Author V.11
Combs, Sean (Puff Daddy) .... Apr 98
Coolio.......................... Sep 96
Cosby, Bill...................... Jan 92
Curtis, Christopher Paul ...... Author V.4;
    Update 00
Dayne, Ron .... Apr 00
Delany, Bessie.................. Sep 99
Delany, Sadie .... Sep 99
Destiny's Child .... Apr 01
Devers, Gail .... Sport V.2
Dove, Rita...................... Jan 94
Draper, Sharon .... Apr 99
Dumars, Joe......... Sport V.3; Update 99
Dunbar, Paul Lawrence .... Author V.8
Edelman, Marian Wright.......... Apr 93
Ellison, Ralph................ Author V.3
Ewing, Patrick .... Jan 95; Update 02
Farrakhan, Louis .... Jan 97
Fielder, Cecil .... Sep 93
Fitzgerald, Ella .... Jan 97
Flake, Sharon............... Author V.13
Flowers, Vonetta.............. Sport V.8
Franklin, Aretha .... Apr 01
Freeman, Cathy .... Jan 01
Garnett, Kevin .... Sport V.6
Gates, Henry Louis, Jr. .... Apr 00
George, Eddie................. Sport V.6
Gillespie, Dizzy.................. Apr 93
Glover, Savion.................. Apr 99
Goldberg, Whoopi .... Apr 94
Griffey, Ken, Jr. .... Sport V.1
Gumbel, Bryant................. Apr 97
Guy, Jasmine.................... Sep 93
Guy, Rosa .... Author V.9
Gwaltney, John Langston ..... Science V.3
Haley, Alex .... Apr 92
Hamilton, Virginia .... Author V.1;
    Author V.12
Hammer .... Jan 92

Hansberry, Lorraine . . . . Author V.5
Hardaway, Anfernee "Penny" . . . Sport V.2
Harris, Bernard . . . . Science V.3
Hernandez, Livan . . . . Apr 98
Hill, Anita . . . . Jan 93
Hill, Grant . . . . Sport V.1
Hill, Lauryn . . . . Sep 99
Holdsclaw, Chamique . . . . Sep 00
Houston, Whitney . . . . Sep 94
Hughes, Langston . . . . Author V.7
Hunter-Gault, Charlayne . . . . Jan 00
Hurston, Zora Neale . . . . Author V.6
Ice-T . . . . Apr 93
Iverson, Allen . . . . Sport V.7
Jackson, Bo . . . . Jan 92; Update 93
Jackson, Jesse . . . . Sep 95; Update 01
Jackson, Shirley Ann . . . . Science V.2
Jamison, Judith . . . . Jan 96
Jemison, Mae . . . . Oct 92
Jeter, Derek . . . . Sport V.4
Johnson, Angela . . . . Author V.6
Johnson, John . . . . Jan 97
Johnson, Lonnie . . . . Science V.4
Johnson, Magic . . . . Apr 92; Update 02
Johnson, Michael . . . . . . Jan 97; Update 00
Jones, James Earl . . . . Jan 95
Jones, Marion . . . . Sport V.5
Jordan, Barbara . . . . Apr 96
Jordan, Michael . . . . Jan 92; Update 93;
    Update 94; Update 95; Update 99; Update
    01
Joyner-Kersee, Jackie . . . . Oct 92; Update
    96; Update 97; Update 98
Kaunda, Kenneth . . . . WorLdr V.2
Kenyatta, Jomo . . . . WorLdr V.2
Kidd, Jason . . . . Sport V.9
Lawrence, Jacob . . . . . Artist V.1; Update 01
Lee, Spike . . . . Apr 92
Lester, Julius . . . . Author V.7
Lewis, Carl . . . . Sep 96; Update 97
Lewis, John . . . . Jan 03
Maathai, Wangari . . . . WorLdr V.1
Mac, Bernie . . . . PerfArt V.1
Mandela, Nelson . . . . Jan 92; Update 94;
    Update 01
Mandela, Winnie . . . . WorLdr V.2
Marsalis, Wynton . . . . Apr 92
Marshall, Thurgood . . . . . Jan 92; Update 93
Martinez, Pedro . . . . Sport V.5
Maxwell, Jody-Anne . . . . Sep 98
McCarty, Oseola . . . . Jan 99; Update 99

McGruder, Aaron . . . . Author V.10
McKissack, Fredrick L. . . . . Author V.3
McKissack, Patricia C. . . . . Author V.3
McNabb, Donovan . . . . Apr 03
Mobutu Sese Seko . . . . WorLdr V.2;
    Update 97
Morgan, Garrett . . . . Science V.2
Morrison, Sam . . . . Sep 97
Morrison, Toni . . . . Jan 94
Moss, Randy . . . . Sport V.4
Mugabe, Robert . . . . WorLdr V.2
Myers, Walter Dean . . . . . Jan 93; Update 94
Ndeti, Cosmas . . . . Sep 95
Nelson, Marilyn . . . . Author V.13
Nkrumah, Kwame . . . . WorLdr V.2
Nyerere, Julius Kambarage . . . WorLdr V.2;
    Update 99
Olajuwon, Hakeem . . . . Sep 95
Oliver, Patsy Ruth . . . . WorLdr V.1
O'Neal, Shaquille . . . . Sep 93
Parks, Gordon . . . . Artist V.1
Parks, Rosa . . . . Apr 92; Update 94
Payton, Walter . . . . Jan 00
Pelé . . . . Sport V.1
Pinkney, Andrea Davis . . . . Author V.10
Pinkney, Jerry . . . . Author V.2
Pippen, Scottie . . . . Oct 92
Powell, Colin . . . . Jan 92; Update 93;
    Update 95; Update 01
Queen Latifah . . . . Apr 92
Rice, Condoleezza . . . . Apr 02
Rice, Jerry . . . . Apr 93
Ringgold, Faith . . . . Author V.2
Roba, Fatuma . . . . Sport V.3
Robinson, David . . . . Sep 96
Robinson, Jackie . . . . Sport V.3
Rodman, Dennis . . . . Apr 96; Update 99
Rowan, Carl . . . . Sep 01
Rudolph, Wilma . . . . Apr 95
Salt 'N' Pepa . . . . Apr 95
Sanders, Barry . . . . Sep 95; Update 99
Sanders, Deion . . . . Sport V.1
Sapp, Warren . . . . Sport V.5
Saro-Wiwa, Ken . . . . WorLdr V.1
Satcher, David . . . . Sep 98
Savimbi, Jonas . . . . WorLdr V.2
Schwikert, Tasha . . . . Sport V.7
Scurry, Briana . . . . Jan 00
Senghor, Léopold Sédar . . . . . . WorLdr V.2
Shabazz, Betty . . . . Apr 98
Shakur, Tupac . . . . Apr 97

Simmons, Ruth . . . . Sep 02
Smith, Emmitt . . . . Sep 94
Smith, Will . . . . Sep 94
Sosa, Sammy . . . . Jan 99; Update 99
Stanford, John . . . . Sep 99
Stewart, Kordell . . . . Sep 98
Swoopes, Sheryl . . . . Sport V.2
Tarvin, Herbert . . . . Apr 97
Taylor, Mildred D. . . Author V.1; Update 02
Thomas, Clarence . . . . Jan 92
Tubman, William V. S. . . . . WorLdr V.2
Tucker, Chris . . . . Jan 01
Usher . . . . PerfArt V.1
Vick, Michael . . . . Sport V.9
Ward, Charlie . . . . Apr 94
Ward, Lloyd D. . . . . Jan 01
Washington, Denzel . . . . Jan 93; Update 02
Wayans, Keenen Ivory . . . . Jan 93
White, Jaleel . . . . Jan 96
White, Reggie . . . . Jan 98
WilderBrathwaite, Gloria . . . . . . Science V.7
Williams, Serena . . . . Sport V.4; Update 00;
    Update 02
Williams, Venus . . . . Jan 99; Update 00;
    Update 01; Update 02
Willingham, Tyrone . . . . Sep 02
Wilson, August . . . . Author V.4
Winans, CeCe . . . . Apr 00
Winfield, Dave . . . . Jan 93
Winfrey, Oprah . . . . Apr 92; Update 00
Woods, Tiger . . . . Sport V.1; Update 00;
    Sport V.6
Woodson, Jacqueline . . . . Author V.7;
    Update 01
Wright, Richard . . . . Author V.5
Blair, Bonnie . . . . Apr 94; Update 95
Blanchard, Rachel . . . . Apr 97
Bledel, Alexis . . . . Jan 03
Blige, Mary J. . . . . Apr 02
Blume, Judy . . . . Jan 92
BMX
    see bicycle riding
bobsledding
    Flowers, Vonetta . . . . Sport V.8
Bonds, Barry . . . . Jan 03
Bosnian
    Filipovic, Zlata . . . . Sep 94
Boulmerka, Hassiba . . . . Sport V.1
Bourke-White, Margaret . . . . Artist V.1
Boutros-Ghali, Boutros . . . . Apr 93;
    Update 98

boxing
    Ali, Muhammad . . . . Sport V.2
Boyd, Candy Dawson . . . . Author V.3
Boyz II Men . . . . Jan 96
Bradbury, Ray . . . . Author V.3
Bradley, Ed . . . . Apr 94
Brady, Tom . . . . Sport V.7
Brandis, Jonathan . . . . Sep 95
Brandy . . . . Apr 96
Brazilians
    da Silva, Fabiola . . . . Sport V.9
    Mendes, Chico . . . . WorLdr V.1
    Pelé . . . . Sport V.1
Breathed, Berke . . . . Jan 92
Brody, Jane . . . . Science V.2
Brooks, Garth . . . . Oct 92
Brooks, Gwendolyn . . . . Author V.3
Brower, David . . . . . WorLdr V.1; Update 01
Brown, Claude . . . . Author V.12
Brown, Ron . . . . Sep 96
Brundtland, Gro Harlem . . . . . . Science V.3
Bryan, Zachery Ty . . . . Jan 97
Bryant, Kobe . . . . Apr 99
Bulgarian
    Christo . . . . Sep 96
Burger, Warren . . . . Sep 95
Burke, Chris . . . . Sep 93
Burmese
    Aung San Suu Kyi . . . . . Apr 96; Update 98;
        Update 01; Update 02
    Ka Hsaw Wa . . . . WorLdr V.3
Burns, Ken . . . . Jan 95
Burnside, Aubyn . . . . Sep 02
Burrell, Stanley Kirk
    see Hammer . . . . Jan 92
Bush, Barbara . . . . Jan 92
Bush, George . . . . Jan 92
Bush, George W. . . . . . . Sep 00; Update 00;
    Update 01; Update 02
Bush, Laura . . . . Apr 03
business
    Bezos, Jeff . . . . Apr 01
    Brown, Ron . . . . Sep 96
    Case, Steve . . . . Science V.5
    Chavez, Julz . . . . Sep 02
    Cheney, Dick . . . . Jan 02
    Combs, Sean (Puff Daddy) . . . . Apr 98
    Diemer, Walter . . . . Apr 98
    Fields, Debbi . . . . Jan 96
    Fiorina, Carly . . . . Sep 01; Update 01;
        Update 02

Fox, Vicente . . . . Apr 03
Fuller, Millard . . . . Apr 03
Gates, Bill . . . . Apr 93; Update 98;
   Update 00; Science V.5; Update 01
Groppe, Laura . . . . Science V.5
Handler, Ruth . . . . Apr 98; Update 02
Iacocca, Lee A. . . . . Jan 92
Jobs, Steven . . . . Jan 92; Science V.5
Johnson, John . . . . Jan 97
Johnson, Lonnie . . . . Science V.4
Kurzweil, Raymond . . . . Science V.2
Land, Edwin . . . . Science V.1
Mars, Forrest Sr. . . . . Science V.4
Mohajer, Dineh . . . . Jan 02
Morgan, Garrett . . . . Science V.2
Morita, Akio . . . . Science V.4
Perot, H. Ross . . . . Apr 92; Update 93
Stachowski, Richie . . . . Science V.3
Swanson, Janese . . . . Science V.4
Thomas, Dave . . . . Apr 96; Update 02
Tompkins, Douglas . . . . WorLdr V.3
Wang, An . . . . Science V.2
Ward, Lloyd D. . . . . Jan 01
Butcher, Susan . . . . Sport V.1
Byars, Betsy . . . . Author V.4
Cabot, Meg . . . . Author V.12
Caldecott Medal
   Cooney, Barbara . . . . Author V.8
   Macauley, David . . . . Author V.2
   McCully, Emily Arnold. . . Jul 92; Update 93
   Myers, Walter Dean. . . . . Jan 93; Update 94
   Sendak, Maurice . . . . Author V.2
   Small, David. . . . . Author V.10
   Van Allsburg, Chris . . . . Apr 92
Calder, Alexander . . . . Artist V.1
Calderone, Mary S. . . . . Science V.3
Cameron, Candace . . . . Apr 95
Campbell, Neve . . . . Apr 98
Canadians
   Bailey, Donovan . . . . Sport V.2
   Blanchard, Rachel . . . . Apr 97
   Campbell, Neve . . . . Apr 98
   Candy, John . . . . Sep 94
   Carrey, Jim . . . . Apr 96
   Dion, Celine . . . . Sep 97
   Galdikas, Biruté . . . . Science V.4
   Gretzky, Wayne . . . . Jan 92; Update 93;
      Update 99
   Howe, Gordie . . . . Sport V.2
   Jennings, Peter . . . . Jul 92
   Johnston, Lynn . . . . Jan 99
   Kielburger, Craig . . . . Jan 00

lang, k.d. . . . . Sep 93
Lemieux, Mario . . . . Jul 92; Update 93
Martin, Bernard . . . . WorLdr V.3
Messier, Mark . . . . Apr 96
Morissette, Alanis . . . . Apr 97
Mowat, Farley . . . . Author V.8
Priestley, Jason . . . . Apr 92
Roy, Patrick . . . . Sport V.7
Sakic, Joe . . . . Sport V.6
Shatner, William . . . . Apr 95
Twain, Shania . . . . Apr 99
Vernon, Mike . . . . Jan 98; Update 02
Watson, Paul . . . . WorLdr V.1
Wolf, Hazel . . . . WorLdr V.3
Yzerman, Steve . . . . Sport V.2
Canady, Alexa . . . . Science V.6
Candy, John . . . . Sep 94
Caplan, Arthur . . . . Science V.6
Capriati, Jennifer . . . . Sport V.6
car racing
   Andretti, Mario . . . . Sep 94
   Earnhardt, Dale . . . . Apr 01
   Gordon, Jeff . . . . Apr 99
   Muldowney, Shirley . . . . Sport V.7
   Petty, Richard . . . . Sport V.2
   Stewart, Tony . . . . Sport V.9
Carey, Mariah . . . . Apr 96
Carle, Eric . . . . Author V.1
Carpenter, Mary Chapin . . . . Sep 94
Carrey, Jim . . . . Apr 96
Carson, Ben . . . . Science V.4
Carson, Rachel . . . . WorLdr V.1
Carter, Aaron . . . . Sep 02
Carter, Chris . . . . Author V.4
Carter, Jimmy . . . . Apr 95; Update 02
Carter, Nick
   see Backstreet Boys . . . . Jan 00
Carter, Vince . . . . Sport V.5; Update 01
cartoonists
   see also animators
   Armstrong, Robb . . . . Author V.9
   Breathed, Berke . . . . Jan 92
   Davis, Jim . . . . Author V.1
   Groening, Matt . . . . Jan 92
   Guisewite, Cathy . . . . Sep 93
   Johnston, Lynn . . . . Jan 99
   Jones, Chuck . . . . Author V.12
   Larson, Gary . . . . Author V.1
   Lee, Stan . . . . Author V.7; Update 02
   McGruder, Aaron . . . . Author V.10

Schulz, Charles .... Author V.2; Update 00
Tartakovsky, Genndy .... Author V.11
Watterson, Bill .... Jan 92
Carvey, Dana .... Jan 93
Case, Steve .... Science V.5
Castro, Fidel .... Jul 92; Update 94
Chagall, Marc................. Artist V.1
Chamberlain, Wilt .... Sport V.4
Champagne, Larry III .... Apr 96
Chan Kwong Sang
  see Chan, Jackie .... PerfArt V.1
Chan, Jackie................. PerfArt V.1
Chasez, JC
  see *N Sync...................... Jan 01
Chastain, Brandi ..... Sport V.4; Update 00
Chavez, Cesar................... Sep 93
Chavez, Julz .... Sep 02
Chavis, Benjamin .... Jan 94; Update 94
Cheney, Dick.................... Jan 02
chess
  Ashley, Maurice .... Sep 99
Childress, Alice .... Author V.1
Chinese
  Chan, Jackie................. PerfArt V.1
  Dai Qing .... WorLdr V.3
  Fu Mingxia .... Sport V.5
  Pei, I.M. .... Artist V.1
  Wang, An .... Science V.2
choreography
  see dance
Christo .... Sep 96
Chung, Connie .... Jan 94; Update 95;
  Update 96
Cisneros, Henry .... Sep 93
civil rights movement
  Chavis, Benjamin....... Jan 94; Update 94
  Edelman, Marian Wright.......... Apr 93
  Jackson, Jesse.......... Sep 95; Update 01
  Lewis, John.................... Jan 03
  Marshall, Thurgood..... Jan 92; Update 93
  Parks, Rosa .... Apr 92
  Shabazz, Betty.................. Apr 98
Clark, Kelly .... Sport V.8
Clarkson, Kelly.................. Jan 03
Clay, Cassius Marcellus, Jr.
  see Ali, Muhammad .... Sport V.2
Cleary, Beverly................. Apr 94
Clements, Andrew............. Author V.13
Clinton, Bill .... Jul 92; Update 94;
  Update 95; Update 96; Update 97; Update 98;
  Update 99; Update 00; Update 01

Clinton, Chelsea .... Apr 96; Update 97;
  Update 01
Clinton, Hillary Rodham .... Apr 93;
  Update 94; Update 95; Update 96; Update
  99; Update 00; Update 01
Cobain, Kurt.................... Sep 94
Cohen, Adam Ezra............... Apr 97
Colfer, Eoin .... Author V.13
Collier, Bryan .... Author V.11
Collins, Eileen .... Science V.4
Collins, Francis .... Science V.6
Columbian
  Shakira .... PerfArt V.1
Combs, Sean (Puff Daddy) .... Apr 98
comedians
  Allen, Tim .... Apr 94; Update 99
  Arnold, Roseanne .... Oct 92
  Candy, John..................... Sep 94
  Carrey, Jim..................... Apr 96
  Carvey, Dana .... Jan 93
  Cosby, Bill..................... Jan 92
  Goldberg, Whoopi .... Apr 94
  Leno, Jay .... Jul 92
  Letterman, David................ Jan 95
  Mac, Bernie .... PerfArt V.1
  O'Donnell, Rosie ...... Apr 97; Update 02
  Seinfeld, Jerry .... Oct 92; Update 98
  Tucker, Chris .... Jan 01
  Wayans, Keenen Ivory .... Jan 93
  Williams, Robin.................. Apr 92
comic strips
  see cartoonists
computers
  Berners-Lee, Tim .... Science V.7
  Bezos, Jeff..................... Apr 01
  Case, Steve .... Science V.5
  Cray, Seymour .... Science V.2
  Engelbart, Douglas........... Science V.5
  Fanning, Shawn ... Science V.5; Update 02
  Fiorina, Carly .... Sep 01; Update 01;
    Update 02
  Flannery, Sarah.............. Science V.5
  Gates, Bill .... Apr 93; Update 98;
    Update 00; Science V.5; Update 01
  Groppe, Laura................ Science V.5
  Hopper, Grace Murray........ Science V.5
  Jobs, Steven ...... Jan 92; Science V.5
  Kurzweil, Raymond .... Science V.2
  Miller, Rand.................. Science V.5
  Miller, Robyn................. Science V.5
  Miyamoto, Shigeru........... Science V.5
  Perot, H. Ross .... Apr 92

Wang, An .... Science V.2
Wozniak, Steve .... Science V.5
Congress
  see representatives
  see senators
conservationists
  see environmentalists
Coolio .... Sep 96
Cooney, Barbara .... Author V.8
Cooney, Caroline B. .... Author V.4
Córdova, France .... Science V.7
Cormier, Robert .... Author V.1; Update 01
Cosby, Bill .... Jan 92
Cousteau, Jacques .... Jan 93; Update 97
Coville, Bruce .... Author V.9
Crawford, Cindy .... Apr 93
Cray, Seymour .... Science V.2
Creech, Sharon .... Author V.5
Crichton, Michael .... Author V.5
Cronin, John .... WorLdr V.3
Cubans
  Castro, Fidel .... Jul 92; Update 94
  Estefan, Gloria .... Jul 92
  Fuentes, Daisy .... Jan 94
  Hernandez, Livan .... Apr 98
  Zamora, Pedro .... Apr 95
Culkin, Macaulay .... Sep 93
Curtis, Christopher Paul ...... Author V.4;
  Update 00
Cushman, Karen .... Author V.5
Czechoslovakians
  Hasek, Dominik .... Sport V.3
  Hingis, Martina .... Sport V.2
  Jagr, Jaromir .... Sport V.5
  Navratilova, Martina .... Jan 93; Update 94
da Silva, Fabiola .... Sport V.9
Dae-jung, Kim
  see Kim Dae-jung .... Sep 01
Dahl, Roald .... Author V.1
Dai Qing .... WorLdr V.3
Dakides, Tara .... Sport V.7
Dalai Lama .... Sep 98
Daly, Carson .... Apr 00
dance
  Abdul, Paula .... Jan 92; Update 02
  de Mille, Agnes .... Jan 95
  Estefan, Gloria .... Jul 92
  Farrell, Suzanne .... PerfArt V.1
  Glover, Savion .... Apr 99
  Hammer .... Jan 92

Jamison, Judith .... Jan 96
Kistler, Darci .... Jan 93
Nureyev, Rudolf .... Apr 93
Danes, Claire .... Sep 97
Daniel, Beth .... Sport V.1
Danziger, Paula .... Author V.6
da Silva, Fabiola .... Sport V.9
Davenport, Lindsay .... Sport V.5
Davis, Jim .... Author V.1
Dayne, Ron .... Apr 00
de Klerk, F.W. .... Apr 94; Update 94
Delany, Bessie .... Sep 99
Delany, Sadie .... Sep 99
de Mille, Agnes .... Jan 95
Democratic Party
  Brown, Ron .... Sep 96
  Carter, Jimmy .... Apr 95; Update 02
  Clinton, Bill .... Jul 92; Update 94;
    Update 95; Update 96; Update 97; Update
    98; Update 99; Update 00; Update 01
  Gore, Al .... Jan 93; Update 96; Update 97;
    Update 98; Update 99; Update 00; Update
    01
  Lewis, John .... Jan 03
dentist
  Delany, Bessie .... Sep 99
Denton, Sandi
  see Salt 'N' Pepa .... Apr 95
dePaola, Tomie .... Author V.5
Destiny's Child .... Apr 01
Devers, Gail .... Sport V.2
Diana, Princess of Wales .... Jul 92;
  Update 96; Update 97; Jan 98
DiCamillo, Kate .... Author V.10
DiCaprio, Leonardo .... Apr 98
Diemer, Walter .... Apr 98
Diesel, Vin .... Jan 03
Dion, Celine .... Sep 97
diplomats
  Albright, Madeleine .... Apr 97
  Annan, Kofi .... Jan 98; Update 01
  Boutros-Ghali, Boutros .... Apr 93;
    Update 98
  Rowan, Carl .... Sep 01
directors
  Burns, Ken .... Jan 95
  Carter, Chris .... Author V.4
  Chan, Jackie .... PerfArt V.1
  Crichton, Michael .... Author V.5
  Farrell, Suzanne .... PerfArt V.1

Jones, Chuck . . . . Author V.12
Lasseter, John . . . . Sep 00
Lee, Spike . . . . Oct 92
Lucas, George . . . . Apr 97; Update 02
Parks, Gordon . . . . Artist V.1
Spielberg, Steven . . . . . . Jan 94; Update 94;
  Update 95
Taymor, Julie . . . . PerfArt V.1
Warhol, Andy . . . . Artist V.1
Wayans, Keenen Ivory . . . . Jan 93
Whedon, Joss . . . . Author V.9
Williamson, Kevin . . . . Author V.6
disabled
Burke, Chris . . . . Sep 93
Dole, Bob . . . . Jan 96
Driscoll, Jean . . . . Sep 97
Grandin, Temple . . . . Science V.3
Gwaltney, John Langston . . . . . Science V.3
Hawking, Stephen . . . . Apr 92
Parkinson, Jennifer . . . . Apr 95
Perlman, Itzhak . . . . Jan 95
Reeve, Christopher . . . . . Jan 97; Update 02
Runyan, Marla . . . . Apr 02
Stepanek, Mattie . . . . Apr 02
Whitestone, Heather . . . Apr 95; Update 02
diving
Fu Mingxia . . . . Sport V.5
Dixie Chicks . . . . PerfArt V.1
doctors
Brundtland, Gro Harlem . . . . . . Science V.3
Calderone, Mary S. . . . . Science V.3
Canady, Alexa . . . . Science V.6
Carson, Ben . . . . Science V.4
Collins, Francis . . . . Science V.6
Fauci, Anthony S. . . . . Science V.7
Harris, Bernard . . . . Science V.3
Healy, Bernadine . . . Science V.1; Update 01
Heimlich, Henry . . . . Science V.6
Ho, David . . . . Science V.6
Jemison, Mae . . . . Oct 92
Kamler, Kenneth . . . . Science V.6
Love, Susan . . . . Science V.3
Nielsen, Jerri . . . . Science V.7
Novello, Antonia . . . . Apr 92
Pippig, Uta . . . . Sport V.1
Richardson, Dot . . . . . Sport V.2; Update 00
Sabin, Albert . . . . Science V.1
Sacks, Oliver . . . . Science V.3
Salk, Jonas . . . . Jan 94; Update 95
Satcher, David . . . . Sep 98

Spelman, Lucy . . . . Science V.6
Spock, Benjamin . . . . Sep 95; Update 98
WilderBrathwaite, Gloria . . . . . . Science V.7
Doherty, Shannen . . . . . . Apr 92; Update 94
Dole, Bob . . . . Jan 96; Update 96
Dole, Elizabeth . . . . Jul 92; Update 96;
  Update 99
Domingo, Placido . . . . Sep 95
Dominicans
Martinez, Pedro . . . . Sport V.5
Sosa, Sammy . . . . Jan 99; Update 99
Dorough, Howie
  see Backstreet Boys . . . . Jan 00
Douglas, Marjory Stoneman . . WorLdr V.1;
  Update 98
Dove, Rita . . . . Jan 94
Dragila, Stacy . . . . Sport V.6
Draper, Sharon . . . . Apr 99
Driscoll, Jean . . . . Sep 97
Duchovny, David . . . . Apr 96
Duff, Hilary . . . . Sep 02
Duke, David . . . . Apr 92
Dumars, Joe . . . . Sport V.3; Update 99
Dumitriu, Ioana . . . . Science V.3
Dunbar, Paul Lawrence . . . . Author V.8
Duncan, Lois . . . . Sep 93
Dunlap, Alison . . . . Sport V.7
Dunst, Kirsten . . . . PerfArt V.1
Dutch
Lionni, Leo . . . . Author V.6
Earle, Sylvia . . . . Science V.1
Earnhardt, Dale . . . . Apr 01
Edelman, Marian Wright . . . . Apr 93
educators
Armstrong, William H. . . . . Author V.7
Calderone, Mary S. . . . . Science V.3
Córdova, France . . . . Science V.7
Delany, Sadie . . . . Sep 99
Draper, Sharon . . . . Apr 99
Forman, Michele . . . . Jan 03
Gates, Henry Louis, Jr. . . . . Apr 00
Giff, Patricia Reilly . . . . Author V.7
Jiménez, Francisco . . . . Author V.13
Simmons, Ruth . . . . Sep 02
Stanford, John . . . . Sep 99
Suzuki, Shinichi . . . . Sep 98
Egyptians
Boutros-Ghali, Boutros . . . . Apr 93;
  Update 98
Sadat, Anwar . . . . WorLdr V.2
Elion, Getrude . . . . Science V.6

Ellerbee, Linda . . . . Apr 94
Ellison, Ralph . . . . Author V.3
Elway, John . . . . Sport V.2; Update 99
Eminem . . . . Apr 03
Engelbart, Douglas . . . . Science V.5
English
   Almond, David . . . . Author V.10
   Amanpour, Christiane . . . . Jan 01
   Attenborough, David . . . . Science V.4
   Barton, Hazel . . . . Science V.6
   Berners-Lee, Tim . . . . Science V.7
   Dahl, Roald . . . . Author V.1
   Diana, Princess of Wales. . . . . Jul 92;
     Update 96; Update 97; Jan 98
   Goodall, Jane. . . . . . Science V.1; Update 02
   Handford, Martin . . . . Jan 92
   Hargreaves, Alison . . . . Jan 96
   Hawking, Stephen . . . . Apr 92
   Herriot, James . . . . Author V.1
   Jacques, Brian. . . . . Author V.5
   Leakey, Louis . . . . Science V.1
   Leakey, Mary. . . . . Science V.1
   Lewis, C. S. . . . . Author V.3
   Macaulay, David . . . . Author V.2
   Moore, Henry. . . . . Artist V.1
   Potter, Beatrix . . . . Author V.8
   Pullman, Philip. . . . . Author V.9
   Radcliffe, Daniel. . . . . Jan 02
   Reid Banks, Lynne . . . . Author V.2
   Rennison, Louise. . . . . Author V.10
   Rowling, J. K. . . . . Sep 99; Update 00;
     Update 01; Update 02
   Sacks, Oliver . . . . Science V.3
   Stewart, Patrick . . . . Jan 94
   Tolkien, J.R.R. . . . . Jan 02
   Watson, Emma. . . . . Apr 03
   Winslet, Kate . . . . Sep 98
environmentalists
   Abbey, Edward. . . . . WorLdr V.1
   Adams, Ansel . . . . Artist V.1
   Askins, Renee. . . . . WorLdr V.1
   Babbitt, Bruce. . . . . Jan 94
   Brower, David. . . . . WorLdr V.1; Update 01
   Brundtland, Gro Harlem . . . . . . Science V.3
   Carson, Rachel . . . . WorLdr V.1
   Cousteau, Jacques . . . . Jan 93
   Cronin, John. . . . . WorLdr V.3
   Dai Qing. . . . . WorLdr V.3
   Douglas, Marjory Stoneman . . WorLdr V.1;
     Update 98
   Earle, Sylvia. . . . . Science V.1

Foreman, Dave. . . . . WorLdr V.1
Gibbs, Lois . . . . WorLdr V.1
Irwin, Steve . . . . Science V.7
Ka Hsaw Wa. . . . . WorLdr V.3
LaDuke, Winona . . WorLdr V.3; Update 00
Leopold, Aldo. . . . . WorLdr V.3
Maathai, Wangari . . . . WorLdr V.1
Martin, Bernard . . . . WorLdr V.3
Mendes, Chico . . . . WorLdr V.1
Mittermeier, Russell A. . . . . WorLdr V.1
Moss, Cynthia . . . . WorLdr V.3
Mowat, Farley . . . . Author V.8
Muir, John. . . . . WorLdr V.3
Murie, Margaret. . . . . WorLdr V.1
Murie, Olaus J. . . . . WorLdr V.1
Nakamura, Leanne. . . . . Apr 02
Nelson, Gaylord. . . . . WorLdr V.3
Oliver, Patsy Ruth . . . . WorLdr V.1
Patrick, Ruth . . . . Science V.3
Peterson, Roger Tory. . . . . WorLdr V.1
Saro-Wiwa, Ken. . . . . WorLdr V.1
Tompkins, Douglas . . . . WorLdr V.3
Watson, Paul . . . . WorLdr V.1
Werbach, Adam. . . . . WorLdr V.1
Wolf, Hazel. . . . . WorLdr V.3
Erdös, Paul . . . . Science V.2
Estefan, Gloria . . . . Jul 92
Ethiopians
   Haile Selassie . . . . WorLdr V.2
   Roba, Fatuma . . . . Sport V.3
Evans, Janet . . . . Jan 95; Update 96
Evert, Chris. . . . . Sport V.1
Ewing, Patrick . . . . Jan 95; Update 02
Fanning, Shawn . . . . Science V.5; Update 02
Farmer, Nancy. . . . . Author V.6
Farrakhan, Louis. . . . . Jan 97
Farrell, Suzanne . . . . PerfArt V.1
Fatone, Joey
   see *N Sync. Jan 01
Fauci, Anthony S. . . . . Science V.7
Favre, Brett . . . . Sport V.2
Fedorov, Sergei. . . . . Apr 94; Update 94
Fernandez, Lisa . . . . Sport V.5
Ficker, Roberta Sue
   see Farrell, Suzanne. . . . . PerfArt V.1
Fielder, Cecil. . . . . Sep 93
Fields, Debbi . . . . Jan 96
Filipovic, Zlata . . . . Sep 94
film critic
   Siskel, Gene . . . . Sep 99

Fiorina, Carly . . . . Sep 01; Update 01; Update 02
First Ladies of the United States
  Bush, Barbara . . . . Jan 92
  Bush, Laura . . . . Apr 03
  Clinton, Hillary Rodham . . . . Apr 93; Update 94; Update 95; Update 96; Update 99; Update 00; Update 01
fishing
  Yelas, Jay . . . . Sport V.9
Fitzgerald, Ella . . . . Jan 97
Fitzhugh, Louise . . . . Author V.3
Flake, Sharon . . . . Author V.13
Flannery, Sarah . . . . Science V.5
Flowers, Vonetta . . . . Sport V.8
football
  Aikman, Troy . . . . Apr 95; Update 01
  Allen, Marcus . . . . Sep 97
  Brady, Tom . . . . Sport V.7
  Dayne, Ron . . . . Apr 00
  Elway, John . . . . Sport V.2; Update 99
  Favre, Brett . . . . Sport V.2
  George, Eddie . . . . Sport V.6
  Griese, Brian . . . . Jan 02
  Harbaugh, Jim . . . . Sport V.3
  Jackson, Bo . . . . Jan 92; Update 93
  Johnson, Jimmy . . . . Jan 98
  Madden, John . . . . Sep 97
  Manning, Peyton . . . . Sep 00
  Marino, Dan . . . . Apr 93; Update 00
  McNabb, Donovan . . . . Apr 03
  Montana, Joe . . . . Jan 95; Update 95
  Moss, Randy . . . . Sport V.4
  Payton, Walter . . . . Jan 00
  Rice, Jerry . . . . Apr 93
  Sanders, Barry . . . . Sep 95; Update 99
  Sanders, Deion . . . . Sport V.1
  Sapp, Warren . . . . Sport V.5
  Shula, Don . . . . Apr 96
  Smith, Emmitt . . . . Sep 94
  Stewart, Kordell . . . . Sep 98
  Vick, Michael . . . . Sport V.9
  Ward, Charlie . . . . Apr 94
  Warner, Kurt . . . . Sport V.4
  Weinke, Chris . . . . Apr 01
  White, Reggie . . . . Jan 98
  Willingham, Tyrone . . . . Sep 02
  Young, Steve . . . . Jan 94; Update 00
Ford, Harrison . . . . Sep 97
Foreman, Dave . . . . WorLdr V.1
Forman, Michele . . . . Jan 03

Fossey, Dian . . . . Science V.1
Fox, Vicente . . . . Apr 03
Frank, Anne . . . . Author V.4
Frankenthaler, Helen . . . . Artist V.1
Franklin, Aretha . . . . Apr 01
Freeman, Cathy . . . . Jan 01
French
  Cousteau, Jacques . . . . . . Jan 93; Update 97
Fresh Prince
  see Smith, Will . . . . Sep 94
Fu Mingxia . . . . Sport V.5
Fuentes, Daisy . . . . Jan 94
Fuller, Millard . . . . Apr 03
Galdikas, Biruté . . . . Science V.4
Galeczka, Chris . . . . Apr 96
Gantos, Jack . . . . Author V.10
Garcia, Jerry . . . . Jan 96
Garcia, Sergio . . . . Sport V.7
Garnett, Kevin . . . . Sport V.6
Garth, Jennie . . . . Apr 96
Gates, Bill . . . . Apr 93; Update 98; Update 00; Science V.5; Update 01
Gates, Henry Louis, Jr. . . . . Apr 00
Geisel, Theodor Seuss
  see Seuss, Dr. . . . . Jan 92
Gellar, Sarah Michelle . . . . Jan 99
Geography Bee, National
  Galeczka, Chris . . . . Apr 96
George, Eddie . . . . Sport V.6
George, Jean Craighead . . . . Author V.3
Germans
  Bethe, Hans A. . . . . Science V.3
  Frank, Anne . . . . Author V.4
  Graf, Steffi . . . . Jan 92; Update 01
  Otto, Sylke . . . . Sport V.8
  Pippig, Uta . . . . Sport V.1
Ghanaians
  Annan, Kofi . . . . Jan 98; Update 01
  Nkrumah, Kwame . . . . WorLdr V.2
Gibbs, Lois . . . . WorLdr V.1
Giff, Patricia Reilly . . . . Author V.7
Gilbert, Sara . . . . Apr 93
Gilbert, Walter . . . . Science V.2
Gillespie, Dizzy . . . . Apr 93
Gilman, Billy . . . . Apr 02
Gingrich, Newt . . . . Apr 95; Update 99
Ginsburg, Ruth Bader . . . . Jan 94
Giuliani, Rudolph . . . . Sep 02
Glenn, John . . . . Jan 99
Glover, Savion . . . . Apr 99
Goldberg, Whoopi . . . . Apr 94

golf
Daniel, Beth . . . . Sport V.1
Garcia, Sergio . . . . Sport V.7
Nicklaus, Jack . . . . Sport V.2
Norman, Greg . . . . Jan 94
Pak, Se Ri . . . . Sport V.4
Sorenstam, Annika . . . . Sport V.6
Webb, Karrie . . . . . . Sport V.5; Update 01;
Update 02
Woods, Tiger . . . . . . Sport V.1; Update 00;
Sport V.6
Goodall, Jane . . . . . . Science V.1; Update 02
Goodman, John . . . . Sep 95
Gorbachev, Mikhail . . . . . Jan 92; Update 96
Gordon, Jeff . . . . Apr 99
Gore, Al . . . . Jan 93; Update 96;
Update 97; Update 98; Update 99; Update 00;
Update 01
Gorey, Edward . . . . Author V.13
Gould, Stephen Jay . . . . Science V.2;
Update 02
governors
Babbitt, Bruce . . . . Jan 94
Bush, George W. . . . . . . Sep 00; Update 00;
Update 01; Update 02
Carter, Jimmy . . . . Apr 95; Update 02
Clinton, Bill . . . . Jul 92; Update 94;
Update 95; Update 96; Update 97; Update
98; Update 99; Update 00; Update 01
Nelson, Gaylord . . . . WorLdr V.3
Ventura, Jesse . . . . Apr 99; Update 02
Graf, Steffi . . . . Jan 92; Update 01
Granato, Cammi . . . . Sport V.8
Grandin, Temple . . . . Science V.3
Granny D
see Haddock, Doris. . . . . Sep 00
Grant, Amy . . . . Jan 95
Gretzky, Wayne . . . . Jan 92; Update 93;
Update 99
Griese, Brian . . . . Jan 02
Griffey, Ken, Jr. . . . . Sport V.1
Griffith Joyner, Florence . . . . Sport V.1;
Update 98
Grisham, John . . . . Author V.1
Groening, Matt . . . . Jan 92
Groppe, Laura . . . . Science V.5
Guatemalan
Menchu, Rigoberta . . . . Jan 93
Guey, Wendy . . . . Sep 96
Guisewite, Cathy . . . . Sep 93

Gumbel, Bryant . . . . Apr 97
Guy, Jasmine . . . . Sep 93
Guy, Rosa . . . . Author V.9
Gwaltney, John Langston . . . . . Science V.3
Gyatso, Tenzin
see Dalai Lama. . . . . Sep 98
gymnastics
Miller, Shannon . . . . Sep 94; Update 96
Moceanu, Dominique . . . . Jan 98
Schwikert, Tasha . . . . Sport V.7
Zmeskal, Kim. . . . . Jan 94
Haddix, Margaret Peterson . . . Author V.11
Haddock, Doris. . . . . Sep 00
Haile Selassie . . . . WorLdr V.2
Haitian
Aristide, Jean-Bertrand . . Jan 95; Update 01
Haley, Alex . . . . Apr 92
Hamilton, Virginia . . . . Author V.1;
Author V.12
Hamm, Mia. . . . . Sport V.2; Update 00
Hammer . . . . Jan 92
Hampton, David . . . . Apr 99
Handford, Martin . . . . Jan 92
Handler, Daniel
see Snicket, Lemony . . . . Author V.12
Handler, Ruth. . . . . Apr 98; Update 02
Hanks, Tom . . . . Jan 96
Hansberry, Lorraine . . . . Author V.5
Hanson . . . . Jan 98
Hanson, Ike
see Hanson . . . . Jan 98
Hanson, Taylor
see Hanson . . . . Jan 98
Hanson, Zac
see Hanson . . . . Jan 98
Harbaugh, Jim . . . . Sport V.3
Hardaway, Anfernee "Penny" . . . Sport V.2
Harding, Tonya . . . . Sep 94
Hargreaves, Alison. . . . . Jan 96
Harris, Bernard. . . . . Science V.3
Hart, Melissa Joan . . . . Jan 94
Hasek, Dominik . . . . Sport V.3
Hassan II . . . . WorLdr V.2; Update 99
Haughton, Aaliyah Dana
see Aaliyah . . . . Jan 02
Hawk, Tony. . . . . Apr 01
Hawking, Stephen. . . . . Apr 92
Healy, Bernadine. . . . . Science V.1; Update 01
Heimlich, Henry . . . . Science V.6
Heinlein, Robert. . . . . Author V.4
Hendrickson, Sue . . . . Science V.7

Henry, Marguerite . . . . Author V.4
Hernandez, Livan . . . . Apr 98
Herriot, James . . . . Author V.1
Hesse, Karen . . . . . . Author V.5; Update 02
Hewitt, Jennifer Love. . . . . Sep 00
Hill, Anita. . . . . Jan 93
Hill, Faith. . . . . Sep 01
Hill, Grant. Sport V.1
Hill, Lauryn . . . . Sep 99
Hillary, Sir Edmund . . . . Sep 96
Hingis, Martina . . . . Sport V.2
Hinton, S.E. . . . . Author V.1
Hispanics
    Aguilera, Christina . . . . Apr 00
    Alba, Jessica. . . . . Sep 01
    Alvarez, Luis W. . . . . Science V.3
    Bledel, Alexis . . . . Jan 03
    Castro, Fidel. . . . . Jul 92; Update 94
    Chavez, Cesar . . . . Sep 93
    Chavez, Julz . . . . Sep 02
    Cisneros, Henry . . . . Sep 93
    Córdova, France . . . . Science V.7
    Domingo, Placido. . . . . Sep 95
    Estefan, Gloria. . . . . Jul 92
    Fernandez, Lisa . . . . Sport V.5
    Fox, Vicente. . . . . Apr 03
    Fuentes, Daisy . . . . Jan 94
    Garcia, Sergio . . . . Sport V.7
    Hernandez, Livan. . . . . Sep 93
    Iglesias, Enrique. . . . . Jan 03
    Jiménez, Francisco. . . . . Author V.13
    Lopez, Charlotte. . . . . Apr 94
    Lopez, Jennifer. . . . . Jan 02
    Martin, Ricky . . . . Jan 00
    Martinez, Pedro . . . . Sport V.5
    Mendes, Chico . . . . WorLdr V.1
    Muniz, Frankie. . . . . Jan 01
    Novello, Antonia . . . . Apr 92
    Ochoa, Ellen . . . . Apr 01; Update 02
    Ochoa, Severo . . . . Jan 94
    Pele . . . . Sport V.1
    Prinze, Freddie, Jr. . . . . Apr 00
    Rivera, Diego . . . . Artist V.1
    Rodriguez, Alex . . . . Sport V.6
    Rodriguez, Eloy. . . . . Science V.2
    Ryan, Pam Muñoz . . . . Author V.12
    Sanchez Vicario, Arantxa . . . . Sport V.1
    Selena . . . . Jan 96
    Shakira . . . . PerfArt V.1
    Soto, Gary . . . . Author V.5
    Toro, Natalia. . . . . Sep 99

Vidal, Christina . . . . PerfArt V.1
Villa-Komaroff, Lydia . . . . Science V.6
Zamora, Pedro . . . . Apr 95
Ho, David . . . . Science V.6
hockey
    Fedorov, Sergei . . . . Apr 94; Update 94
    Granato, Cammi. . . . . Sport V.8
    Gretzky, Wayne . . . . Jan 92; Update 93;
        Update 99
    Hasek, Dominik . . . . Sport V.3
    Howe, Gordie. . . . . Sport V.2
    Jagr, Jaromir . . . . Sport V.5
    Lemieux, Mario. . . . . Jul 92; Update 93
    Messier, Mark . . . . Apr 96
    Roy, Patrick. . . . . Sport V.7
    Sakic, Joe. Sport V.6
    Vernon, Mike . . . . Jan 98; Update 02
    Yzerman, Steve. . . . . Sport V.2
Hogan, Hulk . . . . Apr 92
Holdsclaw, Chamique. . . . . Sep 00
Holmes, Katie . . . . Jan 00
Hooper, Geoff . . . . Jan 94
Hopper, Grace Murray . . . . Science V.5
Horner, Jack . . . . Science V.1
horse racing
    Krone, Julie . . . . Jan 95; Update 00
House of Representatives
    see representatives
Houston, Whitney . . . . Sep 94
Howe, Gordie. . . . . Sport V.2
Hughes, Langston . . . . Author V.7
Hughes, Sarah . . . . Jan 03
Hungarians
    Erdös, Paul . . . . Science V.2
    Seles, Monica. . . . . Jan 96
Hunter-Gault, Charlayne . . . . Jan 00
Hurston, Zora Neale . . . . Author V.6
Hussein, King. . . . . Apr 99
Hussein, Saddam . . . . Jul 92; Update 96;
    Update 01; Update 02
Iacocca, Lee A. . . . . Jan 92
Ice-T . . . . Apr 93
Iglesias, Enrique . . . . Jan 03
illustrators
    Berenstain, Jan. . . . . Author V.2
    Berenstain, Stan. . . . . Author V.2
    Carle, Eric. . . . . Author V.1
    Collier, Bryan. . . . . Author V.11
    Cooney, Barbara . . . . Author V.8
    dePaola, Tomie . . . . Author V.5
    Fitzhugh, Louise . . . . Author V.3

George, Jean Craighead . . . . Author V.3
Gorey, Edward. . . . . Author V.13
Handford, Martin . . . . Jan 92
Konigsburg, E. L. . . . . Author V.3
Lionni, Leo. . . . . Author V.6
Macaulay, David . . . . Author V.2
McCully, Emily Arnold. . Apr 92; Update 93
Peet, Bill . . . . Author V.4
Pinkney, Jerry . . . . Author V.2
Pinkwater, Daniel . . . . Author V.8
Potter, Beatrix . . . . Author V.8
Ringgold, Faith . . . . Author V.2
Rockwell, Norman. . . . . Artist V.1
Scarry, Richard . . . . Sep 94
Sendak, Maurice . . . . Author V.2
Seuss, Dr. . . . . Jan 92
Silverstein, Shel . . . . Author V.3; Update 99
Small, David. . . . . Author V.10
Van Allsburg, Chris . . . . Apr 92
Williams, Garth . . . . Author V.2
in-line skating
see skating (in-line). . . . . Sport V.9
Internet
Berners-Lee, Tim . . . . Science V.7
Bezos, Jeff. Apr 01
Case, Steve . . . . Science V.5
Fanning, Shawn . . . Science V.5; Update 02
Flannery, Sarah. . . . . Science V.5
Groppe, Laura. . . . . Science V.5
Tarbox, Katie . . . . Author V.10
inventors
Alvarez, Luis W. . . . . Science V.3
Berners-Lee, Tim . . . . Science V.7
Cousteau, Jacques . . . . . . Jan 93; Update 97
Diemer, Walter . . . . Apr 98
Engelbart, Douglas. . . . . Science V.5
Fanning, Shawn . . . Science V.5; Update 02
Grandin, Temple . . . . Science V.3
Hampton, David. . . . . Apr 99
Handler, Ruth . . . . Apr 98; Update 02
Heimlich, Henry. . . . . Science V.6
Johnson, Lonnie . . . . Science V.4
Kurzweil, Raymond . . . . Science V.2
Land, Edwin . . . . Science V.1
Lemelson, Jerome. . . . . Science V.3
Mars, Forrest Sr.. . . . . Science V.4
Morgan, Garrett . . . . Science V.2
Ochoa, Ellen . . . . Apr 01; Update 02
Patterson, Ryan. . . . . Science V.7
Stachowski, Richie . . . . Science V.3
Swanson, Janese. . . . . Science V.4

Wang, An . . . . Science V.2
Wozniak, Steve . . . . Science V.5
Iraqi
Hussein, Saddam. . . . . . . Jul 92; Update 96;
Update 01; Update 02
Irish
Colfer, Eoin . . . . Author V.13
Flannery, Sarah. . . . . Science V.5
Lewis, C. S. . . . . Author V.3
Robinson, Mary. . . . . Sep 93
Irwin, Steve. . . . . Science V.7
Israelis
Perlman, Itzhak . . . . Jan 95
Portman, Natalie . . . . Sep 99
Rabin, Yitzhak . . . . Oct 92; Update 93;
Update 94; Update 95
Italians
Andretti, Mario . . . . Sep 94
Krim, Mathilde . . . . Science V.1
Levi-Montalcini, Rita . . . . Science V.1
Iverson, Allen. . . . . Sport V.7
Ivey, Artis, Jr.
see Coolio. Sep 96
Jackson, Bo. . . . . Jan 92; Update 93
Jackson, Jesse . . . . Sep 95; Update 01
Jackson, Shirley . . . . Author V.6
Jackson, Shirley Ann . . . . Science V.2
Jacques, Brian . . . . Author V.5
Jagr, Jaromir . . . . Sport V.5
Jamaicans
Ashley, Maurice . . . . Sep 99
Bailey, Donovan . . . . Sport V.2
Denton, Sandi
see Salt 'N' Pepa. . . . . Apr 95
Ewing, Patrick . . . . Jan 95; Update 02
Maxwell, Jody-Anne . . . . Sep 98
James, Cheryl
see Salt 'N' Pepa . . . . Apr 95
Jamison, Judith . . . . Jan 96
Jansen, Dan. . . . . Apr 94
Japanese
Miyamoto, Shigeru. . . . . Science V.5
Morita, Akio . . . . Science V.4
Suzuki, Shinichi . . . . Sep 98
Uchida, Mitsuko . . . . Apr 99
Javacheff, Christo V.
see Christo . . . . Sep 96
Jemison, Mae . . . . Oct 92
Jennings, Peter . . . . Jul 92
Jeter, Derek. . . . . Sport V.4
Jewel . . . . Sep 98

Jiménez, Francisco . . . . Author V.13
Jobs, Steven . . . . Jan 92; Science V.5
jockey
  Krone, Julie . . . . Jan 95; Update 00
John Paul II . . . . Oct 92; Update 94;
  Update 95
Johns, Jasper. . . . . Artist V.1
Johnson, Angela . . . . Author V.6
Johnson, Jimmy. . . . . Jan 98
Johnson, Johanna. . . . . Apr 00
Johnson, John . . . . Jan 97
Johnson, Lonnie. . . . . Science V.4
Johnson, Magic. . . . . Apr 92; Update 02
Johnson, Michael . . . . Jan 97; Update 00
Johnson, Randy . . . . Sport V.9
Johnston, Lynn . . . . Jan 99
Jones, Chuck . . . . Author V.12
Jones, James Earl. . . . . Jan 95
Jones, Marion. . . . . Sport V.5
Jordan, Barbara . . . . Apr 96
Jordan, Michael . . . . Jan 92; Update 93;
  Update 94; Update 95; Update 99; Update
  01
Jordanian
  Hussein, King . . . . Apr 99
journalists
  Amanpour, Christiane . . . . Jan 01
  Anderson, Terry . . . . Apr 92
  Benson, Mildred. . . . . Jan 03
  Bradley, Ed. . . . . Apr 94
  Brody, Jane . . . . Science V.2
  Chung, Connie . . . . Jan 94; Update 95;
    Update 96
  Dai Qing . . . . WorLdr V.3
  Ellerbee, Linda . . . . Apr 94
  Hunter-Gault, Charlayne . . . . Jan 00
  Jennings, Peter . . . . Jul 92
  Krakauer, Jon. . . . . Author V.6
  Lipsyte, Robert . . . . Author V.12
  Pauley, Jane. . . . . Oct 92
  Roberts, Cokie. . . . . Apr 95
  Rowan, Carl. . . . . Sep 01
  Soren, Tabitha . . . . Jan 97
  Steinem, Gloria. . . . . Oct 92
  Walters, Barbara . . . . Sep 94
Joyner-Kersee, Jackie . . . . . . Oct 92; Update
  96; Update 97; Update 98
Jung, Kim Dae
  see Kim Dae-jung . . . . Sep 01
Ka Hsaw Wa. . . . . WorLdr V.3

Kaddafi, Muammar
  see Qaddafi, Muammar . . . . Apr 97
Kamler, Kenneth . . . . Science V.6
Kaunda, Kenneth . . . . WorLdr V.2
Keene, Carolyne
  see Benson, Mildred. . . . . Jan 03
Kenyans
  Kenyatta, Jomo . . . . WorLdr V.2
  Maathai, Wangari . . . . WorLdr V.1
  Ndeti, Cosmas. . . . . Sep 95
Kenyatta, Jomo . . . . WorLdr V.2
Kerr, M.E.. . . . . Author V.1
Kerrigan, Nancy. . . . . Apr 94
Kidd, Jason. . . . . Sport V.9
Kielburger, Craig . . . . Jan 00
Kilcher, Jewel
  see Jewel . . . . Sep 98
Kim Dae-jung. . . . . Sep 01
King, Stephen . . . . . . Author V.1; Update 00
Kiraly, Karch . . . . Sport V.4
Kirkpatrick, Chris
  see *N Sync. . . . . Jan 01
Kistler, Darci . . . . Jan 93
Klug, Chris . . . . Sport V.8
Knowles, Beyoncé
  see Destiny's Child . . . . Apr 01
Konigsburg, E. L. . . . . Author V.3
Korean
  An Na. Author V.12
  Kim Dae-jung . . . . Sep 01
  Pak, Se Ri . . . . Sport V.4
Krakauer, Jon . . . . Author V.6
Krim, Mathilde . . . . Science V.1
Krone, Julie. . . . . Jan 95; Update 00
Kurzweil, Raymond . . . . Science V.2
Kwan, Michelle . . . . . . Sport V.3; Update 02
Laden, Osama bin
  see bin Laden, Osama . . . . Apr 02
LaDuke, Winona . . . WorLdr V.3; Update 00
Lalas, Alexi . . . . Sep 94
Lama, Dalai
  see Dalai Lama . . . . Sep 98
Land, Edwin . . . . Science V.1
lang, k.d. . . . . Sep 93
Larson, Gary . . . . Author V.1
Lasseter, John.. . . . . Sep 00
Latino/Latina
  see Hispanics
Lawrence, Jacob . . . . . . Artist V.1; Update 01
Leakey, Louis . . . . Science V.1
Leakey, Mary . . . . Science V.1

Lee, Harper . . . . Author V.9
Lee, Jeanette . . . . Apr 03
Lee, Spike . . . . Apr 92
Lee, Stan . . . . Author V.7; Update 02
Le Guin, Ursula K. . . . . Author V.8
Leibovitz, Annie . . . . Sep 96
Lemelson, Jerome . . . . Science V.3
Lemieux, Mario . . . . Jul 92; Update 93
LeMond, Greg . . . . Sport V.1
L'Engle, Madeleine. . . . . Jan 92; Apr 01
Leno, Jay . . . . .Jul 92
Leopold, Aldo . . . . WorLdr V.3
Lester, Julius . . . . Author V.7
Letterman, David . . . . .Jan 95
Levi-Montalcini, Rita . . . . Science V.1
Lewis, C. S. . . . . Author V.3
Lewis, Carl. . . . . Sep 96; Update 97
Lewis, John. Jan 03
Lewis, Shari . . . . Jan 99
Liberian
    Tubman, William V. S. . . . . WorLdr V.2
librarians
    Avi. . . . . Jan 93
    Bush, Laura . . . . Apr 03
    Cleary, Beverly . . . . Apr 94
    Morrison, Lillian . . . . Author V.12
    Morrison, Sam . . . . Sep 97
    Rylant, Cynthia . . . . Author V.1
Libyan
    Qaddafi, Muammar . . . . Apr 97
Limbaugh, Rush. . . . . Sep 95; Update 02
Lin, Maya. . . . . Sep 97
Lindgren, Astrid. . . . . Author V.13
Lionni, Leo. . . . . Author V.6
Lipinski, Tara. . . . . Apr 98
Lipsyte, Robert . . . . Author V.12
Lisanti, Mariangela . . . . Sep 01
Lithuanian
    Galdikas, Biruté. . . . . Science V.4
Littrell, Brian
    see Backstreet Boys. . . . . Jan 00
Lobo, Rebecca . . . . Sport V.3
Locklear, Heather . . . . Jan 95
Lopez, Charlotte. . . . . Apr 94
Lopez, Jennifer . . . . Jan 02
Love, Susan. . . . . Science V.3
Lovell, Jim . . . . Jan 96
Lowe, Alex . . . . Sport V.4
Lowman, Meg. . . . . Science V.4
Lowry, Lois . . . . Author V.4
Lucas, George . . . . Apr 97; Update 02

Lucid, Shannon . . . . Science V.2
luge
    Otto, Sylke . . . . Sport V.8
Lynch, Chris . . . . Author V.13
Ma, Yo-Yo . . . . .Jul 92
Maathai, Wangari . . . . WorLdr V.1
Mac, Bernie . . . . PerfArt V.1
Macaulay, David . . . . Author V.2
MacLachlan, Patricia . . . . Author V.2
Madden, John. . . . . Sep 97
Maddux, Greg . . . . Sport V.3
Maguire, Martie
    see Dixie Chicks . . . . PerfArt V.1
Maines, Natalie
    see Dixie Chicks . . . . PerfArt V.1
Malawian
    Banda, Hastings Kamuzu . . . . WorLdr V.2
Mandela, Nelson . . . . Jan 92; Update 94;
        Update 01
Mandela, Winnie . . . . WorLdr V.2
Mankiller, Wilma . . . . Apr 94
Manning, Peyton. . . . . Sep 00
Mantle, Mickey. . . . . Jan 96
Margulis, Lynn. . . . . Sep 96
Marino, Dan . . . . Apr 93; Update 00
Marrow, Tracy
    see Ice-T . . . . Apr 93
Mars, Forrest Sr.. . . . . Science V.4
Marsalis, Wynton . . . . Apr 92
Marshall, Thurgood . . . . . Jan 92; Update 93
Martin, Ann M.. . . . . Jan 92
Martin, Bernard. . . . . WorLdr V.3
Martin, Ricky. . . . . Jan 00
Martinez, Pedro . . . . Sport V.5
Masih, Iqbal. . . . . Jan 96
mathematicians
    Dumitriu, Ioana . . . . Science V.3
    Erdös, Paul . . . . Science V.2
    Flannery, Sarah. . . . . Science V.5
    Hopper, Grace Murray. . . . . . . Science V.5
    Nash, John Forbes, Jr. . . . . Science V.7
Mathers, Marshall III
    see Eminem . . . . Apr 03
Mathis, Clint. . . . . Apr 03
Mathison, Melissa . . . . Author V.4
Maxwell, Jody-Anne . . . . Sep 98
McCain, John . . . . Apr 00
McCarty, Oseola . . . . Jan 99; Update 99
McCary, Michael
    see Boyz II Men. . . . . Jan 96
McClintock, Barbara . . . . Oct 92

McCully, Emily Arnold .. Jul 92; Update 93
McEntire, Reba. . . . . Sep 95
McGruder, Aaron. . . . . Author V.10
McGwire, Mark . . . . Jan 99; Update 99
McKissack, Fredrick L. . . . . Author V.3
McKissack, Patricia C. . . . . Author V.3
McLean, A. J.
    see Backstreet Boys. . . . . Jan 00
McNabb, Donovan . . . . Apr 03
Mead, Margaret . . . . Science V.2
Meaker, Marijane
    see Kerr, M.E. . . . . Author V.1
Mebarak Ripoll, Shakira Isabel
    see Shakira . . . . PerfArt V.1
Meltzer, Milton. . . . . Author V.11
Menchu, Rigoberta. . . . . Jan 93
Mendes, Chico . . . . WorLdr V.1
Messier, Mark . . . . Apr 96
Mexicans
    Fox, Vicente. . . . . Apr 03
    Jiménez, Francisco. . . . . Author V.13
    Rivera, Diego . . . . Artist V.1
military service
– Israel
    Rabin, Yitzhak . . . . Oct 92
– Libya
    Qaddafi, Muammar . . . . Apr 97
– Somalia
    Aidid, Mohammed Farah . . . WorLdr V.2
– Uganda
    Amin, Idi . . . . WorLdr V.2
– United States
    Hopper, Grace Murray . . . . . . Science V.5
    McCain, John. . . . . Apr 00
    Powell, Colin . . . . Jan 92; Update 93;
        Update 95; Update 01
    Schwarzkopf, H. Norman . . . . Jan 92
    Stanford, John . . . . Sep 99
– Zaire
    Mobutu Sese Seko . . . . WorLdr V.2
Miller, Rand . . . . Science V.5
Miller, Robyn. . . . . Science V.5
Miller, Shannon. . . . . . . Sep 94; Update 96
Milosevic, Slobodan . . . Sep 99; Update 00;
    Update 01; Update 02
Mirra, Dave . . . . Sep 02
Mittermeier, Russell A. . . . . . . WorLdr V.1
Miyamoto, Shigeru. . . . . Science V.5
Mobutu Sese Seko .. WorLdr V.2; Update 97
Moceanu, Dominique . . . . Jan 98

model
    Crawford, Cindy . . . . Apr 93
Mohajer, Dineh. . . . . Jan 02
Monroe, Bill . . . . Sep 97
Montana, Joe . . . . Jan 95; Update 95
Moore, Henry. . . . . Artist V.1
Morgan, Garrett . . . . Science V.2
Morissette, Alanis . . . . Apr 97
Morita, Akio . . . . Science V.4
Moroccan
    Hassan II . . . . WorLdr V.2; Update 99
Morris, Nathan
    see Boyz II Men. . . . . Jan 96
Morris, Wanya
    see Boyz II Men. . . . . Jan 96
Morrison, Lillian . . . . Author V.12
Morrison, Samuel . . . . Sep 97
Morrison, Toni . . . . Jan 94
Moseley, Jonny . . . . Sport V.8
Moses, Grandma. . . . . Artist V.1
Moss, Cynthia . . . . WorLdr V.3
Moss, Randy. . . . . Sport V.4
Mother Teresa
    see Teresa, Mother . . . . Apr 98
mountain climbing
    Hargreaves, Alison . . . . Jan 96
    Hillary, Sir Edmund . . . . Sep 96
    Kamler, Kenneth . . . . Science V.6
    Krakauer, Jon. . . . . Author V.6
    Lowe, Alex . . . . Sport V.4
movies
    see actors/actresses
    see animators
    see directors
    see film critic
    see producers
    see screenwriters
Mowat, Farley. . . . . Author V.8
Mugabe, Robert . . . . WorLdr V.2
Muir, John . . . . WorLdr V.3
Muldowney, Shirley . . . . Sport V.7
Muniz, Frankie . . . . Jan 01
Murie, Margaret . . . . WorLdr V.1
Murie, Olaus J. . . . . WorLdr V.1
Murray, Ty . . . . Sport V.7
music
    Aaliyah . . . . Jan 02
    Abdul, Paula . . . . Jan 92; Update 02
    Adams, Yolanda . . . . Apr 03
    Aguilera, Christina . . . . Apr 00
    Anderson, Marian. . . . . Jan 94

Backstreet Boys . . . . Jan 00
Battle, Kathleen. . . . . Jan 93
Blige, Mary J. Apr 02
Boyz II Men. . . . . Jan 96
Brandy. . . . . Apr 96
Brooks, Garth . . . . Oct 92
Carey, Mariah. . . . . Apr 96
Carpenter, Mary Chapin . . . . Sep 94
Carter, Aaron . . . . Sep 02
Clarkson, Kelly. . . . . Jan 03
Cobain, Kurt. Sep 94
Combs, Sean (Puff Daddy) . . . . Apr 98
Coolio . . . . Sep 96
Destiny's Child . . . . Apr 01
Dion, Celine . . . . Sep 97
Dixie Chicks. . . . . PerfArt V.1
Domingo, Placido . . . . Sep 95
Eminem . . . . Apr 03
Estefan, Gloria . . . . Jul 92
Fitzgerald, Ella. . . . . Jan 97
Franklin, Aretha . . . . Apr 01
Garcia, Jerry. Jan 96
Gillespie, Dizzy. . . . . Apr 93
Gilman, Billy . . . . Apr 02
Grant, Amy . . . . Jan 95
Guy, Jasmine . . . . Sep 93
Hammer . . . . Jan 92
Hanson . . . . Jan 98
Hill, Faith. . . . . Sep 01
Hill, Lauryn. Sep 99
Houston, Whitney . . . . Sep 94
Ice-T . . . . Apr 93
Iglesias, Enrique. . . . . Jan 03
Jewel . . . . Sep 98
Johnson, Johanna . . . . Apr 00
lang, k.d. . . . . Sep 93
Lopez, Jennifer. . . . . Jan 02
Ma, Yo-Yo . . . . Jul 92
Marsalis, Wynton. . . . . Apr 92
Martin, Ricky . . . . Jan 00
McEntire, Reba. . . . . Sep 95
Monroe, Bill. Sep 97
Morissette, Alanis. . . . . Apr 97
*N Sync. . . . . Jan 01
Perlman, Itzhak . . . . Jan 95
Queen Latifah . . . . Apr 92
Rimes, LeAnn . . . . Jan 98
Salt 'N' Pepa. Apr 95
Selena . . . . Jan 96
Shakira . . . . PerfArt V.1

Shakur, Tupac. . . . . Apr 97
Sinatra, Frank. . . . . Jan 99
Smith, Will . . . . Sep 94
Spears, Britney . . . . Jan 01
Stern, Isaac. . . . . PerfArt V.1
Suzuki, Shinichi . . . . Sep 98
Twain, Shania . . . . Apr 99
Uchida, Mitsuko . . . . Apr 99
Usher . . . . PerfArt V.1
Vidal, Christina . . . . PerfArt V.1
Winans, CeCe . . . . Apr 00
Myers, Walter Dean . . . . . Jan 93; Update 94
***N Sync**. . . . . Jan 01
Nakamura, Leanne . . . . Apr 02
Nash, John Forbes, Jr. . . . . Science V.7
Native Americans
 LaDuke, Winona . . WorLdr V.3; Update 00
 Mankiller, Wilma . . . . Apr 94
 Menchu, Rigoberta . . . . Jan 93
Navratilova, Martina . . . . Jan 93; Update 94
Naylor, Phyllis Reynolds. . . . . Apr 93
Ndeti, Cosmas . . . . Sep 95
Nechita, Alexandra. . . . . Jan 98
Nelson, Gaylord . . . . WorLdr V.3
Nelson, Marilyn . . . . Author V.13
Nevelson, Louise. . . . . Artist V.1
New Zealander
 Hillary, Sir Edmund . . . . Sep 96
Newbery Medal
 Alexander, Lloyd . . . . Author V.6
 Armstrong, William H. . . . . Author V.7
 Cleary, Beverly . . . . Apr 94
 Creech, Sharon . . . . Author V.5
 Curtis, Christopher Paul . . . . . . Author V.4;
  Update 00
 Cushman, Karen . . . . Author V.5
 George, Jean Craighead . . . . Author V.3
 Hamilton, Virginia . . . . Author V.1;
  Author V.12
 Hesse, Karen . . . . . . Author V.5; Update 02
 Konigsburg, E. L. . . . . Author V.3
 L'Engle, Madeleine . . . . Jan 92; Apr 01
 MacLachlan, Patricia. . . . . Author V.2
 Naylor, Phyllis Reynolds . . . . Apr 93
 O'Dell, Scott . . . . Author V.2
 Paterson, Katherine . . . . Author V.3
 Peck, Richard. . . . . Author V.10
 Rylant, Cynthia . . . . Author V.1
 Sachar, Louis . . . . Author V.6
 Speare, Elizabeth George Sep95
 Spinelli, Jerry. . . . . Apr 93

Taylor, Mildred D... Author V.1; Update 02
Voight, Cynthia................. Oct 92
Nicklaus, Jack .... Sport V.2
Nielsen, Jerri................ Science V.7
Nigerians
  Olajuwon, Hakeem .... Sep 95
  Saro-Wiwa, Ken............. WorLdr V.1
Nixon, Joan Lowery........... Author V.1
Nixon, Richard.................. Sep 94
Nkrumah, Kwame .... WorLdr V.2
Nobel Prize
  Alvarez, Luis W.............. Science V.3
  Aung San Suu Kyi..... Apr 96; Update 98;
    Update 01; Update 02
  Bardeen, John .... Science V.1
  Bethe, Hans A. .... Science V.3
  Dalai Lama .... Sep 98
  de Klerk, F.W. .... Apr 94
  Elion, Gertrude............. Science V.6
  Gilbert, Walter .... Science V.2
  Gorbachev, Mikhail............... Jan 92
  Kim Dae-jung................... Sep 01
  Levi-Montalcini, Rita........ Science V.1
  Mandela, Nelson....... Jan 92; Update 94;
    Update 01
  McClintock, Barbara............. Oct 92
  Menchu, Rigoberta .... Jan 93
  Morrison, Toni.................. Jan 94
  Nash, John Forbes, Jr. .... Science V.7
  Ochoa, Severo .... Jan 94
  Pauling, Linus .... Jan 95
  Sadat, Anwar .... WorLdr V.2
  Teresa, Mother .... Apr 98
  Watson, James D............. Science V.1
Norman, Greg .... Jan 94
Norwegian
  Brundtland, Gro Harlem ...... Science V.3
Norwood, Brandy
  see Brandy .... Apr 96
Novello, Antonia .... Apr 92; Update 93
***N Sync**.......................... Jan 01
Nureyev, Rudolf .... Apr 93
Nye, Bill..................... Science V.2
Nye, Naomi Shihab.......... Author V.8
Nyerere, Julius Kambarage ... WorLdr V.2;
  Update 99
Ochoa, Ellen .... Apr 01; Update 02
Ochoa, Severo .... Jan 94
O'Connor, Sandra Day............. Jul 92
O'Dell, Scott .... Author V.2

O'Donnell, Rosie....... Apr 97; Update 02
Ohno, Apolo.................. Sport V.8
O'Keeffe, Georgia.............. Artist V.1
Olajuwon, Hakeem.............. Sep 95
Oleynik, Larisa.................. Sep 96
Oliver, Patsy Ruth .... WorLdr V.1
Olsen, Ashley.................... Sep 95
Olsen, Mary Kate................. Sep 95
Olympics
  Ali, Muhammad.............. Sport V.2
  Ammann, Simon .... Sport V.8
  Armstrong, Lance...... Sep 00; Update 00;
    Update 01; Update 02
  Bahrke, Shannon .... Sport V.8
  Bailey, Donovan.............. Sport V.2
  Baiul, Oksana .... Apr 95
  Bird, Larry............. Jan 92; Update 98
  Blair, Bonnie .... Apr 94
  Boulmerka, Hassiba........... Sport V.1
  Capriati, Jennifer .... Sport V.6
  Carter, Vince........ Sport V.5; Update 01
  Chastain, Brandi..... Sport V.4; Update 00
  Clark, Kelly.................. Sport V.8
  Davenport, Lindsay........... Sport V.5
  Devers, Gail .... Sport V.2
  Dragila, Stacy .... Sport V.6
  Dunlap, Alison .... Sport V.7
  Evans, Janet .... Jan 95; Update 96
  Ewing, Patrick .... Jan 95; Update 02
  Fernandez, Lisa .... Sport V.5
  Flowers, Vonetta.............. Sport V.8
  Freeman, Cathy .... Jan 01
  Fu Mingxia .... Sport V.5
  Garnett, Kevin .... Sport V.6
  Granato, Cammi............... Sport V.8
  Griffith Joyner, Florence........ Sport V.1;
    Update 98
  Hamm, Mia........ Sport V.2; Update 00
  Harding, Tonya................. Sep 94
  Hasek, Dominik .... Sport V.3
  Hill, Grant................... Sport V.1
  Hughes, Sarah .... Jan 03
  Jansen, Dan..................... Apr 94
  Johnson, Michael....... Jan 97; Update 00
  Jones, Marion .... Sport V.5
  Joyner-Kersee, Jackie...... Oct 92; Update
    96; Update 97; Update 98
  Kerrigan, Nancy .... Apr 94
  Klug, Chris .... Sport V.8
  Kwan, Michelle...... Sport V.3; Update 02

Lewis, Carl. Sep 96
Lipinski, Tara. . . . . Apr 98
Lobo, Rebecca. . . . . Sport V.3
Miller, Shannon . . . . Sep 94; Update 96
Moceanu, Dominique. . . . . Jan 98
Moseley, Jonny. . . . . Sport V.8
Ohno, Apolo. . . . . Sport V.8
Otto, Sylke . . . . Sport V.8
Pippig, Uta . . . . Sport V.1
Richardson, Dot . . . . . Sport V.2; Update 00
Roba, Fatuma . . . . Sport V.3
Robinson, David . . . . Sep 96
Roy, Patrick. . . . . Sport V.7
Rudolph, Wilma . . . . Apr 95
Runyan, Marla. . . . . Apr 02
Sakic, Joe. . . . . Sport V.6
Sanborn, Ryne . . . . Sport V.8
Sanchez Vicario, Arantxa . . . . Sport V.1
Schwikert, Tasha . . . . Sport V.7
Scurry, Briana. . . . . Jan 00
Shea, Jim, Jr. . . . . Sport V.8
Stockton, John . . . . Sport V.3
Street, Picabo . . . . Sport V.3
Summitt, Pat. . . . . Sport V.3
Swoopes, Sheryl. . . . . Sport V.2
Thompson, Jenny. . . . . Sport V.5
Van Dyken, Amy . . . . Sport V.3; Update 00
Williams, Serena . . . . Sport V.4; Update 00;
    Update 02
Williams, Venus . . . . Jan 99; Update 00;
    Update 01; Update 02
Yamaguchi, Kristi . . . . Apr 92
Zmeskal, Kim. . . . . Jan 94
O'Neal, Shaquille . . . . Sep 93
Opdyke, Irene Gut . . . . Author V.9
Oppenheimer, J. Robert. . . . . . . Science V.1
Otto, Sylke . . . . Sport V.8
painters
    see artists
Pak, Se Ri . . . . Sport V.4
Pakistanis
    Bhutto, Benazir . . . . Apr 95; Update 99
    Masih, Iqbal . . . . Jan 96
Palestinian
    Arafat, Yasir. . . . . Sep 94; Update 94;
        Update 95; Update 96; Update 97; Update
        98; Update 00; Update 01; Update 02
Park, Linda Sue . . . . Author V.12
Parkinson, Jennifer. . . . . Apr 95

Parks, Gordon . . . . Artist V.1
Parks, Rosa . . . . Apr 92; Update 94
Pascal, Francine . . . . Author V.6
Paterson, Katherine . . . . Author V.3
Patrick, Ruth. . . . . Science V.3
Patterson, Ryan . . . . Science V.7
Pauley, Jane. . . . . Oct 92
Pauling, Linus . . . . Jan 95
Paulsen, Gary . . . . Author V.1
Payton, Walter. . . . . Jan 00
Peck, Richard . . . . Author V.10
Peet, Bill. . . . . Author V.4
Pei, I.M. . . . . Artist V.1
Pelé. . . . . Sport V.1
Perlman, Itzhak. . . . . Jan 95
Perot, H. Ross. . . . . Apr 92; Update 93;
    Update 95; Update 96
Perry, Luke. . . . . Jan 92
Peterson, Roger Troy . . . . WorLdr V.1
Petty, Richard. . . . . Sport V.2
philanthropist
    McCarty, Oseola. . . . . Jan 99; Update 99
philosopher
    Caplan, Arthur . . . . Science V.6
Phoenix, River . . . . Apr 94
photographers
    Adams, Ansel . . . . Artist V.1
    Bourke-White, Margaret. . . . . Artist V.1
    Land, Edwin . . . . Science V.1
    Leibovitz, Annie . . . . Sep 96
    Parks, Gordon . . . . Artist V.1
Pierce, Tamora . . . . Author V.13
Pike, Christopher. . . . . Sep 96
pilot
    Van Meter, Vicki . . . . Jan 95
Pine, Elizabeth Michele . . . . Jan 94
Pinkney, Andrea Davis. . . . . . . Author V.10
Pinkney, Jerry . . . . Author V.2
Pinkwater, Daniel . . . . Author V.8
Pinsky, Robert . . . . Author V.7
Pippen, Scottie . . . . Oct 92
Pippig, Uta . . . . Sport V.1
Pitt, Brad . . . . Sep 98
playwrights
    Bennett, Cherie. . . . . Author V.9
    Hansberry, Lorraine . . . . Author V.5
    Hughes, Langston. . . . . Author V.7
    Wilson, August . . . . Author 98
poets
    Brooks, Gwendolyn . . . . Author V.3
    Dove, Rita. Jan 94

Dunbar, Paul Lawrence . . . . Author V.8
Hughes, Langston. . . . . Author V.7
Jewel . . . . Sep 98
Morrison, Lillian . . . . Author V.12
Nelson, Marilyn. . . . . Author V.13
Nye, Naomi Shihab . . . . Author V.8
Pinsky, Robert . . . . Author V.7
Prelutsky, Jack . . . . Author V.2
Senghor, Léopold Sédar . . . . . WorLdr V.2
Silverstein, Shel . . . . Author V.3; Update 99
Sones, Sonya . . . . Author V.11
Soto, Gary . . . . Author V.5
Stepanek, Mattie. . . . . Apr 02

Polish
John Paul II . . . . Oct 92; Update 94;
  Update 95
Opdyke, Irene Gut. . . . . Author V.9

political leaders
Abzug, Bella . . . . Sep 98
Amin, Idi . . . . WorLdr V.2
Annan, Kofi . . . . Jan 98; Update 01
Arafat, Yasir . . . . Sep 94; Update 94;
  Update 95; Update 96; Update 97; Update
  98; Update 00; Update 01; Update 02
Aristide, Jean-Bertrand . . Jan 95; Update 01
Babbitt, Bruce . . . . Jan 94
Baker, James . . . . Oct 92
Banda, Hastings Kamuzu . . . . WorLdr V.2
Bhutto, Benazir. . . . . Apr 95; Update 99;
  Update 02
Boutros-Ghali, Boutros . . Apr 93; Update 98
Brundtland, Gro Harlem . . . . . . Science V.3
Bush, George . . . . Jan 92
Bush, George W. . . . . Sep 00; Update 00;
  Update 01; Update 02
Carter, Jimmy . . . . Apr 95; Update 02
Castro, Fidel. . . . . Jul 92; Update 94
Cheney, Dick . . . . Jan 02
Cisneros, Henry . . . . Sep 93
Clinton, Bill. . . . . Jul 92; Update 94;
  Update 95; Update 96; Update 97; Update
  98; Update 99; Update 00; Update 01
Clinton, Hillary Rodham. . . . . Apr 93;
  Update 94; Update 95; Update 96; Update
  99; Update 00; Update 01
de Klerk, F.W. . . . . Apr 94; Update 94
Dole, Bob . . . . Jan 96; Update 96
Duke, David . . . . Apr 92
Fox, Vicente. . . . . Apr 03
Gingrich, Newt . . . . Apr 95; Update 99

Giuliani, Rudolph . . . . Sep 02
Glenn, John . . . . Jan 99
Gorbachev, Mikhail . . . . . Jan 92; Update 94;
  Update 96
Gore, Al . . . . . Jan 93; Update 96; Update 97;
  Update 98; Update 99; Update 00; Update
  01
Hussein, King . . . . Apr 99
Hussein, Saddam. . . . . . . Jul 92; Update 96;
  Update 01; Update 02
Jackson, Jesse. . . . . Sep 95; Update 01
Jordan, Barbara . . . . Apr 96
Kaunda, Kenneth . . . . WorLdr V.2
Kenyatta, Jomo . . . . WorLdr V.2
Kim Dae-jung . . . . Sep 01
Lewis, John. Jan 03
Mandela, Nelson. . . . . . . Jan 92; Update 94;
  Update 01
McCain, John . . . . Apr 00
Milosevic, Slobodan . . . Sep 99; Update 00;
  Update 01; Update 02
Mobutu Sese Seko . . WorLdr V.2; Update 97
Mugabe, Robert . . . . WorLdr V.2
Nelson, Gaylord. . . . . WorLdr V.3
Nixon, Richard . . . . Sep 94
Nkrumah, Kwame . . . . WorLdr V.2
Nyerere, Julius Kambarage . . . WorLdr V.2;
  Update 99
Perot, H. Ross. . . . . Apr 92; Update 93;
  Update 95; Update 96
Rabin, Yitzhak . . . . Oct 92; Update 93;
  Update 94; Update 95
Rice, Condoleezza. . . . . Apr 02
Robinson, Mary. . . . . Sep 93
Sadat, Anwar . . . . WorLdr V.2
Savimbi, Jonas . . . . WorLdr V.2
Schroeder, Pat . . . . Jan 97
Senghor, Léopold Sédar . . . . . WorLdr V.2
Tubman, William V. S. . . . . WorLdr V.2
Ventura, Jesse . . . . Apr 99; Update 02
Yeltsin, Boris. . . . . Apr 92; Update 93;
  Update 95; Update 96; Update 98; Update
  00

Pope of the Roman Catholic Church
John Paul II. . . . . Oct 92; Update 94;
  Update 95
Portman, Natalie . . . . Sep 99
Potter, Beatrix . . . . Author V.8
Powell, Colin . . . . Jan 92; Update 93;
  Update 95; Update 01

Prelutsky, Jack . . . . Author V.2
presidents
– **Cuba**
    Castro, Fidel . . . . Jul 92; Update 94
– **Egypt**
    Sadat, Anwar . . . . WorLdr V.2
– **Ghana**
    Nkrumah, Kwame . . . . WorLdr V.2
– **Haiti**
    Aristide, Jean-Bertrand . . . . Jan 95;
    Update 01
– **Iraq**
    Hussein, Saddam . . . . . Jul 92; Update 96;
    Update 01
– **Ireland**
    Robinson, Mary . . . . Sep 93
– **Kenya**
    Kenyatta, Jomo . . . . WorLdr V.2
– **Liberia**
    Tubman, William V. S. . . . . . WorLdr V.2
– **Malawi**
    Banda, Hastings Kamuzu . . . WorLdr V.2
– **Republic of South Africa**
    de Klerk, F.W. . . . . Apr 94; Update 9
    Mandela, Nelson . . . . . Jan 92; Update 94;
    Update 01
– **Republic of Tanzania**
    Nyerere, Julius Kambarage . . WorLdr V.2;
    Update 99
– **Russian Federation**
    Yeltsin, Boris . . . . Apr 92; Update 93;
    Update 95; Update 96; Update 98; Update
    00
– **Senegal**
    Senghor, Léopold Sédar . . . . WorLdr V.2
– **South Korea**
    Kim Dae-jung . . . . Sep 01
– **Soviet Union**
    Gorbachev, Mikhail . . . . Jan 92
– **Uganda**
    Amin, Idi . . . . WorLdr V.2
– **United States**
    Bush, George . . . . Jan 92
    Bush, George W. . . . . . Sep 00; Update 00;
    Update 01; Update 02
    Carter, Jimmy . . . . Apr 95; Update 02
    Clinton, Bill . . . . Jul 92; Update 94;
    Update 95; Update 96; Update 97; Update
    98; Update 99; Update 00; Update 01
    Nixon, Richard . . . . Sep 94

– **Yugoslavia**
    Milosevic, Slobodan . . . . Sep 99; Update
    00; Update 01; Update 02
– **Zaire**
    Mobutu Sese Seko . . . . WorLdr V.2;
    Update 97
– **Zambia**
    Kaunda, Kenneth . . . . WorLdr V.2
– **Zimbabwe**
    Mugabe, Robert . . . . WorLdr V.2
Priestley, Jason . . . . Apr 92
prime ministers
– **Israel**
    Rabin, Yitzhak . . . . Oct 92; Update 93;
    Update 94; Update 95
– **Norway**
    Brundtland, Gro Harlem . . . . Science V.3
– **Pakistan**
    Bhutto, Benazir . . . . . . Apr 95; Update 99;
    Update 02
Prinze, Freddie, Jr. . . . . Apr 00
Probst, Jeff . . . . Jan 01
producers
    Barrymore, Drew . . . . Jan 01
    Carter, Chris . . . . Author V.4
    Chan, Jackie . . . . PerfArt V.1
    Combs, Sean (Puff Daddy) . . . . Apr 98
    Cousteau, Jacques . . . . Jan 93
    Groppe, Laura . . . . Science V.5
    Jones, Chuck . . . . Author V.12
    Lucas, George . . . . Apr 97; Update 02
    Spielberg, Steven . . . . Jan 94
    Whedon, Joss . . . . Author V.9
    Williamson, Kevin . . . . Author V.6
Puerto Ricans
    see also Hispanics
    Lopez, Charlotte . . . . Apr 94
    Martin, Ricky . . . . Jan 00
    Novello, Antonia . . . . Apr 92
Puff Daddy
    see Combs, Sean (Puff Daddy) . . . . . Apr 98
Puffy
    see Combs, Sean (Puff Daddy) . . . . . Apr 98
Pullman, Philip . . . . Author V.9
Qaddafi, Muammar . . . . Apr 97
Qing, Dai
    see Dai Qing . . . . WorLdr V.3
Queen Latifah . . . . Apr 92
Quesada, Vicente Fox
    see Fox, Vicente . . . . Apr 03

Quintanilla, Selena
see Selena . . . . Jan 96
Rabin, Yitzhak . . . . Oct 92; Update 93;
Update 94; Update 95
Radcliffe, Daniel . . . . Jan 02
radio
Hunter-Gault, Charlayne . . . . Jan 00
Limbaugh, Rush . . . . Sep 95; Update 02
Roberts, Cokie. . . . . Apr 95
rappers
see music
Raymond, Usher, IV
see Usher . . . . PerfArt V.1
Reeve, Christopher . . . . . . Jan 97; Update 02
Reid Banks, Lynne . . . . Author V.2
religious leaders
Aristide, Jean-Bertrand . . Jan 95; Update 01
Chavis, Benjamin . . . . Jan 94; Update 94
Dalai Lama . . . . Sep 98
Farrakhan, Louis . . . . Jan 97
Jackson, Jesse. . . . . Sep 95; Update 01
Pope John Paul II . . . . . . Oct 92; Update 94;
Update 95
Teresa, Mother . . . . Apr 98
Rennison, Louise . . . . Author V.10
Reno, Janet . . . . Sep 93; Update 98
representatives
Abzug, Bella. . . . . Sep 98
Cheney, Dick . . . . Jan 02
Gingrich, Newt . . . . Apr 95; Update 99
Jordan, Barbara . . . . Apr 96
Lewis, John. . . . . Jan 03
Schroeder, Pat . . . . Jan 97
Republican Party
Baker, James . . . . Oct 92
Bush, George . . . . Jan 92
Bush, George W.. . . . . . . Sep 00; Update 00;
Update 01; Update 02
Cheney, Dick . . . . Jan 02
Gingrich, Newt . . . . Apr 95; Update 99
Giuliani, Rudolph . . . . Sep 02
Nixon, Richard . . . . Sep 94
Rice, Anne . . . . Author V.3
Rice, Condoleezza . . . . Apr 02
Rice, Jerry . . . . Apr 93
Richardson, Dot. . . . . . Sport V.2; Update 00
Richardson, Kevin
see Backstreet Boys. . . . . Jan 00
Ride, Sally . . . . Jan 92
Riley, Dawn . . . . Sport V.4
Rimes, LeAnn . . . . Jan 98
Rinaldi, Ann . . . . Author V.8

Ringgold, Faith . . . . Author V.2
Ripken, Cal, Jr.. . . . . . . Sport V.1; Update 01
Risca, Viviana. . . . . Sep 00
Rivera, Diego . . . . Artist V.1
Roba, Fatuma . . . . Sport V.3
Roberts, Cokie . . . . Apr 95
Roberts, Julia . . . . Sep 01
Robinson, David . . . . Sep 96
Robinson, Jackie . . . . Sport V.3
Robinson, Mary . . . . Sep 93
Robison, Emily
see Dixie Chicks . . . . PerfArt V.1
rock climbing
Allen, Tori . . . . Sport V.9
Rockwell, Norman . . . . Artist V.1
Roddick, Andy . . . . Jan 03
rodeo
Murray, Ty. Sport V.7
Rodman, Dennis. . . . . Apr 96; Update 99
Rodriguez, Alex. . . . . Sport V.6
Rodriguez, Eloy . . . . Science V.2
Romanians
Dumitriu, Ioana . . . . Science V.3
Nechita, Alexandra . . . . Jan 98
Risca, Viviana. . . . . Sep 00
Roper, Dee Dee
see Salt 'N' Pepa . . . . Apr 95
Rosa, Emily . . . . Sep 98
Rose, Pete . . . . Jan 92
Rowan, Carl . . . . Sep 01
Rowland, Kelly
see Destiny's Child . . . . Apr 01
Rowling, J. K. . . . . Sep 99; Update 00;
Update 01; Update 02
Roy, Patrick . . . . Sport V.7
royalty
Diana, Princess of Wales . . . . Jul 92;
Update 96; Update 97; Jan 98
Haile Selassie . . . . WorLdr V.2
Hassan II . . . . WorLdr V.2; Update 99
Hussein, King . . . . Apr 99
Rudolph, Wilma . . . . Apr 95
running
Bailey, Donovan . . . . Sport V.2
Boulmerka, Hassiba . . . . Sport V.1
Freeman, Cathy . . . . Jan 01
Griffith Joyner, Florence . . . . Sport V.1;
Update 98
Johnson, Michael . . . . Jan 97; Update 00
Jones, Marion . . . . Sport V.5
Lewis, Carl. . . . . Sep 96; Update 97

Ndeti, Cosmas. . . . . Sep 95
Pippig, Uta . . . . Sport V.1
Roba, Fatuma . . . . Sport V.3
Rudolph, Wilma . . . . Apr 95
Runyan, Marla. . . . . Apr 02
Webb, Alan . . . . Sep 01
Runyan, Marla . . . . Apr 02
Russians
Chagall, Marc . . . . Artist V.1
Fedorov, Sergei . . . . Apr 94; Update 94
Gorbachev, Mikhail. . . . . Jan 92; Update 96
Nevelson, Louise . . . . Artist V.1
Tartakovsky, Genndy . . . . Author V.11
Yeltsin, Boris. . . . . Apr 92; Update 93;
    Update 95; Update 96; Update 98; Update
    00
Ryan, Nolan . . . . Oct 92; Update 93
Ryan, Pam Muñoz . . . . Author V.12
Ryder, Winona . . . . Jan 93
Rylant, Cynthia. . . . . Author V.1
Sabin, Albert. . . . . Science V.1
Sachar, Louis. . . . . Author V.6
Sacks, Oliver. . . . . Science V.3
Sadat, Anwar . . . . WorLdr V.2
Sagan, Carl . . . . Science V.1
sailing
Riley, Dawn. . . . . Sport V.4
Sakic, Joe. . . . . Sport V.6
Salinger, J.D.. . . . . Author V.2
Salk, Jonas . . . . Jan 94; Update 95
Salt 'N' Pepa . . . . Apr 95
Sampras, Pete. . . . . Jan 97; Update 02
Sanborn, Ryne. . . . . Sport V.8
Sanchez Vicario, Arantxa . . . . Sport V.1
Sanders, Barry. . . . . Sep 95; Update 99
Sanders, Deion . . . . Sport V.1
Sapp, Warren . . . . Sport V.5
Saro-Wiwa, Ken . . . . WorLdr V.1
Satcher, David . . . . Sep 98
Saudi
bin Laden, Osama . . . . Apr 02
Savimbi, Jonas . . . . WorLdr V.2
Scarry, Richard. . . . . Sep 94
Schroeder, Pat . . . . Jan 97
Schulz, Charles M . . Author V.2; Update 00
Schwarzkopf, H. Norman. . . . . Jan 92
Schwikert, Tasha. . . . . Sport V.7
science competitions
Cohen, Adam Ezra . . . . Apr 97
Lisanti, Mariangela. . . . . Sep 01

Patterson, Ryan. . . . . Science V.7
Pine, Elizabeth Michele. . . . . Jan 94
Risca, Viviana. . . . . Sep 00
Rosa, Emily . . . . Sep 98
Toro, Natalia . . . . Sep 99
Vasan, Nina. . . . . Science V.7
scientists
Alvarez, Luis W. . . . . Science V.3
Asimov, Isaac . . . . Jul 92
Askins, Renee. . . . . WorLdr V.1
Attenborough, David. . . . . Science V.4
Ballard, Robert . . . . Science V.4
Bardeen, John . . . . Science V.1
Barton, Hazel . . . . Science V.6
Berners-Lee, Tim . . . . Science V.7
Bethe, Hans A. . . . . Science V.3
Brundtland, Gro Harlem . . . . . . Science V.3
Calderone, Mary S.. . . . . Science V.3
Carson, Ben. . . . . Science V.4
Carson, Rachel . . . . WorLdr V.1
Collins, Francis . . . . Science V.6
Córdova, France . . . . Science V.7
Cray, Seymour . . . . Science V.2
Earle, Sylvia. . . . . Science V.1
Elion, Gertrude . . . . Science V.6
Engelbart, Douglas. . . . . Science V.5
Fauci, Anthony S. . . . . Science V.7
Fossey, Dian . . . . Science V.1
Galdikas, Biruté. . . . . Science V.4
Gilbert, Walter . . . . Science V.2
Goodall, Jane. . . . . . . Science V.1; Update 02
Gould, Stephen Jay . . . . Science V.2;
    Update 02
Grandin, Temple . . . . Science V.3
Gwaltney, John Langston . . . . . Science V.3
Harris, Bernard . . . . Science V.3
Hawking, Stephen . . . . Apr 92
Healy, Bernadine . . . Science V.1; Update 01
Hendrickson, Sue . . . . Science V.7
Ho, David . . . . Science V.6
Horner, Jack . . . . Science V.1
Jackson, Shirley Ann . . . . Science V.2
Jemison, Mae. . . . . Oct 92
Krim, Mathilde . . . . Science V.1
Kurzweil, Raymond . . . . Science V.2
Leakey, Louis . . . . Science V.1
Leakey, Mary. . . . . Science V.1
Levi-Montalcini, Rita . . . . Science V.1
Love, Susan. . . . . Science V.3
Lowman, Meg. . . . . Science V.4

Lucid, Shannon . . . . Science V.2
Margulis, Lynn . . . . Sep 96
McClintock, Barbara . . . . Oct 92
Mead, Margaret . . . . Science V.2
Mittermeier, Russell A. . . . . WorLdr V.1
Moss, Cynthia . . . . WorLdr V.3
Ochoa, Severo . . . . Jan 94
Oppenheimer, J. Robert . . . . Science V.1
Patrick, Ruth . . . . Science V.3
Pauling, Linus . . . . Jan 95
Ride, Sally . . . . Jan 92
Rodriguez, Eloy . . . . Science V.2
Sabin, Albert . . . . Science V.1
Sacks, Oliver . . . . Science V.3
Sagan, Carl . . . . Science V.1
Salk, Jonas . . . . Jan 94; Update 95
Satcher, David . . . . Sep 98
Thomas, Lewis . . . . Apr 94
Tuttle, Merlin . . . . Apr 97
Villa-Komaroff, Lydia . . . . Science V.6
Watson, James D. . . . . Science V.1
Scieszka, Jon . . . . Author V.9
Scottish
Muir, John . . . . WorLdr V.3
screenwriters
Affleck, Ben . . . . Sep 99
Carter, Chris . . . . Author V.4
Crichton, Michael . . . . Author V.5
Mathison, Melissa . . . . Author V.4
Peet, Bill . . . . Author V.4
Whedon, Joss . . . . Author V.9
Williamson, Kevin . . . . Author V.6
sculptors
see artists
Scurry, Briana . . . . Jan 00
Sealfon, Rebecca . . . . Sep 97
Seinfeld, Jerry . . . . Oct 92; Update 98
Selena . . . . Jan 96
Seles, Monica . . . . Jan 96
senators
Clinton, Hillary Rodham . . . . Apr 93;
Update 94; Update 95; Update 96; Update
99; Update 00; Update 01
Dole, Bob . . . . Jan 96; Update 96
Glenn, John . . . . Jan 99
Gore, Al . . . . . . Jan 93; Update 96; Update 97;
Update 98; Update 99; Update 00; Update
01
McCain, John . . . . Apr 00
Nelson, Gaylord . . . . WorLdr V.3
Nixon, Richard . . . . Sep 94

Sendak, Maurice . . . . Author V.2
Senegalese
Senghor, Léopold Sédar . . . . . . WorLdr V.2
Senghor, Léopold Sédar . . . . . . WorLdr V.2
Serbian
Milosevic, Slobodan . . . Sep 99; Update 00;
Update 01; Update 02
Seuss, Dr. . . . . Jan 92
Shabazz, Betty . . . . Apr 98
Shakira . . . . PerfArt V.1
Shakur, Tupac . . . . Apr 97
Shatner, William . . . . Apr 95
Shea, Jim, Jr. . . . . Sport V.8
Shula, Don . . . . Apr 96
Silva, Fabiola da
see da Silva, Fabiola . . . . Sport V.9
Silverstein, Shel . . . . Author V.3; Update 99
Simmons, Ruth . . . . Sep 02
Sinatra, Frank . . . . Jan 99
singers
see music
Siskel, Gene . . . . Sep 99
skateboarding
Hawk, Tony . . . . Apr 01
skating (ice)
Baiul, Oksana . . . . Apr 95
Blair, Bonnie . . . . Apr 94; Update 95
Harding, Tonya . . . . Sep 94
Hughes, Sarah . . . . Jan 03
Jansen, Dan . . . . Apr 94
Kerrigan, Nancy . . . . Apr 94
Kwan, Michelle . . . . . . Sport V.3; Update 02
Lipinski, Tara . . . . Apr 98
Ohno, Apolo . . . . Sport V.8
Yamaguchi, Kristi . . . . Apr 92
skating (in-line)
da Silva, Fabiola . . . . Sport V.9
skeleton
Shea, Jim, Jr. . . . . Sport V.8
skiing
Amman, Simon . . . . Sport V.8
Bahrke, Shannon . . . . Sport V.8
Moseley, Jonny . . . . Sport V.8
Street, Picabo . . . . Sport V.3
Sleator, William . . . . Author V.11
sled-dog racing
Butcher, Susan . . . . Sport V.1
Zirkle, Aliy . . . . Sport V.6
Small, David . . . . Author V.10
Smith, Emmitt . . . . Sep 94
Smith, Will . . . . Sep 94

Smyers, Karen . . . . Sport V.4
Snicket, Lemony . . . . Author V.12
snowboarding
  Clark, Kelly . . . . Sport V.8
  Dakides, Tara . . . . Sport V.7
  Klug, Chris . . . . Sport V.8
soccer
  Chastain, Brandi . . . . . Sport V.4; Update 00
  Hamm, Mia . . . . Sport V.2; Update 00
  Lalas, Alexi . . . . Sep 94
  Mathis, Clint . . . . Apr 03
  Pelé . . . . Sport V.1
  Scurry, Briana . . . . Jan 00
softball
  Fernandez, Lisa . . . . Sport V.5
  Richardson, Dot . . . . . Sport V.2; Update 00
Somalian
  Aidid, Mohammed Farah . . . . . WorLdr V.2
Sones, Sonya . . . . Author V.11
Soren, Tabitha . . . . Jan 97
Sorenstam, Annika . . . . Sport V.6
Sosa, Sammy . . . . Jan 99; Update 99
Soto, Gary . . . . Author V.5
South Africans
  de Klerk, F.W. . . . . Apr 94; Update 94
  Mandela, Nelson . . . . Jan 92; Update 94;
    Update 01
  Mandela, Winnie . . . . WorLdr V.2
South Korean
  Pak, Se Ri . . . . Sport V.4
Spaniards
  Domingo, Placido . . . . Sep 95
  Garcia, Sergio . . . . Sport V.7
  Iglesias, Enrique . . . . Jan 03
  Sanchez Vicario, Arantxa . . . . Sport V.1
Speare, Elizabeth George . . . . Sep 95
Spears, Britney . . . . Jan 01
spelling bee competition
  Andrews, Ned . . . . Sep 94
  Guey, Wendy . . . . Sep 96
  Hooper, Geoff . . . . Jan 94
  Maxwell, Jody-Anne . . . . Sep 98
  Sealfon, Rebecca . . . . Sep 97
  Thampy, George . . . . Sep 00
Spelman, Lucy . . . . Science V.6
Spencer, Diana
  see Diana, Princess of Wales . . . . Jul 92;
    Update 96; Update 97; Jan 98
Spielberg, Steven . . . . Jan 94; Update 94;
  Update 95

Spinelli, Jerry . . . . Apr 93
Spock, Dr. Benjamin . . . . Sep 95; Update 98
sports
  Aaron, Hank . . . . Sport V.1
  Abdul-Jabbar, Kareem . . . . Sport V.1
  Agassi, Andre . . . . Jul 92
  Aikman, Troy . . . . Apr 95; Update 01
  Ali, Muhammad . . . . Sport V.2
  Allen, Marcus . . . . Sep 97
  Allen, Tori . . . . Sport V.9
  Ammann, Simon . . . . Sport V.8
  Andretti, Mario . . . . Sep 94
  Armstrong, Lance . . . . . . Sep 00; Update 00;
    Update 01; Update 02
  Ashe, Arthur . . . . Sep 93
  Bahrke, Shannon . . . . Sport V.8
  Bailey, Donovan . . . . Sport V.2
  Baiul, Oksana . . . . Apr 95
  Barkley, Charles . . . . Apr 92; Update 02
  Beachley, Layne . . . . Sport V.9
  Bird, Larry . . . . Jan 92; Update 98
  Bird, Sue . . . . Sport V.9
  Blair, Bonnie . . . . Apr 94
  Bonds, Barry . . . . Jan 03
  Boulmerka, Hassiba . . . . Sport V.1
  Brady, Tom . . . . Sport V.7
  Bryant, Kobe . . . . Apr 99
  Butcher, Susan . . . . Sport V.1
  Capriati, Jennifer . . . . Sport V.6
  Carter, Vince . . . . Sport V.5; Update 01
  Chamberlain, Wilt . . . . Sport V.4
  Chastain, Brandi . . . . . Sport V.4; Update 00
  Clark, Kelly . . . . Sport V.8
  Dakides, Tara . . . . Sport V.7
  Daniel, Beth . . . . Sport V.1
  da Silva, Fabiola . . . . Sport V.9
  Davenport, Lindsay . . . . Sport V.5
  Dayne, Ron . . . . Apr 00
  Devers, Gail . . . . Sport V.2
  Dragila, Stacy . . . . Sport V.6
  Driscoll, Jean . . . . Sep 97
  Dumars, Joe . . . . Sport V.3; Update 99
  Dunlap, Alison . . . . Sport V.7
  Earnhardt, Dale . . . . Apr 01
  Elway, John . . . . Sport V.2; Update 99
  Evans, Janet . . . . Jan 95
  Evert, Chris . . . . Sport V.1
  Ewing, Patrick . . . . Jan 95; Update 02
  Favre, Brett . . . . Sport V.2
  Fedorov, Sergei . . . . Apr 94; Update 94

Fernandez, Lisa . . . . Sport V.5
Flowers, Vonetta. . . . . Sport V.8
Freeman, Cathy . . . . Jan 01
Fu Mingxia . . . . Sport V.5
Garcia, Sergio . . . . Sport V.7
Garnett, Kevin . . . . Sport V.6
George, Eddie. . . . . Sport V.6
Gordon, Jeff. . . . . Apr 99
Graf, Steffi. . . . . Jan 92; Update 01
Granato, Cammi. . . . . Sport V.8
Gretzky, Wayne . . . . Jan 92; Update 93;
   Update 99
Griese, Brian. . . . . Jan 02
Griffey, Ken, Jr. . . . . Sport V.1
Griffith Joyner, Florence. . . . . Sport V.1;
   Update 98
Hamm, Mia. . . . . Sport V.2; Update 00
Harbaugh, Jim . . . . Sport V.3
Hardaway, Anfernee "Penny" . . . Sport V.2
Harding, Tonya. . . . . Sep 94
Hasek, Dominik . . . . Sport V.3
Hawk, Tony. . . . . Apr 01
Hernandez, Livan. . . . . Apr 98
Hill, Grant . . . . Sport V.1
Hingis, Martina . . . . Sport V.2
Hogan, Hulk . . . . Apr 92
Holdsclaw, Chamique. . . . . Sep 00
Howe, Gordie. . . . . Sport V.2
Hughes, Sarah . . . . Jan 03
Iverson, Allen . . . . Sport V.7
Jackson, Bo . . . . Jan 92; Update 93
Jagr, Jaromir . . . . Sport V.5
Jansen, Dan. . . . . Apr 94
Jeter, Derek . . . . Sport V.4
Johnson, Jimmy. . . . . Jan 98
Johnson, Magic . . . . Apr 92; Update 02
Johnson, Michael. . . . . . . Jan 97; Update 00
Johnson, Randy . . . . Sport V.9
Jones, Marion . . . . Sport V.5
Jordan, Michael. . . . . Jan 92; Update 93;
   Update 94; Update 95; Update 99; Update
   01
Joyner-Kersee, Jackie. . . . . . Oct 92; Update
   96; Update 97; Update 98
Kerrigan, Nancy . . . . Apr 94
Kidd, Jason . . . . Sport V.9
Kiraly, Karch . . . . Sport V.4
Klug, Chris . . . . Sport V.8
Kwan, Michelle. . . . . . . Sport V.3; Update 02
Lalas, Alexi . . . . Sep 94
Lee, Jeanette . . . . Apr 03

Lemieux, Mario. . . . . Jul 92; Update 93
LeMond, Greg . . . . Sport V.1
Lewis, Carl. . . . . Sep 96; Update 97
Lipinski, Tara. . . . . Apr 98
Lobo, Rebecca. . . . . Sport V.3
Lowe, Alex . . . . Sport V.4
Madden, John . . . . Sep 97
Maddux, Greg. . . . . Sport V.3
Manning, Peyton . . . . Sep 00
Mantle, Mickey . . . . Jan 96
Marino, Dan . . . . Apr 93; Update 00
Martinez, Pedro . . . . Sport V.5
Mathis, Clint . . . . Apr 03
McGwire, Mark . . . . Jan 99; Update 99
McNabb, Donovan. . . . . Apr 03
Messier, Mark . . . . Apr 96
Miller, Shannon . . . . Sep 94; Update 96
Mirra, Dave . . . . Sep 02
Moceanu, Dominique. . . . . Jan 98
Montana, Joe . . . . Jan 95; Update 95
Moseley, Jonny. . . . . Sport V.8
Moss, Randy . . . . Sport V.4
Muldowney, Shirley. . . . . Sport V.7
Murray, Ty. . . . . Sport V.7
Navratilova, Martina . . . . Jan 93; Update 94
Ndeti, Cosmas. . . . . Sep 95
Nicklaus, Jack . . . . Sport V.2
Ohno, Apolo. . . . . Sport V.8
Olajuwon, Hakeem . . . . Sep 95
O'Neal, Shaquille . . . . Sep 93
Otto, Sylke . . . . Sport V.8
Pak, Se Ri . . . . Sport V.4
Payton, Walter . . . . Jan 00
Pelé . . . . Sport V.1
Petty, Richard . . . . Sport V.2
Pippen, Scottie . . . . Oct 92
Pippig, Uta . . . . Sport V.1
Rice, Jerry. Apr 93
Richardson, Dot . . . . . Sport V.2; Update 00
Riley, Dawn. . . . . Sport V.4
Ripken, Cal, Jr. . . . . . . Sport V.1; Update 01
Roba, Fatuma . . . . Sport V.3
Robinson, David . . . . Sep 96
Robinson, Jackie . . . . Sport V.3
Roddick, Andy . . . . Jan 03
Rodman, Dennis . . . . Apr 96; Update 99
Rodriguez, Alex . . . . Sport V.6
Rose, Pete . . . . Jan 92
Roy, Patrick. . . . . Sport V.7
Rudolph, Wilma . . . . Apr 95
Runyan, Marla. . . . . Apr 02

Ryan, Nolan. . . . . Oct 92; Update 93
Sakic, Joe. . . . . Sport V.6
Sampras, Pete. . . . . Jan 97; Update 02
Sanchez Vicario, Arantxa . . . . Sport V.1
Sanders, Barry . . . . Sep 95; Update 99
Sanders, Deion. . . . . Sport V.1
Sapp, Warren . . . . Sport V.5
Schwikert, Tasha . . . . Sport V.7
Scurry, Briana. . . . . Jan 00
Seles, Monica. . . . . Jan 96
Shea, Jim, Jr. . . . . Sport V.8
Shula, Don. Apr 96
Smith, Emmitt. . . . . Sep 94
Smyers, Karen . . . . Sport V.4
Sorenstam, Annika . . . . Sport V.6
Sosa, Sammy . . . . Jan 99; Update 99
Stewart, Kordell . . . . Sep 98
Stewart, Tony . . . . Sport V.9
Stiles, Jackie . . . . Sport V.6
Stockton, John . . . . Sport V.3
Street, Picabo . . . . Sport V.3
Summitt, Pat. . . . . Sport V.3
Swoopes, Sheryl. . . . . Sport V.2
Thompson, Jenny. . . . . Sport V.5
Van Dyken, Amy . . . . Sport V.3; Update 00
Ventura, Jesse . . . . Apr 99; Update 02
Vernon, Mike . . . . Jan 98; Update 02
Vick, Michael . . . . Sport V.9
Ward, Charlie . . . . Apr 94
Warner, Kurt. . . . . Sport V.4
Webb, Alan . . . . Sep 01
Webb, Karrie . . . . Sport V.5; Update 01;
    Update 02
Weinke, Chris . . . . Apr 01
White, Reggie. . . . . Jan 98
Williams, Serena . . . . Sport V.4; Update 00;
    Update 02
Williams, Ted . . . . Sport V.9
Williams, Venus . . . . Jan 99; Update 00;
    Update 01; Update 02
Willingham, Tyrone . . . . Sep 02
Winfield, Dave. . . . . Jan 93
Woods, Tiger . . . . Sport V.1; Update 00;
    Sport V.6
Yamaguchi, Kristi . . . . Apr 92
Yelas, Jay. Sport V.9
Young, Steve . . . . Jan 94; Update 00
Yzerman, Steve. . . . . Sport V.2
Zirkle, Aliy. . . . . Sport V.6
Zmeskal, Kim. . . . . Jan 94
Stachowski, Richie . . . . Science V.3

Stanford, John . . . . Sep 99
Steinem, Gloria . . . . Oct 92
Stern, Isaac. . . . . PerfArt V.1
Stewart, Kordell . . . . Sep 98
Stewart, Patrick. . . . . Jan 94
Stewart, Tony. . . . . Sport V.9
Stiles, Jackie. . . . . Sport V.6
Stine, R.L. . . . . Apr 94
Stockman, Shawn
    see Boyz II Men. . . . . Jan 96
Stockton, John . . . . Sport V.3
Strasser, Todd . . . . Author V.7
Street, Picabo . . . . Sport V.3
Strug, Kerri . . . . Sep 96
Summitt, Pat. . . . . Sport V.3
Supreme Court
    Blackmun, Harry . . . . Jan 00
    Burger, Warren . . . . Sep 95
    Ginsburg, Ruth Bader . . . . Jan 94
    Marshall, Thurgood. . . . . Jan 92; Update 93
    O'Connor, Sandra Day . . . . Jul 92
    Thomas, Clarence . . . . Jan 92
surfer
    Beachley, Layne . . . . Sport V.9
Suzuki, Shinichi . . . . Sep 98
Swanson, Janese . . . . Science V.4
Swedish
    Lindgren, Astrid . . . . Author V.13
    Sorenstam, Annika . . . . Sport V.6
swimming
    Evans, Janet . . . . Jan 95; Update 96
    Thompson, Jenny. . . . . Sport V.5
    Van Dyken, Amy . . . . Sport V.3; Update 00
Swiss
    Ammann, Simon . . . . Sport V.8
Swoopes, Sheryl . . . . Sport V.2
Taiwanese
    Ho, David . . . . Science V.6
Tan, Amy. . . . . Author V.9
Tanzanian
    Nyerere, Julius Kambarage . . . WorLdr V.2;
        Update 99
Tarbox, Katie. . . . . Author V.10
Tartakovsky, Genndy . . . . Author V.11
Tartar
    Nureyev, Rudolph . . . . Apr 93
Tarvin, Herbert . . . . Apr 97
Taylor, Mildred D. . . . . Author V.1;
    Update 02
Taymor, Julie . . . . PerfArt V.1

teachers

see educators

television

Alba, Jessica . . . . Sep 01
Allen, Tim . . . . Apr 94; Update 99
Alley, Kirstie . . . . Jul 92
Amanpour, Christiane . . . . Jan 01
Anderson, Gillian . . . . Jan 97
Aniston, Jennifer. . . . . Apr 99
Arnold, Roseanne . . . . Oct 92
Attenborough, David . . . . Science V.4
Bergen, Candice . . . . Sep 93
Bialik, Mayim . . . . Jan 94
Blanchard, Rachel . . . . Apr 97
Bledel, Alexis . . . . Jan 03
Brandis, Jonathan . . . . Sep 95
Brandy . . . . Apr 96
Bryan, Zachery Ty . . . . Jan 97
Burke, Chris. Sep 93
Burns, Ken . . . . Jan 95
Cameron, Candace. . . . . Apr 95
Campbell, Neve . . . . Apr 98
Candy, John. Sep 94
Carter, Chris. . . . . Author V.4
Carvey, Dana . . . . Jan 93
Chung, Connie . . . . Jan 94; Update 95;
    Update 96
Clarkson, Kelly. . . . . Jan 03
Cosby, Bill. . . . . Jan 92
Cousteau, Jacques . . . . Jan 93
Crawford, Cindy . . . . Apr 93
Crichton, Michael . . . . Author V.5
Daly, Carson . . . . Apr 00
Doherty, Shannen . . . . . Apr 92; Update 94
Duchovny, David . . . . Apr 96
Duff, Hilary . . . . Sep 02
Ellerbee, Linda . . . . Apr 94
Fuentes, Daisy . . . . Jan 94
Garth, Jennie. . . . . Apr 96
Gellar, Sarah Michelle. . . . . Jan 99
Gilbert, Sara . . . . Apr 93
Goldberg, Whoopi . . . . Apr 94
Goodman, John . . . . Sep 95
Groening, Matt . . . . Jan 92
Gumbel, Bryant. . . . . Apr 97
Guy, Jasmine. . . . . Sep 93
Hart, Melissa Joan . . . . Jan 94
Hewitt, Jennifer Love. . . . . Sep 00
Holmes, Katie . . . . Jan 00
Hunter-Gault, Charlayne . . . . Jan 00

Irwin, Steve . . . . Science V.7
Jennings, Peter . . . . Jul 92
Leno, Jay . . . . Jul 92
Letterman, David. . . . . Jan 95
Lewis, Shari . . . . Jan 99
Limbaugh, Rush . . . . Sep 95; Update 02
Locklear, Heather . . . . Jan 95
Mac, Bernie . . . . PerfArt V.1
Madden, John . . . . Sep 97
Muniz, Frankie. . . . . Jan 01
Nye, Bill. . . . . Science V.2
O'Donnell, Rosie . . . . . . Apr 97; Update 02
Oleynik, Larisa . . . . Sep 96
Olsen, Ashley . . . . Sep 95
Olsen, Mary Kate . . . . Sep 95
Pauley, Jane. Oct 92
Perry, Luke. . . . . Jan 92
Priestley, Jason . . . . Apr 92
Probst, Jeff . . . . Jan 01
Roberts, Cokie. . . . . Apr 95
Sagan, Carl . . . . Science V.1
Seinfeld, Jerry . . . . Oct 92; Update 98
Shatner, William. . . . . Apr 95
Siskel, Gene. Sep 99
Smith, Will. . . . . Sep 94
Soren, Tabitha . . . . Jan 97
Stewart, Patrick . . . . Jan 94
Tartakovsky, Genndy . . . . Author V.11
Thiessen, Tiffani-Amber . . . . Jan 96
Thomas, Jonathan Taylor. . . . . Apr 95
Vidal, Christina . . . . PerfArt V.1
Walters, Barbara . . . . Sep 94
Watson, Barry . . . . Sep 02
Wayans, Keenen Ivory . . . . Jan 93
Whedon, Joss . . . . Author V.9
White, Jaleel. Jan 96
Williams, Robin. . . . . Apr 92
Williamson, Kevin. . . . . Author V.6
Winfrey, Oprah. . . . . Apr 92; Update 00
Zamora, Pedro . . . . Apr 95

tennis

Agassi, Andre . . . . Jul 92
Ashe, Arthur . . . . Sep 93
Capriati, Jennifer . . . . Sport V.6
Davenport, Lindsay . . . . Sport V.5
Evert, Chris . . . . Sport V.1
Graf, Steffi. . . . . Jan 92; Update 01
Hingis, Martina . . . . Sport V.2
Navratilova, Martina . . . . Jan 93; Update 94
Roddick, Andy . . . . Jan 03
Sampras, Pete. . . . . Jan 97; Update 02

Sanchez Vicario, Arantxa . . . . Sport V.1
Seles, Monica . . . . Jan 96
Williams, Serena . . . . Sport V.4; Update 00;
  Update 02
Williams, Venus . . . . Jan 99; Update 00;
  Update 01; Update 02
Tenzin Gyatso
  see Dalai Lama . . . . Sep 98
Teresa, Mother . . . . Apr 98
Thampy, George . . . . Sep 00
Thiessen, Tiffani-Amber . . . . Jan 96
Thomas, Clarence . . . . Jan 92
Thomas, Dave . . . . Apr 96; Update 02
Thomas, Jonathan Taylor . . . . Apr 95
Thomas, Lewis . . . . Apr 94
Thompson, Jenny . . . . Sport V.5
Tibetan
  Dalai Lama . . . . Sep 98
Timberlake, Justin
  see *N Sync . . . . Jan 01
Tolkien, J.R.R. . . . . Jan 02
Tompkins, Douglas . . . . WorLdr V.3
Toro, Natalia . . . . Sep 99
track
  Bailey, Donovan . . . . Sport V.2
  Devers, Gail . . . . Sport V.2
  Dragila, Stacy . . . . Sport V.6
  Griffith Joyner, Florence . . . . Sport V.1;
    Update 98
  Freeman, Cathy . . . . Jan 01
  Johnson, Michael . . . . Jan 97; Update 00
  Jones, Marion . . . . Sport V.5
  Joyner-Kersee, Jackie . . . . . . Oct 92; Update
    96; Update 97; Update 98
  Lewis, Carl . . . . Sep 96; Update 97
  Rudolph, Wilma . . . . Apr 95
  Runyan, Marla . . . . Apr 02
Travers, P.L. . . . . Author V.2
triathalon
  Smyers, Karen . . . . Sport V.4
Trinidadian
  Guy, Rosa . . . . Author V.9
Tubman, William V. S. . . . . WorLdr V.2
Tucker, Chris . . . . Jan 01
Tuttle, Merlin . . . . Apr 97
Twain, Shania . . . . Apr 99
Uchida, Mitsuko . . . . Apr 99
Ugandan
  Amin, Idi . . . . WorLdr V.2
Ukrainians
  Baiul, Oksana . . . . Apr 95
  Stern, Isaac . . . . PerfArt V.1

United Nations
– **Ambassadors to**
  Albright, Madeleine . . . . Apr 97
  Bush, George . . . . Jan 92
– **Secretaries General**
  Annan, Kofi . . . . Jan 98; Update 01
  Boutros-Ghali, Boutros . . . . Apr 93;
    Update 98
United States
– **Attorney General**
  Reno, Janet . . . . Sep 93; Update 98
– **First Ladies**
  Bush, Barbara . . . . Jan 92
  Bush, Laura . . . . Apr 03
  Clinton, Hillary Rodham . . . . Apr 93;
    Update 94; Update 95; Update 96; Update
    99; Update 00; Update 01
– **Joint Chiefs of Staff, Chairman**
  Powell, Colin . . . . Jan 92; Update 93;
    Update 95; Update 01
– **National Institutes of Health**
  Collins, Francis . . . . Science V.6
  Fauci, Anthony S. . . . . Science V.7
  Healy, Bernadine . . . . Science V.1;
    Update 01
– **National Security Advisor**
  Rice, Condoleezza . . . . Apr 02
– **Nuclear Regulatory Commission**
  Jackson, Shirley Ann . . . . Science V.2
– **Presidents**
  Bush, George . . . . Jan 92
  Bush, George W. . . . . . . Sep 00; Update 00;
    Update 01; Update 02
  Carter, Jimmy . . . . Apr 95; Update 02
  Clinton, Bill . . . . Jul 92; Update 94;
    Update 95; Update 96; Update 97; Update
    98; Update 99; Update 00; Update 01
  Nixon, Richard . . . . Sep 94
– **Secretary of Commerce**
  Brown, Ron . . . . Sep 96
– **Secretary of Defense**
  Cheney, Dick . . . . Jan 02
– **Secretary of Housing and
  Urban Development**
  Cisneros, Henry . . . . Sep 93
– **Secretary of Interior**
  Babbitt, Bruce . . . . Jan 94
– **Secretary of Labor**
  Dole, Elizabeth Hanford . . . . Jul 92;
    Update 96; Update 99

– Secretaries of State
  Albright, Madeleine . . . . Apr 97
  Baker, James. . . . . Oct 92
– Secretary of Transportation
  Dole, Elizabeth . . . . Jul 92; Update 96;
  Update 99
– Secretary of Treasury
  Baker, James. . . . . Oct 92
– Senate Majority Leader
  Dole, Bob. . . . . Jan 96; Update 96
– Speaker of the House of
  Representatives
  Gingrich, Newt. . . . . . . Apr 95; Update 99
– Supreme Court Justices
  Blackmun, Harry . . . . Jan 00
  Burger, Warren . . . . Sep 95
  Ginsburg, Ruth Bader . . . . Jan 94
  Marshall, Thurgood . . . Jan 92; Update 93
  O'Connor, Sandra Day. . . . . Jul 92
  Thomas, Clarence. . . . . Jan 92
– Surgeons General
  Novello, Antonia . . . . . Apr 92; Update 93
  Satcher, David . . . . Sep 98
– Vice-Presidents
  Bush, George . . . . Jan 92
  Cheney, Dick . . . . Jan 02
  Gore, Al . . . . Jan 93; Update 96;
  Update 97; Update 98; Update 99; Up-
  date 00; Update 01
  Nixon, Richard. . . . . Sep 94
Usher. . . . . PerfArt V.1
Van Allsburg, Chris . . . . Apr 92
Van Draanen, Wendelin. . . . . . Author V.11
Van Dyken, Amy. . . . . Sport V.3; Update 00
Van Meter, Vicki . . . . Jan 95
Vasan, Nina . . . . Science V.7
Ventura, Jesse. . . . . Apr 99; Update 02
Vernon, Mike. . . . . Jan 98; Update 02
veterinarians
  Herriot, James . . . . Author V.1
  Spelman, Lucy . . . . Science V.6
Vice-Presidents
  Bush, George . . . . Jan 92
  Cheney, Dick . . . . Jan 02
  Gore, Al . . . . Jan 93; Update 96;
  Update 97; Update 98; Update 99; Update
  00; Update 01
  Nixon, Richard . . . . Sep 94
Vick, Michael. . . . . Sport V.9
Vidal, Christina . . . . PerfArt V.1

Villa-Komaroff, Lydia . . . . Science V.6
Vincent, Mark
  see Diesel, Vin. . . . . Jan 03
Voigt, Cynthia . . . . Oct 92
volleyball
  Kiraly, Karch. . . . . Sport V.4
Vonnegut, Kurt, Jr. . . . . Author V.1
Wa, Ka Hsaw
  see Ka Hsaw Wa. . . . . WorLdr V.3
Walters, Barbara. . . . . Sep 94
Wang, An. . . . . Science V.2
Ward, Charlie . . . . Apr 94
Ward, Lloyd D. . . . . Jan 01
Warhol, Andy. . . . . Artist V.1
Warner, Kurt. . . . . Sport V.4
Washington, Denzel . . . . Jan 93; Update 02
Watson, Barry . . . . Sep 02
Watson, Emma . . . . Apr 03
Watson, James D.. . . . . Science V.1
Watson, Paul . . . . WorLdr V.1
Watterson, Bill. . . . . Jan 92
Wayans, Keenen Ivory . . . . Jan 93
Webb, Alan. Sep 01
Webb, Karrie . . . . Sport V.5; Update 01;
  Update 02
Weinke, Chris. . . . . Apr 01
Werbach, Adam . . . . WorLdr V.1
Whedon, Joss . . . . Author V.9
White, E.B.. . . . . Author V.1
White, Jaleel. . . . . Jan 96
White, Reggie . . . . Jan 98
White, Ruth . . . . Author V.11
Whitestone, Heather . . . . Apr 95; Update 02
Wilder, Laura Ingalls. . . . . Author V.3
WilderBrathwaite, Gloria . . . . . Science V.7
Williams, Garth . . . . Author V.2
Williams, Michelle
  see Destiny's Child . . . . Apr 01
Williams, Robin. . . . . Apr 92
Williams, Serena . . . . Sport V.4; Update 00;
  Update 02
Williams, Ted. . . . . Sport V.9
Williams, Venus. . . . . . . Jan 99; Update 00;
  Update 01; Update 02
Williamson, Kevin. . . . . Author V.6
Willingham, Tyrone . . . . Sep 02
Wilson, August. . . . . Author V.4
Wilson, Mara . . . . Jan 97
Winans, CeCe . . . . Apr 00
Winfield, Dave . . . . Jan 93

Winfrey, Oprah . . . . Apr 92; Update 00
Winslet, Kate . . . . Sep 98
Witherspoon, Reese . . . . Apr 03
Wojtyla, Karol Josef
  see John Paul II . . . . Oct 92; Update 94;
    Update 95
Wolf, Hazel. . . . . WorLdr V.3
Wolff, Virginia Euwer . . . . Author V.13
Wood, Elijah . . . . Apr 02
Woods, Tiger . . . . Sport V.1; Update 00;
    Sport V.6
Woodson, Jacqueline . . . . Author V.7;
    Update 01
World Wide Web
  see **Internet**
Wortis, Avi
  see **Avi** . . . . Jan 93
Wozniak, Steve . . . . Science V.5
Wrede, Patricia C.. . . . . Author V.7
wrestling
  Hogan, Hulk . . . . Apr 92
  Ventura, Jesse . . . . Apr 99; Update 02

Wright, Frank Lloyd. . . . . Artist V.1
Wright, Richard . . . . Author V.5
Yamaguchi, Kristi . . . . Apr 92
Yelas, Jay. . . . . Sport V.9
Yeltsin, Boris . . . . Apr 92; Update 93;
    Update 95; Update 96; Update 98; Update 00
Yep, Laurence . . . . Author V.5
Yolen, Jane. . . . . Author V.7
Young, Steve . . . . Jan 94; Update 00
Yzerman, Steve . . . . Sport V.2
Zairian
  Mobutu Sese Seko . . . . WorLdr V.2;
    Update 97
Zambian
  Kaunda, Kenneth . . . . WorLdr V.2
Zamora, Pedro . . . . Apr 95
Zimbabwean
  Mugabe, Robert . . . . WorLdr V.2
Zindel, Paul . . . . Author V.1; Update 02
Zirkle, Aliy . . . . Sport V.6
Zmeskal, Kim . . . . Jan 9

Places of Birth Index

The following index lists the places of birth for the individuals profiled in *Biography Today*. Places of birth are entered under state, province, and/or country.

Alabama

Aaron, Hank – *Mobile* . . . . Sport V.1
Allen, Tori – *Auburn* . . . . Sport V.9
Barkley, Charles – *Leeds* . . . . Apr 92
Flowers, Vonetta – *Birmingham* . . Sport V.8
Fuller, Millard – *Lanett* . . . . Apr 03
Hamm, Mia – *Selma* . . . . Sport V.2
Hurston, Zora Neale
  – *Notasulga* . . . . Author V.6
Jackson, Bo – *Bessemer* . . . . Jan 92
Jemison, Mae – *Decatur* . . . . Oct 92
Johnson, Angela – *Tuskegee* . . . . Author V.6
Johnson, Lonnie – *Mobile* . . . . . Science V.4
Lee, Harper – *Monroeville* . . . . . . Author V.9
Lewis, Carl – *Birmingham* . . . . Sep 96
Lewis, John – *Pike County* . . . . Jan 03
Parks, Rosa – *Tuskegee* . . . . Apr 92
Rice, Condoleezza – *Birmingham* . . . Apr 02
Satcher, David – *Anniston* . . . . Sep 98
Whitestone, Heather – *Dothan* . . . . . Apr 95

Algeria

Boulmerka, Hassiba
  – *Constantine* . . . . Sport V.1

Angola

Savimbi, Jonas – *Munhango* . . . WorLdr V.2

Arizona

Chavez, Cesar – *Yuma* . . . . Sep 93
Chavez, Julz – *Yuma* . . . . Sep 02
Farmer, Nancy – *Phoenix* . . . . . . Author V.6
Morrison, Sam – *Flagstaff* . . . . Sep 97
Murray, Ty – *Phoenix* . . . . Sport V.7
Strug, Kerri – *Tucson* . . . . Sep 96

Arkansas

Bates, Daisy – *Huttig* . . . . Apr 00
Clinton, Bill – *Hope* . . . . Jul 92
Clinton, Chelsea – *Little Rock* . . . . . . Apr 96
Grisham, John – *Jonesboro* . . . . . Author V.1
Johnson, John – *Arkansas City* . . . . . Jan 97
Pippen, Scottie – *Hamburg* . . . . Oct 92

Australia

Beachley, Layne – *Sydney* . . . . Sport V.9
Freeman, Cathy – *Mackay,*
  Queensland . . . . Jan 01
Irwin, Steve – *Victoria* . . . . Science V.7
Norman, Greg – *Mt. Isa, Queensland* Jan 94
Travers, P.L. – *Maryborough,*
  Queensland . . . . Author V.2
Webb, Karrie – *Ayr, Queensland* . . Sport V.5

Bosnia-Herzogovina

Filipovic, Zlata – *Sarajevo* . . . . Sep 94

Brazil

da Silva, Fabiola – *Sao Paulo* . . . . . Sport V.9
Mendes, Chico – *Xapuri, Acre* . . WorLdr V.1
Pelé – *Tres Coracoes,*
  Minas Gerais . . . . Sport V.1

Bulgaria

Christo – *Gabrovo* . . . . Sep 96

Burma

Aung San Suu Kyi – *Rangoon* . . . . . . Apr 96
Ka Hsaw Wa – *Rangoon* . . . . WorLdr V.3

California

Abdul, Paula – *Van Nuys* . . . . Jan 92
Adams, Ansel – *San Francisco* . . . . Artist V.1
Affleck, Ben – *Berkeley* . . . . Sep 99
Aikman, Troy – *West Covina* . . . . Apr 95
Alba, Jessica – *Pomona* . . . . Sep 01
Allen, Marcus – *San Diego* . . . . Sep 97
Alvarez, Luis W. – *San*
  Francisco . . . . Science V.3
Aniston, Jennifer – *Sherman Oaks* . . . Apr 99
Babbitt, Bruce – *Los Angeles* . . . . Jan 94
Bahrke, Shannon – *Tahoe City* . . . Sport V.8
Barrymore, Drew – *Los Angeles* . . . . . Jan 01
Bergen, Candice – *Beverly Hills* . . . . . Sep 93
Bialik, Mayim – *San Diego* . . . . Jan 94
Bonds, Barry – *Riverside* . . . . Jan 03
Brady, Tom – *San Mateo* . . . . Sport V.7
Breathed, Berke – *Encino* . . . . Jan 92
Brower, David – *Berkeley* . . . . . . WorLdr V.1

217

Cameron, Candace . . . . Apr 95
Carter, Chris – *Bellflower* . . . . . . Author V.4
Chastain, Brandi – *San Jose* . . . . . . Sport V.4
Coolio – *Los Angeles* . . . . Sep 96
Dakides, Tara – *Mission Viejo* . . . . Sport V.7
Davenport, Lindsay
   – *Palos Verdes* . . . . Sport V.5
DiCaprio, Leonardo – *Hollywood* . . . Apr 98
Dragila, Stacy – *Auburn* . . . . Sport V.6
Evans, Janet – *Fullerton* . . . . Jan 95
Fernandez, Lisa – *Long Beach* . . . . Sport V.5
Fielder, Cecil – *Los Angeles* . . . . Sep 93
Fields, Debbi – *East Oakland* . . . . Jan 96
Fossey, Dian – *San Francisco* . . . Science V.1
Garcia, Jerry – *San Francisco* . . . . Jan 96
Gilbert, Sara – *Santa Monica* . . . . Apr 93
Gordon, Jeff – *Vallejo* . . . . Apr 99
Griffith Joyner, Florence – *Los
   Angeles* . . . . Sport V.1
Hammer – *Oakland* . . . . Jan 92
Hanks, Tom – *Concord* . . . . Jan 96
Hawk, Tony – *San Diego* . . . . Apr 01
Jackson, Shirley – *San Francisco* . . Author V.6
Jobs, Steven – *San Francisco* . . . . Jan 92;
   Science V.5
Johnson, Johanna . . . . Apr 00
Johnson, Randy – *Walnut Creek* . . Sport V.9
Jones, Marion – *Los Angeles* . . . . . . Sport V.5
Kidd, Jason – *San Francisco* . . . . . . Sport V.9
Kistler, Darci – *Riverside* . . . . Jan 93
Kwan, Michelle –*Torrance* . . . . Sport V.3
LaDuke, Winona – *Los Angeles* . . WorLdr V.3
Lasseter, John – *Hollywood* . . . . Sep 00
Le Guin, Ursula K. – *Berkeley* . . . Author V.8
LeMond, Greg – *Los Angeles* . . . . . Sport V.1
Locklear, Heather – *Los Angeles* . . . . . Jan 95
Lucas, George – *Modesto* . . . . Apr 97
Mathison, Melissa . . . . Author V.4
McGwire, Mark – *Pomona* . . . . Jan 99
Moceanu, Dominique – *Hollywood* . . Jan 98
Nixon, Joan Lowery – *Los
   Angeles* . . . . Author V.1
Nixon, Richard – *Yorba Linda* . . . . . . Sep 94
Ochoa, Ellen – *Los Angeles* . . . . Apr 01
O'Dell, Scott – *Terminal Island* . . Author V.2
Oleynik, Larisa – *San Fancisco* . . . . . . Sep 96
Olsen, Ashley . . . . Sep 95
Olsen, Mary Kate . . . . Sep 95
Prinze, Freddie, Jr. – *Los Angeles* . . . Apr 00
Ride, Sally – *Encino* . . . . Jan 92
Runyan, Marla – *Santa Maria* . . . . . . Apr 02

Ryan, Pam Muñoz –
   Bakersfield . . . . Author V.12
Snicket, Lemony – *San
   Francisco* . . . . Author V.12
Soto, Gary – *Fresno* . . . . Author V.5
Stachowski, Richie . . . . Science V.3
Swanson, Janese – *San Diego* . . . Science V.4
Tan, Amy – *Oakland* . . . . Author V.9
Thiessen, Tiffini-Amber – *Modesto* . . . Jan 96
Werbach, Adam – *Tarzana* . . . . WorLdr V.1
White, Jaleel – *Los Angeles* . . . . Jan 96
Williams, Ted – *San Diego* . . . . Sport V.9
Williams, Venus – *Lynwood* . . . . Jan 99
Wilson, Mara – *Burbank* . . . . Jan 97
Woods, Tiger – *Long Beach* . . . . . . Sport V.1,
   Sport V.6
Wozniak, Steve – *San Jose* . . . . . Science V.5
Yamaguchi, Kristi – *Fremont* . . . . Apr 92
Yep, Laurence – *San Francisco* . . Author V.5
Canada
Blanchard, Rachel – *Toronto, Ontario* Apr 97
Campbell, Neve – *Toronto, Ontario* . . Apr 98
Candy, John – *Newmarket, Ontario* . . Sep 94
Carrey, Jim – *Newmarket, Ontario* . . . Apr 96
Dion, Celine – *Charlemagne, Quebec* . Sep 97
Gretzky, Wayne – *Brantford, Ontario* Jan 92
Howe, Gordie – *Floral,
   Saskatchewan* . . . . Sport V.2
Jennings, Peter – *Toronto, Ontario* . . . . Jul 92
Johnston, Lynn – *Collingwood,
   Ontario* . . . . Jan 99
Kielburger, Craig – *Toronto, Ontario* . . Jan 00
lang, k.d. – *Edmonton, Alberta* . . . . . . Sep 93
Lemieux, Mario – *Montreal, Quebec* . . Jul 92
Martin, Bernard – *Petty Harbor,
   Newfoundland* . . . . WorLdr V.3
Messier, Mark – *Edmonton, Alberta* . . Apr 96
Morissette, Alanis – *Ottawa, Ontario* Apr 97
Mowat, Farley – *Belleville,
   Ontario* . . . . Author V.8
Priestley, Jason – *Vancouver,
   British Columbia* . . . . Apr 92
Roy, Patrick – *Quebec City,
   Quebec* . . . . Sport V.7
Sakic, Joe – *Burnbary,
   British Columbia* . . . . Sport V.6
Shatner, William – *Montreal, Quebec* Apr 95
Twain, Shania – *Windsor, Ontario* . . . Apr 99
Vernon, Mike – *Calgary, Alberta* . . . . . Jan 98
Watson, Paul – *Toronto, Ontario* . . WorLdr V.1

Wolf, Hazel – *Victoria,*
  British Columbia . . . . WorLdr V.3
Yzerman, Steve – *Cranbrook,*
  British Columbia . . . . Sport V.2

China
Chan, Jackie – *Hong Kong* . . . . . . PerfArt V.1
Dai Qing – *Chongqing* . . . . WorLdr V.3
Fu Mingxia – *Wuhan* . . . . Sport V.5
Lucid, Shannon – *Shanghai* . . . . Science V.2
Paterson, Katherine – *Qing Jiang,*
  Jiangsu . . . . Author 97
Pei, I.M. – *Canton* . . . . Artist V.1
Wang, An – *Shanghai* . . . . Science V.2

Colombia
Shakira – *Barranquilla* . . . . PerfArt V.1

Colorado
Allen, Tim – *Denver* . . . . Apr 94
Bryan, Zachery Ty – *Aurora* . . . . Jan 97
Dunlap, Alison – *Denver* . . . . Sport V.7
Handler, Ruth – *Denver* . . . . Apr 98
Klug, Chris – *Vail* . . . . Sport V.8
Patterson, Ryan – *Grand*
  Junction . . . . Science V.7
Stachowski, Richie – *Denver*. . . Science V.3
Toro, Natalia – *Boulder* . . . . Sep 99
Van Dyken, Amy – *Englewood* . . . Sport V.3

Connecticut
Brandis, Jonathan – *Danbury* . . . . Sep 95
Bush, George W. – *New Haven* . . . . . Sep 00
dePaola, Tomie – *Meriden* . . . . . Author V.5
Land, Edwin – *Bridgeport* . . . . . . Science V.1
Leibovitz, Annie – *Waterbury* . . . . . . Sep 96
Lobo, Rebecca – *Hartford* . . . . Sport V.3
McClintock, Barbara – *Hartford* . . . . . Oct 92
Shea, Jim, Jr. – *Hartford* . . . . Sport V.8
Spelman, Lucy – *Bridgeport* . . . . Science V.6
Spock, Benjamin – *New Haven* . . . . . Sep 95
Tarbox, Katie – *New Canaan* . . . Author V.10

Cuba
Castro, Fidel – *Mayari, Oriente* . . . . . . Jul 92
Estefan, Gloria – *Havana* . . . . Jul 92
Fuentes, Daisy – *Havana* . . . . Jan 94
Hernandez, Livan – *Villa Clara* . . . . . Apr 98
Zamora, Pedro . . . . Apr 95

Czechoslovakia
Albright, Madeleine – *Prague* . . . . . . Apr 97
Hasek, Dominik – *Pardubice* . . . . . Sport V.3
Hingis, Martina – *Kosice* . . . . Sport V.2
Jagr, Jaromir – *Kladno* . . . . Sport V.5
Navratilova, Martina – *Prague* . . . . . . Jan 93

Delaware
Heimlich, Henry – *Wilmington* . . Science V.6
Dominican Republic
Martinez, Pedro – *Manoguayabo* . . Sport V.5
Sosa, Sammy – *San Pedro de Macoris* . . Jan 99
Egypt
Arafat, Yasir – *Cairo* . . . . Sep 94
Boutros-Ghali, Boutros – *Cairo* . . . . . Apr 93
Sadat, Anwar – *Mit Abu*
  al-Kum . . . . WorLdr V.2
England
Almond, David – *Newcastle* . . . Author V.10
Amanpour, Christiane – *London* . . . . Jan 01
Attenborough, David – *London* . . Science V.4
Barton, Hazel – *Bristol* . . . . Science V.6
Berners-Lee, Tim – *London* . . . . Science V.7
Diana, Princess of Wales – *Norfolk* . . Jul 92;
  Jan 98
Goodall, Jane – *London* . . . . Science V.1
Handford, Martin – *London* . . . . Jan 92
Hargreaves, Alison – *Belper* . . . . Jan 96
Hawking, Stephen – *Oxford* . . . . Apr 92
Herriot, James – *Sunderland* . . . . Author V.1
Jacques, Brian – *Liverpool* . . . . . . Author V.5
Leakey, Mary – *London* . . . . Science V.1
Macaulay, David
  – *Burton-on-Trent* . . . . Author V.2
Moore, Henry – *Castleford* . . . . Artist V.1
Pottter, Beatrix – *London* . . . . . . Author V.8
Pullman, Philip – *Norwich* . . . . . Author V.9
Radcliffe, Daniel – *London* . . . . Jan 02
Reid Banks, Lynne – *London* . . . Author V.2
Rennison, Louise – *Leeds* . . . . . Author V.10
Rowling, J. K. – *Bristol* . . . . Sep 99
Sacks, Oliver – *London* . . . . Science V.3
Stewart, Patrick – *Mirfield* . . . . Jan 94
Winslet, Kate – *Reading* . . . . Sep 98
Ethiopia
Haile Selassie – *Ejarsa Goro,*
  Harar . . . . WorLdr V.2
Roba, Fatuma – *Bokeji* . . . . Sport V.3
Florida
Carter, Aaron – *Tampa* . . . . Sep 02
Carter, Vince – *Daytona Beach* . . . . Sport V.5
Dorough, Howie – *Orlando* . . . . Jan 00
Evert, Chris – *Ft. Lauderdale* . . . . . Sport V.1
Griese, Brian – *Miami* . . . . Jan 02
McLean, A.J. – *West Palm Beach* . . . . Jan 00
Reno, Janet – *Miami* . . . . Sep 93
Richardson, Dot – *Orlando* . . . . . . Sport V.2
Robinson, David – *Key West* . . . . Sep 96

Sanders, Deion – *Ft. Myers* . . . . . . Sport V.1
Sapp, Warren – *Plymouth* . . . . Sport V.5
Smith, Emmitt – *Pensacola* . . . . Sep 94
Tarvin, Herbert – *Miami* . . . . Apr 97

France
Córdova, France – *Paris* . . . . Science V.7
Cousteau, Jacques – *St. Andre-de-
Cubzac* . . . . Jan 93
Ma, Yo-Yo – *Paris* . . . . Jul 92

Georgia
Carter, Jimmy – *Plains* . . . . Apr 95
Grant, Amy – *Augusta* . . . . Jan 95
Hogan, Hulk – *Augusta* . . . . Apr 92
Johns, Jasper – *Augusta* . . . . Artist V.1
Lee, Spike – *Atlanta* . . . . Apr 92
Mathis, Clint – *Conyers* . . . . Apr 03
Roberts, Julia – *Atlanta* . . . . Sep 01
Robinson, Jackie – *Cairo* . . . . Sport V.3
Rowland, Kelly – *Atlanta* . . . . Apr 01
Thomas, Clarence – *Pin Point* . . . . Jan 92
Tucker, Chris – *Decatur* . . . . Jan 01
Ward, Charlie – *Thomasville* . . . . Apr 94

Germany
Bethe, Hans A. – *Strassburg* . . . . Science V.3
Frank, Anne – *Frankfort* . . . . Author V.4
Galdikas, Biruté – *Wiesbaden* . . . Science V.4
Graf, Steffi – *Mannheim* . . . . Jan 92
Otto, Sylke – *Karl-Marx Stad
(Chemnitz)* . . . . Sport V.8
Pippig, Uta – *Berlin* . . . . Sport V.1

Ghana
Annan, Kofi – *Kumasi* . . . . Jan 98
Nkrumah, Kwame – *Nkrofro*. . . WorLdr V.2

Guatemala
Menchu, Rigoberta – *Chimel,
El Quiche* . . . . Jan 93

Haiti
Aristide, Jean-Bertrand – *Port-Salut*. . . Jan 95

Hawaii
Case, Steve – *Honolulu* . . . . Science V.5
Lowry, Lois – *Honolulu* . . . . Author V.4
Nakamura, Leanne – *Honolulu* . . . . . Apr 02
Tuttle, Merlin – *Honolulu* . . . . Apr 97
Yelas, Jay – *Honolulu* . . . . Sport V.9

Holland
Lionni, Leo –
Watergraafsmeer . . . . Author V.6

Hungary
Erdös, Paul – *Budapest* . . . . Science V.2

Idaho
Street, Picabo – *Triumph* . . . . Sport V.3

Illinois
Anderson, Gillian – *Chicago* . . . . Jan 97
Bauer, Joan – *River Forest* . . . . . Author V.10
Blackmun, Harry – *Nashville* . . . . Jan 00
Boyd, Candy Dawson – *Chicago*. Author V.3
Bradbury, Ray – *Waukegan* . . . . . Author V.3
Clinton, Hillary Rodham – *Chicago* . . Apr 93
Crawford, Cindy – *De Kalb* . . . . Apr 93
Crichton, Michael – *Chicago*. . . . Author V.5
Cushman, Karen – *Chicago* . . . . Author V.5
Ford, Harrison – *Chicago* . . . . Sep 97
Garth, Jennie – *Urbana* . . . . Apr 96
Gorey, Edward – *Chicago* . . . . . Author V.13
Granato, Cammi –
Downers Grove . . . . Sport V.8
Hansberry, Lorraine – *Chicago*. . Author V.5
Hendrickson, Sue – *Chicago* . . . Science V.7
Joyner-Kersee, Jackie – *East
St. Louis* . . . . Oct 92
Mac, Bernie – *Chicago* . . . . PerfArt V.1
Margulis, Lynn – *Chicago* . . . . Sep 96
McCully, Emily Arnold – *Galesburg* . . Jul 92
McGruder, Aaron – *Chicago*. . . Author V.10
McNabb, Donovan – *Chicago* . . . . . . Apr 03
Park, Linda Sue – *Urbana*. . . . . Author V.12
Peck, Richard – *Decatur* . . . . . . Author V.10
Silverstein, Shel – *Chicago* . . . . . Author V.3
Siskel, Gene – *Chicago* . . . . Sep 99
Van Draanen, Wendelin –
Chicago . . . . Author V.11
Watson, James D. – *Chicago* . . . Science V.1
Williams, Michelle – *Rockford* . . . . . . Apr 01
Wrede, Patricia C. – *Chicago* . . . Author V.7

Indiana
Bird, Larry – *West Baden* . . . . Jan 92
Cabot, Meg – *Bloomington* . . . . Author V.12
Davis, Jim – *Marion*. . . . . Author V.1
Letterman, David – *Indianapolis*. . . . . Jan 95
Naylor, Phyllis Reynolds – *Anderson* Apr 93
Pauley, Jane – *Indianapolis* . . . . Oct 92
Peet, Bill – *Grandview* . . . . Author V.4
Stewart, Tony – *Rushville*. . . . . Sport V.9
Vonnegut, Kurt – *Indianapolis* . . Author V.1

Iowa
Benson, Mildred – *Ladora* . . . . Jan 03
Leopold, Aldo – *Burlington* . . . . WorLdr V.3
Warner, Kurt – *Burlington* . . . . Sport V.4
Wood, Elijah – *Cedar Rapids* . . . . . . Apr 02

Iraq
Hussein, Saddam – *al-Auja* . . . . Jul 92

Ireland, Northern
  Lewis, C. S. – *Belfast* . . . . Author V.3
Ireland, Republic of
  Colfer, Eoin – *Wexford* . . . . Author V.13
  Flannery, Sarah – *Blarney,*
    County Cork . . . . Science V.5
  Robinson, Mary – *Ballina* . . . . Sep 93
Israel
  Perlman, Itzhak – *Tel Aviv* . . . . Jan 95
  Portman, Natalie – *Jerusalem* . . . . Sep 99
  Rabin, Yitzhak – *Jerusalem* . . . . Oct 92
Italy
  Andretti, Mario – *Montona* . . . . Sep 94
  Krim, Mathilde – *Como* . . . . Science V.1
  Levi-Montalcini, Rita – *Turin* . . Science V.1
Jamaica
  Ashley, Maurice – *St. Andrew* . . . . . . Sep 99
  Bailey, Donovan – *Manchester* . . . Sport V.2
  Denton, Sandi – *Kingston* . . . . Apr 95
  Ewing, Patrick – *Kingston* . . . . Jan 95
  Maxwell, Jody-Anne – *St. Andrew* . . Sep 98
Japan
  Miyamoto, Shigeru – *Sonobe* . . . Science V.5
  Morita, Akio – *Kasugaya* . . . . . . Science V.4
  Suzuki, Shinichi – *Nagoya* . . . . Sep 98
  Uchida, Mitsuko – *Tokyo* . . . . Apr 99
Jordan
  Hussein, King – *Amman* . . . . Apr 99
Kansas
  Alley, Kirstie – *Wichita* . . . . Jul 92
  Ballard, Robert – *Wichita* . . . . . . Science V.4
  Brooks, Gwendolyn – *Topeka* . . . Author V.3
  Dole, Bob – *Russell* . . . . Jan 96
  Parks, Gordon – *Fort Scott* . . . . Artist V.1
  Patrick, Ruth . . . . Science V.3
  Probst, Jeff – *Wichita* . . . . Jan 01
  Sanders, Barry – *Wichita* . . . . Sep 95
  Stiles, Jackie – *Kansas City* . . . . Sport V.6
Kentucky
  Ali, Muhammad – *Louisville* . . . . . Sport V.2
  Littrell, Brian – *Lexington* . . . . Jan 00
  Monroe, Bill – *Rosine* . . . . Sep 97
  Morgan, Garrett – *Paris* . . . . Science V.2
  Richardson, Kevin – *Lexington* . . . . . . Jan 00
Kenya
  Leakey, Louis – *Nairobi* . . . . Science V.1
  Kenyatta, Jomo – *Ngenda* . . . . . WorLdr V.2
  Maathai, Wangari – *Nyeri* . . . . . WorLdr V.1
  Ndeti, Cosmas – *Machakos* . . . . Sep 95
Liberia
  Tubman, William V. S.
    – *Harper City* . . . . WorLdr V.2

Libya
  Qaddafi, Muammar . . . . Apr 97
Louisiana
  Dumars, Joe – *Natchitoches* . . . . . . Sport V.3
  Gumbel, Bryant – *New Orleans* . . . . . Apr 97
  Manning, Peyton – *New Orleans* . . . . Sep 00
  Marsalis, Wynton – *New Orleans* . . . Apr 92
  Rice, Anne – *New Orleans* . . . . . . Author V.3
  Roberts, Cokie – *New Orleans* . . . . . . Apr 95
  Spears, Britney – *Kentwood* . . . . Jan 01
  Stewart, Kordell – *Marrero* . . . . Sep 98
  Witherspoon, Reese – *New Orleans* . . Apr 03
Macedonia
  Teresa, Mother – *Skopje* . . . . Apr 98
Maine
  King, Stephen – *Portland* . . . . . . Author V.1
Malawi
  Banda, Hastings Kamuzu
    – *Chiwengo, Nyasaland* . . . . . WorLdr V.2
Maryland
  Atwater-Rhodes, Amelia
    – *Silver Spring* . . . . Author V.8
  Collier, Bryan – *Salisbury* . . . . . Author V.11
  Hesse, Karen – *Baltimore* . . . . . . Author V.5
  Marshall, Thurgood – *Baltimore* . . . . . Jan 92
  Ripken, Cal, Jr. – *Havre de Grace* . . Sport V.1
  Sleator, William –
    Havre de Grace . . . . Author V.11
  Stepanek, Mattie – *Upper Marlboro* . . Apr 02
Massachusetts
  Bush, George – *Milton* . . . . Jan 92
  Butcher, Susan – *Cambridge* . . . . . Sport V.1
  Caplan, Arthur – *Boston* . . . . Science V.6
  Cormier, Robert – *Leominister* . . Author V.1
  Fanning, Shawn – *Brockton* . . . . Science V.5
  Gilbert, Walter – *Cambridge* . . . . Science V.2
  Grandin, Temple – *Boston* . . . . . Science V.3
  Guey, Wendy – *Boston* . . . . Sep 96
  Guy, Jasmine – *Boston* . . . . Sep 93
  Kerrigan, Nancy – *Woburn* . . . . Apr 94
  Krakauer, Jon – *Brookline* . . . . . . Author V.6
  Lynch, Chris – *Boston* . . . . Author V.13
  Meltzer, Milton – *Worcester* . . . Author V.11
  Pine, Elizabeth Michele – *Boston* . . . . Jan 94
  Robison, Emily – *Pittsfield* . . . . . PerfArt V.1
  Scarry, Richard – *Boston* . . . . Sep 94
  Seuss, Dr. – *Springfield* . . . . Jan 92
  Sones, Sonya – *Boston* . . . . Author V.11
  Speare, Elizabeth George
    – *Melrose* . . . . Sep 95
  Taymor, Julie – *Newton* . . . . PerfArt V.1

Thompson, Jenny – *Georgetown* . . Sport V.5
Voigt, Cynthia – *Boston*. . . . . Oct 92
Walters, Barbara – *Boston*. . . . . Sep 94

Mexico
Fox, Vicente – *Mexico City* . . . . Apr 03
Jiménez, Francisco – *San Pedro,
Tlaquepaque,* . . . . Author V.13
Rivera, Diego – *Guanajuato* . . . . . . Artist V.1

Michigan
Applegate, K.A. . . . . Jan 00
Askins, Renee. . . . . WorLdr V.1
Canady, Alexa – *Lansing* . . . . . . Science V.6
Carson, Ben – *Detroit*. . . . . Science V.4
Curtis, Christopher Paul – *Flint* Author V.4
Galeczka, Chris – *Sterling Heights* . . . Apr 96
Johnson, Magic – *Lansing* . . . . Apr 92
Kiraly, Karch – *Jackson* . . . . Sport V.4
Krone, Julie – *Benton Harbor*. . . . . . . Jan 95
Lalas, Alexi – *Royal Oak* . . . . Sep 94
Mohajer, Dineh – *Bloomfield Hills* . . . Jan 02
Riley, Dawn – *Detroit*. . . . . Sport V.4
Scieszka, Jon – *Flint* . . . . Author V.9
Shabazz, Betty – *Detroit* . . . . Apr 98
Small, David – *Detroit* . . . . Author V.10
Van Allsburg, Chris – *Grand Rapids*. . Apr 92
Ward, Lloyd D. – *Romulus* . . . . Jan 01
Watson, Barry – *Traverse City* . . . . . . Sep 02
Webb, Alan – *Ann Arbor* . . . . Sep 01
Williams, Serena – *Saginaw* . . . . . Sport V.4
Winans, CeCe – *Detroit* . . . . Apr 00

Minnesota
Burger, Warren – *St. Paul*. . . . . Sep 95
Douglas, Marjory Stoneman
– *Minneapolis*. . . . . WorLdr V.1
Madden, John – *Austin*. . . . . Sep 97
Mars, Forrest, Sr. – *Minneapolis* Science V.4
Murie, Olaus J. . . . . WorLdr V.1
Paulsen, Gary – *Minneapolis* . . . Author V.1
Ryder, Winona – *Winona* . . . . Jan 93
Schulz, Charles – *Minneapolis* . . Author V.2
Scurry, Briana – *Minneapolis*. . . . . . . Jan 00
Ventura, Jesse – *Minneapolis*. . . . . . . Apr 99
Weinke, Chris – *St. Paul*. . . . . Apr 01
Winfield, Dave – *St. Paul*. . . . . Jan 93

Mississippi
Bass, Lance – *Clinton*. . . . . Jan 01
Brandy – *McComb*. . . . . Apr 96
Favre, Brett – *Gulfport* . . . . Sport V.2
Forman, Michele – *Biloxi*. . . . . Jan 03
Hill, Faith – *Jackson* . . . . Sep 01

Jones, James Earl – *Arkabutla
Township* . . . . Jan 95
McCarty, Oseola – *Wayne County* . . . Jan 99
Payton, Walter – *Columbia* . . . . Jan 00
Rice, Jerry – *Crawford* . . . . Apr 93
Rimes, LeAnn – *Jackson*. . . . . Jan 98
Taylor, Mildred D. – *Jackson* . . . . Author V.1
Winfrey, Oprah – *Kosciusko*. . . . . Apr 92
Wright, Richard – *Natchez* . . . . . Author V.5

Missouri
Angelou, Maya – *St. Louis* . . . . Apr 93
Champagne, Larry III – *St. Louis*. . . . Apr 96
Eminem – *Kansas City* . . . . Apr 03
Goodman, John – *Affton* . . . . Sep 95
Heinlein, Robert – *Butler* . . . . . . Author V.4
Hughes, Langston – *Joplin* . . . . . Author V.7
Lester, Julius – *St. Louis* . . . . Author V.7
Limbaugh, Rush – *Cape Girardeau* . . Sep 95
Miller, Shannon – *Rolla* . . . . Sep 94
Nye, Naomi Shihab – *St. Louis* . . Author V.8

Montana
Carvey, Dana – *Missoula*. . . . . Jan 93
Horner, Jack – *Shelby* . . . . Science V.1
Lowe, Alex – *Missoula* . . . . Sport V.4

Morocco
Hassan II – *Rabat* . . . . WorLdr V.2

Myanmar
see Burma

Nebraska
Cheney, Dick – *Lincoln* . . . . Jan 02
Roddick, Andy – *Omaha* . . . . Jan 03

Nevada
Agassi, Andre – *Las Vegas* . . . . Jul 92
Schwikert, Tasha – *Las Vegas* . . . . Sport V.7

New Hampshire
Zirkle, Aliy – *Manchester* . . . . Sport V.6

New Jersey
Blume, Judy . . . . Jan 92
Carpenter, Mary Chapin
– *Princeton*. . . . . Sep 94
Clements, Andrew – *Camden* . . Author V.13
Dunst, Kirsten – *Point Pleasant* . . PerfArt V.1
Earle, Sylvia – *Gibbstown* . . . . . . Science V.1
Glover, Savion – *Newark* . . . . Apr 99
Gwaltney, John Langston –
Orange . . . . Science V.3
Hill, Lauryn – *South Orange*. . . . . . . Sep 99
Houston, Whitney – *Newark* . . . . Sep 94
Ice-T – *Newark* . . . . Apr 93
Jeter, Derek – *Pequannock* . . . . Sport V.4
Lawrence, Jacob – *Atlantic City* . . Artist V.1

Love, Susan – *Long Branch* . . . . Science V.3
Martin, Ann M. – *Princeton* . . . . Jan 92
Morrison, Lillian – *Jersey City*. . Author V.12
Muniz, Frankie – *Ridgewood* . . . . Jan 01
O'Neal, Shaquille – *Newark*. . . . . . . Sep 93
Pinsky, Robert – *Long Branch* . . Author V.7
Queen Latifah – *Newark* . . . . Apr 92
Rodman, Dennis – *Trenton* . . . . Apr 96
Schwarzkopf, H. Norman – *Trenton*. . Jan 92
Sinatra, Frank – *Hoboken*. . . . . Jan 99
Thomas, Dave – *Atlantic City* . . . . . . Apr 96

New Mexico
Bezos, Jeff – *Albuquerque* . . . . Apr 01
Foreman, Dave – *Albuquerque*. . . WorLdr V.1
Villa-Komaroff, Lydia –
    Las Vegas. . . . . Science V.6

New York State
Aaliyah – *Brooklyn* . . . . Jan 02
Abdul-Jabbar, Kareem
    – *New York City* . . . . Sport V.1
Abzug, Bella – *Bronx*. . . . . Sep 98
Aguilera, Christina – *Staten Island* . . Apr 00
Anderson, Laurie Halse –
    Potsdam . . . . Author V.11
Avi – *New York City* . . . . Jan 93
Baldwin, James
    – *New York City* . . . . Author V.2
Bennett, Cherie – *Buffalo* . . . . . . Author V.9
Bird, Sue – *Syosset* . . . . Sport V.9
Blair, Bonnie – *Cornwall*. . . . . Apr 94
Blige, Mary J. – *Yonkers* . . . . Apr 02
Bourke-White, Margaret
    – *New York City* . . . . Artist V.1
Brody, Jane – *Brooklyn* . . . . Science V.2
Brown, Claude
    – *New York City* . . . . Author V.12
Burke, Chris – *New York City*. . . . . . . Sep 93
Burns, Ken – *Brooklyn* . . . . Jan 95
Bush, Barbara – *New York City* . . . . . . Jan 92
Calderone, Mary S.
    – *New York City* . . . . Science V.3
Capriati, Jennifer – *Long Island* . . . Sport V.6
Carey, Mariah – *New York City* . . . . . Apr 96
Carle, Eric – *Syracuse*. . . . . Author V.1
Carter, Nick – *Jamestown*. . . . . Jan 00
Cohen, Adam Ezra – *New York City* Apr 97
Collins, Eileen – *Elmira* . . . . Science V.4
Combs, Sean (Puff Daddy)
    – *New York City* . . . . Apr 98
Cooney, Barbara – *Brooklyn* . . . . Author V.8

Cooney, Caroline B. – *Geneva*. . . Author V.4
Coville, Bruce – *Syracuse*. . . . . . . Author V.9
Cronin, John – *Yonkers*. . . . . WorLdr V.3
Culkin, Macaulay – *New York City* . . Sep 93
Danes, Claire – *New York City*. . . . . . Sep 97
de Mille, Agnes – *New York City* . . . . Jan 95
Diesel, Vin – *New York City* . . . . Jan 03
Duchovny, David – *New York City* . . Apr 96
Elion, Gertrude
    – *New York City* . . . . Science V.6
Farrakhan, Louis – *Bronx* . . . . Jan 97
Fatone, Joey – *Brooklyn* . . . . Jan 01
Fauci, Anthony S. – *Brooklyn*. . . Science V.7
Frankenthaler, Helen
    – *New York City* . . . . Artist V.1
Gellar, Sarah Michelle
    – *New York City*. . . . . Jan 99
Giff, Patricia Reilly – *Queens*. . . . Author V.7
Ginsburg, Ruth Bader – *Brooklyn* . . . . Jan 94
Giuliani, Rudolph – *Brooklyn*. . . . . . Sep 02
Goldberg, Whoopi
    – *New York City* . . . . Apr 94
Gould, Stephen Jay
    – *New York City* . . . . Science V.2
Haley, Alex – *Ithaca* . . . . Apr 92
Hart, Melissa Joan – *Smithtown* . . . . . Jan 94
Healy, Bernadine – *Queens* . . . . Science V.1
Holdsclaw, Chamique – *Queens*. . . . . Sep 00
Hopper, Grace Murray
    – *New York City* . . . . Science V.5
Hughes, Sarah – *Great Neck* . . . . Jan 03
James, Cheryl – *New York City* . . . . . Apr 95
Jordan, Michael – *Brooklyn* . . . . Jan 92
Kamler, Kenneth
    – *New York City* . . . . Science V.6
Kerr, M.E. – *Auburn* . . . . Author V.1
Konigsburg, E.L.
    – *New York City* . . . . Author V.3
Kurzweil, Raymond
    – *New York City* . . . . Science V.2
Lee, Jeanette – *Brooklyn* . . . . Apr 03
Lee, Stan – *New York City* . . . . . Author V.7
Lemelson, Jerome – *Staten
    Island*. Science V.3
L'Engle, Madeleine – *New York
    City* . . . . Jan 92; Apr 01
Leno, Jay – *New Rochelle* . . . . Jul 92
Lewis, Shari – *New York City* . . . . Jan 99
Lipsyte, Robert
    – *New York City* . . . . Author V.12

Lisanti, Mariangela – *Bronx* . . . . Sep 01
Lopez, Jennifer – *Bronx* . . . . Jan 02
Lowman, Meg – *Elmira* . . . . Science V.4
Mirra, Dave – *Syracuse* . . . . Sep 02
Mittermeier, Russell A.
 – *New York City* . . . . WorLdr V.1
Moses, Grandma – *Greenwich* . . . Artist V.1
Moss, Cynthia – *Ossining* . . . . . WorLdr V.3
O'Donnell, Rosie – *Commack* . . . . . . Apr 97
Oppenheimer, J. Robert
 – *New York City* . . . . Science V.1
Pascal, Francine
 – *New York City* . . . . Author V.6
Peterson, Roger Tory
 – *Jamestown* . . . . WorLdr V.1
Pike, Christopher – *Brooklyn* . . . . Sep 96
Powell, Colin – *New York City* . . . . . Jan 92
Prelutsky, Jack – *Brooklyn* . . . . . . Author V.2
Reeve, Christopher – *Manhattan* . . . . Jan 97
Rinaldi, Ann – *New York City* . . . Author V.8
Ringgold, Faith – *New York City* . Author V.2
Rockwell, Norman
 – *New York City* . . . . Artist V.1
Rodriguez, Alex – *New York City* . . Sport V.6
Roper, Dee Dee – *New York City* . . . . Apr 95
Sachar, Louis – *East Meadow* . . . Author V.6
Sagan, Carl – *Brooklyn* . . . . Science V.1
Salinger, J.D. – *New York City* . . Author V.2
Salk, Jonas – *New York City* . . . . Jan 94
Sealfon, Rebecca – *New York City* . . . Sep 97
Seinfeld, Jerry – *Brooklyn* . . . . Oct 92
Sendak, Maurice – *Brooklyn* . . . . Author V.2
Shakur, Tupac – *Bronx* . . . . Apr 97
Strasser, Todd – *New York City* . . Author V.7
Vidal, Christina – *Queens* . . . . . . PerfArt V.1
Washington, Denzel – *Mount Vernon* . . Jan 93
Wayans, Keenen Ivory
 – *New York City* . . . . Jan 93
White, E.B. – *Mount Vernon* . . . . Author V.1
WilderBrathwaite, Gloria
 – *Brooklyn* . . . . Science V.7
Williams, Garth – *New York City* . Author V.2
Yolen, Jane – *New York City* . . . . Author V.7
Zindel, Paul – *Staten Island* . . . . . Author V.1

New Zealand
Hillary, Sir Edmund – *Auckland* . . . . Sep 96
Nigeria
Olajuwon, Hakeem – *Lagos* . . . . Sep 95
Saro-Wiwa, Ken – *Bori,*
 Rivers State . . . . WorLdr V.1

North Carolina
Bearden, Romare – *Charlotte*. . . . . Artist V.1
Burnside, Aubyn – *Hickory* . . . . Sep 02
Byars, Betsy – *Charlotte* . . . . . . Author V.4
Chavis, Benjamin – *Oxford* . . . . Jan 94
Delany, Bessie – *Raleigh* . . . . Sep 99
Dole, Elizabeth Hanford – *Salisbury* . . Jul 92
Earnhardt, Dale – *Kannapolis* . . . . Apr 01
Petty, Richard – *Level Cross* . . . . . . Sport V.2
Williamson, Kevin – *New Bern* . . Author V.6
Willingham, Tyrone – *Kinston* . . . . . . Sep 02
Norway
Brundtland, Gro Harlem
 – *Baerum* . . . . Science V.3
Ohio
Anderson, Terry – *Lorain* . . . . Apr 92
Battle, Kathleen – *Portsmouth* . . . . . . Jan 93
Berry, Halle – *Cleveland* . . . . Jan 95
Creech, Sharon – *Mayfield*
 Heights . . . . Author V.5
Dove, Rita – *Akron* . . . . Jan 94
Draper, Sharon – *Cleveland* . . . . Apr 99
Dunbar, Paul Laurence
 – *Dayton* . . . . Author V.8
Farrell, Suzanne – *Cincinnati* . . . PerfArt V.1
Glenn, John – *Cambridge* . . . . Jan 99
Guisewite, Cathy – *Dayton* . . . . Sep 93
Haddix, Margaret Peterson
 – *Washington Court House* . . . Author V.11
Hamilton, Virginia – *Yellow*
 Springs . . . . Author V.1, Author V.12
Hampton, David . . . . Apr 99
Harbaugh, Jim – *Toledo* . . . . Sport V.3
Holmes, Katie – *Toledo* . . . . Jan 00
Lin, Maya – *Athens* . . . . Sep 97
Lovell, Jim – *Cleveland* . . . . Jan 96
Morrison, Toni – *Lorain* . . . . Jan 94
Nelson, Marilyn – *Cleveland* . . . Author V.13
Nicklaus, Jack – *Columbus* . . . . Sport V.2
Nielsen, Jerri – *Salem* . . . . Science V.7
Perry, Luke – *Mansfield* . . . . Jan 92
Rose, Pete – *Cincinnati* . . . . Jan 92
Shula, Don – *Grand River* . . . . Apr 96
Spielberg, Steven – *Cincinnati* . . . . . . Jan 94
Steinem, Gloria – *Toledo* . . . . Oct 92
Stine, R.L. – *Columbus* . . . . Apr 94
Tompkins, Douglas
 – *Conneaut* . . . . WorLdr V.3
Woodson, Jacqueline
 – *Columbus* . . . . Author V.7

Oklahoma

Brooks, Garth – *Tulsa* . . . . Oct 92
Duke, David – *Tulsa* . . . . Apr 92
Ellison, Ralph – *Oklahoma City* . . Author V.3
Hanson, Ike – *Tulsa* . . . . Jan 98
Hanson, Taylor – *Tulsa* . . . . Jan 98
Hanson, Zac – *Tulsa* . . . . Jan 98
Hill, Anita – *Morris* . . . . Jan 93
Hinton, S.E. – *Tulsa*. . . . . Author V.1
Mankiller, Wilma – *Tahlequah*. . . . . . Apr 94
Mantle, Mickey – *Spavinaw* . . . . Jan 96
McEntire, Reba – *McAlester* . . . . Sep 95
Pitt, Brad – *Shawnee* . . . . Sep 98

Oregon

Cleary, Beverly – *McMinnville* . . . . . . Apr 94
Engelbart, Douglas – *Portland* . . Science V.5
Groening, Matt – *Portland* . . . . Jan 92
Harding, Tonya – *Portland* . . . . Sep 94
Hooper, Geoff – *Salem* . . . . Jan 94
Pauling, Linus – *Portland* . . . . Jan 95
Phoenix, River – *Madras* . . . . Apr 94
Schroeder, Pat – *Portland* . . . . Jan 97
Wolff, Virginia Euwer
 – *Portland* . . . . Author V.13

Pakistan

Bhutto, Benazir – *Karachi*. . . . . Apr 95
Masih, Iqbal . . . . Jan 96

Palestine

Perlman, Itzhak – *Tel Aviv* . . . . Jan 95
Rabin, Yitzhak – *Jerusalem* . . . . Oct 92

Panama

McCain, John – *Panama*
 Canal Zone . . . . Apr 00

Pennsylvania

Abbey, Edward – *Indiana* . . . . . WorLdr V.1
Alexander, Lloyd – *Philadelphia*. Author V.6
Anderson, Marian – *Philadelphia* . . . . Jan 94
Armstrong, Robb – *Philadelphia*. . Author V.9
Berenstain, Jan – *Philadelphia* . . Author V.2
Berenstain, Stan – *Philadelphia* . Author V.2
Bradley, Ed – *Philadelphia* . . . . Apr 94
Bryant, Kobe – *Philadelphia*. . . . . . . Apr 99
Calder, Alexander – *Lawnton* . . . . Artist V.1
Carson, Rachel – *Springdale* . . . WorLdr V.1
Chamberlain, Wilt – *Philadelphia* . . Sport V.4
Cosby, Bill. . . . . Jan 92
DiCamillo, Kate – *Philadelphia* . . Author V.10
Diemer, Walter – *Philadelphia*. . . . . . Apr 98
Duncan, Lois – *Philadelphia*. . . . . . . Sep 93
Flake, Sharon – *Philadelphia*. . . Author V.13

Gantos, Jack – *Mount Pleasant* . . Author V.10
George, Eddie – *Philadelphia*. . . . . Sport V.6
Gingrich, Newt – *Harrisburg* . . . . Apr 95
Griffey, Ken, Jr. – *Donora*. . . . . Sport V.1
Iacocca, Lee A. – *Allentown*. . . . . Jan 92
Jamison, Judith – *Philadelphia* . . . . . Jan 96
Kirkpatrick, Chris – *Clarion* . . . . Jan 01
Lipinski, Tara – *Philadelphia* . . . . Apr 98
Maguire, Martie – *York* . . . . PerfArt V.1
Marino, Dan – *Pittsburgh* . . . . Apr 93
McCary, Michael – *Philadelphia* . . . . . Jan 96
Mead, Margaret – *Philadelphia* . Science V.2
Montana, Joe – *New Eagle*. . . . . Jan 95
Morris, Nathan – *Philadelphia* . . . . . . Jan 96
Morris, Wanya – *Philadelphia* . . . . Jan 96
Pierce, Tamora – *Connellsville* . . Author V.13
Pinkney, Jerry – *Philadelphia* . . . Author V.2
Smith, Will – *Philadelphia* . . . . Sep 94
Smyers, Karen – *Corry* . . . . Sport V.4
Stanford, John – *Darby*. . . . . Sep 99
Stockman, Shawn – *Philadelphia* . . . . Jan 96
Thomas, Jonathan Taylor
 – *Bethlehem* . . . . Apr 95
Van Meter, Vicki – *Meadville* . . . . Jan 95
Warhol, Andy. . . . . Artist V.1
Wilson, August – *Pittsburgh* . . . . Author V.4

Poland

John Paul II – *Wadowice*. . . . . Oct 92
Opdyke, Irene Gut – *Kozienice* . . Author V.9
Sabin, Albert – *Bialystok*. . . . . . . Science V.1

Puerto Rico

Lopez, Charlotte. . . . . Apr 94
Martin, Ricky – *Santurce* . . . . Jan 00
Moseley, Jonny – *San Juan* . . . . . . Sport V.8
Novello, Antonia – *Fajardo* . . . . Apr 92

Rhode Island

Clark, Kelly – *Newport* . . . . Sport V.8
Gilman, Billy – *Westerly* . . . . Apr 02

Romania

Dumitriu, Ioana – *Bucharest* . . . Science V.3
Nechita, Alexandra – *Vaslui* . . . . Jan 98
Risca, Viviana – *Bucharest* . . . . Sep 00

Russia

Asimov, Isaac – *Petrovichi* . . . . Jul 92
Chagall, Marc – *Vitebsk* . . . . Artist V.1
Fedorov, Sergei – *Pskov* . . . . Apr 94
Gorbachev, Mikhail – *Privolnoye* . . . . Jan 92
Nevelson, Louise – *Kiev* . . . . Artist V.1
Nureyev, Rudolf . . . . Apr 93
Tartakovsky, Genndy
 – *Moscow*. . . . . Author V.11
Yeltsin, Boris – *Butka* . . . . Apr 92

Saudi Arabia
bin Laden, Osama – *Riyadh* . . . . Apr 02
Scotland
Muir, John – *Dunbar* . . . . WorLdr V.3
Senegal
Senghor, Léopold Sédar – *Joal*. . . WorLdr V.2
Serbia
Milosevic, Slobodan – *Pozarevac* . . . . Sep 99
Seles, Monica – *Novi Sad* . . . . Jan 96
Somalia
Aidid, Mohammed Farah . . . . . WorLdr V.2
South Africa
de Klerk, F.W. – *Mayfair* . . . . Apr 94
Mandela, Nelson – *Umtata, Transkei*. . Jan 92
Mandela, Winnie
– *Pondoland, Transkei* . . . . WorLdr V.2
Tolkien, J.R.R. – *Bloemfontein* . . . . Jan 02
South Carolina
Childress, Alice – *Charleston* . . . Author V.1
Daniel, Beth – *Charleston*. . . . . . . Sport V.1
Edelman, Marian Wright
– *Bennettsville* . . . . Apr 93
Garnett, Kevin – *Greenville* . . . . . . Sport V.6
Gillespie, Dizzy – *Cheraw* . . . . Apr 93
Hunter-Gault, Charlayne
– *Due West*. Jan 00
Jackson, Jesse – *Greenville* . . . . Sep 95
South Korea
An Na. Author V.12
Kim Dae-jung – *Hugwang* . . . . Sep 01
Pak, Se Ri – *Daejeon*. . . . . Sport V.4
Spain
Domingo, Placido – *Madrid*. . . . . . . Sep 95
Garcia, Sergio – *Castellon* . . . . Sport V.7
Iglesias, Enrique – *Madrid* . . . . Jan 03
Ochoa, Severo – *Luarca*. . . . . Jan 94
Sanchez Vicario, Arantxa
– *Barcelona* . . . . Sport V.1
Sweden
Lindgren, Astrid – *Vimmerby* . . Author V.13
Sorenstam, Annika – *Stockholm* . . . Sport V.6
Taiwan
Ho, David – *Taichung*. . . . . Science V.6
Tanzania
Nyerere, Julius Kambarage. . . . WorLdr V.2
Tennessee
Andrews, Ned – *Oakridge* . . . . Sep 94
Doherty, Shannen – *Memphis*. . . . . . Apr 92
Fitzhugh, Louise – *Memphis*. . . . Author V.3
Franklin, Aretha – *Memphis*. . . . . Apr 01

Hardaway, Anfernee "Penny"
– *Memphis* . . . . Sport V.2
McKissack, Fredrick L.
– *Nashville* . . . . Author V.3
McKissack, Patricia C. – *Smyrna* . Author V.3
Pinkwater, Daniel – *Memphis* . . Author V.8
Rowan, Carl T. – *Ravenscroft* . . . . Sep 01
Rudolph, Wilma – *St. Bethlehem* . . . . Apr 95
Summitt, Pat – *Henrietta* . . . . Sport V.3
Timberlake, Justin – *Memphis*. . . . . . . Jan 01
White, Reggie – *Chattanooga* . . . . Jan 98
Texas
Adams, Yolanda – *Houston* . . . . Apr 03
Armstrong, Lance – *Plano* . . . . Sep 00
Baker, James – *Houston*. . . . . Oct 92
Bledel, Alexis – *Houston* . . . . Jan 03
Bush, Laura – *Midland* . . . . Apr 03
Cisneros, Henry – *San Antonio* . . . . . Sep 93
Clarkson, Kelly – *Burleson*. . . . . Jan 03
Duff, Hilary – *Houston* . . . . Sep 02
Ellerbee, Linda – *Bryan* . . . . Apr 94
Fiorina, Carly – *Austin* . . . . Sep 01
Groppe, Laura – *Houston*. . . . . . . Science V.5
Harris, Bernard – *Temple* . . . . . . Science V.3
Hewitt, Jennifer Love – *Waco*. . . . . . . Sep 00
Hill, Grant – *Dallas*. . . . . Sport V.1
Johnson, Jimmy – *Port Arthur*. . . . . . . Jan 98
Johnson, Michael – *Dallas* . . . . Jan 97
Jordan, Barbara – *Houston* . . . . Apr 96
Knowles, Beyoncé – *Houston*. . . . . . . Apr 01
Maddux, Greg – *San Angelo* . . . . . Sport V.3
Maines, Natalie – *Lubbock* . . . . . PerfArt V.1
O'Connor, Sandra Day – *El Paso* . . . . Jul 92
Oliver, Patsy Ruth – *Texarkana*. . WorLdr V.1
Perot, H. Ross – *Texarkana* . . . . Apr 92
Rodriguez, Eloy – *Edinburg* . . . . Science V.2
Ryan, Nolan – *Refugio*. . . . . Oct 92
Selena – *Lake Jackson*. . . . . Jan 96
Simmons, Ruth – *Grapeland* . . . . Sep 02
Soren, Tabitha – *San Antonio* . . . . . . Jan 97
Swoopes, Sheryl – *Brownfield* . . . . Sport V.2
Thampy, George – *Houston* . . . . Sep 00
Usher – *Dallas* . . . . PerfArt V.1
Zmeskal, Kim – *Houston* . . . . Jan 94
Tibet
Dalai Lama – *Takster, Amdo* . . . . Sep 98
Trinidad
Guy, Rosa – *Diego Martin* . . . . . . Author V.9
Uganda
Amin, Idi – *Koboko* . . . . WorLdr V.2

Ukraine

Baiul, Oksana – *Dnepropetrovsk*. . . . . Apr 95
Stern, Isaac – *Kreminiecz*. . . . . . . PerfArt V.1

USSR – Union of Soviet
Socialist Republics

Asimov, Isaac – *Petrovichi, Russia* . . . . Jul 92
Baiul, Oksana – *Dnepropetrovsk,*
  Ukraine . . . . Apr 95
Fedorov, Sergei – *Pskov, Russia* . . . . . Apr 94
Gorbachev, Mikhail – *Privolnoye,*
  Russia . . . . Jan 92
Nureyev, Rudolf – *Russia*. . . . . Apr 93
Yeltsin, Boris – *Butka, Russia* . . . . Apr 92

Utah

Arnold, Roseanne – *Salt Lake City* . . Oct 92
Jewel – *Payson* . . . . Sep 98
Young, Steve – *Salt Lake City* . . . . Jan 94

Vermont

Muldowney, Shirley – *Burlington* . . Sport V.7

Virginia

Armstrong, William H.
  – *Lexington*. . . . . Author V.7
Ashe, Arthur – *Richmond* . . . . Sep 93
Collins, Francis – *Staunton* . . . . . Science V.6
Dayne, Ron – *Blacksburg* . . . . Apr 00
Delany, Sadie – *Lynch's Station* . . . . . Sep 99
Fitzgerald, Ella – *Newport News* . . . . . Jan 97
Iverson, Allen – *Hampton* . . . . Sport V.7
Rylant, Cynthia – *Hopewell*. . . . . Author V.1
Vick, Michael – *Newport News* . . . Sport V.9
White, Ruth – *Whitewood*. . . . . Author V.11

Wales

Dahl, Roald – *Llandaff*. . . . . Author V.1

Washington, D.C.

Brown, Ron . . . . Sep 96
Chasez, JC. . . . . Jan 01
Chung, Connie. Jan 94
Danziger, Paula. . . . . Author V.6
George, Jean Craighead . . . . Author V.3
Gore, Al . . . . Jan 93
Jackson, Shirley Ann . . . . Science V.2
Nye, Bill. Science V.2
Pinkney, Andrea Davis. . . . . . . Author V.10
Sampras, Pete . . . . Jan 97
Vasan, Nina. . . . . Science V.7
Watterson, Bill . . . . Jan 92

Washington State

Cobain, Kurt – *Aberdeen*. . . . . Sep 94
Devers, Gail – *Seattle* . . . . Sport V.2
Elway, John – *Port Angeles* . . . . . . Sport V.2

Gates, Bill – *Seattle* . . . . Apr 93; Science V.5
Jones, Chuck – *Spokane*. . . . . . . Author V.12
Larson, Gary – *Tacoma* . . . . Author V.1
Murie, Margaret – *Seattle* . . . . . WorLdr V.1
Ohno, Apolo – *Seattle* . . . . Sport V.8
Stockton, John – *Spokane*. . . . . Sport V.3

West Virginia

Gates, Henry Louis, Jr. – *Keyser* . . . . Apr 00
Moss, Randy – *Rand* . . . . Sport V.4
Myers, Walter Dean
  – *Martinsburg*. . . . . Jan 93
Nash, John Forbes, Jr.
  – *Bluefield* . . . . Science V.7

Wisconsin

Bardeen, John – *Madison* . . . . . . Science V.1
Cray, Seymour – *Chippewa Falls* . Science V.2
Driscoll, Jean – *Milwaukee* . . . . Sep 97
Henry, Marguerite – *Milwaukee* Author V.4
Jansen, Dan – *Milwaukee*. . . . . Apr 94
Nelson, Gaylord – *Clear Lake* . . WorLdr V.3
O'Keeffe, Georgia – *Sun Prairie* . . Artist V.1
Wilder, Laura Ingalls – *Pepin* . . . Author V.3
Wright, Frank Lloyd
  – *Richland Center*. . . . . Artist V.1

Wyoming

MacLachlan, Patricia
  – *Cheyenne*. . . . . Author V.2

Yugoslavia

Filipovic, Zlata – *Sarajevo,*
  Bosnia-Herzogovina . . . . Sep 94
Milosevic, Slobodan – *Pozarevac,*
  Serbia. . . . . Sep 99
Seles, Monica – *Novi Sad, Serbia* . . . . Jan 96

Zaire

Mobutu Sese Seko – *Lisala* . . . . WorLdr V.2

Zambia

Kaunda, Kenneth – *Lubwa* . . . . WorLdr V.2

Zimbabwe

Mugabe, Robert – *Kutama*. . . . . WorLdr V.2

Birthday Index

January		Year
1	Salinger, J.D.	1919
2	Asimov, Isaac	1920
3	Fuller, Millard	1935
	Tolkien, J.R.R.	1892
4	Naylor, Phyllis Reynolds	1933
	Runyan, Marla	1969
	Shula, Don	1930
6	Van Draanen, Wendelin	?
7	Hurston, Zora Neale	?1891
	Rodriguez, Eloy	1947
8	Hawking, Stephen W.	1942
	Spelman, Lucy	1963
9	Garcia, Sergio	1980
	McLean, A.J.	1978
	Menchu, Rigoberta	1959
	Nixon, Richard	1913
11	Leopold, Aldo	1887
12	Amanpour, Christiane	1958
	Bezos, Jeff	1964
	Lasseter, John	?1957
	Limbaugh, Rush	1951
13	Burnside, Aubyn	1985
	Webb, Alan	1983
14	Lucid, Shannon	1943
15	Werbach, Adam	1973
16	Aaliyah	1979
	Fossey, Dian	1932
	Lipsyte, Robert	1938
17	Carrey, Jim	1962
	Cormier, Robert	1925
	Jones, James Earl	1931
	Lewis, Shari	?1934
	Tartakovsky, Genndy	1970
18	Ali, Muhammad	1942
	Chavez, Julz	1962
	Messier, Mark	1961
19	Askins, Renee	1959
	Johnson, John	1918
21	Domingo, Placido	1941
	Nicklaus, Jack	1940
	Olajuwon, Hakeem	1963

		Year
22	Chavis, Benjamin	1948
	Ward, Lloyd D.	1949
23	Elion, Gertrude	1918
	Thiessen, Tiffani-Amber	1974
24	Haddock, Doris (Granny D)	1910
25	Alley, Kirstie	1955
26	Carter, Vince	1977
	Morita, Akio	1921
	Siskel, Gene	1946
	Tarbox, Katie	1982
27	Lester, Julius	1939
	Vasan, Nina	1984
28	Carter, Nick	1980
	Fatone, Joey	1977
	Gretzky, Wayne	1961
	Wood, Elijah	1981
29	Abbey, Edward	1927
	Gilbert, Sara	1975
	Hasek, Dominik	1965
	Peet, Bill	1915
	Winfrey, Oprah	1954
30	Alexander, Lloyd	1924
	Cheney, Dick	1941
	Engelbart, Douglas	1925
31	Collier, Bryan	1967
	Flannery, Sarah	1982
	Robinson, Jackie	1919
	Ryan, Nolan	1947
	Timberlake, Justin	1981

February		Year
1	Cabot, Meg	1967
	Hughes, Langston	1902
	Spinelli, Jerry	1941
	Yeltsin, Boris	1931
2	Shakira	1977
3	Heimlich, Henry	1920
	Nixon, Joan Lowery	1927
	Rockwell, Norman	1894
	Sanborn, Ryne	1989
4	Parks, Rosa	1913
5	Aaron, Hank	1934

February (continued)   Year

6 Leakey, Mary 1913
    Rosa, Emily 1987
    Zmeskal, Kim 1976
7 Brooks, Garth 1962
    Wang, An 1920
    Wilder, Laura Ingalls 1867
8 Grisham, John 1955
9 Love, Susan 1948
10 Konigsburg, E.L. 1930
    Norman, Greg 1955
11 Aniston, Jennifer 1969
    Brandy 1979
    Rowland, Kelly 1981
    Yolen, Jane 1939
12 Blume, Judy 1938
    Kurzweil, Raymond 1948
    Small, David 1945
    Woodson, Jacqueline . . . . ?1964
13 Moss, Randy 1977
    Sleator, William 1945
15 Groening, Matt 1954
    Jagr, Jaromir 1972
    Sones, Sonya 1952
    Van Dyken, Amy 1973
16 Freeman, Cathy 1973
17 Anderson, Marian 1897
    Hargreaves, Alison 1962
    Jordan, Michael 1963
18 Morrison, Toni 1931
19 Tan, Amy 1952
20 Adams, Ansel 1902
    Barkley, Charles 1963
    Cobain, Kurt 1967
    Crawford, Cindy 1966
    Hernandez, Livan 1975
    Littrell, Brian 1975
21 Carpenter, Mary Chapin 1958
    Hewitt, Jennifer Love 1979
    Jordan, Barbara 1936
    Lewis, John 1940
    Mugabe, Robert 1924
22 Barrymore, Drew 1975
    Fernandez, Lisa 1971
    Gorey, Edward 1925
23 Brown, Claude 1937
24 Jobs, Steven 1955
    Vernon, Mike 1963
    Whitestone, Heather 1973

25 Voigt, Cynthia 1942
26 Thompson, Jenny 1973
27 Clinton, Chelsea 1980
    Hunter-Gault, Charlayne 1942
28 Andretti, Mario 1940
    Pauling, Linus 1901

March   Year

1 Ellison, Ralph Waldo 1914
    Murie, Olaus J. 1889
    Nielsen, Jerri 1952
    Rabin, Yitzhak 1922
    Zamora, Pedro 1972
2 Gorbachev, Mikhail 1931
    Satcher, David 1941
    Seuss, Dr. 1904
3 Hooper, Geoff 1979
    Joyner-Kersee, Jackie 1962
    MacLachlan, Patricia 1938
4 Armstrong, Robb 1962
    Morgan, Garrett 1877
5 Margulis, Lynn 1938
6 Ashley, Maurice 1966
7 McCarty, Oseola 1908
8 Prinze, Freddie Jr. 1976
10 Guy, Jasmine 1964
    Miller, Shannon 1977
    Wolf, Hazel 1898
12 Hamilton, Virginia 1936
    Nye, Naomi Shihab 1952
13 Van Meter, Vicki 1982
14 Dayne, Ron 1977
    Hanson, Taylor 1983
    Williamson, Kevin 1965
15 Ginsburg, Ruth Bader 1933
    White, Ruth 1942
16 O'Neal, Shaquille 1972
17 Hamm, Mia 1972
    Nureyev, Rudolf 1938
18 Blair, Bonnie 1964
    de Klerk, F.W. 1936
    Griese, Brian 1975
    Queen Latifah 1970
19 Blanchard, Rachel 1976
20 Lee, Spike 1957
    Lowry, Lois 1937
    Sachar, Louis 1954
21 Gilbert, Walter 1932
    O'Donnell, Rosie 1962
22 Shatner, William 1931

March (continued)	Year
23 Kidd, Jason	1973
24 Manning, Peyton	1976
25 Dragila, Stacy	1971
Franklin, Aretha	1942
Granato, Cammi	1971
Lovell, Jim	1928
Park, Linda Sue	1960
Steinem, Gloria	1934
Swoopes, Sheryl	1971
26 Allen, Marcus	1960
Erdös, Paul	1913
O'Connor, Sandra Day	1930
Stockton, John	1962
Witherspoon, Reese	1976
27 Carey, Mariah	1970
Wrede, Patricia C.	1953
28 James, Cheryl	
McEntire, Reba	1955
Tompkins, Douglas	1943
29 Capriati, Jennifer	1976
30 Dion, Celine	1968
Hammer	1933
31 Caplan, Arthur	1950
Chavez, Cesar	1927
Gore, Al	1948
Howe, Gordie	1928

April	Year
1 Maathai, Wangari	1940
2 Carvey, Dana	1955
3 Garth, Jennie	1972
Goodall, Jane	1934
Street, Picabo	1971
4 Angelou, Maya	1928
Mirra, Dave	1974
5 Peck, Richard	1934
Powell, Colin	1937
6 Watson, James D.	1928
7 Chan, Jackie	1954
Douglas, Marjory Stoneman	1890
Forman, Michele	1946
8 Annan, Kofi	1938
9 Haddix, Margaret Peterson	1964
10 Madden, John	1936
12 Cleary, Beverly	1916
Danes, Claire	1979
Doherty, Shannen	1971
Hawk, Tony	1968
Letterman, David	1947
Soto, Gary	1952

		Year
13	Brandis, Jonathan	1976
	Henry, Marguerite	1902
14	Collins, Francis	1950
	Gellar, Sarah Michelle	1977
	Maddux, Greg	1966
	Rose, Pete	1941
15	Martin, Bernard	1954
	Watson, Emma	1990
16	Abdul-Jabbar, Kareem	1947
	Atwater-Rhodes, Amelia	1984
	Selena	1971
	Williams, Garth	1912
17	Champagne, Larry III	1985
18	Hart, Melissa Joan	1976
20	Brundtland, Gro Harlem	1939
21	Muir, John	1838
22	Levi-Montalcini, Rita	1909
	Oppenheimer, J. Robert	1904
23	Watson, Barry	1974
24	Clarkson, Kelly	1982
25	Fitzgerald, Ella	1917
26	Giff, Patricia Reilly	1935
	Nelson, Marilyn	1946
	Pei, I.M.	1917
27	Wilson, August	1945
28	Alba, Jessica	1981
	Baker, James	1930
	Duncan, Lois	1934
	Hussein, Saddam	1937
	Kaunda, Kenneth	1924
	Lee, Harper	1926
	Leno, Jay	1950
29	Agassi, Andre	1970
	Earnhardt, Dale	1951
	Seinfeld, Jerry	1954
30	Dunst, Kirsten	1982

May		Year
2	Hughes, Sarah	1985
	Spock, Benjamin	1903
4	Bass, Lance	1979
5	Lionni, Leo	1910
	Maxwell, Jody-Anne	1986
	Opdyke, Irene Gut	1922
	Strasser, Todd	1950
	WilderBrathwaite, Gloria	1964
7	Land, Edwin	1909
8	Attenborough, David	1926
	Iglesias, Enrique	1975
	Meltzer, Milton	1915

May (continued)	Year
9	Bergen, Candice 1946
	Yzerman, Steve 1965
10	Cooney, Caroline B............. 1947
	Curtis, Christopher Paul 1953
	Galdikas, Biruté 1946
	Jamison, Judith 1944
	Ochoa, Ellen 1958
11	Farrakhan, Louis............... 1933
12	Mowat, Farley 1921
13	Pascal, Francine 1938
	Rodman, Dennis............... 1961
14	Lucas, George 1944
	Smith, Emmitt................. 1969
15	Albright, Madeleine............ 1937
	Almond, David................. 1951
	Johns, Jasper 1930
	Zindel, Paul................... 1936
16	Coville, Bruce.................. 1950
17	Paulsen, Gary 1939
18	John Paul II 1920
19	Brody, Jane 1941
	Garnett, Kevin................. 1976
	Hansberry, Lorraine 1930
20	Stewart, Tony.................. 1971
21	Robinson, Mary................ 1944
22	Ohno, Apolo................... 1982
23	Bardeen, John 1908
	Jewel 1974
	O'Dell, Scott 1898
24	Beachley, Layne............... 1972
	Dumars, Joe 1963
	Gilman, Billy................... 1988
26	Hill, Lauryn 1975
	Ride, Sally 1951
27	Carson, Rachel 1907
	Kerr, M.E. 1927
28	Giuliani, Rudolph 1944
	Johnston, Lynn 1947
	Shabazz, Betty................. 1936
29	Clements, Andrew 1949
30	Cohen, Adam Ezra 1979
?	McGruder, Aaron 1974

June	Year
1	Lalas, Alexi 1970
	Morissette, Alanis 1974
4	Kistler, Darci 1964
	Nelson, Gaylord 1916
5	Scarry, Richard 1919

6	Rylant, Cynthia 1954
7	Brooks, Gwendolyn 1917
	Iverson, Allen 1975
	Oleynik, Larisa 1981
8	Berners-Lee, Tim............... 1955
	Bush, Barbara 1925
	Davenport, Lindsay 1976
	Edelman, Marian Wright 1939
	Wayans, Keenen Ivory 1958
	Wright, Frank Lloyd 1869
9	Portman, Natalie................ 1981
10	Frank, Anne 1929
	Lipinski, Tara.................. 1982
	Sendak, Maurice 1928
	Shea, Jim, Jr. 1968
11	Cousteau, Jacques.............. 1910
	Montana, Joe.................. 1956
12	Bush, George.................. 1924
13	Allen, Tim 1953
	Alvarez, Luis W................ 1911
	Christo....................... 1935
	Nash, John Forbes, Jr........... 1928
14	Bourke-White, Margaret 1904
	Graf, Steffi 1969
	Summitt, Pat 1952
	Yep, Laurence 1948
15	Horner, Jack 1946
	Jacques, Brian................. 1939
16	McClintock, Barbara........... 1902
	Shakur, Tupac 1971
17	Gingrich, Newt 1943
	Jansen, Dan................... 1965
	Williams, Venus 1980
18	da Silva, Fabiola 1979
	Johnson, Angela 1961
	Morris, Nathan 1971
	Van Allsburg, Chris............ 1949
19	Abdul, Paula 1962
	Aung San Suu Kyi.............. 1945
	Muldowney, Shirley............ 1940
20	Goodman, John................ 1952
21	Bhutto, Benazir 1953
	Breathed, Berke................ 1957
22	Bradley, Ed.................... 1941
	Daly, Carson 1973
	Warner, Kurt 1971
23	Rudolph, Wilma 1940
	Thomas, Clarence............. 1948

June (continued)   **Year**
25   Carle, Eric 1929
     Gibbs, Lois. 1951
26   Ammann, Simon 1981
     Harris, Bernard 1956
     Jeter, Derek 1974
     LeMond, Greg. 1961
     Vick, Michael 1980
27   Babbitt, Bruce 1938
     Dunbar, Paul Laurence 1872
     Perot, H. Ross 1930
28   Elway, John 1960
29   Jiménez, Francisco 1943
30   Ballard, Robert 1942

July   **Year**
1   Brower, David 1912
     Calderone, Mary S. 1904
     Diana, Princess of Wales 1961
     Duke, David 1950
     Lewis, Carl. 1961
     McCully, Emily Arnold. 1939
2   Bethe, Hans A. 1906
     Fox, Vicente 1942
     Gantos, Jack 1951
     George, Jean Craighead 1919
     Lynch, Chris 1962
     Marshall, Thurgood 1908
     Petty, Richard 1937
     Thomas, Dave 1932
3   Simmons, Ruth 1945
5   Watterson, Bill. 1958
6   Bush, George W. 1946
     Dalai Lama 1935
     Dumitriu, Ioana 1976
7   Chagall, Marc 1887
     Heinlein, Robert 1907
     Kwan, Michelle. 1980
     Otto, Sylke. 1969
     Sakic, Joe 1969
     Stachowski, Richie 1985
8   Hardaway, Anfernee "Penny" 1971
     Sealfon, Rebecca 1983
9   Farmer, Nancy. 1941
     Hanks, Tom. 1956
     Hassan II 1929
     Krim, Mathilde 1926
     Lee, Jeanette 1971
     Sacks, Oliver 1933
10   Ashe, Arthur 1943
     Benson, Mildred. 1905
     Boulmerka, Hassiba 1969

11   Cisneros, Henry 1947
     White, E.B. 1899
12   Bauer, Joan 1951
     Cosby, Bill 1937
     Johnson, Johanna 1983
     Yamaguchi, Kristi 1972
13   Ford, Harrison 1942
     Stewart, Patrick. 1940
15   Aristide, Jean-Bertrand. 1953
     Ventura, Jesse. 1951
16   Johnson, Jimmy 1943
     Sanders, Barry 1968
17   An Na. 1972
     Stepanek , Mattie 1990
18   Diesel, Vin 1967
     Glenn, John 1921
     Lemelson, Jerome 1923
     Mandela, Nelson. 1918
19   Tarvin, Herbert. 1985
20   Hillary, Sir Edmund 1919
21   Chastain, Brandi 1968
     Reno, Janet 1938
     Riley, Dawn 1964
     Stern, Isaac. 1920
     Williams, Robin. 1952
22   Calder, Alexander 1898
     Dole, Bob. 1923
     Hinton, S.E. 1948
23   Haile Selassie 1892
     Williams, Michelle 1980
24   Abzug, Bella 1920
     Bonds, Barry 1964
     Krone, Julie 1963
     Lopez, Jennifer. 1970
     Moss, Cynthia 1940
     Wilson, Mara. 1987
25   Payton, Walter 1954
26   Berenstain, Jan 1923
     Clark, Kelly 1983
27   Dunlap, Alison. 1969
     Rodriguez, Alex. 1975
28   Davis, Jim. 1945
     Pottter, Beatrix 1866
29   Burns, Ken. 1953
     Creech, Sharon 1945
     Dole, Elizabeth Hanford. 1936
     Jennings, Peter 1938
     Morris, Wanya. 1973
30   Allen, Tori 1988
     Hill, Anita 1956
     Moore, Henry 1898
     Schroeder, Pat. 1940

July (continued)

		Year
31	Cronin, John	1950
	Radcliffe, Daniel	1989
	Reid Banks, Lynne	1929
	Rowling, J. K.	1965
	Weinke, Chris	1972

August

		Year
1	Brown, Ron	1941
	Coolio	1963
	Garcia, Jerry	1942
2	Baldwin, James	1924
	Healy, Bernadine	1944
3	Brady, Tom	1977
	Roper, Dee Dee	?
	Savimbi, Jonas	1934
4	Gordon, Jeff	1971
5	Córdova, France	1947
	Ewing, Patrick	1962
	Jackson, Shirley Ann	1946
6	Cooney, Barbara	1917
	Robinson, David	1965
	Warhol, Andy	?1928
7	Byars, Betsy	1928
	Duchovny, David	1960
	Leakey, Louis	1903
	Villa-Komaroff, Lydia	1947
8	Boyd, Candy Dawson	1946
	Chasez, JC	1976
9	Anderson, Gillian	1968
	Holdsclaw, Chamique	1977
	Houston, Whitney	1963
	McKissack, Patricia C.	1944
	Sanders, Deion	1967
	Travers, P.L.	?1899
11	Haley, Alex	1921
	Hogan, Hulk	1953
	Rowan, Carl T.	1925
	Wozniak, Steve	1950
12	Barton, Hazel	1971
	Martin, Ann M.	1955
	McKissack, Fredrick L.	1939
	Myers, Walter Dean	1937
	Sampras, Pete	1971
13	Battle, Kathleen	1948
	Castro, Fidel	1927
14	Berry, Halle	?1967
	Johnson, Magic	1959
	Larson, Gary	1950

		Year
15	Affleck, Benjamin	1972
	Ellerbee, Linda	1944
16	Farrell, Suzanne	1945
	Fu Mingxia	1978
	Robison, Emily	1972
	Thampy, George	1987
18	Danziger, Paula	1944
	Murie, Margaret	1902
19	Clinton, Bill	1946
	Soren, Tabitha	1967
20	Chung, Connie	1946
	Dakides, Tara	1975
	Milosevic, Slobodan	1941
21	Chamberlain, Wilt	1936
	Draper, Sharon	1952
	Toro, Natalia	1984
22	Bradbury, Ray	1920
	Dorough, Howie	1973
	Schwarzkopf, H. Norman	1934
23	Bryant, Kobe	1978
	Novello, Antonia	1944
	Phoenix, River	1970
24	Arafat, Yasir	1929
	Dai Qing	1941
	Ripken, Cal, Jr.	1960
25	Case, Steve	1958
	Wolff, Virginia Euwer	1937
26	Burke, Christopher	1965
	Culkin, Macaulay	1980
	Sabin, Albert	1906
	Teresa, Mother	1910
	Tuttle, Merlin	1941
27	Adams, Yolanda	1961
	Moseley, Jonny	1975
	Nechita, Alexandra	1985
	Rinaldi, Ann	1934
28	Dove, Rita	1952
	Evans, Janet	1971
	Peterson, Roger Tory	1908
	Priestley, Jason	1969
	Rimes, LeAnn	1982
	Twain, Shania	1965
29	Grandin, Temple	1947
	Hesse, Karen	1952
	McCain, John	1936
30	Earle, Sylvia	1935
	Roddick, Andy	1982
	Williams, Ted	1918
31	Perlman, Itzhak	1945

September	Year
1 Estefan, Gloria	1958
Guy, Rosa	1925
Smyers, Karen	1961
2 Bearden, Romare	?1912
Galeczka, Chris	1981
Lisanti, Mariangela	1983
Mohajer, Dineh	1972
Yelas, Jay	1965
3 Delany, Bessie	1891
4 Knowles, Beyoncé	1981
Wright, Richard	1908
5 Guisewite, Cathy	1950
6 Fiorina, Carly	1954
7 Lawrence, Jacob	1917
Moses, Grandma	1860
Pippig, Uta	1965
Scurry, Briana	1971
8 Prelutsky, Jack	1940
Scieszka, Jon	1954
Thomas, Jonathan Taylor	1982
10 Gould, Stephen Jay	1941
Johnson, Randy	1963
13 Johnson, Michael	1967
Monroe, Bill	1911
Taylor, Mildred D.	1943
14 Armstrong, William H.	1914
Stanford, John	1938
15 dePaola, Tomie	?1934
Marino, Dan	1961
16 Bledel, Alexis	1981
Dahl, Roald	1916
Gates, Henry Louis, Jr.	1950
17 Burger, Warren	1907
18 Armstrong, Lance	1971
Carson, Ben	1951
de Mille, Agnes	1905
Fields, Debbi	1956
Nakamura, Leanne	1982
19 Delany, Sadie	1889
21 Fielder, Cecil	1963
Hill, Faith	1967
Jones, Chuck	1912
King, Stephen	1947
Nkrumah, Kwame	1909
22 Richardson, Dot	1961
23 Nevelson, Louise	1899
24 George, Eddie	1973
Ochoa, Severo	1905

25 Gwaltney, John Langston	1928
Locklear, Heather	1961
Lopez, Charlotte	1976
Pinkney, Andrea Davis	1963
Pippen, Scottie	1965
Reeve, Christopher	1952
Smith, Will	1968
Walters, Barbara	1931
26 Mandela, Winnie	1934
Stockman, Shawn	1972
Williams, Serena	1981
27 Handford, Martin	1956
28 Cray, Seymour	1925
Duff, Hilary	1987
Pak, Se Ri	1977
29 Berenstain, Stan	1923
Guey, Wendy	1983
Gumbel, Bryant	1948
30 Hingis, Martina	1980
Moceanu, Dominique	1981

October	Year
1 Carter, Jimmy	1924
McGwire, Mark	1963
2 Leibovitz, Annie	1949
3 Campbell, Neve	1973
Herriot, James	1916
Richardson, Kevin	1972
Winfield, Dave	1951
4 Cushman, Karen	1941
Kamler, Kenneth	1947
Rice, Anne	1941
5 Fitzhugh, Louise	1928
Hill, Grant	1972
Lemieux, Mario	1965
Lin, Maya	1959
Roy, Patrick	1965
Winslet, Kate	1975
6 Bennett, Cherie	1960
Lobo, Rebecca	1973
7 Ma, Yo-Yo	1955
8 Jackson, Jesse	1941
Ringgold, Faith	1930
Stine, R.L.	1943
Winans, CeCe	1964
9 Bryan, Zachery Ty	1981
Senghor, Léopold Sédar	1906
Sorenstam, Annika	1970
10 Favre, Brett	1969
Saro-Wiwa, Ken	1941

October (continued)

		Year
11	Murray, Ty	1969
	Perry, Luke	?1964
	Young, Steve	1961
12	Childress, Alice	?1920
	Jones, Marion	1975
	Maguire, Martie	1969
	Ward, Charlie	1970
13	Carter, Chris	1956
	Kerrigan, Nancy	1969
	Rice, Jerry	1962
14	Daniel, Beth	1956
	Maines, Natalie	1974
	Mobutu Sese Seko	1930
	Usher	1978
15	Iacocca, Lee A.	1924
16	Stewart, Kordell	1972
17	Eminem	1972
	Jemison, Mae	1956
	Kirkpatrick, Chris	1971
18	Bird, Sue	1980
	Foreman, Dave	1946
	Marsalis, Wynton	1961
	Navratilova, Martina	1956
	Suzuki, Shinichi	1898
19	Pullman, Philip	1946
20	Kenyatta, Jomo	?1891
	Mantle, Mickey	1931
	Pinsky, Robert	1940
21	Gillespie, Dizzy	1956
	Le Guin, Ursula K.	1929
22	Hanson, Zac	1985
23	Anderson, Laurie Halse	1961
	Crichton, Michael	1942
	Pelé	1940
25	Martinez, Pedro	1971
26	Clinton, Hillary Rodham	1947
27	Anderson, Terry	1947
	Morrison, Lillian	1917
28	Gates, Bill	1955
	Roberts, Julia	1967
	Salk, Jonas	1914
29	Flowers, Vonetta	1973
	Ryder, Winona	1971
31	Candy, John	1950
	Paterson, Katherine	1932
	Patterson, Ryan	1983
	Pauley, Jane	1950
	Tucker, Chris	1973

November

		Year
2	lang, k.d.	1961
3	Arnold, Roseanne	1952
	Ho, David	1952
	Kiraly, Karch	1960
4	Bush, Laura	1946
	Combs, Sean (Puff Daddy)	1969
	Handler, Ruth	1916
7	Bahrke, Shannon	1980
	Canady, Alexa	1950
8	Mittermeier, Russell A.	1949
9	Denton, Sandi	
	Sagan, Carl	1934
10	Bates, Daisy	?1914
11	Blige, Mary J.	1971
	DiCaprio, Leonardo	1974
	Vonnegut, Kurt	1922
12	Andrews, Ned	1980
	Blackmun, Harry	1908
	Harding, Tonya	1970
	Sosa, Sammy	1968
13	Goldberg, Whoopi	1949
14	Boutros-Ghali, Boutros	1922
	Hussein, King	1935
	Lindgren, Astrid	1907
	Rice, Condoleezza	1954
15	O'Keeffe, Georgia	1887
	Pinkwater, Daniel	1941
16	Baiul, Oksana	1977
	Miyamoto, Shigeru	1952
17	Fuentes, Daisy	1966
	Hanson, Ike	1980
18	Driscoll, Jean	1966
	Klug, Chris	1972
	Mankiller, Wilma	1945
	Vidal, Christina	1981
19	Collins, Eileen	1956
	Devers, Gail	1966
	Glover, Savion	1973
	Strug, Kerri	1977
21	Aikman, Troy	1966
	Griffey, Ken, Jr.	1969
	Schwikert, Tasha	1984
	Speare, Elizabeth George	1908
24	Ndeti, Cosmas	1971
25	Grant, Amy	1960
	Mathis, Clint	1976
	McNabb, Donovan	1976
	Thomas, Lewis	1913

November (continued)   Year
26 Patrick, Ruth 1907
    Pine, Elizabeth Michele 1975
    Schulz, Charles 1922
27 Nye, Bill 1955
    White, Jaleel 1977
29 L'Engle, Madeleine 1918
    Lewis, C. S. 1898
    Tubman, William V. S. 1895
30 Jackson, Bo 1962
    Parks, Gordon 1912

December   Year
2 Hendrickson, Sue 1949
    Macaulay, David 1946
    Seles, Monica 1973
    Spears, Britney 1981
    Watson, Paul 1950
3 Kim Dae-jung . . . . ?1925
    Filipovic, Zlata 1980
5 Muniz, Frankie 1985
6 Risca, Viviana 1982
7 Bird, Larry 1956
    Carter, Aaron 1987
8 Rivera, Diego 1886
9 Hopper, Grace Murray 1906
12 Bialik, Mayim 1975
    Frankenthaler, Helen 1928
    Sinatra, Frank 1915
13 Fedorov, Sergei 1969
    Pierce, Tamora 1954
14 Jackson, Shirley 1916
15 Aidid, Mohammed Farah 1934
    Mendes, Chico 1944
    Taymor, Julie 1952

16 Bailey, Donovan 1967
    McCary, Michael 1971
    Mead, Margaret 1901
17 Kielburger, Craig 1982
18 Aguilera, Christina 1980
    Holmes, Katie 1978
    Pitt, Brad 1964
    Sanchez Vicario, Arantxa 1971
    Spielberg, Steven 1947
19 Morrison, Sam 1936
    Sapp, Warren 1972
    White, Reggie 1961
20 Uchida, Mitsuko 1948
    Zirkle, Aliy 1969
21 Evert, Chris 1954
    Griffith Joyner, Florence 1959
    Stiles, Jackie 1978
    Webb, Karrie 1974
22 Pinkney, Jerry 1939
23 Avi 1937
    Harbaugh, Jim 1963
    Lowman, Meg 1953
24 Fauci, Anthony S. 1940
    Flake, Sharon 1955
    Lowe, Alex 1958
    Martin, Ricky 1971
25 Ryan, Pam Muñoz 1951
    Sadat, Anwar 1918
26 Butcher, Susan 1954
27 Roberts, Cokie 1943
28 Lee, Stan 1922
    Washington, Denzel 1954
30 Willingham, Tyrone 1953
    Woods, Tiger 1975

Biography Today

General Series

For ages 9 and above

iography Today **General Series** includes a unique combination of current biographical profiles that teachers and librarians — and the readers themselves — tell us are most appealing. The **General Series** is available as a 3-issue subscription; hardcover annual cumulation; or subscription plus cumulation.

Within the **General Series**, your readers will find a variety of sketches about:

- Authors
- Musicians
- Political leaders
- Sports figures
- Movie actresses & actors
- Cartoonists
- Scientists
- Astronauts
- TV personalities
- and the movers & shakers in many other fields!

"*Biography Today* **will be useful in elementary and middle school libraries and in public library children's collections where there is a need for biographies of current personalities. High schools serving reluctant readers may also want to consider a subscription.**"
— *Booklist,* American Library Association

"**Highly recommended for the young adult audience. Readers will delight in the accessible, energetic, tell-all style; teachers, librarians, and parents will welcome the clever format, intelligent and informative text. It should prove especially useful in motivating 'reluctant' readers or literate nonreaders.**"
— *MultiCultural Review*

"**Written in a friendly, almost chatty tone, the profiles offer quick, objective information. While coverage of current figures makes *Biography Today* a useful reference tool, an appealing format and wide scope make it a fun resource to browse.**" — *School Library Journal*

"**The best source for current information at a level kids can understand.**"
— Kelly Bryant, School Librarian, Carlton, OR

"**Easy for kids to read. We love it! Don't want to be without it.**"
— Lynn McWhirter, School Librarian, Rockford, IL

ONE-YEAR SUBSCRIPTION
- 3 softcover issues, 6" x 9"
- Published in January, April, and September
- 1-year subscription, $57
- 150 pages per issue
- 8-10 profiles per issue
- Contact sources for additional information
- Cumulative General, Places of Birth, and Birthday Indexes

HARDBOUND ANNUAL CUMULATION
- Sturdy 6" x 9" hardbound volume
- Published in December
- $58 per volume
- 450 pages per volume
- 25-30 profiles — includes all profiles found in softcover issues for that calendar year
- Cumulative General, Places of Birth, and Birthday Indexes
- Special appendix features current updates of previous profiles

SUBSCRIPTION AND CUMULATION COMBINATION
- $99 for 3 softcover issues plus the hardbound volume

239

1992

Paula Abdul
Andre Agassi
Kirstie Alley
Terry Anderson
Roseanne Arnold
Isaac Asimov
James Baker
Charles Barkley
Larry Bird
Judy Blume
Berke Breathed
Garth Brooks
Barbara Bush
George Bush
Fidel Castro
Bill Clinton
Bill Cosby
Diana, Princess of Wales
Shannen Doherty
Elizabeth Dole
David Duke
Gloria Estefan
Mikhail Gorbachev
Steffi Graf
Wayne Gretzky
Matt Groening
Alex Haley
Hammer
Martin Handford
Stephen Hawking
Hulk Hogan
Saddam Hussein
Lee Iacocca
Bo Jackson
Mae Jemison
Peter Jennings
Steven Jobs
Pope John Paul II
Magic Johnson
Michael Jordon
Jackie Joyner-Kersee
Spike Lee
Mario Lemieux
Madeleine L'Engle
Jay Leno
Yo-Yo Ma
Nelson Mandela
Wynton Marsalis
Thurgood Marshall
Ann Martin
Barbara McClintock
Emily Arnold McCully
Antonia Novello

Sandra Day O'Connor
Rosa Parks
Jane Pauley
H. Ross Perot
Luke Perry
Scottie Pippen
Colin Powell
Jason Priestley
Queen Latifah
Yitzhak Rabin
Sally Ride
Pete Rose
Nolan Ryan
H. Norman
   Schwarzkopf
Jerry Seinfeld
Dr. Seuss
Gloria Steinem
Clarence Thomas
Chris Van Allsburg
Cynthia Voigt
Bill Watterson
Robin Williams
Oprah Winfrey
Kristi Yamaguchi
Boris Yeltsin

1993

Maya Angelou
Arthur Ashe
Avi
Kathleen Battle
Candice Bergen
Boutros Boutros-Ghali
Chris Burke
Dana Carvey
Cesar Chavez
Henry Cisneros
Hillary Rodham Clinton
Jacques Cousteau
Cindy Crawford
Macaulay Culkin
Lois Duncan
Marian Wright Edelman
Cecil Fielder
Bill Gates
Sara Gilbert
Dizzy Gillespie
Al Gore
Cathy Guisewite
Jasmine Guy
Anita Hill
Ice-T
Darci Kistler

k.d. lang
Dan Marino
Rigoberta Menchu
Walter Dean Myers
Martina Navratilova
Phyllis Reynolds Naylor
Rudolf Nureyev
Shaquille O'Neal
Janet Reno
Jerry Rice
Mary Robinson
Winona Ryder
Jerry Spinelli
Denzel Washington
Keenen Ivory Wayans
Dave Winfield

1994

Tim Allen
Marian Anderson
Mario Andretti
Ned Andrews
Yasir Arafat
Bruce Babbitt
Mayim Bialik
Bonnie Blair
Ed Bradley
John Candy
Mary Chapin Carpenter
Benjamin Chavis
Connie Chung
Beverly Cleary
Kurt Cobain
F.W. de Klerk
Rita Dove
Linda Ellerbee
Sergei Fedorov
Zlata Filipovic
Daisy Fuentes
Ruth Bader Ginsburg
Whoopi Goldberg
Tonya Harding
Melissa Joan Hart
Geoff Hooper
Whitney Houston
Dan Jansen
Nancy Kerrigan
Alexi Lalas
Charlotte Lopez
Wilma Mankiller
Shannon Miller
Toni Morrison
Richard Nixon
Greg Norman
Severo Ochoa

River Phoenix
Elizabeth Pine
Jonas Salk
Richard Scarry
Emmitt Smith
Will Smith
Steven Spielberg
Patrick Stewart
R.L. Stine
Lewis Thomas
Barbara Walters
Charlie Ward
Steve Young
Kim Zmeskal

1995

Troy Aikman
Jean-Bertrand Aristide
Oksana Baiul
Halle Berry
Benazir Bhutto
Jonathan Brandis
Warren E. Burger
Ken Burns
Candace Cameron
Jimmy Carter
Agnes de Mille
Placido Domingo
Janet Evans
Patrick Ewing
Newt Gingrich
John Goodman
Amy Grant
Jesse Jackson
James Earl Jones
Julie Krone
David Letterman
Rush Limbaugh
Heather Locklear
Reba McEntire
Joe Montana
Cosmas Ndeti
Hakeem Olajuwon
Ashley Olsen
Mary-Kate Olsen
Jennifer Parkinson
Linus Pauling
Itzhak Perlman
Cokie Roberts
Wilma Rudolph
Salt 'N' Pepa
Barry Sanders
William Shatner
Elizabeth George
   Speare

Dr. Benjamin Spock
Jonathan Taylor
    Thomas
Vicki Van Meter
Heather Whitestone
Pedro Zamora

1996

Aung San Suu Kyi
Boyz II Men
Brandy
Ron Brown
Mariah Carey
Jim Carrey
Larry Champagne III
Christo
Chelsea Clinton
Coolio
Bob Dole
David Duchovny
Debbi Fields
Chris Galeczka
Jerry Garcia
Jennie Garth
Wendy Guey
Tom Hanks
Alison Hargreaves
Sir Edmund Hillary
Judith Jamison
Barbara Jordan
Annie Leibovitz
Carl Lewis
Jim Lovell
Mickey Mantle
Lynn Margulis
Iqbal Masih
Mark Messier
Larisa Oleynik
Christopher Pike
David Robinson
Dennis Rodman
Selena
Monica Seles
Don Shula
Kerri Strug
Tiffani-Amber Thiessen
Dave Thomas
Jaleel White

1997

Madeleine Albright
Marcus Allen
Gillian Anderson
Rachel Blanchard
Zachery Ty Bryan
Adam Ezra Cohen
Claire Danes
Celine Dion
Jean Driscoll
Louis Farrakhan
Ella Fitzgerald
Harrison Ford
Bryant Gumbel
John Johnson
Michael Johnson
Maya Lin
George Lucas
John Madden
Bill Monroe
Alanis Morissette
Sam Morrison
Rosie O'Donnell
Muammar el-Qaddafi
Christopher Reeve
Pete Sampras
Pat Schroeder
Rebecca Sealfon
Tupac Shakur
Tabitha Soren
Herbert Tarvin
Merlin Tuttle
Mara Wilson

1998

Bella Abzug
Kofi Annan
Neve Campbell
Sean Combs (Puff
    Daddy)
Dalai Lama (Tenzin
    Gyatso)
Diana, Princess of Wales
Leonardo DiCaprio
Walter E. Diemer
Ruth Handler
Hanson
Livan Hernandez
Jewel
Jimmy Johnson
Tara Lipinski
Jody-Anne Maxwell
Dominique Moceanu
Alexandra Nechita

Brad Pitt
LeAnn Rimes
Emily Rosa
David Satcher
Betty Shabazz
Kordell Stewart
Shinichi Suzuki
Mother Teresa
Mike Vernon
Reggie White
Kate Winslet

1999

Ben Affleck
Jennifer Aniston
Maurice Ashley
Kobe Bryant
Bessie Delany
Sadie Delany
Sharon Draper
Sarah Michelle Gellar
John Glenn
Savion Glover
Jeff Gordon
David Hampton
Lauryn Hill
King Hussein
Lynn Johnston
Shari Lewis
Oseola McCarty
Mark McGwire
Slobodan Milosevic
Natalie Portman
J. K. Rowling
Frank Sinatra
Gene Siskel
Sammy Sosa
John Stanford
Natalia Toro
Shania Twain
Mitsuko Uchida
Jesse Ventura
Venus Williams

2000

Christina Aguilera
K.A. Applegate
Lance Armstrong
Backstreet Boys
Daisy Bates
Harry Blackmun
George W. Bush
Carson Daly
Ron Dayne
Henry Louis Gates, Jr.
Doris Haddock
    (Granny D)
Jennifer Love Hewitt
Chamique Holdsclaw
Katie Holmes
Charlayne Hunter-Gault
Johanna Johnson
Craig Kielburger
John Lasseter
Peyton Manning
Ricky Martin
John McCain
Walter Payton
Freddie Prinze, Jr.
Viviana Risca
Briana Scurry
George Thampy
CeCe Winans

2001

Jessica Alba
Christiane Amanpour
Drew Barrymore
Jeff Bezos
Destiny's Child
Dale Earnhardt
Carly Fiorina
Aretha Franklin
Cathy Freeman
Tony Hawk
Faith Hill
Kim Dae-jung
Madeleine L'Engle
Mariangela Lisanti
Frankie Muniz
*N Sync
Ellen Ochoa
Jeff Probst
Julia Roberts
Carl T. Rowan
Britney Spears
Chris Tucker
Lloyd D. Ward
Alan Webb
Chris Weinke

2002

Aaliyah
Osama bin Laden
Mary J. Blige
Aubyn Burnside
Aaron Carter
Julz Chavez
Dick Cheney
Hilary Duff
Billy Gilman
Rudolph Giuliani
Brian Griese
Jennifer Lopez
Dave Mirra
Dineh Mohajer
Leanne Nakamura
Daniel Radcliffe
Condoleezza Rice
Marla Runyan
Ruth Simmons
Mattie Stepanek
J.R.R. Tolkien
Barry Watson
Tyrone Willingham
Elijah Wood

2003

Yolanda Adams
Mildred Benson
Alexis Bledel
Barry Bonds
Laura Bush
Kelly Clarkson
Vin Diesel
Eminem
Michele Forman
Vicente Fox
Millard Fuller
Sarah Hughes
Enrique Iglesias
Jeanette Lee
John Lewis
Clint Mathis
Donovan McNabb
Andy Roddick
Emma Watson
Reese Witherspoon

Biography Today
Subject Series

For ages 9 and above

Expands and complements the General Series and targets specific subject areas ...

Our readers asked for it! They wanted more biographies, and the *Biography Today* **Subject Series** is our response to that demand. Now your readers can choose their special areas of interest and go on to read about their favorites in those fields. Priced at just $39 per volume, the following specific volumes are included in the *Biography Today* Subject Series:

- **Artists**
- **Authors**
- **Performing Artists**
- **Scientists & Inventors**
- **Sports**
- **World Leaders**
  Environmental Leaders
  Modern African Leaders

FEATURES AND FORMAT

- Sturdy 6" x 9" hardbound volumes
- Individual volumes, $39 each
- 200 pages per volume
- 10-12 profiles per volume — targets individuals within a specific subject area
- Contact sources for additional information
- Cumulative General, Places of Birth, and Birthday Indexes

NOTE: There is *no duplication of entries* between the **General Series** of *Biography Today* and the **Subject Series**.

AUTHORS

"A useful tool for children's assignment needs." — *School Library Journal*

"The prose is workmanlike: report writers will find enough detail to begin sound investigations, and browsers are likely to find someone of interest." — *School Library Journal*

SCIENTISTS & INVENTORS

"The articles are readable, attractively laid out, and touch on important points that will suit assignment needs. Browsers will note the clear writing and interesting details." — *School Library Journal*

"The book is excellent for demonstrating that scientists are real people with widely diverse backgrounds and personal interests. The biographies are fascinating to read." — *The Science Teacher*

SPORTS

"This series should become a standard resource in libraries that serve intermediate students." — *School Library Journal*

ENVIRONMENTAL LEADERS #1

"A tremendous book that fills a gap in the biographical category of books. This is a great reference book." — *Science Scope*

243

Artists

VOLUME 1

Ansel Adams
Romare Bearden
Margaret Bourke-White
Alexander Calder
Marc Chagall
Helen Frankenthaler
Jasper Johns
Jacob Lawrence
Henry Moore
Grandma Moses
Louise Nevelson
Georgia O'Keeffe
Gordon Parks
I.M. Pei
Diego Rivera
Norman Rockwell
Andy Warhol
Frank Lloyd Wright

Authors

VOLUME 1

Eric Carle
Alice Childress
Robert Cormier
Roald Dahl
Jim Davis
John Grisham
Virginia Hamilton
James Herriot
S.E. Hinton
M.E. Kerr
Stephen King
Gary Larson
Joan Lowery Nixon
Gary Paulsen
Cynthia Rylant
Mildred D. Taylor
Kurt Vonnegut, Jr.
E.B. White
Paul Zindel

VOLUME 2

James Baldwin
Stan and Jan Berenstain
David Macaulay
Patricia MacLachlan
Scott O'Dell
Jerry Pinkney
Jack Prelutsky

Lynn Reid Banks
Faith Ringgold
J.D. Salinger
Charles Schulz
Maurice Sendak
P.L. Travers
Garth Williams

VOLUME 3

Candy Dawson Boyd
Ray Bradbury
Gwendolyn Brooks
Ralph W. Ellison
Louise Fitzhugh
Jean Craighead George
E.L. Konigsburg
C.S. Lewis
Fredrick L. McKissack
Patricia C. McKissack
Katherine Paterson
Anne Rice
Shel Silverstein
Laura Ingalls Wilder

VOLUME 4

Betsy Byars
Chris Carter
Caroline B. Cooney
Christopher Paul Curtis
Anne Frank
Robert Heinlein
Marguerite Henry
Lois Lowry
Melissa Mathison
Bill Peet
August Wilson

VOLUME 5

Sharon Creech
Michael Crichton
Karen Cushman
Tomie dePaola
Lorraine Hansberry
Karen Hesse
Brian Jacques
Gary Soto
Richard Wright
Laurence Yep

VOLUME 6

Lloyd Alexander
Paula Danziger
Nancy Farmer
Zora Neale Hurston

Shirley Jackson
Angela Johnson
Jon Krakauer
Leo Lionni
Francine Pascal
Louis Sachar
Kevin Williamson

VOLUME 7

William H. Armstrong
Patricia Reilly Giff
Langston Hughes
Stan Lee
Julius Lester
Robert Pinsky
Todd Strasser
Jacqueline Woodson
Patricia C. Wrede
Jane Yolen

VOLUME 8

Amelia Atwater-Rhodes
Barbara Cooney
Paul Laurence Dunbar
Ursula K. Le Guin
Farley Mowat
Naomi Shihab Nye
Daniel Pinkwater
Beatrix Potter
Ann Rinaldi

VOLUME 9

Robb Armstrong
Cherie Bennett
Bruce Coville
Rosa Guy
Harper Lee
Irene Gut Opdyke
Philip Pullman
Jon Scieszka
Amy Tan
Joss Whedon

VOLUME 10

David Almond
Joan Bauer
Kate DiCamillo
Jack Gantos
Aaron McGruder
Richard Peck
Andrea Davis Pinkney
Louise Rennison
David Small
Katie Tarbox

VOLUME 11

Laurie Halse Anderson
Bryan Collier
Margaret Peterson
  Haddix
Milton Meltzer
William Sleator
Sonya Sones
Genndy Tartakovsky
Wendelin Van Draanen
Ruth White

VOLUME 12

An Na
Claude Brown
Meg Cabot
Virginia Hamilton
Chuck Jones
Robert Lipsyte
Lillian Morrison
Linda Sue Park
Pam Muñoz Ryan
Lemony Snicket
  (Daniel Handler)

VOLUME 13

Andrew Clements
Eoin Colfer
Sharon Flake
Edward Gorey
Francisco Jiménez
Astrid Lindgren
Chris Lynch
Marilyn Nelson
Tamora Pierce
Virginia Euwer Wolff

Performing Artists

VOLUME 1

Jackie Chan
Dixie Chicks
Kirsten Dunst
Suzanne Farrell
Bernie Mac
Shakira
Isaac Stern
Julie Taymor
Usher
Christina Vidal

244

Scientists & Inventors

VOLUME 1

John Bardeen
Sylvia Earle
Dian Fossey
Jane Goodall
Bernadine Healy
Jack Horner
Mathilde Krim
Edwin Land
Louise & Mary Leakey
Rita Levi-Montalcini
J. Robert Oppenheimer
Albert Sabin
Carl Sagan
James D. Watson

VOLUME 2

Jane Brody
Seymour Cray
Paul Erdös
Walter Gilbert
Stephen Jay Gould
Shirley Ann Jackson
Raymond Kurzweil
Shannon Lucid
Margaret Mead
Garrett Morgan
Bill Nye
Eloy Rodriguez
An Wang

VOLUME 3

Luis W. Alvarez
Hans A. Bethe
Gro Harlem Brundtland
Mary S. Calderone
Ioana Dumitriu
Temple Grandin
John Langston
    Gwaltney
Bernard Harris
Jerome Lemelson
Susan Love
Ruth Patrick
Oliver Sacks
Richie Stachowski

VOLUME 4

David Attenborough
Robert Ballard
Ben Carson
Eileen Collins
Biruté Galdikas
Lonnie Johnson
Meg Lowman
Forrest Mars Sr.
Akio Morita
Janese Swanson

VOLUME 5

Steve Case
Douglas Engelbart
Shawn Fanning
Sarah Flannery
Bill Gates
Laura Groppe
Grace Murray Hopper
Steven Jobs
Rand and Robyn Miller
Shigeru Miyamoto
Steve Wozniak

VOLUME 6

Hazel Barton
Alexa Canady
Arthur Caplan
Francis Collins
Gertrude Elion
Henry Heimlich
David Ho
Kenneth Kamler
Lucy Spelman
Lydia Villa-Komaroff

VOLUME 7

Tim Berners-Lee
France Córdova
Anthony S. Fauci
Sue Hendrickson
Steve Irwin
John Forbes Nash, Jr.
Jerri Nielsen
Ryan Patterson
Nina Vasan
Gloria WilderBrathwaite

Sports

VOLUME 1

Hank Aaron
Kareem Abdul-Jabbar
Hassiba Boulmerka
Susan Butcher
Beth Daniel
Chris Evert
Ken Griffey, Jr.
Florence Griffith Joyner
Grant Hill
Greg LeMond
Pelé
Uta Pippig
Cal Ripken, Jr.
Arantxa Sanchez Vicario
Deion Sanders
Tiger Woods

VOLUME 2

Muhammad Ali
Donovan Bailey
Gail Devers
John Elway
Brett Favre
Mia Hamm
Anfernee "Penny"
    Hardaway
Martina Hingis
Gordie Howe
Jack Nicklaus
Richard Petty
Dot Richardson
Sheryl Swoopes
Steve Yzerman

VOLUME 3

Joe Dumars
Jim Harbaugh
Dominik Hasek
Michelle Kwan
Rebecca Lobo
Greg Maddux
Fatuma Roba
Jackie Robinson
John Stockton
Picabo Street
Pat Summitt
Amy Van Dyken

VOLUME 4

Wilt Chamberlain
Brandi Chastain
Derek Jeter
Karch Kiraly
Alex Lowe
Randy Moss
Se Ri Pak
Dawn Riley
Karen Smyers
Kurt Warner
Serena Williams

VOLUME 5

Vince Carter
Lindsay Davenport
Lisa Fernandez
Fu Mingxia
Jaromir Jagr
Marion Jones
Pedro Martinez
Warren Sapp
Jenny Thompson
Karrie Webb

VOLUME 6

Jennifer Capriati
Stacy Dragila
Kevin Garnett
Eddie George
Alex Rodriguez
Joe Sakic
Annika Sorenstam
Jackie Stiles
Tiger Woods
Aliy Zirkle

VOLUME 7

Tom Brady
Tara Dakides
Alison Dunlap
Sergio Garcia
Allen Iverson
Shirley Muldowney
Ty Murray
Patrick Roy
Tasha Schwiker

VOLUME 8

Simon Ammann
Shannon Bahrke
Kelly Clark
Vonetta Flowers
Cammi Granato
Chris Klug
Jonny Moseley
Apolo Ohno
Sylke Otto
Ryne Sanborn
Jim Shea, Jr.

VOLUME 9

Tori Allen
Layne Beachley
Sue Bird
Fabiola da Silva
Randy Johnson
Jason Kidd
Tony Stewart
Michael Vick
Ted Williams
Jay Yelas

World Leaders

VOLUME 1:
Environmental
Leaders 1

Edward Abbey
Renee Askins
David Brower
Rachel Carson
Marjory Stoneman
    Douglas
Dave Foreman
Lois Gibbs
Wangari Maathai
Chico Mendes
Russell A. Mittermeier
Margaret and Olaus J.
    Murie
Patsy Ruth Oliver
Roger Tory Peterson
Ken Saro-Wiwa
Paul Watson
Adam Werbach

VOLUME 2:
Modern African
Leaders

Mohammed Farah
    Aidid
Idi Amin
Hastings Kamuzu Banda
Haile Selassie
Hassan II
Kenneth Kaunda
Jomo Kenyatta
Winnie Mandela
Mobutu Sese Seko
Robert Mugabe
Kwame Nkrumah
Julius Kambarage
    Nyerere
Anwar Sadat
Jonas Savimbi
Léopold Sédar Senghor
William V. S. Tubman

VOLUME 3:
Environmental
Leaders 2

John Cronin
Dai Qing
Ka Hsaw Wa
Winona LaDuke
Aldo Leopold
Bernard Martin
Cynthia Moss
John Muir
Gaylord Nelson
Douglas Tompkins
Hazel Wolf